LESSONS IN LOVE AND ROMANCE

THE FUNNIEST ROMCOM YOU'LL READ THIS YEAR!

KIRSTY GREENWOOD

For Christine, my mum, who makes everything better.

CHAPTER ONE

To attract the right sort of chap, a woman must exude allure yet remain virtuous. Modesty is necessary if she intends to receive a proposal of marriage!

***Matilda Beam's Guide to Love and Romance*, 1955**

I have done many unwise things in my life. And while sex with the new neighbour less than two hours after meeting him is definitely not the most ridiculous of those things, it's quite high up on the list. As is losing my contact lenses during the mistimed throes of our clumsy copulation, leaving myself blind in his bed this sticky-hot July morning.

Stupid, delicious pear cider, I cannot resist thee.

Somewhere in the room my phone gives off a muffly buzz. Shit, I bet I'm late. The big meeting is today and I swore to Summer that I absolutely, definitely would not be late.

I can't quite remember my neighbour's name, though I have a strong feeling that it's Jim. Or maybe Timothy. Whatever he's called, his partially hidden face is snoring away beside me, blissfully oblivious to my presence. If I had the power of sight I would just find my clothes and creep across the corridor without having to acknowledge him in any way. At least until the inevitable bumping into him in the hall bit, at which point I'd simply shriek and leg it. But without contacts in I can only see about six inches in front of me.

'Wake up ... ' *Jim? Timothy?* ' ... boy,' I croak, nudging neighbour's burly shoulder with my elbow. 'Rise and shine! It's a magical new day and all that jazz. Come on. Time to get up now.'

He mumbles something that sounds like 'mnnneblurp', grabs my hand and plonks it onto his willy, clearly hopeful of a repeat performance.

No, ta.

I remove my hand from his junk and use it to punch his arm.

Jumping upright, he blinks once as if stunned by the sight of a real live woman in his bed. I squint at him. His brawny, muscular body looks oddly out of proportion with his head. What a tiny head he has. I probably thought it was a fascinating head last night. Everything's fascinating after that much booze. I disguise my *What the blazing arse was I thinking?* grimace with an extravagant yawn.

Whipping up the blanket, neighbour discovers that I'm still naked. He smirks, sliding closer. 'Oh, *hellooo*, Jess from next door,' he says, wetting his pale lips with his pale tongue. 'Do you have a ... *cup of sugar* I could borrow?'

He gazes at me for a moment, eyes narrowed, top lip lifted in a half-grin. I suspect he thinks it's a sexually alluring facial arrangement, but in reality it gives him the aura of a man restraining a fart.

I do an army roll over to the other side of the bed.

'*Sugar*,' he cracks again, beaming. 'D'y geddit? Ha-ha. Like a euphemism? For sex? Ha-ha. Ha.'

Good God. My standards – which, let's face it, were never mega high – have really dropped recently. First Mickey the Butcher, who wasn't even really a butcher, and then Rupert, who only loved me because I let him take sepia-filtered Instagram pics of my feet. And now *this* guy, whose name eludes me.

'Hey ... fella,' I improvise. 'I'm so sorry to wake you, but I'm late and probably in trouble with my boss. I've lost my contact lenses and I'm completely short-sighted without them. Would you mind helping find my clothes and walking me back to my flat?'

He stretches his thick arms above his head and raises an eyebrow. 'Where we're going ... we don't need clothes.'

'I think we do. I really think we do.'

'I'd like it much better if you just stayed naked.'

'That's very flattering. But I think I'd like *you* much better if you did me a lovely favour and found my stuff.'

He sighs and slithers out of the bed, grabs some stripy cotton boxers and a creased vest from a half-unpacked suitcase and pulls them on. It only takes him a moment to find my clothes, which have been artlessly flung onto his computer desk. My knickers are curled around the handle of an errant mug. He hands them over and watches as I dress.

Yanking up my skinny jeans, I pull the zipper before fastening the safety pin that's there in place of the button I lost last week.

Everything is so blurry. I really must remember to start carrying a spare pair of glasses in my bag. I must also remember to start carrying a bag.

'So, do you want my number, Jess?' neighbour asks,

linking his arm with mine and leading me slowly out of his bedroom, down a hall and through a curry-scented kitchen area. 'I feel a real rapport here. Romantic potential, like. I'd love to get to know you more.'

We trail through a sparse living room, the shockingly bright rays of sunshine blaring through the window making me squint.

'Thanks and all,' I say, sidestepping a stack of unpacked boxes on the floor, 'but I'm not really the "getting to know you more" type. I mean, maybe I'll get round to doing the whole relationship thing in twenty years or so when my body's gone to shit and most of the fun of life has already been had. But right now? *Nope.* Ta for the offer, though.'

'Right, yeah, totally agree, totally agree,' he says as we leave his flat. 'I'm exactly the same. Fucking hate relationships. Relationships can go suck long balls for all I care. Ha. Listen to this: I like ships, yeah? But wanna know what my least favourite type of ship is?

'A relationship.'

'You got it! Ha-ha. So you being all *independent lady* and that, well, it could make us the perfect match, when you think about it. Something to consider?'

'Hmm-hmm.'

We plod out into the communal hall and down the corridor for the twenty seconds it takes us to reach my flat. I fish inside my back pocket for the door key.

'Thanks a lot for helping me home.'

'Oh, always happy to accompany a pretty young thang like yourself.'

'Right.' I nod. 'Cool, well, take care then. Probably see you around the flats sometime!'

I wave and give him my *goodbye* smile. He does not leave.

'Um, so yeah, I'll see you around sometime!' I repeat.

Still he does not leave.

Why doesn't he leave?

'You know, Jess,' he says thoughtfully, thumb hooked in the band of his boxers, crotch thrusting slightly in my direction. 'I think you should at least take my number for neighbourly purposes. Like, in case you get burgled or something. Or locked in. Or locked out. Or maybe one day you might need some help with your tinned goods shopping bags. Or what if, right, what if you're indoors alone one day and your washing machine just breaks? Explodes, like KABLAM, flooding all of your things and you need a helping hand? Or what if – ' his nostrils flare slightly – 'what if you find yourself feeling lonely, eh? Very lonely, but of course no one knows how lonesome you are because you pretend your job at the B&Q warehouse fulfils you and you put on your glad face at the Wednesday-night poker tournaments, but underneath the charade you're bored and alone and in dire, wretched need of soft, comforting human warmth ... '

Woah.

Seeing such raw desperation for companionship makes me feel extra grateful that I have no such urges. The art of a successful one-night stand is dead simple: Do Not Emotionally Attach, OK? I also find this to be an excellent motto for life in general.

Poor guy, with that shrunken head as well.

'All right, then,' I say, feeling bad for him. 'I'll take that number. Just in case my washing machine does, you know, explode.'

Grinning, he crosses the personal space threshold and hovers by my shoulder, watching as I enter the number he recites.

And then it gets to the bit where I'm supposed to type his name into my phone.

I scrunch up my eyes, hand poised over the screen.

Jim or Timothy?

Jim or Timothy?

If I get this wrong, it could be considered a genuinely skanky moment.

'Um, Jessica,' he mumbles, smile fading, 'do you not know my name?'

I snort and do an over-the-top eye roll. 'I know it,' I say breezily. 'Obviously I know your name!'

Jim or Timothy? It's a simple fifty-fifty call, Jess. Make the call.

'*Obviously* your name is Jjjjiiiiim ... '

His brow dips.

' ... mmmothy?'

He does a tiny gasp.

'Did you just call me *Jimothy*?'

'Errrrrr.'

'My name is *Paul*.'

He throws me a deeply offended look, mutters 'slapper' under his breath and stomps off back down the hall.

Paul. Pea-head Paul. *Of course.*

CHAPTER TWO

Being late is never, ever fashionable.
***Matilda Beam's Good Woman Guide*, 1959**

Before I get a chance to turn the key in the lock, the front door is yanked open by my boss, flatmate and *Celebrity Rear of the Year Runner-Up 2011*, Summer Spencer.

'Did the new neighbour just call you a slapper?' she asks, observing his retreating form.

'I prefer sexually cheerful.'

'I suppose that's one way to put it.' She raises a fashionably thick dark eyebrow. 'How are you even late, Jess? Seriously. Today of all days? Possibly the biggest day of my – of our – entire career? We've got to leave for London in less than half an hour and you're a mess, *quelle surpreeeeze*.'

Mr Belding, our tiny black and white kitten, winds his way around my legs. Picking him up, I hold him close, like a protective shield against Summer's grump bullets. I look at his head. What's she done to him this time?

'I know.' I grimace. 'Sorry, Sum. I did mean to have an

early night. I even wrote it on my hand. Look!' I hold out my palm to show her the smudged blue biro scrawl reading *Have early night!* 'I just ... after you left, the beer garden got dead busy and everyone was playing Twister and it was so sunny and warm and they do that lovely pear cider . . .' I rub my eyes. 'I can barely see right now, I lost my conta—'

'Yeah, I'm sure it's all another delightful adventure in the amazing responsibility-free world of Jessica Beam.' She blows the air out through her cheeks. 'But maybe you can tell me on the train down south? Just shower, will you?' Leaning forward, she gives me a delicate little sniff. 'You reek.'

'Do I have time for a quick run first? Twenty minutes max? Just to clear away the cobwebs? I feel a bit pukey.'

'No! Jesus, Jess.'

Summer holds her arms out to take Mr Belding back. He scrambles up me, his paws clinging desperately to my top. She narrows her eyes in deep suspicion.

'Hmm. I don't get why he likes you so much when I'm the one who spends so much time with him. Styles him, manages his career.'

Mr Belding is a burgeoning Internet star. A model cat. Summer dresses him up in little outfits and together they pose for pictures, which she posts online for likes and retweets.

I pointedly eye the specially made feline top hat that Mr Belding is wearing. 'I don't know,' I say innocently. 'Maybe he just wants to grapple back a little creative control?'

Summer tuts. 'Oh, it's all *such* a laugh, isn't it? Just hurry up, will you?' She sighs loudly, spins on her heel and clicks back across the hardwood floor, closing the living room door more forcefully than usual.

She's *so* moody lately.

I grasp tightly onto the dado rail and feel along it until I reach my cosy, cupboard-sized bedroom, where I finally put on my old faithful tortoiseshell glasses.

'Praise be!' I cry to the ceiling as sight is restored.

Plugging my iPhone into the docking station, I flick on my favourite rock anthems playlist – which never fails to get me in a brilliant mood – and speedily pull off last night's clothes, chucking them in the general direction of the already overflowing laundry basket. Really must get round to putting some washing on.

Tomorrow.

Definitely tomorrow.

Jumping into the shower, I do the fastest shampoo I've ever done in my life because Summer has already used this week's quota of hot water for the twice daily holistic baths she's been reading about on *goop* and the water is turning into icicles before it even hits me. From downstairs she yells:

'Double-brush your teeth, Jess. Maybe triple.'

'Absolutely!' I call back in a shivery voice, immediately reaching outside the shower screen for my toothbrush and getting to work on an extreme mouth cleansing.

'Don't forget to wear underwear today,' Summer shouts again, this time from outside my bedroom door. I half expect her to suddenly appear in the bathroom Ninja-Cat style to make sure I've cleaned behind my ears.

'Definitely will wear pants!' I call back.

I wonder if it's normal to be a little bit afraid of your best friend? Not like in a murdery way, of course, but sometimes, when Summer gives me this stony-eyed, ice-cold look, my heart plummets to my knees. If I'm extra tiddly or extra flirty or extra gobby, Summer's frosty stare comes out, and that's when I know I should probably rein in it. Every so often I try to get sensible. I go cold turkey on fun: stop with the boy crazy, end the boozing, press pause on eating only Pot Noodles with a side order of McCoy's crisps and a pudding of Haribo for dinner, and start going with her to the horrendous Saturday spinning class and taking my make-up off before I go to sleep and trying to understand that fashion is about much more than which sparkly top makes my boobs look the most awesome. I usually manage fine for a few days. But then, soon enough, life feels quite grey and empty without a party going on, and whether I like it or not I'm back to what Summer refers to as my 'ridiculous Jessica Beam adventures'. She reckons I'm still living life like I'm eighteen instead of twenty-eight, but what's so wrong with that? As Tulisa Contostavlos sang so soulfully, 'we're young, we're young, we're young'. And as I always say: life is too blummin' short not to have a giggle while you can.

'Jess! Get a move on!'

'Five mins!'

I try to super-speedily shave my legs, which is a grave error of judgement and leads to unsightly shin cuts that sting like a mofo. I hop about and mutter all the swear words until the pain subsides.

A sweet prog rock keyboardist I saw for a few weeks last year asked me why on earth I cared so much about what Summer Spencer thought. And I told him exactly why: Summer was there for me at a time when no one else was. Which sounds dramatic, I know, but it's a true fact. Because when I was eighteen my mum, Rose, died. I was in my first year at Manchester university and Summer was on the same English Lit course as me. When I'd failed to turn up to lectures for three weeks, she came to my halls to find out why I'd disappeared. To be fair, up until then I'd been helping her with the assignments (I still don't know how she got on the course – she thought George Eliot was a dude), and she'd been getting rubbish marks in my absence. But still, out of everyone, Summer was the only person who'd even noticed I was missing.

When she discovered me holed up in my room eating an undercooked frozen garlic bread, doing a *Rosemary & Thyme* DVD marathon and swigging shit boxed wine directly from the plastic tap on the box, she said to me, 'This is the saddest scene I've ever witnessed. Put on some lipstick, let's go out and get ridiculously fucked.' Which, at the time, I thought was the worst, most insensitive idea in the world. But as it turned out, going out and having fun was the most effective distraction I'd had in weeks. From then on we were inseparable. Summer took me under her wing and introduced me to her crowd of cool friends, who eventually became my crowd of cool friends too.

I'd never met anyone like Summer Spencer before. Even at eighteen years old she was the most confident, popular person in most rooms. She'd wear stylish new hairdos and fashion before they even hit the magazines, always had an innate sense of where the best parties were going on, and the fact that she wanted to hang out with me was supremely flattering. Still is. And I didn't mind writing the odd essay for her, or even doing what eventually turned out to be most of her dissertation – I loved the books we were studying, and a stressed-out Summer was nowhere near as much fun. And I'll never forget that if she hadn't dragged me out of my bedroom that day, I'd probably still be in there now, going mouldy.

Outside the bathroom door I hear the growly opening riffs of one of my favourite Led Zeppelin songs blare out of the iPhone. I can't resist a quick air-guitar moment before rinsing the conditioner off my head.

So, after graduation, Summer and I lost touch for a few years. She was super busy in New York trying to make it as a fashion designer and dating Anderson Warner – he of the twinkly eyes and MTV movie award fame – and I was travelling across Europe, not really trying to make it as anything but having some pretty epic adventures along the way. Later, when Summer's fashiony dreams didn't quite come off and Anderson chucked her for a South Korean model, she came back to the UK and set up a blog called *Summer in the City*.

In the beginning it was mostly just daily duck-faced selfies of Summer at different parties and product launches. It barely had any traffic, and no income to speak of. She called me and asked if I'd like to write for her. I was in Morocco at the time having a ball, but she needed a favour and I owed her big time. And now here we are. The wages aren't quite enough for me to rent my own pad, but Summer lets me live cheaply in the Castlefield apartment Anderson bought her. This is where I've been ever since, and over the past two years of working together, *Summer in the City* has become this gorgeous, popular lifestyle blog based on Summer's adventures in Manchester. I do the bulk of the writing, but Summer's the tastemaker. I mooch along to all the restaurants, cocktail bars, boutiques, gigs and product parties, and together we blog about it. Me the voice, and Summer the face. The work's easy-peasy, and we get to go out a lot for free. I never really made any grand plans for a career, so to have fallen into this, I've got to admit, is a sweet deal.

Hopefully it's about to get even sweeter because today we're going to London to pitch to Valentina Smith – non-fiction editor at the Southbank Press. They're interested in turning *Summer in the City* into a glossy lifestyle book!

OK: clothes.

I dry myself off with the only towel I can find until I do some washing – a teeny green hand towel – and open my wardrobe door to find that the line of plastic coat hangers that are supposed to hold my clothes are all empty except for one, which displays a slutty Cleopatra costume from last Halloween.

Probably not that.

Rifling through my drawers I find, amongst the odd DVD case, a half-empty bottle of rum, the beloved gold bra I thought I'd lost, a slightly crumpled, kind of low-cut but otherwise perfectly all right turquoise and pink floral cotton dress.

Is this even mine?

I give it a sniff.

Not bad ...

I liberally spritz it with Febreze just in case and pull it on. It's quite short, just about covering my bum and fully exposing my razor-doomed legs.

Dammit. I probably should have prepared better for this. The dress does look kind of awesome, though, as long as everyone's eyes remain firmly above the waist.

'Jess! Hurry uuuuuup!'

Right, it'll just have to do.

'Sorry, Summer! Nearly there!'

I dab loo roll on the cuts, blast my white-blonde hair extensions dry, draw in my eyebrows, put on my favourite silver flip-flops and head out to an increasingly impatient Summer.

* * *

'What are you wearing? No. *Noooooooo*.' Summer panics as soon as she sees me.

She's in our living room looking perfectly groomed in a coral shift dress and a short leather bolero jacket with some high-heeled ankle boots. Her dark ombre'd hair is softly waved and swept over to one side. Around her neck she's wearing a necklace with a gold Sonic the Hedgehog charm. *I* don't get it, but we wrote about it on the blog last week and apparently it's really 'on trend'. Behind her, draped across our faux-distressed leather sofa, is Summer's boyfriend Holden. He looks me up and down over the top of his big square knobhead glasses which make him look like a knobhead.

'I'm wearing a dress, like you said to!' I explain, fingering the short skirt.

'That's not a dress, sweetpea, it's a tragedy.'

Holden sniggers. I shoot him my best withering glance, which I've checked out in the mirror a few times. It's pretty withering.

'But isn't it your dress?' I ask. 'I don't think it's mine ... '

She's offended by the mere suggestion. 'Why didn't you just buy a new one like I asked you to?'

Shitbags. She did ask me to get a new one just last week. I wrote it on my arm. *Buy sensible dress!*

'Is this really so bad?' I ask. 'It's all floral and shit. You like flowery things, don't you? That designer person you said you love ... Cath Kidston! It looks exactly like that.'

'I did not say I love Cath Kidston,' Summer fumes, tapping a foot speedily against the floor. 'I said loathe. I loathe Cath Kidston. *Loathe.* And why are you wearing your glasses? Put your contacts in.'

I push my glasses up my nose. 'Oh, I lost my contacts last night. Haven't had a chance to order some more yet.'

'Most people order these things in advance!'

'Do they? Don't worry. If 80s teen comedies have taught me anything, it's that people wearing glasses are much cleverer than other people. Glasses make me look more bookish. They are perfect for a trip to a publisher!'

'This isn't a *trip*, Jess. It could be the difference between being winners in life or sad losers. I know which one *I'm* going to be. This is important. Why can't you take just one thing seriously?'

I roll my eyes, but I do know how important it is. I've worked really hard on the pitch for today. Nonetheless, as my mum always used to say, if you want something too much, it'll probably go wrong. So I'm going to do what I always do. I'm going to be cool. Cool like a fool in a swimming pool.

'Don't stress so much, Sum.' I pat her on the arm. 'They probably won't even notice what we're wearing. They're interested in us for our *brains*.'

Summer tuts, glances at her retro Minnie Mouse watch (I'll never understand why people wear naff old things when they can get shiny new things) and stalks over to the coat cupboard. 'It's too late to change you now, though you'd think my sartorial finesse might have rubbed off just a teensy bit after all these years following me around. And your legs. The fake tan is all patchy around the knees and ... is your shin *bleeding*?'

I peer down at my legs.

'Oh, um, yeah. It was bleeding a teeny bit, but it's stopped now. You can hardly even notice it. It could be just a bit of red fluff for all anyone knows.'

'Red fluff? Why would you have red fluff on your shin?'

'Errr ... '

I can think of no believable reason.

'Here. Put this on.' She flings me my long black cashmere winter coat, the sheer weight of which makes me stumble backwards into the wall.

'But it's July!' I eye the heavy fabric with horror. 'I'll stew in my own juices.'

Summer puts hand to slender hip and glares at me.

'I'm going to make the wild assumption that you have no other clean clothes ready, and you absolutely can't wear jeans for this. I'm, like, a model-tall size eight, maybe even a six now, and you're a five-foot-three size ten, so it's not like anything of mine will fit you. Shit, Jess. Just put the coat on. We need to go.'

Fuck. She's getting really upset.

Before I've even got one arm in the sleeve of the coat I can feel the beads of sweat begin to form on my forehead. My estimation for full slide-offage of eyebrows is approximately ten minutes.

'Have fun in Londonski, guys,' Holden twangs from the sofa, lighting his Gauloises cigarette. 'Say hi to the ol' LDN from me, yeah? Good town. Good town.'

Summer sashays over to give him a kiss, being careful not to get her eye poked out by the drumstick he keeps tucked behind his ear. 'Wish us luck!' she trills.

'Good luck,' he purrs, taking a sip from his jam jar of artisan beer before pulling her onto his knee for a full-on snog. 'Go do you, babydoll. Go do you.'

'I love you more than tea and kittens and apricot gin,' Summer murmurs, making a heart shape with her hands and giggling as Mr Belding jumps between the two of them with a hiss.

'I love you more than Mumford and Sons,' Holden says solemnly.

My body starts feeling itchy, like it always does when

anyone gets overly emotional in my presence. I have no problem with public displays of affection; I have partaken in many varieties in all different kinds of locations. But public declarations of everlasting love? Yeuch. Get me outta here.

'See you laters, Crocodeelios,' Holden croons, smirking as Summer finally leaves his knee. As she turns away, he blows me a moustachioed kiss and a pervy wink.

Barf.

'Come on, Summer,' I say, flipping Holden the bird behind Summer's back. 'Let's go to London and seek our fortune!'

UNTITLED

Rose Beam's Diary
17th April 1985

Almost got caught tonight! Knocked *Gulliver's Travels* off the windowsill climbing back through the window. Luckily I managed to dive back into bed and pull the covers over my head before Mum came nosying about the room to catch me out in this minuscule lace Madonna dress. Twenty-five years old and still sneaking out of my parents' house to go to a nightclub. Christ.

I'm itching to get a proper acting job so that I can afford to get out of here and be independent. Mum and Dad are steadfastly refusing to believe that I need to, especially with Nigel flipping Pemberton sniffing around with his oily hair and 'I've got a tiny penis' car and his stupid boring stock portfolio. Hello! It's 1985 now! Women staying still until a marriage proposal approved by their parents is utterly archaic. It's like a flipping Austen novel. Working at the gallery is horrendously dull and there's no money in it, but at least I can escape this place for a little while every day while I figure out what I really and truly want to do with my one wild and precious life!

Anyway, I'm pretty tipsy (isn't crème de menthe delicious?) and writing about things that are not even interesting. Victoria has invited me out again on Friday night to a rad new club called the Blue Canary. It's in Soho. Father would die. Hah! I absolutely can't wait. I love dancing. I love the colourful lights. I love going out with Victoria, she's such a buzz and not at all stuffy like Anna and Claire-Marie.

Must sleep and dream now. Work in the morning. Boooo. REMEMBER, ROSE! You must hide flat pumps outside next time. Climbing on these balconies is dangerous even without the five-inch heels!

R x

CHAPTER THREE

When travelling by train, eat only light, plain food. Strong, lingering smells are a nuisance ...

Apart from a friendly greeting, train mates usually don't speak. If you are a lady alone, take a book or enjoy the view out of your window.

***Matilda Beam's Good Woman Guide*, 1959**

What I want to know is why everyone's so obsessed with the Quiet Zone on trains? They announce their preference for it reverentially. 'Oh, I *always* book Quiet Zone, I do,' they say, as if their ears are super delicate and simply cannot handle both human noise and high-speed travel at the same time. And then these peculiar people spend the entire journey miserable and twitchy with anticipation, ears pricked, watching and waiting for the tiniest sniffle or crunch of a biscuit that will break the silence and ruin that special Quiet Zone magic forever.

I open my beloved old laptop and place it on the plastic train table as Summer, sitting opposite me, angrily rolls her eyes at a child a few rows down who's loudly trying to decide whether his favourite colour is blue like the sky or dandelion yellow.

'Ugh. Doesn't the little shit know we're in Quiet Zone?' she hisses, much to the chagrin of the man on the seat to her left who tells Summer to hush, thus setting off a cacophony of tuts and grumbles and high-pitched whispers throughout the whole carriage. It sounds like school assembly. I cough, even though I don't really need to, and get the urge to shout 'MASSIVE WANG' at the top of my voice.

Because of Summer's sensitivity to train noise, we're going to rehearse our pitch silently via the power of instant message, or IM as we hip new media kids call it. As the train creaks out of Manchester Piccadilly, I pay for and connect to the WiFi Internet on both our computers.

SUMMER SPENCER: OK. Let's go over everything one final time. We're already behind.

MS BEAMBASTIC: Agreed. But can I get a pasty first? I'm starving. Do you want one? My treat?

SUMMER: A pasty? No thank you. It being eleven a.m. and all.

MS BEAMBASTIC. I'm a bit rough. I'm going to nip to the food cart and get one. Back in a mo.

Summer does the frosty-glare thing as I stumble my way down the narrow aisle and into the next carriage, the infinitesimal sound of my flip-flops on the carpet causing the other Quiet Zone passengers to wince and shoot me daggers. I eagerly grab my beef Ginsters from the lightly humming refrigerator and peruse the crisps selection. Hula Hoops, Skips or McCoy's salt and vinegar? It's a very tough choice. The sulky young fella behind the counter stares at me and utters a loud sigh.

'What do you think I should get?' I ask cheerily. He stares blankly at me and shrugs.

'You're absolutely right,' I say to him. 'McCoys are *clearly* superior.'

I grab a bag and plonk them onto the counter as well as a Green & Black's ginger and dark chocolate bar for Summer.

'I'll have a Lilt as well, I think. And a vodka. Hair of the dog and all that.'

When I get back to my seat, Summer frowns and starts to type.

SUMMER SPENCER: Vodka? What??

MS BEAMBASTIC: Hair of the dog.

SUMMER SPENCER: Classy. And crisps? We're in Quiet Zone.

MS BEAMBASTIC: I'll lick them first so they won't crunch as loud.

SUMMER SPENCER: Ugh! You are such a scruff.

MS BEAMBASTIC:

I open my pasty and take a huge bite, sighing with pleasure as the juicy beef brings the pink colour back into my chalky, hungover cheeks.

. . .

SUMMER SPENCER: That stinks. You're upsetting the entire train.

I scan the carriage and notice the other passenger sniffing and pulling faces of horror. I put my pasty down on the table and type.

MS BEAMBASTIC: But it tastes really good! They're just jealous of my pasty.

Summer dramatically holds her nose for the whole time I'm eating the pasty. I gobble it down as quickly as I can and attempt to stifle the resulting burp. I don't do a good job, though, and it rings out in the silence, causing a collective gasp throughout the train coach. I cringe and expect an outcry, or even to get kicked off, but no one says a thing. They can't, for they are in Quietzonia, land of the aggresively mute. I stand up from my seat, take a bow and do a royal wave with my most annoying flared nostril smile. They fume. They quietly fume!

* * *

Once we've gone over our pitch – refining key sentences, making sure the slide show of our website pages are all there and triple-checking the order we're going to speak in – Summer plugs a pair of headphones into her laptop to watch a movie. It's *True Bromance*, the smash hit 'buddy comedy' Anderson Warner was filming when they met in New York, the premier for which she accompanied him to. This film in particular holds special memories for her. Not only is it a reminder of how she and Anderson met (one of her fashiony friends was a wardrobe assistant for the movie and invited Summer to visit the set), but it was also at that time that she started getting a bit famous. There was actually a period of about six months when she couldn't go out without getting papped whether Anderson was with her or not. You always read about celebs hating the paparazzi, but Summer thrived on it, on occasion tipping them off about her whereabouts. She's even got Manila folders of all her press cuttings. Of course she doesn't know I know that – I saw them one night when Mr Belding got trapped under her bed in a cowboy outfit and I was performing a rescue mission.

When Anderson dumped her, the interest in America all but disappeared, but a few of the UK fashion blogs still fawn over her. She's cool, you know – wears white ankle socks with lavender-coloured brogues and has a huge fringe, both vertically and horizontally.

I yawn and give her a smile, but she doesn't notice. She's got that weird dreamy expression she always gets when she's thinking about Anderson.

Jeez.

My mum used to say that love made people crazy, and she was right. Not that I've personally ever been in love. But for someone who's usually so focused and razor-sharp, Summer turns into a wibbly wreck of a woman when it comes to that guy. It doesn't seem to matter that he got his PA to dump her by email, or that he's now officially dating Emma Watson. She still thinks of him as the one that got away, and if he were ever to come back I reckon she'd drop Holden in a nanosecond, which wouldn't necessarily be a bad thing, since Holden is a proper turd.

Sinking back against the train seat, I get started on my Lilt and vodka, watch the gorgeous greens and golds of the English countryside whizz past through the window, and wonder what life will be like when I'm the rich and famous co-author of a bestselling book. I'll finally be able to go travelling again without having to worry about money. I could open a bar somewhere exotic and far away. Maybe Bali. Or St Lucia, even. Somewhere full of happy, relaxed people who just want to chill out and have fun and dance in the glow of the moon and that sort of shit. Somewhere I could live in my bikini, throw amazing, life-changing parties every night and just enjoy myself without any pressure or questions or obligations to anyone. Complete and utter freedom without a worry in the world.

I can't wait.

CHAPTER FOUR

When meeting new female friends, be friendly and interested, but not too interested as this will cause suspicion.

***MATILDA BEAM'S GOOD WOMAN GUIDE*, 1959**

The Southbank Press lobby is so fancy: a mixture of majestic London architecture, with its high ceilings and intricate cornicing, blended with modern minimalist decor. The walls are vast and white and lined with framed images of book covers, each one lit by soft, glowy uplighting like in an art gallery. It's busier than I thought it would be, with people bustling about in and out of lifts and lounging on huge sofas reading sheaves of paper and biting biros insightfully. On one wall, a huge cinema-sized TV screen blasts out glossy promotional videos of famous authors talking about their books.

'Shit on a stick,' I whisper as I spot the recent Booker Prize-winning Davis Arthur Montblanc hurrying into the lifts. He was on BBC's *Question Time* just a few nights ago. And now he's here! 'Look, Summer! It's Davis Arthur

Montblanc. I didn't know the Southbank Press published him!'

Summer rolls her eyes and pushes me along the expanse of lobby. 'Of course they publish him. They publish practically every *Sunday Times* bestseller in the country.'

'Fuck.'

'Will you stop swearing?'

As I watch the electronic doors whoosh closed behind Davis Arthur Montblanc, the magnitude of where we are hits me. Blimey. This is a Real Thing. Potentially the big time. A swarm of excitable butterflies make themselves known in the pit of my belly and the sudden blast of nerves somehow reminds my body to start sweating again. Stupid massive coat.

Oh no. I've just had the most shitty thought. What if I sweat onto the desk in the meeting? Onto an important manuscript? Oh. My. God. What if I sweat onto Davis Arthur Montblanc's award-winning manuscript? Jesus-God, no.

'Are you absolutely sure I shouldn't take the coat off?' I ask Summer as a droplet of perspiration slides off my forehead and trickles its way down my nose.

'Yes, I'm sure. Not in that ridiculous dress. You'll make a horrible impression.'

I protest a little but keep the coat on – because Summer is the fashion genius and I wouldn't know a Louboutin if it were flung at my head – and frantically fan my crimson face as we reach the reception desk.

'Good afternoon,' says a friendly-looking young woman in a crisp, cream cotton shirt. 'Welcome to Southbank Press. How may I help you?'

'Hello there,' Summer says with her usual supreme confidence. 'Summer Spencer here for Valentina Smith.'

'And Jessica Beam too. I'm also here to see Valentina Smith.'

Summer throws me her withering look which, I'm peeved to admit, is a great deal more withering than my withering look.

The receptionist nods curtly, hands us plastic 'Guest' lanyards and instructs us to take a seat while she calls down Valentina Smith.

'Right,' Summer says once we're perched on the plush purple sofas. 'We're going to storm this, OK? We have to. Anderson will rue the day he decided to dump a bestselling author!'

I imagine Anderson is probably poolside in LA right now, cheerily snorting cocaine off a model's teeny arse cheek, thinking about how mega loaded and successful he is. If the topless selfies Summer texts to him when she's had a few haven't got his attention already, then I'm not sure a book will. Poor Summer.

'They won't be able to say no,' I agree in my most confident voice. 'We've got a mega pitch. And a great, unique lifestyle website. We're basically a fucking dream team, Sum. Practically the ... Cannon and Ball of fashion-slash-lifestyle blogging. No, wait, Cannon and Ball haven't worked as a dream team comparison for years. Torvill and Dean? No. Er ... Kenan and Kel? No ... um ... '

'Shush.' Summer opens up her yellow Mulberry purse and pulls out the well-worn picture of the time she met her idol, Alexa Chung, at a fashion show in New York. She inhales and breathes out extra slowly through her mouth before closing her eyes.

'I call upon the power of Chung to see me through this important life moment. To inspire me to be my freshest, most stylish self. To help me to rock it in a super-hot way.

To allow my star power to rise to the surface and shine brightly like a super, super star.'

She opens her eyes, strokes Alexa Chung's luminous cheek and carefully tucks the photograph back into her bag.

'Fuck. I'm a bit nervous,' I huff, picking up an abandoned copy of the *Guardian* to fan myself with.

'No swearing, Jess!'

'Shit, did I swear again? Shitballs, sorry. I don't even know I'm doing it anybloodymore. Maybe we should get a swear jar in the flat. But not a jar, something nicer. A swear mug? A swear vase? Some cool kind of vessel, anyway – what do you th—'

'It's fine. Shush. Just be extra careful in the meeting.'

An intern appears and indicates that we should follow her into the lifts.

Summer smiles, a steely look in her big brown eyes. She leans in close.

'Don't fuck this one up, Jess.'

* * *

Valentina Smith, non-fiction editorial director, is one very polished-looking woman. She's in her mid-thirties and really attractive: long, deeply tanned and willowy, and wearing clothes in camel, taupe and biscuit, which everyone knows is basically light beige, dark beige and medium beige. Her long, blown-out hair is highlighted in exactly the same three-tone colour as her outfit, her lips are painted a look-at-my-mouth! postbox red, and her only jewellery is a pair of understated, elegant, white-gold studs. There's an awkward moment with my gigantic coat: Valentina insists I take it off immediately on account of this absurdly hot summer weather, but I'm conscious of Summer's instructions to keep it on no matter what so that the dress underneath never sees the light of day. I don't know what to do! Valentina starts to pull the coat off my shoulders, but I hiss 'No!' and clutch onto it fiercely, and then we have a kind of coat tug-of-war until Valentina – who I suspect usually gets what she wants – wins out and the coat is removed. Now my floral dress is revealed in all its hideous glory. Summer looks as if she's mere seconds away from dying of embarrassment.

'Oh, I am loving that dress!' Valentina Smith says, her bright blue eyes appraising the outfit. 'Very "Jen" from *Dawson's Creek*, but just a touch slaggier. In an ironic way, of course. I was reading an article about the whole ironic fashion trend in the *Observer* last month. I'm not sure I could ever quite pull it off myself, but you do it beautifully, Jess! Kudos.'

'Thank you, Valentina Smith!'

I haven't a clue what she's talking about, but it all seems to be very positive. I *knew* this dress wasn't so bad.

Summer and I sit down on a stiff buttercream sofa and I take a good look around at what I think is the most gorgeous office I've ever seen. It's as stylish as Valentina is – all glass surfaces and huge windows, with bursts of colour coming only from vases of exotic-looking flowers and the beautifully glossy hardback books that fill up the entire back wall. If this were my office, I would have it exactly the same way. Except I'd probably add some fairy lights to brighten things up just a touch, and maybe a few beanbags to hang out and read all the books on. Ooh, and an amazing sound system so we could play some music and have a dance whenever the mood struck. Maybe even a funky disco ball ...

Valentina pours fancy bottled water into three tall crystal glasses. I'm super thirsty from the blistering July heat, so I pick up one of the glasses right away and down the refreshingly cool liquid. Summer and Valentina watch as I gulp it all eagerly.

'Aaaaaah! Necked it in one!' I whisper, muffling a petite burp with my hand.

Summer gives me the frosty look. What's up with her?

'Quite!' Valentina laughs and sits down behind her big desk. 'So! How much do I adore *Summer in the City*? The answer is *a lot*. It's so "of the now". So springy and fresh. We *love* it.'

Summer and I smile excitedly at each other. This is so cool. They love our site!

'Obviously Summer here is the eponymous Summer of the website. Jessica, can you clarify what role you play in things?

'Oh, I'm mainly the writer, but I do a bit of community management too – you know, look after the social media and admin-type stuff.'

Valentina glances at Summer, her brow puckered slightly. 'Ah! OK! So you don't actually write any of the content, Summer?'

Summer mumbles. 'I, er ... well ... '

The last time I heard Summer mumble was back in uni when the lecturer asked her a question about one of the assignments I'd written for her. Luckily we were sitting together and I was able to scribble the answer on my Pukka Pad for her to see before anyone realized. She flushes red. I can't bear it.

'We write together,' I interject quickly. 'Totally equal. Isn't that right, Sum?'

Summer nods vigorously and swallows before saying, 'Right, yes. And I'm the face of the site too. And I decide what and who exactly we write about.'

'Great!' Valentina smiles, showing off beautifully white,

perfectly straight teeth. 'I couldn't be more excited to hear your pitch.'

So we begin.

* * *

It's all going well. Really well. Summer is performing the first half of the presentation as planned, and I'm flicking the projector monitor through screen-grabs of *Summer in the City* and all of our recent analytics. The page that shows our steep traffic climb over the past year elicits a gasp of delight from Valentina Smith, and her tongue almost lolls with pleasure when we show her how many of our product click-throughs result in a direct sale of that product. Summer is on fire – unwavering and poised. I get a tickle of pride as I watch her talk about our site.

It's getting close to my turn to speak. I'm trying to stay cool, but my hands shake a little, something that's never happened before. Since when did I start getting nervous? I clasp them together to keep them steady.

You can do this, Jess. Just picture the distant mountains of Peru, the hot bearded boy travellers, the beach parties, a whole new life. You could have it all if you get this book deal ...

I take a deep breath, open my mouth and ...

Summer doesn't stop talking.

My first thought is that I'm trying to jump in too early. I look down at the notes. But no. She's saying my words. She's doing my bit of the pitch!

I cough lightly to get her attention as non-intrusively as possible, but she doesn't notice, just continues speaking the words I've been going over the whole way here.

What is she doing? I watch her, and the feeling of pride

I had a moment ago turns to one of despair. Maybe she's nervous? Or is she just so in the flow that she can't stop?

When Summer finishes up with the excellent joke I wrote about the difference between Flickr and Pinterest, I don't quite know whether to feel pissed off that I didn't get my chance to speak or pleased that Valentina doesn't seem to have noticed the hiccup.

I give Summer a 'What the hell?' look when she sits back down, but she doesn't seem to see me, just smiles serenely at Valentina.

'Great,' Valentina enthuses, tucking a golden-blonde lock behind her ear. 'You've clearly got a handle on your audience. And your retail relationships are to *die* for.'

'Thanks!' Summer smiles. 'It's something I've taken super seriously.'

'Jess, we've not heard from you yet.' Valentina turns to me. 'Traditionally a lifestyle book like this is meant for the coffee table. But us old publishing stalwarts have to think about the exciting new digital revolution. How do *you* think a *Summer in the City* book would flourish as a digital entity?'

I stand up, my knees all wibbly. Shit. We didn't prepare for this question, though it seems so obvious now that we should have. I give Summer a look of terror. She shrugs discreetly.

Fuck.

'Well, um ... ' I cough and push my glasses up my sweaty nose. 'I ... I think the best thing to do would be to transfer ideas from the book into all mediums.' I reach down for my glass of water and take a huge gulp, not quite sure where I'm going with this. 'Er, as you heard from Summer, we already have quite a good social media following. We could up our YouTube content with spoken extracts from the book or podcast interviews with the designers and establishments we feature?'

Valentina nods, her eyes slightly narrowed. OK. She's not trying to kick me out of the room yet.

'With an e-book, we would—' I start.

' I know sooo many amazing Manchester-based business owners that would be up for featuring,' Summer interrupts. 'They're good friends of mine – it's a really *connected* scene. I could call them up and ask—'

'Oh, I don't think Jess was quite finished,' Valentina says with a polite smile. I risk a glance at Summer. She's gone ruby red. Shit. I clear my throat and pause for a second before continuing.

'Um, well, with an e-book we would have the capacity to make the book interactive on a tablet device.'

'Interactive? Super!' Valentina tilts her head encouragingly. I lift my chin.

'We could embed retail details in the images. Link to video content or even run it from directly inside the book. We could have Facebook comments working as an app through the chapters. Ooh, or we could entitle the chapters with hashtags, so that people who are reading the same bits of the book can have a natter about it on Twitter. Could the images be turned into gifs, do you think? Our audience on Tumblr really love gifs! And we could run snippets of music by the bands we mention. Summer knows loads of bands. Let's allow the readers to instantly see and hear and buy exactly what it is we're talking about!'

I stop, aware that I'm getting overexcited and might not be fully making sense.

Valentina Smith clasps her hands together and gives me a wide grin.

'Fantastic ideas, Jess. Well done, lovely energy there. Kudos!'

I give Summer a look as if to say 'Phew', but she's gone pale and is staring at me, her mouth gaping open.

'You know ... ' Valentina says thoughtfully. 'We're having a launch tonight for Davis Arthur Montblanc's fabulous new novel. Why don't you girls come along? Meet a few of the Southbank team?'

We nod eagerly. Wow. Davis Arthur Montblanc's party!

'Of course, I can't *promise* anything yet,' Valentina continues, 'but ... ' and then she looks straight at me. 'I think you'd fit in very well here. Very well indeed.'

Aw yeeeah.

CHAPTER FIVE

Your attire should always suit the event for which it's worn. Plan as far in advance as possible!

***Matilda Beam's Guide to Love and Romance*, 1955**

Summer's been dead weird ever since we got out of the meeting with Valentina. I asked her why she didn't let me say my bit of the pitch, and she told me it was down to an attack of the nerves, although she didn't look nervous at all to me. Then she was quiet and evasive for the entire Tube journey to Carnaby Street. I don't know. Maybe she's processing everything. The whole meeting was pretty intense, to be fair.

She doesn't even balk when I pull her into Primark, a place she usually swears brings her out in a polyester rash.

I pick a nice bright pair of pink feather earrings off a stand.

'What do you think?' I ask Summer.

'I can't even begin to explain how much they offend me.'

I inspect them. What's wrong with them? How can a pair of pink feathery earrings offend a person? Fashion is even more confusing to me than trying to eat spaghetti bolognese without getting sauce on my chest. Bugger it. I like the earrings. I plonk them in my basket and carry on through the store, Summer trailing behind sullenly.

'Ooh, look!' I say. 'Onesies are three for two!'

I love onesies so much. What could be more comfortable than an adult Babygro! When I'm properly hung-over, the only thing that will cure me is sprawling across the sofa with an 80s film and two cans of icy-cold Fanta, all bundled up in a onesie.

I pick up a hooded cow-print one, a leopard-print one with a neon-pink zip, and a plain yellow one, excitedly adding them to the basket.

We pay for my stuff in Primark and continue walking towards Carnaby Street and a fancy boutique Summer wants to go to. I glance over at her.

'Are you OK, Sum?'

She shrugs prettily.

I put my arm round her. 'You did a really fucking excellent job in there, you know. I was really proud of you.'

She pauses mid-walk and gives me her look.

'Yeah, I'm not sure Valentina *got* me. Then again ... I didn't exactly have a chance to impress her, with you prattling on about all that digital technological stuff the whole time. What was that? We didn't agree to talk about that. It wasn't in the notes you wrote.'

'Oh, Sum, what else was I supposed to do? She asked me a blummin' question. I totally had to wing it.'

'Right. Well, thank God for clever old Jess!' she says

with an odd smile before walking ahead of me into the fancy shop.

* * *

It's after six and we're back at the hotel getting ready for the Davis Arthur Montblanc party. Summer has perked up a bit: the shop assistant at the boutique – a huge Anderson Warner fan – recognized her, something that hasn't happened for a while, and gave her a discount on the long black velvet dress she bought.

'How does it look?' she says now, posing by the hotel bed, hand on hip, one foot crossed over the other red-carpet style.

'Beautiful. You look really beautiful,' I say. She does. She's a five eight-size eight with legs like a baby giraffe and Jennifer Aniston-level toned arms. Her brunette to caramel dip-dyed hair is thick and wavy over her angular shoulders, her big brown eyes are enhanced by perfectly applied bronze shadow and she's painted her lips a very dark, very chic blood red. The necklace she's wearing does have a dismembered Barbie's head on it, though. But it's from a really exclusive shop, so even though I'm not keen, it's almost certainly a very cool fashiony choice which everyone will be impressed with.

'What about my arse?' She turns around to show me her bum.

'It looks wonderful.'

'Better than Carol Vorderman's?' She frowns, twisting her head round so she can see her bum in the full-length mirror. Carol Vorderman is Summer's arch nemesis: the woman who stole 2011's Rear of the Year award from under her nose and didn't even have the grace to respond when

Summer sent her a tweet that said: '*Congrats hun, the best woman won :D <3 #rearoftheyear #noregrets.*'

'Way better than Carol Vorderman,' I say enthusiastically. 'Vorderman's arse is a ... a sack of porridge compared to yours.'

'OK, good,' she mumbles, grabbing her iPhone and taking a series of selfies in the mirror, which she proceeds to post immediately to Twitter and Instagram and Facebook.

I ended up finding something in the posh boutique too. It's a pale grey silk jumpsuit with tiny little metal studs dotted round the halter-neck. It's a bit smarter than I'd usually wear, but the store assistant insisted that I couldn't go to a fancy book launch in H&M, and the jumpsuit was on sale so it didn't completely ransack my overdraft. Well, maybe a tiny bit, but a book deal means money, therefore the jumpsuit is really just an investment in my career. As are the metallic purple high heels I bought to go with it.

I plug my iPhone into the hotel-room speakers, crank up a bit of Britpop and throw some shapes. Summer pours two glasses of Merlot from the minibar and we sit side by side, companionably finishing off our make-up. As Summer rustles around in her tote in search of her favourite mascara, an envelope falls out of the bag and onto the carpet. It's thick and seashell-coloured, with Summer's name written on it in gold-embossed script. A wedding invitation.

'Ooh, who's getting mawwied?' I lean over to get a better look. Summer snatches the envelope up and holds it to her chest.

'Oh, no one you know,' she says nonchalantly.

'Sum, we know all the same people.'

'Um ...' She starts to shove the envelope back into her bag.

A secret wedding!

'Oi! What the bloody hell are you hiding?' I rugby-tackle her and grab the envelope from her manicured hands. 'Let me see it!'

'Jess, you freak! You'll mess up my hair. Give me that back.'

I chuckle and open the envelope. 'Now, now, let me see, who is Summer's new friend? Summer's special secret wedding friend!'

I pull out the creamy invitation and unfold the stiff paper. It's an invite for Amy Keyplass's wedding to Mark Chunder. Old friends of ours from uni.

'Oh, it's just Amy and Mark. Should be a good knees-up. Why wouldn't you show me this? Is there an RSVP date?' I scan the text. 'Remind me to find my invite when we get back – must be somewhere in the post pile. Actually, have you got a pen? I'll write it on my hand. *RSVP Amy and Mark.*'

'You haven't got one.' Summer coughs.

'Huh?'

'An invitation. You haven't got an invitation. You're kind of not invited to the wedding.'

'Oh ... just the reception bit then?'

'Yeeeaaah ... no. You're not invited to any of it.'

'Just like Amy, forgetting. She'd forget her own head if it wasn't screwed on.' I roll my eyes. 'They must be dead busy with all the planning. I'll give her a ring over the weekend!'

Summer puts down her mascara and sighs. 'You're not getting it, petal. Amy hasn't forgotten. They ... just don't want you there.'

I frown, confused. 'Whaaat? Why on earth wouldn't they want me there? I'm the *life* of the party. A wedding isn't a proper wedding until I've cha-cha slid solo on the dance floor. Everyone knows that. Amy and me are top mates! I introduced her to Mark!'

'You got her arrested, Jess.'

'Er, that was a year ago. And it's not like *I* lifted her top up and flashed her boobs at the cast of Corrie on their Christmas meal out. She did that all by herself. Tyrone loved it, but Rita had to go and call the police, didn't she? Typical fucking Rita.'

'You provided the tequila and double-dared Amy to do it. Mark thinks you're a bad influence.'

'Mark Chunder's a ginormous dork. Just because I haven't got a stick lodged up my bum like he has. Jeez. Amy was such a good giggle at uni.' I sigh nostalgically at the lovely fun times Amy and I once had.

Summer shakes her head delicately. 'We're not at university any more, though, Jess. They're, like, getting *married*. They're renovating a town house in Surrey. You know – growing up, committing, being responsible. You might want to try it sometime.'

I feel the familiar uncomfortable itch spread across my body. *Renovating a town house in Surrey? Gross.*

I think of Amy and what fun she was back in the day. Totally mental and giggly and up for anything. And now she's just like the rest of them. It's like *The Walking Dead*, but instead of a zombie apocalypse, it's a boring person apocalypse. Everybody's changing.

'Yeah, well,' I say breezily, feeling an odd lurch in my stomach, 'weddings suck anyway. I'm *glad* I'm not invited. It'll probably be full of shithead couply couples talking about babies and stamp duty and the garden centre. Chuh. Pledging to spend your entire life with one boring person for ever and ever? It's so daft, when you think about it. You never know what's going to happen. How do you know that you won't get fed up of them? That they won't leave you? That you won't get shafted? It's absurd.'

Summer rolls her eyes at me in the mirror. 'It's not absurd, Jess. Most people don't get "shafted" by falling in love. Most people don't ... well, they don't end up like your mum.'

I tut. Summer reckons that every bloody thing I think or do has some woo-woo subconscious connection to my mum. Which is blatantly daft and annoying, not to mention downright untrue. I wouldn't mind, but the extent of Summer's psychological knowledge is that she once saw Dr Linda Papadopoulos off *This Morning* in M&S Food.

I swallow, and it feels like there's an annoying little splinter stuck in my throat. 'Pass us my wine, will you, Sum. What time is it? We should probably get a move on. We can't be late for Davis Arthur Montblanc! Ooh, wonder if they'll have a posh buffet on ... '

* * *

I spend ages restraightening my hair extensions before backcombing extensively at the top and pulling it all into a tight, high ponytail. Then I attach two pairs of fake eyelashes and do some glittery gold eyeliner so that my eyes stand out behind my specs.

In the bathroom, I change into my new silky jumpsuit, feeling a little flutter of pleasure as the cold, smooth material skims its way across my body. I'm quite short at five foot three, but it makes me look at least an inch taller. I spin round in the mirror. All the running and partying I've been doing recently has eradicated the little beer belly I've been carrying around for the past few years. I look pretty good, actually – I think the word is lithe. And I reckon jumpsuits suit me! Maybe when I move to some exotic country I'll buy more silk jumpsuits in all different colours. Summer is always going on about 'signature looks'. Could jumpsuits be my signature look? Jumpsuit Jess? 'Here comes Jumpsuit Jess,' people would say. 'Now the party can *really* start.'

'Ta-da!' I sing as I leave the bathroom. 'I'm blummin' uncomfortable because my thong keeps riding up my arse, *but* ... ' I twirl round and do jazz hands in the mirror.

'Oh! You look different. *Yay*!' Summer scoops the wine glasses up from the bedside table. 'Super awesome. Let's finish this wine – we need to get going.' She strides forward on her high heels and holds one glass-carrying hand out to me. I reach to take it from her when somehow, suddenly, the wine glass is out of her hands –

'Fuuuuck!'

And its contents are on my brand-new jumpsuit.

Shit! Did Summer trip up? No. She's perfectly upright. How did ... ?

'Oh dear!' Summer says, carefully putting down the other wine glass on the coffee table and grabbing a facial wipe from her make-up bag. 'I'm *such* a klutz!'

'What are you talking about? You're the least klutzy person on earth. What the heck?'

'I think there was something on the carpet. I totally stumbled over something. Sorreeeee!'

Summer dabs frantically at the wine now dripping off my arm and spreading into a violent-looking stain across my silk-covered abdomen. I look like an extra in a prom-based horror movie.

'Oh dear.' Summer repeats. 'It's not coming out. Red wine just does not come out. Soooo annoying.'

Shit!

I jog to the bathroom, strip off the jumpsuit and run it

under the tap, rubbing furiously at the fabric with a towel. Nothing happens. The stain sits there stubbornly.

'I need to call the taxi now!' Summer informs me worriedly. 'You're going to have to put something else on quickly or we'll be late. I'm really sorry, sweetpea.'

I feel a lurch in my stomach. I don't know why I'm even bothered about it. It's just clothes, after all.

I pick up today's floral 90s dress from the corner of the bedroom where I flung it earlier. This will have to do.

'You can't wear that again!' Summer barks, tapping the cab number into her mobile. 'Valentina already saw it!'

'She seemed to like it before.' I yank it over my head. 'It'll be all right.'

Summer stalks over and tugs on it with a grimace. 'It smells a bit, J.'

I give it a sniff. She's right. The Febreze has worn off and the original damp mothbally smell is now evident. It stinks.

'But I have nothing else!'

Summer frowns and squints her eyes like she's thinking really hard. I don't know what genius plan she thinks she's going to come up with. The only other choice of outfit I have is—

'Onesie!' Summer breathes as if it's the most obvious idea ever to generate in a brain. 'You could wear one of your new onesies.'

'A onesie?' I screw my face up. I know bugger all about clothes, and I do love onesies, obviously, but I'm pretty sure that they're not suitable garb for posh literary bashes. 'Nah. I don't think so, Summer ... '

'Just hear me out!' she urges. 'It'll be so cool. A onesie is kind of like a jumpsuit when you really think about it. You can roll up the legs and still wear your new high heels. With all your hair and make-up, so ... glam, it'll look super fresh. Totally.'

Hmmm. I suppose they *are* really nice onesies ... and really very comfortable ...

'Ooh, ooh,' Summer continues, opening the Primark bag by my bed. 'You could wear those new spangly pink feather earrings too!'

'You didn't like those when we were in the shop.'

'I do like them! I was just pissed off that you saw them first. Trust me – you'll look amazing.'

The front desk calls to let us know that our cab is here. Crap.

'Erm ... '

I guess I did see someone from *Geordie Shore* wearing a onesie at a product launch in Manchester, and I do love that show. But that was a lad. Would it work on a woman?

'Don't you trust me?' Summer says, hurt pooling in her large brown eyes. 'After everything we've been through? Look, maybe you should just stay here while I go ... I don't mind.'

Hmm. Summer *does* know everything about fashion. And she is my best friend. She wouldn't make me look stupid.

'Course I trust you, you big geek,' I say, pulling the furry leopard-skin onesie with the neon-pink zip out of the carrier bag. 'Summer and Jess take on the world, right?'

Summer grins in recognition of our university motto. 'Oh, totes.'

CHAPTER SIX

A well-mixed manhattan at a social gathering is one of life's pleasures. But know your alcohol limits, ladies. No Good Man ever wanted to marry a wild girl!

MATILDA BEAM'S GUIDE TO LOVE AND ROMANCE, 1955

I'm not entirely sure a onesie was the right move.

Summer and I strut though the discreetly glamorous Berkeley Rooms in Soho; her on the hunt for Valentina Smith, me on the hunt for someone else rocking leisurewear to make friends with. As we push through the impeccably dressed and intelligently talkative crowds, I notice eyes bulging in horror as I pass by. Shitballs. Is that Benedict Cumberbatch? And there's Helena Bonham Carter chatting away to Davis Arthur Montblanc. Damn. This do is way, way too fancy for my onesie. As I make my way though the room, a lofty ginger guy in a sharp suit drawls, 'Looks like the entertainment has arrived, folks.'

I throw him my very best withering glance, but he's

already turned back to his cronies and doesn't get the benefit.

Gad. Why the blazing arse did I agree to wear this?

'I'm starting to think this onesie was a really fucking shitty idea!' I hiss at Summer as she accepts a glass of champagne from a passing waiter.

'You look great, Jess. Honestly. These people wouldn't know a bold fashion choice if it stabbed them in the back.'

I look around distractedly for the bar, but I can't see one. I could really do with a drink. A big important party can often be a bit daunting, and especially so if you've arrived wearing your pyjamas.

'I'm going to have *one* drink,' I say firmly to Summer. 'We need to keep a clear head, so just the one. No Jessica Beam adventures tonight. I promise.'

'That'll be the day,' Summer scoffs. I smile sadly. There was a time when it was Summer and Jess adventures. Where did she go? And why, oh why did I agree to wear the onesie? Did that man over there just point at me and laugh? Oh Christ. He *is* laughing at me, he's clutching his belly and full-on crying with laughter. Wait, why is he pointing his phone in my direction? Is he *filming* me?

God.

I half jog after the retreating waiter and tap him on the shoulder.

'Yo, you got any pear cider?' I ask him frantically.

He smirks and looks pointedly at his tray of tall champagne flutes glistening snootily beneath the lit-up chandelier.

'No, miss.'

'Any blue Wickeds in the back?'

'I'm afraid not. But I'm sure this 1995 vintage Bollinger will suffice?'

I sigh. Vintage shit. What's the obsession with old stuff? It's 2014, people!

'Fine. Don't worry. I'll take a fizz, then. Only the one, though. If I come back to you for another glass, tell me to just fuck off, OK?'

The waiter smiles politely and hands me a glass of champagne. 'Enjoy your evening, miss.'

'Thank you. Just don't let me have any more after this one. Promise me, OK? Promise.'

But the waiter is already zooming back off through the crowds, glancing back at me with a frightened expression on his young face.

Damn.

I take a teeny sip of the champagne. Blerg. I'll never understand why people go so nuts over champagne. It's so self-satisfied and way too gassy, and you're expected to act all excited about drinking it for the whole time you're drinking it. It's such a lot of pressure. Plus everyone knows that champagne causes a hangover worse than any of the other boozes, but still, the facade continues. Maybe if the *Summer in the City* book goes well they would commission me for another? *The Champagne Conspiracy: An Exposé by Jessica Beam.*

I miss you, pear cider.

Finding my way back to Summer, I discover her deep in conversation with Valentina Smith, who is wearing a silk wrap dress the colour of mustard.

'Hey,' I say brightly. 'Lovely do, isn't it?'

Valentina's mouth drops open as she takes in my get-up. Squirming under her overt scrutiny, I smile widely and nod, confidently trying to own it. I bet she thinks I'm a real chump.

'That's quite an ensemble, Jess' she says, studying my feather earrings.

Is it my imagination, or is Summer smirking?

'Yeah, we had a massive disaster with my other outfit,' I explain with an apologetic cringe.

Valentina takes a sip of her champagne, sighing with immense pleasure (a potential interviewee for *The Champagne Conspiracy*?). She narrows her eyes and looks me up and down for what seems like ages.

Shit. She's going to kick me out of the party. I clearly don't belong here.

'It's so ... on the money,' she eventually declares, shaking her head in wonder. 'All of us in dull black tie and here you are, vibrant like a beautiful fashionista parrot. Or should I say leopard! Bold move, lady. I respect it.' *Is she kidding?* 'Yes, I get it,' she goes on, tilting her head to the side, a finger to her chin, examining me like I'm a work of art. 'I really do. Pseudo-chav. Ironic. Northern, yes?'

'Er ... '

'I like you, Jessica Beam,' she says. 'You're very current.'

'Cheers.' I wonder what on earth she's talking about. 'It was a last-minute decision, to be honest.'

'Modest, too.' She grins warmly as if I am the cleverest, most interesting person to walk the earth. I give Summer a discreet thumbs-up, which she returns with a lukewarm smile.

'So, Valentina.' Summer stands slightly in front of me. 'Do I see Leo Frost over there talking to Davis Arthur Montblanc?'

'What? Leo Frost? Where?' Valentina's voice has gone all weird and strangled.

Valentina and I peer over to where Summer is looking and spot Davis Arthur Montblanc himself in conversation with the tall red-headed twonk who nastily called me the entertainment. The twonk is stroking his chin and nursing a glass of whisky. I wonder how that idiot got hold of a non-champagne-based beverage?

'Must be someone important,' I mutter, resentfully taking another sip of champagne.

'Oh, *of course* you know who Leo Frost is, Jess?' Summer says, gathering her hair up and letting it fall back over her shoulders. 'Artistic Director at Woolf Frost?'

I give her a blank look. 'Nope. Never heard of the guy.'

'Leo Frost, advertising wunderkind?' She says it slowly, like I'm being thick. When I give no reaction, she goes on, 'His dad owns the famous ad agency? Montblanc's nephew? Broke Kate Middleton's heart at St Andrews before she rebounded to Wills?'

I shrug and wonder how the hell he got that whisky. I wonder if he'll get me some, because this champagne really sucks.

'He's the man of the moment, super enigmatic and mysterious.' Summer's eyes light up. 'Anderson knows him quite well, actually. I once met him at this amazing party in Brooklyn. I am – *was* – totally in love with Anderson, but Leo Frost ... well, I could have been tempted. He has this power, this magnetic power, you know, like Alexa Chung has. But he totally abuses it. He's a real womanizer.' She gazes over at him with blatant admiration.

'Leo Frost is a vindictive, arrogant shit!' Valentina suddenly spits, her face flushing cherry red to match her lipstick. She sucks in a huge lungful of breath and exhales, her mouth in a tight 'O' shape. 'Apologies. I shouldn't have said that.'

Her eyes water with barely restrained fury as she glares at him. Wow. She really hates this bloke. We all stare at Leo

Frost. He must sense it because he turns round and gives Valentina an arrogant wink.

Valentina makes a weird sound somewhere in the middle of a sob and a squeak.

'What's the story there?' I ask nosily.

Valentina sniffs and takes an enormous gulp of her champagne. 'Oh, nothing, nothing.' She pauses for a beat. 'Well, apart from the six weeks we dated and he basically destroyed my heart *and* my self-esteem.'

Eek.

'Harsh beans,' Summer says with a grimace.

'I don't fall easily,' Valentina explains, anger making her eyes glint. 'But I fell for him hard. Really hard. He made me feel like I was something special. Reeled me in. I thought we were serious, or getting there at least, and then I found out he was seeing three other women. Yes, three. He fucked a trio of women behind my back. A *trio*.'

'Nooo.'

'Yes,' Valentina nods sadly. 'It was horrendous.' Her nostrils flare and she shakes her head really quickly as if trying to clear away a bad memory. Woah. She has literally just transformed from a confident Elle McPherson-alike top editor to a broken wreck in the space of two minutes. More evidence of Mum's wisdom: love shits on you.

'I'm sorry, Valentina. That sounds properly crap.'

Ordinarily I'd tell a woman this messed-up over some idiot to get a grip. She's crazy for putting herself into a situation that, essentially, puts an open target on your heart. But this particular woman has the potential to, you know, make our dreams come true and she's clearly very damaged by this shithead, so I keep my mouth shut and try to empathize.

Valentina clings onto her champagne flute, clearly getting into her ranting stride. 'Just last week he was in the

Observer, spouting about how he'll never get married, how he sees himself as an "intrepid explorer of women".' She makes air quotes. 'What does that even mean? I simply cannot believe I wasted six weeks on him. I could have been doing something far more fulfilling with my time. Six weeks! I might have learned a new language in six weeks! German. Ya! Instead I let him do this – ' she points at herself – 'to me. He's a bloody horror show.'

'That is shitty,' I say.

'How awful,' Summer agrees.

'Gosh. I'm seriously sorry, guys.' Valentina takes out a compact mirror and checks her perfect make-up. 'I had no clue he was going to be here. His Twitter feed said he'd be in New York, so it's really thrown me to see him out of the blue.' She grabs another drink from a passing waiter and guzzles it back.

'Well, if it makes you feel any better, I really don't see what the fuss is about. I don't think he's hot at all,' I declare, finishing up my drink.

Valentina and Summer goggle at me.

I examine Leo Frost once more to see if I'm missing this supposed 'magnetism'. But I'm not. He's lanky and pale, and his coppery-coloured hair is arranged into a quiff halfway between Danny Zuko and Don Draper. His eyes are pure green and crafty-looking, and his nose is too long. Why haven't his friends explained to him about Fake Bake? Seems to me that they're not really his friends at all.

'I think he's super hot. Looks just like Tom Hiddleston,' Summer says reluctantly. 'Sorry, Valentina.'

Hmmm. I suppose he does have a Captain America jawline, and what I suspect underneath the navy suit is a pretty nice bod. But he doesn't look like Tom Hiddleston. Not *that* much, anyway.

Valentina hands me another flute of champagne. 'No thanks,' I say firmly. 'I'm, er, not much of a drinker.'

Summer raises her thick fashiony eyebrows.

'You may as well celebrate, sweet Jess,' Valentina says to me with a tipsy wink. 'I'm sure you'll soon have an official reason to.' She gives a little hiccup.

Whaaaaaat? Is she saying what I think she's saying? That the *Summer in the City* book is pretty much a done deal? I do an excited face at Summer, but she doesn't see it – she's busy waving at some blonde guy in sunglasses she seems to recognize.

'Oh, go on, then,' I chuckle, taking the glass from Valentina. 'Just *one* more couldn't hurt.'

* * *

It's a matter of pride for me that I can find a way to have fun in most situations: tram queues, blogger meet-ups, smear tests can all be turned into entertaining social occasions with enough booze and the right banter. But I'm sorry to say that there is zero fun to be had at this book launch. Nil. I feel like I've been here for many days and it's never going to end. There have been approximately fifteen speeches by literary people totally sucking up to Davis Arthur Montblanc, and to be quite frank his new book doesn't sound very entertaining at all. It's called *The Beekeeper*, but it isn't even about bees, just bees as a motif for capitalism. Pah. This is not my crowd. To make matters worse, Valentina is one hundred per cent the only person in this room to appreciate the leopard-print onesie. Everyone else is looking at me like I'm planning to either mug them or offer them class B drugs.

I've thought about slipping out and going back to the

hotel: order some room-service pear cider, chat up the cute, twinkly-eyed concierge, see if he can get me late-night access to the Jacuzzi, but Summer's having such a great time telling everyone about her Barbie-head necklace and the time Anderson took her to the MTV movie awards and James Franco said she had 'presence'.

And in any case, if I left early it would reflect badly on us, especially since we haven't officially signed any book contracts yet, despite Valentina's exciting hints.

Also ... I'm a bit drunk. I know, I know. I didn't mean to be. I truly didn't. But people kept showing up with champagne, and the champagne, although shit-tasting, is free, and there was nothing else to drink and I was thirsty and this party really is a snooze-fest – there isn't even any music playing! And somehow, two glasses of champagne turned into seven glasses of champagne, and all the excitement of the day means I've forgotten to eat anything more substantial than this morning's delicious beef pasty. Anyway, I'm all in now, no point in stopping.

I look around for the smarmy ginger guy who had the whisky. Leo Frost. I wonder if he'll get *me* some whisky.

Oh, there he is, standing by a table piled high with copies of *The Beekeeper*. He's deep in a conversation with three women. I say conversation: the women are all talking over one another while he basks in their adoration. And he's now drinking *a beer*! How on earth did he get a beer? I would so love a beer right now. Ooh, I wonder if he knows where they're keeping the pear cider too? He's obviously part of the inner circle.

I get up from my seat and wobble tipsily on my new purple high heels. Shuffling across the Berkeley Rooms, I reach Leo Frost's little crowd and nudge my way in.

'Hello, everyone! How's it going?' I say with a friendly smile and a wave.

The group give me a cursory glance before their eyes slide away, uninterested. They go right back to their conversation.

Oh.

'Yah, I just loved that Mercedes campaign,' one of the women gushes to Leo Frost. '*Drive. Alive*. It really called to me, you know? I saw it in *Vogue* and bought that car the very next day. I had to!'

'Genius,' a slim, smart-looking Indian woman agrees. 'Just genius work. How on earth did you—'

'*Drive Alive*?' I scoff with a slight hiccup. 'You mean that advert that's up on every bloody billboard I see in my life? You are kidding? That advert sucks. It sucks so hard. Come on, guys. We can be honest. I won't tell anyone.' I push my glasses up my nose with my forefinger. 'Am I right or am I right?'

The group abruptly cease talking and glare at me as if I've just announced I'm going to nick all *The Beekeeper* copies and use them for toilet paper.

Leo Frost frowns and stares down his long nose at me. 'Tell me, what did you not like about the work?'

'*Drive Alive*?' I chuckle. 'It doesn't even *mean* anything. It's basically as if some goon used the first word they could think of that rhymed with drive and called it a concept. Drive Alive. Of course you're alive when you drive. It's a basic requirement of the Highway Code. And why is the woman driving the car wearing nothing but a diamond bikini? I just don't get it. Isn't she cold? Where is she *going*? None of my mates drive in diamond bikinis.'

Leo Frost swallows hard and looks me up and down. 'That ad was my piece,' he says in smooth, deep voice.

'Ah. Oops. Sorry,' I say, feeling a bit guilty.

'Don't worry yourself,' he smirks, eyes travelling pointedly over my onesie. 'It's high-end work. You're hardly the target audience.'

They all laugh at me and then Leo Frost gives me exactly the same infuriating wink he gave to Valentina. 'Run along now, there's a good girl.'

Oh no he did not.

'What a fucking knob-prince!' I hiss. Only it doesn't come out as a 'hiss' but as an indignant shout.

The whole room falls silent. Shit. Did I just shout 'knob-prince' at a Booker-prizewinner's book launch? 'Knob-prince' isn't even a real swear. I just made it up right this minute! And it's not as insulting as I meant it to be. It actually sounds quite complimentary. Shit. What a waste of the word 'knob', Jess.

'Sorry, everyone,' I say, holding my hands up. 'Sorry to interrupt your big night. Sorry, Davis Arthur Montblanc.' Davis Arthur Montblanc looks at me aghast. People are whispering behind their hands and throwing disgusted glances my way. Benedict Cumberbatch shakes his head at me furiously.

Leo Frost takes a leisurely sip of his beer and laughs. He laughs!

'I think you ought to go home,' he says, staring at me with his obnoxious green eyes before wandering off into the crowd, the group of clever, beautiful women trailing behind him.

What an absolute ... knob-prince!

'KNOB-PRINCE!' I call out after him.

Shit! I just did it again. He turns round, a look of pure astonishment on his face. One of the women nudges him and whispers something in his ear. They both laugh super snidely, shake their heads at me and turn away into another huddle of fancy, clever people. Who does he bloody think he is?

Ugh! I march towards him, determined to let him know that he is *not* as cool as he thinks he is, that it was really cruel of him to call me *the entertainment* when I first got here, and that he looks absolutely nothing at all like Tom Hiddleston. But just before I reach him, the waiter (who incidentally failed in his promise not to let me have any more booze), carrying a full tray of champagne, appears out of nowhere. I don't have time to slow down my indignant advance towards Leo Frost and, oh fuck, crash smack-bang into the waiter and his tray.

'Oof,' I groan as his unfeasibly sharp elbow digs into my ribs and I fall to the floor, legs akimbo. I can only watch, mesmerized, as the silver tray frisbees upwards and the flutes upon it sail off through the air like expensive, shit-tasting, heat-seeking missiles.

'Oh, cockwaffle,' I whisper, surveying the carnage from my spot on the floor. Leo Frost has champagne dripping off of his ginger quiff and into his eyes. He's blinking furiously, using his fancy mauve tie to dab at his face. The sour-faced Indian woman has champagne on her lovely posh dress; she's crying soundlessly, her mouth gaping open in distress. The skinny waiter is scrambling up off the floor and racing behind the bar in disgrace. Benedict Cumberbatch has a large champagne spill in the crotch area. And worst of all, the pile of *The Beekeeper* books are absolutely soaked through. Davis Arthur Montblanc picks one up forlornly, dangling the dripping hardback between finger and thumb and trying to shake off the liquid. Oh jeez. This is so much worse than sweating onto his manuscript. I put a hand to my head. Fuck.

Leo Frost, prying his champagne-sticky eyes open with his fingers, catches sight of me on the floor and heads my way. He holds a neatly manicured hand out to help me up. Pretty gracious of him, considering.

'Thank you,' I say earnestly. 'I am so, so sorry. The Bollinger storm was a complete accident. I didn't see the waiter at all – he just blasted into me out of nowhere. Crap. Are your eyes all ri—'

'I haven't a clue who you are or why you think you should be here – ' he interrupts furiously, impressive baritone voice projecting across the room. Why is he talking so loudly? – 'but you're an absolute disgrace. You're dressed inappropriately, you're rude and ... and loutish, and you have ruined a very important night for a lot of people. I suggest you leave immediately before I call the authorities.'

I blink. My stomach churns. I try to say something, anything, but my mouth just opens and closes like a PG Tips monkey. This could be the first time in my life that I'm lost for words. I don't like it one bit. I'm usually so full of words. I love them and cherish them, yet now, when I really need them, they desert me. My cheeks glow with heat as one of the surrounding party attendees begins a slow clap in support of Leo Frost's speech. Then a nearby woman adds her slow clap too, and soon the whole crowd is applauding. *Damn it.* For such a long time I've aspired to be involved in a real-life spontaneous slow clap, but I can hardly join in on this one when its intention is to show me what a div I am. Can I? No. No, I definitely shouldn't.

This feels horrible. They actually hate me. So many people I admire in this room, and they hate me. Leo Frost continues his little public address, turning ceremoniously to the crowd of people, arms flung wide.

'Of course, we mustn't let one unsavoury character ruin

what has been an otherwise wonderful evening, and I'd like to personally extend my sincere apologies for the interruption in tonight's celebrations of my esteemed uncle, Davis Arthur Montblanc. There are many wonderful writers here tonight. Let's just see this little diversion as potential future copy, shall we?'

A scatter of polite laughter.

Unsavoury? *Unsavoury?*

'What the fuck are you doing?' Summer spits, arriving at my side. She grabs hold of my elbow and drags me towards the door. 'Jesus. You're such a let-down, Jess! Why do you do this? You're like a damn teenager.'

'I ... I ... The waiter appeared out of nowhere. It was a complete accident. Where's Valentina? I need to apologize.' I crane my neck, trying to find Valentina in the crowd. She's not there. Instead, Leo Frost, leaning against the bar, catches my eye and looks me up and down in a really condescending way. Ugh!

'No way. No Valentina,' Summer hisses, dragging me out into the busy London street. 'She'll never want us now! It's over.'

CHAPTER SEVEN

Save your tears for the pillowcase.

***Matilda Beam's Good Housewife Guide*, 1957**

Three days later there had been no word from Valentina Smith or anyone at the Southbank Press. On day two, Summer locked herself in her bedroom and refused to come out. I set up camp outside her door and tried to convince her that everyone at the publisher was probably still hungover from all that free party champagne and simply not up for making celebratory phone calls. Summer didn't answer, though, just sent Holden back and forth for organic nut snacks and elderflower cordial and an instruction to absolutely ignore me no matter what I said, even when I sang 'Please let me in, I've been a massive turd, but I'm a turd who is soooo sorreeee!' in my best singing voice. I tried to bribe her out by telling her how much Mr Belding was missing her, even though the truth was that he seemed to be much happier prowling around our flat in the nude.

Five days after the launch, and with still no word from the publisher, it eventually sinks in that I may have fucked things up in a massive way. I can't believe it. Valentina was so enthusiastic about everything. Could that really have changed so quickly? Leo Frost *is* a really big deal in London. Maybe he's like a sort of mafia don and, by offending him, all the doors I try to get through for the rest of my life will be mysteriously shut in my face, and one day, who knows when, the head of a noble stallion will be resting on the foot of my bed.

'I'm going to ring up Valentina,' I say determinedly through Summer's door at lunchtime on Tuesday. 'We had a rapport, I think. I'm going to try and fix this, OK? Apologize to her for my stupid behaviour. She can't punish you for what I've done – it's not fair.'

I take out my iPhone, but before I can look up Valentina's number online, Summer's door clicks open and she emerges at last. She doesn't look dishevelled and tear-stained like I thought she would after holing herself up for almost a week. She looks fresh. Bright-eyed and clean and sparky and ... happy?

'Have you heard something?' I ask, getting up from my spot on the hall floor, my heart leaping. 'Oh my God. You have, haven't you? Good news?'

I've not messed it up. We've got the book deal. Summer's fine. I'll have enough money for a decent flight!

My body floods with hot, bright relief.

'Jess ... we need to talk,' Summer says.

'God, we really do!' I agree, following her downstairs to the living room. 'It's been five days! Feels weird us not speaking for so long. I don't expect you to forgive me straight away. I know how mad you are. But I'll make it up to—'

'We didn't get the book deal,' Summer cuts in, perching neatly on the huge leather sofa.

'We – we didn't? Oh shit. *Shit.*' I plonk down beside her. 'Let me ring Valentina, Sum. God.'

'I've already spoken to Valentina.'

'What? When? When did she ring? What did she say? Why don't they want us? They loved us last week!'

'She said the decision wasn't just down to her ... that a whole team has to decide these things.'

'Oh God. Did she say it was my fault?'

Summer looks me squarely in the eyes and nods. 'Yes. She did.'

Fuck.

'God, I'm so sorry. I didn't mean to call Leo Frost a knob-prince. He just completely rubbed me up the wrong way. He talked to me like I was crap on his overly shined shoe. It made me so cross, I couldn't help myself.'

'Yeah, that's why we need to talk.'

'To figure out a plan? Good idea. We can do that. Shall I get my laptop? We can approach another publisher, can't we? I'll write a better pitch. I'm sure I can fix—'

'Jess, I want you to move out.'

My throat tightens. 'What?'

'And I don't think you should work on *Summer in the City* any more.'

Whaaaat?

My head snaps up. 'You're – you're sacking me? And kicking me out? *On the same day*?'

Summer slowly shrugs one shoulder. 'I just want you to know that it's not been an easy decision for me. I've been thinking about things *super* hard these past few days. I talked to everyone about us, and they all think—'

'Talked to everyone? Who? I don't understand.'

'They all agree. Everyone says you're dragging me down. You've *been* dragging me down.'

I clasp my hands together and rub my thumb into my palm. Did our friends really say that about me? Is that true?

'Look, I know I messed up at the launch. I feel like a real dick about it. But my writing? Isn't that what counts? I've worked really hard on our site, Summer. I know this *particular* opportunity might have gone south, and it's my fault, but I promise I'll get us another one. I swear I'll—'

'*My* site.'

'Sorry?'

'You said *our* site. But it's mine.' Summer tilts her head to the side. 'It's *mine*, Jess.'

'But ... but ... I came up with the entire editorial calendar. I wrote practically every post, got us to 30,000 Twitter followers. I've spent every day, night and weekend of the last two years on this. *Summer in the City* is you and *me*.'

Summer chews her lip for a moment. '*Technically* it isn't. You didn't sign a contract.'

Oh my God, she's right. I didn't. She said she only needed my help for a few months, and when I mentioned that we should maybe sign something, she said that our friendship was the only contract we needed and did I want anything from the bar. It felt silly to push it any further than that, and so I didn't. I didn't think I needed to.

My chest burns with indignation.

'Come on, Summer, that's not fair! You said we didn't need a contract!'

'Did I?' She squints for a moment. 'I don't think I did.'

'You absolutely did. And either way, the website was shit before we partnered up. It was getting fifteen views a day! *And they weren't even unique!*'

Summer gasps sharply as if she's been scorched. 'You liar. It was getting way more views than that!' She scratches her nose. 'You seem to have forgotten it, but this was *my* life you walked into. I did you a favour, employing you, giving you a place to live, and I was happy to. You're a lost soul and I'm a really giving person. I was happy to give you a jump-start, but you never fucking jumped. You're still here. Hijacking everything and making me look bad!'

'What are you talking about, hijacking? I came back from Morocco to help you!

'You were broke in Morocco.'

'I was happy in Morocco. I ... I thought I was doing *you* a favour.' I rub my eyes. 'Where has this all come from? Just a few days ago we were going to sign a book deal together.' With a heavy sigh, I plop down onto the sofa beside Summer. 'Shit. I know you're mad at me, I do. And I'm really sorry. Let's just fucking ... go out, all right? Talk this through. Do an all-dayer at the pub. Summer? We'll have one of our random adventures and just forget this horribleness.'

Summer frowns, shaking her head. 'You don't get it. I don't *want* to do all-dayers any more. I don't want to get so drunk that we forget this conversation. You mess up every opportunity you get before it can really mean anything. You don't even know you're doing it . . . You've had a rough time with your mum, I know. But now your emotional mess is, like, *affecting* me.'

I swallow and lift my chin. 'I think you're going a bit over the top. Kicking me out *and* sacking me? It's really harsh. We're *best friends*.'

'You don't know how to be a friend, Jess,' Summer scoffs. 'You know how to be a mate, and as long as it's fun and daft and easy and a giggle, you're great. But the minute things get serious, you just don't want to know.'

That's not true. OK, fine, I might not *always* be great at listening to her deep feelings and dramas and relationship quandaries. But I wanted that book deal as much as she did. I worked hard for it.

Summer's eyes meet mine. She looks different. Colder.

'Look, Jess. You've been a really useful and fun part of my journey as a person and I appreciate your help on the site. But ... we're going in different directions now and I feel like I'm destined for bigger things on my own. I feel like you're grabbing my spotlight for all the wrong reasons and it's time for me to cut the cord. I'm sorry, you know? But I've got to do what's best for *me*. And ... well, you're no longer a part of that.'

I blink in disbelief. She doesn't look sorry at all. What the fuck is happening?

My whole body vibrating with adrenalin and confusion, I get up from the sofa and walk calmly out of the living room, clicking the door softly shut behind me.

* * *

I'm ten years older now, but the feeling that comes with being left behind feels pretty much the same way it did the first time – like standing on the edge of something very high up and knowing that someone is behind you, just about to push.

I'd been at university for six months and was just about getting to grips with the thought that Mum might manage just fine without me – so far, so good and all that. When she didn't answer my regular lunchtime phone call one wintery

Tuesday, I wasn't too mithered about it. Mum occasionally took to her bed and ignored my calls; it just meant she was having one of her days. And besides, last night she'd been in lovely high spirits; we'd chatted on the phone about my course and giggled over some ridiculous magician on the *Royal Variety* show. But at about four p.m. I was at the library when I saw the number of Mum's community psychiatric nurse flash up on my mobile. CPNs only ever called me when something was wrong.

'Hiya, Pam,' I said as I answered the call. 'Go on. What's she done now?' I rolled my eyes, trailing my fingers along the shelf before selecting the copy of *The Canterbury Tales* I had to read for my course. 'No, wait, let me guess. Drunk and cursing the man who broke her heart? Chucked her medicine down the toilet? Another trip to the loony bin? We've not had one of those in a while!'

I was kidding about – even Mum sometimes joked about her episodes – but behind the casual messing, my heart was hammering hard in my ribcage.

'Jessica. Maybe you should sit down.'

And of course then I knew. Everyone knows what *maybe you should sit down* means.

'Er, OK,' I said, my legs turning to liquid. Sinking down onto the carpeted floor, I leant my head back against the books and squeezed the phone in my hand.

'Jessica. I'm afraid I have some awful news,' Pam said, sounding like someone on the telly. Like this was *East-Enders*. 'I'm afraid that Rose, I mean, your mum ... she . . . she's passed away.'

I held my breath and nodded very quickly, my stomach tilting as if I were on the top of a roller coaster. 'When? H-how?'

'It was late this morning. She ... she ... it was an overdose. I was calling round for my monthly appointment. The front door was ajar and ...' Pam trailed off, a wobble in her usually calm voice.

I dropped *The Canterbury Tales* onto my lap and watched the image of it blur against the tartan skirt of my dress.

'But she was all right the last time she did that. They used that pump thingy in the hospital. She was laughing last night. I don't understand. Are you sure she's ... ? She sounded so *well*. She was ... happy.'

And then it hit me. I knew why Mum was so cheerful last night. Why she'd suddenly seemed bright and positive and like a normal mum. She'd known exactly what she was going to do. She'd known she was leaving, and she'd left the door open for Pam to find her.

I knew I shouldn't have left her. I *knew* I should have stayed at home. She wouldn't have done this if I were at home.

I dropped the phone onto the carpet and stared at the rows of books in front of me, heard the clicking of the keyboards and hushed murmurs of students, all of them unaware that here in the corner, on the floor, my heart had just fractured.

I bit my bottom lip until I tasted blood and felt as if I should start crying. That was the expected thing, wasn't it? There were supposed to be tears and wailing and tearing of hair and a library assistant carting me out, shouting, 'Everyone move out of the way, there's nothing to see here, show's over!' But none of that came. Instead, I got up off the floor, gently slid the book back onto the shelf in its right place and left the building. I stumbled back to halls, and in my room I turned off all the lights and got into bed, where I stared at the dark and waited patiently for my insides to stop twisting. That's pretty much where I stayed until Summer found me.

I didn't cry the day my mum killed herself. I haven't cried since.

CHAPTER EIGHT

Public houses and liquor bars are the residence of ne'er-do-wells. They are no place for a Good Woman. And certainly never an unmarried lady.

***Matilda Beam's Good Woman Guide*, 1959**

The Trap Inn is located at the end of our road. It's a real dive of a pub. The seats are stained and threadbare, there are tooth marks on the beer mats and it smells like egg. But needs must, and it's very close by, so, for now, the Trap Inn will be my place of solitude. I order a bottle of pear cider from the thin, gap-toothed barmaid who, from what I can gather, goes by the name of Skanky Elaine.

'Pear cider?' she says with a blink. 'Pear? Cider? *Pear Cider?*'

'It's just like normal cider, but pear-flavoured. It's delicious, trust me. Don't worry, I can see you don't have any. Just a beer will do, thanks.'

She nods and grabs me a bottle of Corona from one of the fridges. I take a couple of hefty swigs, hop onto the high stool at the bar, put my head in my hands and sigh long and low.

Well that was all a bit fucking intense.

I don't know quite how to feel. Part of me feels really mad that Summer's kicked me out of my own bloody home. But more of me feels sad that I've clearly upset her so much. It's an uncomfortable rolling guilt feeling in my belly. I've not had that feeling since Mum. I can't bear it. Summer's been mad at me plenty of times, but she's never, ever kicked me out. Not least because of the fact that, however much I get on her nerves sometimes, she still needs me to do the work. Ordinarily I'd leave it a couple of hours and then talk to her when she's calmed down, but I get the feeling that that's not going to work this time.

I peek up at the TV in the corner of the pub. *Kirstie's Vintage Home*. More twee 'let's own a crumbly house and source old wooden apple crates for a coffee table' crap. Great. Today is turning out to be a real shithead of a day.

Where the arses am I going to go now? I scroll through the contacts list on my phone. Well, Amy Keyplass and Mark Chunder are obviously out of the question.

Ooh, look. I'll try Betty. Betty's our journalist friend. She's lovely and funny and her house is in Didsbury, which could be a cool place to hang for a while.

I pull out my phone and call her.

'Yo, it's J-dawg!' I say faux brightly.

'Who?'

'Jess.'

' ... Jess?'

'Jess Beam! Betty, you big dope. What are you up to? It sounds loud there. Is that "Old Macdonald Had a Farm" I can hear?'

'Yeah, I'm just arriving at Baby Sensory with Henry.'

'Oh yeah, Henry! How old is he now?'

'Eight months old. You've never met him.'

Yikes. She sounds pissed off. Is it really *that* big a deal that I haven't met her baby? I mean, what would we even talk about?

'Guess what, Bets? Now I *can* meet him. Summer's gone and kicked me out and I need a place to crash. If I stayed with you I could babysit Henry whenever you liked. I mean, if your other babysitters weren't available or if I didn't already have any other plans, maybe ... Hmmm, does Henry know how to dance yet? I could teach him to rock out to Bon Jovi!'

'Why did Summer kick you out?' she says flatly. 'What did you do?'

'Nothing! Why do you naturally assume it's me in the wrong?'

Silence from Betty.

'OK, I might have caused a tiny little scene at a book party. It was all a complete accident, but Summer's having none of it. I'm sure she'll calm down soon, but I think it'll probably be best for me to just do one for a bit.'

'I'm not sure I really want to get in the middle of all that, Jess.'

I hear the baby wail in the background.

'Come on, just for a night or two, Betty Boo. Come ooooon. It'll be like old times. I'll bring some canned margarita and the Kings of Leon live DVD. Ooh, you've got the big house. We could – we could have a party! An epic house party!' My mind wanders as I think about a special Spotify playlist for the party. Betty loves reggae music. I'll Google 'best reggae songs' and put all of them on the playlist for her. I grab my trusty bic biro from my coat pocket and start scribbling 'house party playlist epic' on my arm. I manage to write 'house' before Betty shuts me down.

'Um, as much ... fun ... as that sounds, I'm not sure my infant son will appreciate an epic house party. I'm sorry, Jess. I don't think it's such a good idea for you to stay. Good luck, though. We're actually having a *birthday* party for Henry in August. I'd love for him to meet his auntie Jessica. I'll text you the details nearer the time, shall I?'

'Oh! Yeah, definitely...' I say, feeling itchy at the words 'auntie' and 'Jessica' in the same sentence. 'Sounds great!'

Not.

We end the conversation a tad stiffly, and I scroll frantically through the rest of my phone book. I call each of the people I consider to be my closest mates, but it turns out to be one bloody disaster after the next. Emily, who I met in Tunisia, is far too busy to put me up because of her her high-pressure job as a human rights lawyer. Callum, a web design buddy, is properly mad at me for forgetting to answer his texts, especially after we slept together last new year. And my good mate Michelle, the bisexual bass guitar player, turns out to not want to be good mates any more, since apparently I'm not *there* for her enough 'when it comes to the real, meta issues' in her life.

'I'll have a tequila, straight up, please,' I say to Skanky Elaine. She yanks her eyes away from the telly and idly pours one out into a little shot glass.

'Bit early in the day for tequila, eh, love? Sommat troubling you?' She hands over the drink with a bony hand missing its little finger. I down it and nod towards the bottle for an immediate top-up.

'This is a tequila emergency,' I declare. 'My friends have deserted me, I have less than a hundred quid in the bank, I lost my job and I think I might be homeless.'

Skanky Elaine looks horrified, which oddly makes me feel a bit better. I take the refilled glass from her.

'You know, I just don't see what everyone's problem is. Folk have different friends for different things, don't they? They knew what I was like when they met me. I'm the care-free, fun, adventurous buddy, not the talk-about-your-emotions-and-cry-like-a-chump friend. Why do people suddenly expect me to be a different person? I'm no good with all that daft touchy-feely stuff.'

Skanky Elaine shrugs as I knock back the shot, her eyes flicking back up to the TV. 'Just go and live with your mam and dad for a bit, flower,' she says, as if it's all so simple. 'They'll sort you out.'

I sigh. 'I can't. That's the problem! My mum died yonks ago. I've never met my dad. All I know is that he was a horrible trickster of a bloke who left my mum before I was even born and broke her heart into a million pieces, from which she never recovered.' I shake my head and down another shot. 'I was planning on travelling the world again, but that's all gone to pot now! Maaan.'

'You poor love.'

Downing the next shot, I feel a satisfying warmth in my cheeks and everything softens around the edges. I examine Skanky Elaine. She seems nice. Not that skanky at all.

'Can I stay with you at your house, Skanky Elaine? I could help out at the bar? I've always thought it'd be quite cool to live in a pub.'

'No, love,' she says. 'I don't think so.'

I nod and hiccup, graciously accepting her rejection. 'Can I have another drink then?'

'There's an offer on doubles, love.' She points up to the blackboard signage behind her.

'Brill. Hit me up.'

She pours out the double. 'Do you not have an auntie you can go to, duck? A granny? A godmother? A cousin? An ex?'

I shake my head. 'Nope. I don't have anyone.' I sigh. 'I'm a loner. All alone in this stone-cold worl ... Oh, although ... I think I do have a grandma, actually. Or at leasht I *did*. I've never met her. I don't even know if she's alive. I mean, she wasn't at Mum's funeral . . . at least, I don't remember seeing her there, but then I don't remember a whole lot about that day. Matilda, I think her name was... Thas right. Matilda Beam.'

'You don't even know your own granny? That's bloody sad, that is, flower.' Skanky Elaine gives a grimace, revealing a set of matt, green-tinged teeth and what I suspect is the reason for her nickname.

I rub my eyes, starting to feel a bit drunk. 'Yeah, I s'pose it is sad.' She and Mum never spoke, though I'm not sure why, come to think of it. ''pparently Grandma was shuper-rich, lived in this massive, fancy house in—'

Wait a minute.

I quickly grab my iPhone back out of my jacket and connect to the Internet browser with suddenly shaking hands. It takes me a little while because the tequila has made my fingers clumsy, but after three attempts I finally manage to google 'Matilda Beam + Kensington'

The 192 website pops up. I click on it and scroll down blearily.

Gasp. There's a Matilda Beam! Living at somewhere called Bonham Square in Kensington. The electoral roll shows the year 2014 as the most recent one registered and the age seventy-seven. That's got to be her. It *has* to be. Matilda Beam is hardly a common name.

'You fucking genius,' I breathe, digging into my jeans pocket for some money.

'What's that, love?' Skanky Elaine says, one gammy eye on Kirstie Allsop simpering into the camera.

'You, you're a – hic – geniush. You're absolutely right. I *do* have a Grandma. An alive Grandma. And I think, well, I think she might be loaded. Man, I should have thought of this ages ago! Wow, I wonder how much time I've wasted.' I hurriedly pay the bar bill and hop down off the bar stool with a wobble. 'She'll be able to lend me some money. A loan or sommat. I'll be able to go travelling straight away. I'll go to flippin' Jamaica! Yasssss! I'm going to go home, pack an overnight bag and catch the train back to London right away. There ish no time to lose.'

'Hmmm.' Skanky Elaine frowns. 'You've had a fair amount to drink, love. You sure this is the best idea?'

'No, I'm not sure, Skanky Elaine. I'm not sure at all. But's the only bloody idea I've got.'

* * *

Going on the hunt for your long-lost grandma when you're sad and drunk on a Tuesday afternoon is an unusual idea. In the back alleys of my mind, I know that perhaps I should be thinking this whole thing through more carefully: maybe making a few phone calls, verifying that Grandma actually still lives at the Kensington address I found on Google, or is definitely, absolutely still, you know, alive. But desperation plus tequila equals mental things, and I *am* desperate and so full of tequila. My decision to do one is further solidified when I arrive back home to pack and find that Summer has guests over. I've only been out of the house for an hour or so, and now I can hear them giggling in the kitchen. The unmistakable pop of a champagne cork echoes out through the hallway.

What the fuck?

Are they *celebrating*?

Jeez. She must really want me out! I hurry wonkily to my room, flop onto the bed for a moment and try to have a cry. I do my best to squeeze out a tear, just one teensy little tear, but of course it doesn't happen. As expected, I remain cryless.

Unable to find any proper luggage, I hurriedly pack a bin liner of clothes, grab my laptop bag and sneak back down the stairs and past the giggling festivities in the kitchen. As I reach the front door, Mr Belding darts out of the living room, a curious look upon his fluffy face. He's wearing a tiny purple pork pie hat today in aid of the hours of pictures Summer will be taking of him later for her Instagram page. Poor thing. Destined for a life of preening and posing instead of playing and purring.

I hear another burst of laughter from the kitchen and the clinking of glasses in a toast. Someone, Holden, I think, calls out, 'Here's to the rise of Summer!' Christ. They're congratulating her on getting rid of me. Today really has taken the grimmest turn.

I exhale steadily, a hot flicker of resentment piercing my chest. Then, without really thinking about what I'm doing, I scoop our kitten up under one arm and leave the flat.

* * *

Spending the last of my life funds on a ticket, I catch the train to London for the second time in less than a week. Which, when you're pissed, carrying a huge bin bag of dirty clothes , a laptop bag and smuggling a kitten inside your leather bomber jacket, is not the most joyful of experiences. *Especially* when the bin liner gets a hole in it and the gusset area of your bobbly grey thong is poking out for everyone to see, including the guy you were sadly yet stoically eyeing up at Euston.

Now I'm standing outside a massive white stucco-fronted house in Kensington.

This is it: Grandma's house.

I take a few rapid deep breaths and press a little silver buzzer on the wall. Almost immediately, a high-pitched female voice sounds out through the intercom speaker.

'Hello?'

It's a bit crackly. Grandma, or not Grandma?

I haven't got a clue.

Shit, I don't even know this woman. Can I really just show up and ask for a loan when we've never even met? I look down to where Mr Belding purrs contentedly from inside my coat as if maybe he knows the answer. He doesn't. He knows nothing.

What am I doing? The booze has pretty much worn off now and all that remains is the harsh reality of who I really am: a kitten-nicking, book-deal-ruiner with a bag of skanky clothes and a bit of tequila-induced acid reflux.

'Um, I hope y'all don't mind me asking but w-what are you doing out there? Can I help you? Are – are you in trouble?'

I startle as the intercom crackles back into life.

'Er ... ' I lean forward and speak into the intercom. 'Hello. Uh ... I thought my gran lived here. But you're young and American, and I think she's old and English, so I'm guessing she's probably not here any more. So I'll go. Sorry to have bothered you.'

Brill. I've spent the last pounds I have in the world on

some ridiculous grandma goose chase. I hate myself right now. *Damn it, Jess.*

'Is Matilda Beam your grandma?' the squeaky voice asks.

'Er, yeah. I'm Jessica. Jess.'

Immediately there's a low buzz and a clicking noise as the shiny black door swiftly unlocks.

Shit! My grandma *is* here?

'We're the second and third floor,' the intercom woman says in a lilting southern American cadence. 'Downstairs is a medical clinic.'

'Oh! Right! OK, cheers, great. See you in a sec, then!'

I push open the heavy door to find myself in a grand-looking lobby with a black and white chequered floor and, from what I can gather, a whole load of stairs. I bypass them straight away – lifts are always the easy and best option, I feel, and particularly so when I'm carrying a cat and a bursting plastic bag.

Oh, wait. No. There doesn't appear to be a lift.

'Knobs and bollocks,' I grumble to myself, dropping the bin bag on the floor in despair. I cry to the heavens: '*Knobs and bollocks.*'

I hate stairs at the best of times, but with all this stuff too? It's going to be so haaard. Mr Belding snuffles in agreement.

A door to the left of me opens and the head of a short, curly-haired man pops out. He looks a little younger than me and is wearing a starchy white doctor's coat alongside his confused expression.

'Can I help you?' he says in a melodic Scottish accent, examining me and my wares with a suspicious frown.

'Oh, yes please,' I say. 'I'm looking for the lift. Do you know where it is?'

He clears his throat. 'Um, this place was built mid-nineteenth century. It's stairs only.''Knobs. And. Bollocks,' I grumble again as my worries are confirmed. 'All this stuff is so heavy.'

'You can't say knobs and bollocks in here!'

'Oh? And why is that?' I peer at him. 'Are you the boss of the whole building?'

'Um, no.'

'Then why?'

'Well, because this is Doctor Qureshi's cardiothoracic clinic. We're treating people with problematic hearts. I don't think those people want to hear "knobs and bollocks" being wailed outside the door when they're already anxious and unwell and have quite enough to worry about.'

He lifts his chin a little.

'Oh,' I say, guilt sweeping over me. 'Yeah, I can see how that might be a bit annoying for them. I'm sorry. No more swearing. Are you Doctor Qureshi?'

'No. I'm Doctor Abernathy. I work for Doctor Qureshi.'

'Right. Cool. You fancy helping me with these bags, then?'

'No, not really. I'm very busy at work – wait, who on earth are you?' He narrows his eyes.

'Your worst nightmare.' I answer.

I say this mostly because I've always wanted to say it and this seems like as good a time as any. Also because I still seem to be a tiny bit drunk.

'Hmm, yes, I thought so,' he mutters, before leaning forward to peer at my boobs, eyes growing wide with astonishment. What the hell is this? What is he doing? I mean, to be fair, mine are pretty awesome boobs and have drawn many an admiring glance, though never so overt. Gross.

He's really staring. What a megaperv. I throw him my finest withering glance. 'Ugh.' I spit.

'I'm sorry,' he says, leaning in further still. 'But ... do you know that there's ... there's a *cat* in your jacket? *Wearing a hat?*'

Aha, he's only spotted Mr Belding. Not megaperving. I peek down and see Mr Belding's little face popping out at the top of my coat. I give his ears a little tickle.

'Yeah, thanks for the heads-up, Doctor Seuss. You know, I don't even know why he's there.'

'Sorry, *what?*'

'I mean, I don't know why I brought him here. I adopted him with my friend, but then I got a bit pissed and I was mad at her so I just kind of ... took him. *Anyway,* don't worry about all that. Will you please help me with my stuff?'

The doctor looks at his watch before stepping out of the clinic door and closing it gently behind him.

'Fine. But this does not make me an accomplice to the animal theft.' He takes the bin bag and the laptop bag and leads the way up the stairs. 'I will expect you to testify to that.'

'I'll swear on the Holy Bible that you knew nothing about it,' I reply solemnly as Mr Belding snuggles himself back down into the soft satin lining of my jacket and dozes off. 'Unless they offer me some kind of lighter sentence deal.'

'Great, thanks. So you're going upstairs to see Old Lady Beam?'

'I am. She's my gran.'

'Ah. I didn't know she had any family... I've never seen anyone visit ... um, sorry for calling her Old Lady Beam.'

'Oh, I don't mind.' I lower my voice. 'To be honest, I'd

actually kind of forgotten she existed until, ooh, about five hours ago. I've never met her before. She doesn't even know I'm coming!'

'Wow. So you don't know anything about her ... '

'Nope. Zip. It's kind of cool when you think about it. Like, *Surprise Surprise*, but, you know, not shit.'

'Yes. Right.'

When we finally reach the top of the stairs, the doctor drops the bags, holds out his hand and says, slightly breathlessly. 'I'm Jamie. Dr Jamie Abernathy.'

'Hey.' I take his hand and give it a hearty shake. 'I'm Jess. Ms Jessica Beam.'

'Good luck in there, Ms Jessica Beam.'

'Why would I need luck?' I adjust my glasses on my perspiring nose. 'I'm her *granddaughter*. Grandmas love granddaughters, it's basic human nature.'

Why is he raising an eyebrow like that?

CHAPTER NINE

Coarse language must not ever cross the lips of a well-bred Good Woman! 'Gosh, darn it' may occasionally be acceptable at times of high frustration.

***Matilda Beam's Guide to Love and Romance*, 1955**

'You must be Jessica.'

I recognize the timid voice from the intercom as a heavy-set girl with a shy, slightly buck-toothed smile and a dusting of freckles across her nose opens the door. She's in her mid-twenties and pretty in a scrubbed, wholesome, countryside kind of a way. She's wearing a cream-coloured apron over her long skirt and huge navy T-shirt, and her frizzy, mousy brown hair is tied back into a thick plait.

'I'm Peach.' She doesn't quite make eye contact but offers a chubby hand, the nails short and painted with clear varnish.

'Nice to meet you,' I say, taking her hand. 'Though I'm

not feeling quite so peachy, I'm afraid.' I indicate the now almost fully ripped bin bag.

'No, no. Um, my *name* is Peach,' she says quietly, rounded cheeks turning blotchy red. 'Um, Peach Carmichael. I'm Mrs Beam's assistant.'

'Oh! Cool name.'

Grandma has staff!

'Mrs Beam will receive y'all in the parlour.'

She'll receive me in the parlour? I snort and look around, half expecting Cousin Matthew to pop out from under the stairs. I'd totally do Cousin Matthew.

We head into the flat and the beautiful, magnificent dwelling I was expecting to see, based on the outside appearance of the building, does not materialize. At all. The entrance way is grand and wide, of course, but it's really dingy too. I peer at the ceiling and see a huge, extravagant crystal chandelier, but only one of the bulbs is lit up – the other eight are busted. We turn a corner and walk down a dimly lit hallway. Wow. There's clutter everywhere. It's absolutely chockablock with stuff. Loads and loads of stuff. I bump into a stone bust of some dude's head, and then stumble backwards into a clunky old vacuum cleaner, finally tripping up on a tall stack of newspapers. It's like playing hallway Mousetrap. I topple over and land on my bum, my face squashed up against a misshapen tennis racket.

'Hallllp.'

Peach spins round in horror. 'Oh my.'

'I thought I was messy!' I yelp, peeling my face off the racket and pressing on my ankle to check for damage. Peach holds out a hand to pull me up.

'Are you hurt? I'm ever so sorry. I'm so used to weavin' and dodgin' about this hallway, I forget it's an obstacle course for guests.' She shrugs slightly. 'Not that we have many guests, mind you, besides Gavin the postman.'

'I'm all right.' I scramble back up and brush down my skinny jeans.

Stepping carefully over an intricate mother-of-pearl grandfather clock face, I look around me in astonishment. This hallway is David Dickinson's wet dream. Which might be the grossest thought I've ever had.

'Wow, you guys should do a *Cash in the Attic*.'

Peach looks serious. 'We can't even get the attic door open. Mrs Beam ... well, Mrs Beam likes her belongings around her.'

'Yeah, I can see that.' I negotiate a side table with two old, unplugged telephones on it. What the actual fuck?

And then Peach opens another big door and ushers me into a large, grand room. The ceilings are just as high as in the hallway, and one claret-coloured wall is festooned with a gallery of gilt-framed oil paintings. The other three walls are taken up with crammed-to-the-brim bookcases. I hear the wails of that creepy 1950s Bobby Helms song 'My Special Angel' echoing out from an old-fashioned record player by the huge sash window. And there in the far corner of the room, sitting primly on a stiff-looking duck-egg-blue chair, head buried in a book, is my grandma. She's thin, and although she's sitting down, I can tell that she's tall. Her silvery white hair is styled in what I reckon is supposed to be a Grace Kelly-style chignon, but there's a mass of frizzy tendrils escaping at the temples, creating a kind of wild halo effect. Grandma peers curiously up from her book and I see that, like me, she's wearing glasses. Only hers aren't cool tortoiseshell ones but big red ones that are winged at the corners with those super-thick lenses that make eyes look cartoon-massive. She looks a bit like a Tim Burton creation. And not in the good way.

'Um, Mrs Beam, Jessica Beam is here to see you.'

The old woman gasps.

Eek.

A grandma. *My* grandma.

This is bizarre.

This is too freaking bizarre.

What am I bloody doing here?

It was such a ridiculous idea.

That stupid uncomfortable itch starts to crawl over my scalp.

OK, chill out, Jess. Keep it casual, keep it light. Get her to like you, get her to lend you some of her megabucks, go to Jamaica. Ooh, or maybe New Zealand. Send her a nice post-card, pay her back, ring her at Christmas, blah blah, fly to Peru or St Lucia, live happily ever after, amen, etc. All good in the hood.

'Er, hello. I'm Jessica. Jess,' I say, awkwardly trying to shove my hands into the pockets of my skinny jeans before realizing that they're those trendy fake pockets and I'm essentially just rubbing myself up. 'I'm Rose's daughter. Your granddaughter, actually. Sorry to turn up out of the blue uninvited, but ... I couldn't stay away. Er ... I couldn't fight it.'

Did I just quote an Adele song? Why am I acting weird?

'I'll leave y'all to it,' Peach murmurs so gently that I barely hear her, then she lumbers, shoulders hunched, back out of the room.

Grandma squints at me and places her book onto the mahogany side table before standing up from the chair more fluidly than I thought she would, considering the whole being a gazillion years old thing. She's wearing a stiff-looking pink wool skirt and a long-sleeved white silk blouse. One of the buttons on the blouse has a frayed piece of cotton trailing from it.

'J-Jessica? Baby Jessica? Is it ... is it really you?' she exclaims in the most ridiculously posh accent. She presses a wrinkly hand to her chest, gigantic eyes blinking rapidly. 'Oh my goodness me, you're here!'

At fucking last! Someone on this earth is pleased to see me.

'Yes!' I say grandly, with a beatific smile. 'I am here ... Here I am.'

'Oh, Jessica,' she wails, a bit dramatically if we're being honest. She looks up towards her intricately corniced ceiling and, shaking her head, says, 'Thank you, God! Thank you for bringing her to me.'

Wow. OK. This woman is dead happy to see me. Why was I even worried about coming here for help? I can already taste the Sex on the Beach, feel the sun-warmed sand between my toes, the hands of a well-hung Australian hottie rubbing factor fifteen on my back. Summer can do one. She doesn't need me any more? Well, I don't need her. I've got a *grandma* now.

'Yeah, it's top, isn't it?' I grin. 'I don't know why we left it so long. To be completely truthful, I didn't really think about you at all until this morning. Mum never really talked about ... '

I trail off as I notice Grandma is on the move. She's inching towards me with her arms outstretched. Is she ... is she coming in for a hug? She must be. On the telly, grandmas are always hugging people. Hugging and pinching cheeks and kissing you on the mouth.

Oh no.

As she gets closer, I notice her gigantic eyes are full of

tears. Huge old-lady tears. My most prominent instinct is to back away, protect my cheeks from her bony, pinching hands, my lips from her lips. I am living my nightmare. I want to shout 'Stay right where you are!', but I know I mustn't. It would be really mean to reject her emotional advance.

I'm just going to have to style it out.

Grandma moves with surprising speed and before I know it she is here, right in front of me. She grabs my face. Her hands are cold. As cold as ice.

'Poor, orphaned, homeless Jessica. I've waited years for you. What a terrible time you've been through.' She examines me with an expression of pure pity. '*Look* at you, you poor, impoverished creature.'

Huh? How on earth does she know I'm homeless and impoverished? And what is she on about – 'waited years'? I'm all over the bloody Internet. If it meant that much then surely she could have tracked me down by now? It took me less than five minutes to find her.

Before I get the chance to ask what the fuck is occurring, her long thin arms close around me.

Grandma is a dementor.

I squeeze my eyes shut, hold my breath as she pulls me close and—

'-REEEEAAAOOWWW!'

'*Good heavens!*'

'Shiiiit!'

Mr Belding leaps out of my leather jacket.

Cockwaffle. I'd completely forgotten he was there! He darts up into the air, hissing, quite understandably, at the fact that he's just been almost squished to death in a me-and-Grandma sandwich. Then he lands on my shoulder, claws piercing my décolletage in what I suspect is one of the most physically painful events of my life so far.

'ARGH, MR BELDING, YOU SHITHEAD!'

My swear bounces off the walls of the huge room and echoes back at me. Grandma waddles quickly backwards in surprise, her nostrils flaring. Her lips wobble again. She's got wobbly lips. Her face is now full on Cullen white.

'Good grief,' she croaks, reaching out for the arm of her chair to steady herself. '*Good grief.*'

'Holy shit, I'm sorry,' I mutter, trying to peel Mr Belding off my shoulder. 'I forgot he was in there!'

'Why ... why on earth do you have a cat about your person?' She points a long finger at Mr Belding balancing on my shoulder. 'I can't bear it! Is it some sort of street thing? A trick?'

'Street thing? Whaaa?'

'Oh goodness, do you use its body for warmth? To elicit sympathy when, dear God ... when you're begging for coins? Is that why it's wearing a hat?'

Begging for coins? Wait – does she think I'm properly homeless?

I did not I expect that *I* would be the confused party in this scenario, yet right at this moment I'm even more puzzled than I am any time a character in *EastEnders* sleeps with Phil Mitchell.

I successfully unhook Mr Belding from my shoulder and set him down on the floor. He saunters towards Grandma but she shoos him away with a neatly folded copy of The *Lady*.

'I'm not actually homeless!' I say. 'Well, I suppose I am, technically, *sort of* homeless. But not in the, er, the tramp way. At least not yet . . . Why the heck would you—'

'You don't need to hide it, Jessica. I may be elderly but I am *not* senile. I certainly know a down-and-out when I see one. Only a vagrant would carry their worldly possessions in an old, shabby plastic bag. Only a vagabond would be forced to wear a pair of child-sized trousers. The coarse language, the scent of rough liquor ... ' She wrinkles her nose. '*The unwashed clothing* ... ' I peek down and spot the grey thong once again peeping out of the top of the bin bag. Shit. I thought I'd stuffed that back in.

'You've got the wrong idea about—'

'As if it wasn't already clear enough, you have written the word "house" on your hand.'

I look down at where I started writing 'house party playlist epic' on my hand. I rub at the biro before plonking down onto a navy velvet chair by the window.

'Look, I think we've totally got our wires crossed. I'm one hundred per cent not a street dweller. I promise. These are not a child's denim trousers. They are awesome skinny jeans. They're *supposed* to be super tight. It's sexy! And I've had a really shitty day, ergo the smell of tequila – you know how life gets. I'm using a bin bag because I was in a mad rush and couldn't find a suitcase. See? A complete misunderstanding. Can we please start over again?'

Grandma doesn't answer. Just bites her lip, fiddles with the cotton thread on her blouse and stares at me through narrowed, watery eyes.

Fuck. This is *not* going to plan. I need to recover the situation. Warm things up a bit before I ask to borrow money. I shall use my sunny disposition.

'Your house is really lovely,' I say with my sunniest, most granddaughterly smile. 'Properly fancy.' Peering around, I notice, on the wall, a portrait of a grand-looking woman sitting regally beside a Dalmatian. 'I like your picture.' I point up at it. 'What a stunning girl! That bone structure. Gorgeous. She's the absolute image of Kiera Knightley!'

'That is my *father*. Your great-grandfather.'

'Oh God, I'm sorry. The cheekbones ... I just thought . . . ' I swallow the words down, my face buzzing with heat. 'What's your book?' I swiftly change the subject, noticing the hardback resting on her side table. Good old books: always a safe topic.

I wander over and pick it up. *Lady Chatterley's Lover*. I immediately picture Sean Bean's bum. 'Ooh, saucy,' I say in an odd drawl that sounds a bit pervy. Argh.

I cough. 'I do love to read, you know. Must run in the family! I read everything. Not just books. Also newspapers, magazines, leaflets, posters ... er, greetings cards, road signs, books again. *Minds*. Ha-ha. Only kidding ... or am I ... ?' Grandma's mouth drops open. I clear my throat again. 'Yeah, yeah ... Read, read, read, that's me! Might as well call me Jessica Beam Reading Machine. Or Jessica Beam Madam Readalot. Um. Something like that, anyway... er ... '

'Oh, dear me.' Grandma's eyes brim with fat tears once more. 'I do believe you're experiencing some kind of emotional crisis. This is not a surprise, considering . . . ' She clasps her bony hands together. 'Where is your husband, Jessica? Where is he to help you?' She looks frantically around the room as if this husband might suddenly magic up from behind the walnut dresser.

I snort. 'I promise you I'm not having an "emotional crisis" – *so* not my thing. And as for a husband? I'm only twenty-eight. I *obviously* don't have a husband.'

Grandma purses her lips extra tightly so that the edges of them turn as white as her face. 'You are one of those ... career women?'

'Er, actually, nope. I lost my job as a blogger today.' I

give a sad shrug. 'Which was extra rubbish because I lived with my boss. Who *was* my best friend. So I lost my house too.'

'A blogger? *Dear God.*' She sways slightly.

I wonder what she thinks a blogger is? Now is probably not the time to explain.

'I can fix all of this,' she whispers, almost to herself. 'You did the best thing to come to me. Let me redeem myself. Let me help you.'

She wants to help me! This is it. This is my cue.

'Well, Mrs Beam, *Grandma*, there *is* something I wanted to ask you, actually. It's a bit random, I know, but, well ... is there any chance I could borrow some cash? Obviously I will pay back every single penny as soon as I get myself sorted out. I promise. But as you can probably tell, I'm in a bit of a tight spot and a little money would help to get me back on my feet again. And I know that we're practically strangers, so maybe I could leave something of mine with you as insurance. Like a deposit-type thing. How about Mr Belding? Or this high-quality genuine leather bomber jacket? Whatever you want. What do you think? I'd be ever so grateful.'

Grandma lifts her elegant chin, silver eyebrows dipped, and gives a precise shake of her head. 'Oh, Jessica, of course I will help you in any way I can – ' *Yessss* – 'but . . . I shan't lend you money.' *Nooooo.*

'Oh. Right.'

My stomach clunks with disappointment. I've well and truly buggered this up. *Of course* she isn't going to give me money. Why on earth would she? I've literally rocked up unannounced, perved on *Lady Chatterley's Lover*, insulted her dad, revealed my most skanky set of grey knickers, had my stolen kitten jump out and scare the living daylights out of her and then topped it off with a casual loan request. What else did I expect her to say?

Fuck.

'I won't give you money, Jessica, but of course you should stay here with me.' Grandma flings her arms around the grand living room to demonstrate 'here' before propping her red glasses back onto her nose. Her massive eyes stare me out. 'I will help you through this.' She gives me a worried, imploring-type look and steps forward, skinny arms reaching towards me once more.

I back away, escaping the embrace. I might well be in a gigantic life-pickle right now, but I'm pretty sure that living here with this bizarre, teary-eyed old lady who thinks she ought to 'fix' me is my actual worst nightmare. Yes, we may be related, but I know nothing about this woman and she knows even less about me. Mum, for whatever reason, made sure of that.

However ... I'm all out of options. Really, truly out of options.

I stifle a yawn, pull out my iPhone and check the time. It's already after bloody eight. Shit. What else am I going to do now? I suppose I *could* stay here for a couple of nights, just while I make some proper plans. I mean, who knows, maybe Summer will have cooled down in a few days. In fact, by then, she'll have realized that *Summer in the City* is nowhere near as good without all my work and she'll be begging me to come back ...

I meet Grandma's intense gaze.

'Maybe I could stay for a couple of nights?' I fight another yawn. 'If, er, that's all right with you?'

She breaks into a full-on smile. It transforms her face. She looks just like my mum.

Something tilts uncomfortably inside my chest and the

itch on my head spreads over my whole body. *This is not a good idea.*

Taking a little white porcelain bell from her side table, Grandma gives it a delicate shake. Peach, a solemn look on her round face, materializes super quickly, almost as if she's been earwigging outside the door.

'Peach, Jessica will be staying with us for a while—'

'Just a couple of nights.'

'Please show her to the front guest room and help her to unpack her belongings—'

'I don't need to unpack.' I pick up my bin bag. 'No point, if I'm just going to leave again in two days.'

Grandma continues talking to Peach as if I hadn't spoken. Her voice is Mary Poppins-ish. 'There are plenty of clothes hangers in the wardrobe.' Glancing down at my bag, she wrinkles her nose. 'And a little laundry might be in order too.' She steps closer and I tense up as I think she's about to attempt hug 2.0., but instead she just really meaningfully examines my face. I shrink away from the intensity of her gaze. Her lips start wobbling again.

'What a terrible time you've had, Jessica. But we will fix it. I will not stop until I have fixed this.'

Eeeeek. She's totally nuts. I get a mighty urge to run out of the front door and never return.

Take a deep breath. Be sensible, Jess. It's just a couple of days. You have no other choice.

'Um ... OK then.' I shrug one shoulder. 'Thank you.'

'You are very tired, dear. I think a warm bath and an early night will be just the ticket.' Grandma points a finger in the air. 'A Good Woman must always get her beauty sleep! Breakfast is at seven a.m. and not a moment later.'

What is she talking about? Is – is she sending me to bed? Now? It's not even nine o' clock. Not that *I* want to sit up and talk to Grandma about what we've been up to for our *whole entire lives*, but I kind of thought *she* would. Especially since I'll be gone soon and, let's be honest, will probably never return.

And then, as if everything that has just happened is completely normal and not at all bizarre and awkward and maybe even a bit life-changing, Grandma returns to her chair and back into the sexually charged world of her book.

Sean Bean's Bum.

CHAPTER TEN

Gossip is inelegant. A Good Woman minds her own business.

***Matilda Beam's Good Woman Guide*, 1959**

'This will be your room for the night.' Peach opens a door on the second floor and shows me inside.

'Oh no!' I whisper, jogging backwards out of the bedroom with a terrified moan. I've never moaned in fright before, but this shit just got real. The room is filled with dolls. Not cute, toy dolls that wee themselves like you have when you're a kid, but those serious-looking oldey-timey porcelain dolls that are as creepy as hell. There are loads of them lined up against the three huge floor-to-ceiling windows and sitting on top of a set of antique drawers. At least twenty of them are standing on the hardwood floors in various positions of activity. One of the dolls is holding a tiny doll replica of itself. I am gripped by fear.

'Why?' I say, venturing cautiously back inside. 'Why so many dolls? Why would anyone do this?'

Peach gives a small shrug. 'I don't know. But I think they're awful cute. That one's my favourite. I call her Felicity.' She points to a ringletted brunette doll sitting on a human-sized gold and blue striped armchair. It's wearing little glass glasses and looking worriedly into a small book. I hate it. I hate Felicity.

The centre of the room holds what I suspect is London's largest bed. It's triple the size of my bed in Manchester and has a massive cushioned headboard upholstered in silk, the colour of which Summer would refer to as *dove grey*. Ordinarily I'd take a run up and fling myself onto it, have a good bounce. But after everything that's happened today, I'm just not in the mood.

'Well, that was fucking weird.' I lie down on the bed, arms and legs spread out like a starfish. 'I feel like I'm in some ridiculous abstract nightmare. Matilda Beam is crazy. I can't believe we're related. No offence. I mean, what was she talking about, "fixing me" and "redeeming herself". She's odd isn't she?'

'Oh, that's just her way,' Peach says softly, delicately emptying my bag of clothes. I offer to help, but she shakes her head no. 'Matilda feels things very strongly. She's a woman who is full of heart.'

'Not *that* full of heart,' I grumble. 'I don't mean to self–pity, but I lost my house and my best mate and my job *and* my – my pride today. I only wanted to borrow a bit of money, which she clearly has loads of and which I absolutely would have paid back, and she said no. Just like that! Without even a thought!'

'Oh no, that's nothin' to do with you. Matilda Beam is completely and utterly broke.' Peach suddenly clasps my blue lacy top to her bosom and uses the other hand to clamp to her head. 'Oh jeepers. I did *not* mean to let that slip. Please forget I said anything. Oh d-dear.'

I sit up again.

'Broke? Grandma is *skint*?' I indicate the grand room, the fancy antique furniture. 'How?'

'Hmmm.' Peach frowns, loping over to the huge window and opening a balcony door. 'I'll let some air in, shall I?'

'Oi, don't worry.' I scooch over to the edge of the bed and dangle my legs off. 'You can tell me!' I do my trustworthy smile. 'I'm part of the *family*. I have a right to know. Plus I'm leaving not tomorrow but the day after. She'll never know you told me. Come on. Why is she broke? Isn't this house worth, like, a million quid?'

'Five million,' Peach replies promptly, a look of guilt flitting across her earnest face. She looks down. 'Oh dear, I really shouldn't ... Mrs Beam always says that gossip is the height of inelegance.'

'Er, it's not gossip if it's *true*, though. Tell me, Lady P!'

She smiles slightly at the nickname, her defences wilting. 'I ... I guess you *are* leaving soon ... '

'No diggity, no doubt, I will be out of here in two days.'

'Oh ... all right then, I suppose it won't do any harm. Well, you see, the truth is that Jack, your grandpa, left Matilda with an awful debt. He was a drinker, made some terrible investments over the years and lost all of their money.' She hesitates. 'I don't think I should be ... '

'Go on, Lady P, don't worry.'

She bites her lip. 'W-well ... When he died, Matilda sold the bottom floor and remortgaged the rest so that she could pay off the enormous debts, and what was left she has used to keep going. But now the money has almost completely run out.'

'Shit.' I blink. Mr Belding – who has followed me upstairs – climbs onto my lap and I idly stroke his ears. 'Why doesn't she just move house? It must cost a fortune to run this place. She should just sell up. I don't get what the big deal is.'

Peach nods, eyes wide. 'You're right, the bills here are huge, but Matilda Beam is, well, she's about as stubborn as a mule. She won't give up this house. It's been in the Beam family for years and years and *then* some. It was supposed to be passed down to her daughter and their daughter and—'

'Me! The daughter's daughter, that's me!'

Peach gasps. 'Of course, I guess it is.'

'This house could possibly one day be mine?' I jump up from the bed and walk around the room, trying my best to ignore the dolls. I get a vision of me as lady of the manor. Wafting about like I own the place, which I would. I could throw some truly game-changing parties in this house.

Peach gives me a grave look and I realize that my fantasizing is pretty inappropriate, given the story she's telling me.

I lean forward. 'How do you know all the goss anyway?'

She looks down at her loafer-encased feet. 'I've been here for five years now. Mrs Beam ain't much of a sharer, but I suppose you can't help but pick these things up.'

'I hope you don't mind me asking, but how does she afford you if she's so skint?'

Peach glances at her hands, red-faced. 'I'm afraid she barely does at the moment. I have room and board. Room, mostly. But she lets me have days off whenever I need them, and, well, I can hardly leave her now. She needs me. I've been in l-love with London since I was a girl and by working for Matilda I get to *live* here. And it's not every girl from Alabama gets to live at one of the finest addresses in the world.' She juts her soft chin. 'Anyhow, she's fixin' to get her books republished and then, hopefully, everything will be all right. Someone's coming tomo—'

'*Books republished*? What books?'

'Her *Good Woman* guides?'

I give Peach a blank look.

'Oh, you must know?' she says quietly, fingering the hem of her apron. 'Mrs Beam wrote them way back in the 1950s, before you and I were a twinkle in anyone's eye. Surely you know about those?' Her mouth drops open in disbelief when I say no. 'You really don't know, do you? Those books were practically an institution. My own dear memaw back in Alabama had all five of them. I couldn't believe it when I realized who I was working for. Thought I might get some tips straight from the source, thought it might help my c-confidence – I'm a little shy, you see – but, well, Mrs Beam doesn't talk right much about the old days. I can't believe you didn't know about her books ... '

'I had absolutely no clue,' I say in astonishment.

Wow. Grandma is a writer too. A published writer. This is such a massive piece of information to not know. It strikes me that Mum really told me absolutely nothing about my grandparents. For the first time in my life I wonder what on earth happened for them to become so estranged?

'It's been exciting,' Peachy goes on, taking coat hangers out of the wardrobe. 'The publishers are sending some big gun round here tomorrow to talk about the possibility of reprinting. And then, hopefully, everything will be all right.'

I nod, mind blown. Wow.

Peachy sighs and gathers the heap of clothes up in her arms. 'I best get these clothes laundered. I'll run you that tub too, shall I? You wash the day away and I'll get some newspaper and milk for the kitty. What's his name?'

'Mr Belding,' I answer. Which reminds me, I should probably let Summer know he's with me. She'll be worried by now, I muse guiltily.

'I loved that show. I always wanted a bedroom like Kelly Kapowski.' Peachy smiles dreamily, her slightly protruding teeth making her look like a timid little rabbit. 'Would you like anything to eat before I go, not that we've got a great selection, mind. A pot of tea? A glass of warm milk? I'll be making one of those for Mrs Beam anyway, so it's no trouble.'

I yawn again, overcome with a feeling of bone-tiredness. Today has been pretty damn overwhelming.

'I don't need anything to eat, but that bath sounds perfect right now, Peach. Thank you.'

'No problem.' She opens the door and then turns back round. She doesn't meet my eye but smiles, almost to herself. 'I – I liked talking with you.' And before I can reply she hurries out of the room, clicking the door shut behind her.

* * *

I must be very knackered because I end up falling asleep in the bath, and when I wake up, all the fluffy lavender-scented bubbles have disappeared and the water is cold.

I climb out of the large, roll-top tub, wrap myself in a huge soft blue towel and trot, shivering, back into the bedroom. Wrapping another towel turban-style around my head, I take my blue-checked pyjamas – some of the few clean items of clothing I brought with me – out of the bin bag and pull them on before climbing into the huge mega bed. I pick up my iPhone from the side table to text Summer and let her know that Mr Belding is with me, but before I can press the text message icon, my last visited site – Facebook – pops up with a fresh notification. Summer Spencer has written a new status. I click on the red circle.

Summer Spencer

Guys, I'm utterly THRILLED to announce that I have an American TV development deal with Seth Astrow's production company for Summer in the City! Success has been a looooong time coming and it feels like an utter dream come true. Woop! #noregrets #summerinthecity

What the hell is this?

I don't understand.

I stare at the phone, my heart thudding. An American TV development deal? Huh? Has this *just* happened? But this morning ... I click open the comments – there are loads of them – and frantically scroll down. Everyone we have ever known is leaving *congratulations* and *best wishes* and *always knew you'd be famous* comments. Someone has written 'Amazing, Summer! But I thought you were going for a book deal?!'

Yeah, me bloody too, mate. I click further down for Summer's reply.

I know Seth Astrow from when I was with Anderson, I saw him again at a book party I was at last week! He loves SITC and wants to put it

on TV in America. He said Rachel Bilson might be interested in playing me. I can't believe it!

Last week? My back stiffens. I get a flashback to the blonde guy in sunglasses Summer was talking to all night at the Davis Arthur Montblanc party. She said he was someone she knew through Anderson. Oh my God. Was that Seth Astrow? My heart drops as it all slots into place. The champagne popping from this morning probably had nothing to do with me and everything to do with this fancy telly deal that Summer made behind my back. Why on earth would she do this without me? And why so sneakily?

Another comment pops up from a mutual university friend.

Bet Jess is thrilled! You guys are so clever!

And then an immediate reply from Summer.

Jess has decided to go in another direction, which is probably for the best...

What the fuck? I don't want to go in another direction!

She said, this morning, that she was destined for bigger things and didn't need me any more. Was she talking about this TV thing? I know I fucked up at the party, and I know she's super ambitious, but surely she's not that mean. She's literally just kicked me out of the way.

The towel falls off my head and my wet hair drips onto my face, creating makeshift tears instead of the real ones that elude me. It's not like there's anything I can do about it. I own none of the site, I signed nothing. Not even an employment contract. I feel like such a dick. Telly is *way* more lucrative that books. With an irritated grumble, I switch off my phone. I won't send Summer the text message just yet. She can stew a little longer about the whereabouts of Mr Belding, for all I care. Not that she seems to have noticed, now that she's going to be a celebrity TV person.

'Son of a bitch,' I hiss to myself and punch the pillow like people always suggest you should do when you're feeling stressed. It's a high-quality pillow and my hand just bounces right off, which is really unsatisfying. I lie back on the huge bed and one of the springs uncoils, poking me sharply in the hip.

I don't want to be melodramatic or anything, but I think this might be the second worst day of my life.

UNTITLED

Rose Beam's Diary
19th April 1985

Is it frivolous to reckon that I've met the man I'm going to spend the rest of my life with? Oh, I don't fricking care if it is frivolous. My whole body is fizzing. Even my elbows. It's 3 a.m. and I don't know how I'll ever sleep with this feeling. It's not just lust. Maybe a little lust, but mostly it's a connection. I actually felt it like it was a physical thing! I sound so silly, I know, but I'm allowed to sound silly here, aren't I? Let me tell you about him – I need to get it out onto this page so that I don't forget. Ignore the scrawly handwriting!

So ... his name is Thomas Truman. Thom. And I met him just five hours ago. Thom Truman. Isn't that like the coolest name? I was at the Blue Canary with Victoria and we were dancing to this daft, energetic song by Whitney Houston. Then a tall, eccentric-looking guy strode across the dance floor and, of course, I assumed he was heading for Victoria because, well, they always do. But he came straight to me and leant in close. He said:

'I'll never forgive myself if I don't dance with you tonight. Even if it is to this horrible song.'

Which is a tad excessive, I know, but he said it in such a non-sleazy, genuine kind of way. He had a northern accent, which I think helped with the sincerity. He's not my usual type. His hair is dark and wavy and down to his chin! And he was wearing a patterned cravat, which I would normally loathe on any man, but on him it just looked cool and stylish. I would say he was a cross between Rob Lowe and Adam Ant, with a dash of David Bowie. But much better, if that makes sense? Of course I said yes, and we danced for the next three songs while looking at each other's faces constantly. Later, Victoria was chatting up the DJ and so I sat down for a drink with Thom Truman. And you'll never guess what? He's an actor. I know! And not a jobless/resting/wannabe actor like me. He's playing the part of Benvolio in *Romeo and Juliet* at The Old Vic! He's invited me to go and see him next week, and I don't think I have ever been as excited for anything in my life. I hoped he would kiss me before V and I left for home, but he didn't and now I feel like I will never have a good day again until I know how his lips taste.

Wow, listen to me. Probably in years to come I'll look back on these diaries and think myself such a loser for getting so caught up with a man just five hours after meeting him. But I hope not. Something tells me I'm going to be seeing a lot more of Thomas Truman.

My arm is aching now so I shall leave you and get to bed where I will dream of TT's dancing green eyes and try to get the Whitney Houston song out of my head.

R x

CHAPTER ELEVEN

A well-rested woman is a Good Woman! A fruitful beauty sleep can be aided by a silk scarf around your hair, cold cream on your face and a glass of lightly warmed milk by your bedside.

MATILDA BEAM'S GOOD WOMAN GUIDE, 1959

I've been trying to get to sleep for the past forty minutes, and it's just not happening. It's still light outside, this bed is really lumpy, Mr Belding is a properly loud purrer and, quite frankly, my head is in a bit of a mess. Thinking about how to fix *all* the things in your life does not make for a happy, restful night. Anxiety snakes its way through my body, igniting every nerve ending and causing my foot to tap repeatedly against the old mattress.

Man, I need a cigarette. I know I absolutely shouldn't because it might, you know, kill me and all that. But I need *something*.

I creep out of the bed, careful not to disturb Mr Belding, who is sprawled across the pillow next to me, and grab a

Marlboro out of the emergency ten in my leather jacket pocket. I pull on the skinny jeans and blue lacy top I was wearing earlier and head out into the hall. It's silent apart from the ticking of at least three unsynchronized clocks. Peach and Grandma are probably sound asleep. Pulling the key from a mahogany wall hanger, I creep out and tiptoe down the ruby-carpeted stairs. Getting through the hall without making a sound is difficult. I dip and curve and wind my way around useless objects, being careful not to trip. I do quite a good job actually. I'm like Catherine Zeta-Jones and her sexy laser-dodging in *Entrapment*.

Opening up the door to the building, I descend two of the front steps and sit out on the third one, stone still warm from the sun. It's half past ten and it's not even dark yet. A gorgeous golden-pink glow illuminates the plush private park opposite Grandma's house. Blimey. To live here. With a park on your front doorstep. The nearest park to me in Greater Manchester is also the hang-out of crackhead Jimmy, the local crackhead, and all his crackhead buddies.

I light up, and a minute or two later I hear the door click open behind me. I scooch over so that whoever it is can get down the steps.

'I'd prefer it if you didn't smoke out here,' says a Scottish voice beside me. I turn round to see the young curly-haired guy from before. The know-it-all doctor. Exactly who I wanted to see. *Not*.

'Have you come outside just to tell me that?' I ask with an exaggerated sigh as he stands in front of me, blocking my pleasant view of the park.

'Yes. I'm afraid so.'

'Were you, like, *watching* me out of the window or something?'

'Um, no,' he mumbles. 'The clinic window is open and

the dirty smell was wafting in. I couldn't concentrate on my work.'

I stub out the cigarette underfoot. 'Why are you still at work? Isn't it a bit late?'

'I'm studying for a summer school exam. Doctor Qureshi lets me use the building.

'What exam?'

'Well, I, ah, I will be doing a wet lab aortic dissection on a cadaveric porcine model in a few weeks and I want to get the theory down pat.'

'Ooh. OK, that makes no sense to me, but it sounds hard.'

'It is.'

'Porcine ... does that mean pig?'

'Yes.'

'You're operating on a pig?'

'Porcine models are preferable for trainees, who are prone to making mistakes. Wouldn't want to practise surgery on a human. At least not yet.'

'Ew. Is the pig going to be alive?'

'No. It's a cadaver.'

'Poor thing.'

He guffaws out loud as if I've just said something hilarious.

'Why can't you revise at your house?' I ask.

He rubs his eyes. 'My housemates are newly-weds . They're doing what newly-weds do and it's tough to concentrate with all their ... sounds'

'What sounds?' I ask innocently.

'Love sounds, etcetera.' He frowns and then stares pointedly at my cigarette on the floor, the last orange embers dying out to grey.

'Gad. What is it now?'

'You can't just leave that there.'

'Jeez. No swearing, no smoking, no leaving something on the floor for A TINY MINUTE. Who are you? The … Life Police?'

'Um, no. But it's littering. I don't know if you've noticed, but this is a really nice street. It should be kept that way.'

'God, man.' I pick up the cigarette with the tips of my fingers, mosey across the empty road to a racing-green litter bin and drop it in. I cross back over, indicate the now clear spot on the floor and put my hands on my hips. 'Happy now?'

'Yes, thank you. You're keeping Britain tidy.'

I glare at him, willing him to leave me alone. I really would like to get back to my one-woman pity party on the stoop.

He fiddles with his white coat for a moment.

'Would you, ah, would you like a wee cup of tea?' he says eventually. 'I could actually do with a break.'

He shuffles from one foot to the other and puts his hands in his pockets. The tips of his ears turn red.

Aaaah, I know that look. The doctor totally fancies me. Blue lacy top – works every time.

I squint at him. He's quite cute-looking, I guess. Bit short, but nice glossy dark, curly hair and warm, long-lashed brown eyes. Nerdy. But really quite cute.

I suppose a little kissing might be a reasonable way to cheer me up, help me relax after the stress of the day.

'You got any booze?' I say.

He looks surprised. 'Er … Doctor Qureshi is Muslim, so no. No booze.'

'Fair enough. Tea will do.'

He nods brusquely and we go back into the lobby of the building. He opens up the door to the clinic and we walk in, past a posh waiting room with lots of big comfy-looking tub chairs and oil paintings of gross squelchy- hearts on the walls.

We enter a small dark room. The windows are flung open, and a light breeze makes the blinds turn from side to side so that they look as if they're doing the twist. Along one wall are two hefty filing cabinets, and in the centre of the room is a desk covered in textbooks and papers with scientific diagrams of heart stuff on them. I hop onto the corner of the desk and dangle my legs down.

'Is this your office then, Doc?'

'It is.'

'It's teeny. How do you treat people in here? I can barely fit in. What if you have to treat a larger person? What if you have to treat a wrestler?'

'I don't actually treat patients on my own, so a cupboard-sized office isn't a problem because nobody is in here but me. I'm a part-time assistant. Mostly admin, to be honest, but it looks good on my CV while I'm doing my specialist cardiothoracic training, and I get to be around a genius surgeon every day.

'Why the white coat, then, if you're just here to do admin?'

Jamie goes a little pink in the cheeks. 'I'm still a doctor.'

'Yeah, but you're not doing any doctoring here.'

'I, ah ... I suppose I like how it looks,' he admits with a self-conscious shrug before pouring bottled water into a small kettle.

I laugh. Jamie responds with an embarrassed chuckle.

'So you're going to be a heart surgeon too?' I ask, as he pulls two mugs from his desk drawer. One of them is an NHS mug and the other has little pink hearts dotted all over it. Man, this guy loves hearts so much.

'Yeah, that's the plan.'

'Sounds like hard work.'

'It bloody is. But I love it.' He rubs a hand over his five o'clock shadow. 'What's your profession, Jess?'

Hmm. What *is* my profession? Best friend dragger-downer? Grandma-botherer? Future best mate of crackhead Jimmy? Who the fuck knows any more?

I swiftly change the subject to something much easier.

'You don't have to actually make the tea, you know,' I say, indicating the boiling kettle.

'Excuse me?' Jamie turns round. 'I thought you said you want—'

'We could just get straight to the kissing bit?'

'I'm sorry?' He drops a spoon; it clatters onto the floor. 'I don't quite ... '

'Come on, Doc. Didn't you invite me in here because you fancy me?'

He stutters and fiddles with a teabag. 'Er ... well ... yes. I suppose I did, but—'

'It's fine. Chill. I'm not like most girls. You don't have to woo me and all that fluff.'

He raises his eyebrows and looks down at his feet.

After a very long and awkward moment, I sigh and hop down off the desk.

'Listen, Doc. Thanks for the offer of tea and all—'

But before I can finish the sentence, Jamie has scuffled over and gently pushes me back onto the desk.

'That kissing bit sounds rather nice,' he says, taking hold of my hand.

'Yeah,' I shrug. 'It usually is.'

And so we do the kissing bit.

* * *

Doctor Jamie is standing in front of me while I'm sitting on his desk. We're snogging. Like, really full-on snogging. He's pawing every inch of my body as if he's never had a woman before. He pulls back and looks at me with a serious expression. I don't know, maybe he never *has* had a woman before. He *is* pretty awkward. Maybe I'm his virgin voyage. Gad. Maybe he'll want to cuddle afterwards. Must find a way to escape before that happens.

Either way, I can't deny that having sexy times is, as I expected, the most excellent distraction from the whole failing-at-life thing.

Jamie runs his hands down my back and pulls me off the desk so that I'm on my feet. Grabbing my bum, he draws me closer to him. I feel his hard-on press against me and get a flutter of excitement. He runs a hand through my hair and tugs a little on my ponytail.

Oooh, OK. Definitely not his first time. Though I hope he doesn't tug much harder, else he'll pull out my hair extensions and that would really ruin the moment. *Wait, stop, give me my hair back.*

'I've never done anything like this,' he murmurs, panting and pink of cheek.

'Like what?' I breathe, kissing his neck.

'Not knowing a person before ... but you ... I can't believe this is happening. How the hell did we ... ? At work, of all places ... I can't believe what is happening right now ... '

He trails off and steps back to unbutton his shirt, eyes glassy with le horn.

'How are you finding it?' I say, using his shirt collar to yank him back towards me.

'Super.' He nods decisively. 'Excellent, actually.'

We start kissing again and things move at speed. It feels

so great to let loose, to not feel worried and guilty about things, to feel the comfort of surprisingly strong arms around me. Isn't sex fucking brilliant?

We stumble into another room connected to Jamie's office, some kind of examination/storage room with a high single bed covered in blue paper and tons of boxes and metal trolleys

I unbuckle Jamie's belt and he tugs off my blue lacy top and my bra. He presses his palm against my boob and lets out a groan. Pulling down his trousers, he steps out of one leg, still kissing me with an eagerness the level of which I have not encountered on my sexual adventures thus far. The other trouser legs seems to be stuck. He hops around a bit trying to get it off.

I laugh. 'Hurry up, Doc.'

'I'm trying. Trust me.'

Leaning forward at the waist, he clutches the bottom of the trouser leg, but then somehow bends too far and topples over into a metal trolley.

'Owww!' He falls to the floor and a bedpan boinks him on the ear.

'Holy shit, are you OK?' I hurry over and try not to laugh. What a twit.

'Ouch,' he says, rubbing his elbow and then his ear.

'I hope you're more coordinated than this in the operating theatre.'

'*Ouch!*' He says again, pouting up at me pointedly and grumpily clutching his arm.

'Show me the damage.'

He rolls up his shirt sleeve to reveal an emerging bruisey bump on his elbow. His eyes are watering.

'Fucking hell,' he groans.

'You can't say fucking hell in here,' I say in a ropey Scottish accent.

He gives me a wry smile.

'Shall we stop?' I indicate our state of undress.

'No. No,' he says valiantly. 'I think I'll make it.'

'So brave.'

Then, without another word, he scrambles back up and kisses me as if his life depends on it.

* * *

It's just after 9.30 the following morning and Doctor Jamie and I are frantically trying to get dressed and cleaned-up before Jamie's boss arrives and the clinic opens up at ten. We pretty much did sex the entire night through. Well, until about five this morning, when we slumped onto one of the clinic beds, exhausted and dazed. It was good, too, in a surprising kind of way. Doctor Jamie had sex the way I expect he does most things, with deep concentration, a touch of awkward politeness and lots of enthusiasm.

'I can't find my bra!' I mutter, wriggling into my top in a panic. 'Dammit. I love that bra.'

'It's here.' Jamie grabs it from beneath the sheet of the clinic bed and flings it my way. 'I used it as a pillow.'

I don't have time to take my top back off and put the bra on, so instead I just wrap the strap around my wrist.

'I have to go. I think breakfast was, like, two hours ago,' I say, dragging my skinny jeans up my legs as quickly as it's possible to drag skinny jeans up legs, which isn't very.

Jamie nods and runs his hands through his wet curls. 'OK, yeah. Uh ... are you around for the rest of the week?'

I think about explaining to him that I'll be leaving tomorrow and that I'll probably never see him again because my life is in turmoil and I have zero friends in the world and what does that all say about me? But the mood is light and I don't want – let alone have the time – to explain my shitty situation to a one-night stand.

'Sure, sure. I'll be around.'

'Good. Right. I'll, er, call for you, shall I?'

'Call for me?' I grin. 'OK, I'll ask my nan if I'm allowed to play out.'

He goes pink at the ears again. I chuckle. 'See you later,' I say more kindly. 'I enjoyed us doing "it".'

He waves me off with a very big *I've just had a great deal of sex* grin on his sleep-crumpled face.

Bless.

* * *

I hurry back into the lobby and up the stairs. Why are there so many stairs? The muscles in my thighs burn with each step.

'Ow. Ow. Ow ... Ow,' I hiss to myself as I make my way up. Must do a warm-up next time I intend to make lurve for an entire night.

Ow.

God, I'm so late.

At the sound of the door opening, Peach comes running out of the kitchen and into the hallway of doom, a pretty floral saucer in her hand. 'Where have you been?' she whispers, sidestepping an old KitchenAid, her eyes wide with apprehension. 'We thought you'd left! Mrs Beam's been very upset.'

'Oh sorry. I, er, I just went for a ... early morning run.'

'A three-hour run?'

'I like to run.' I shrug a shoulder casually. 'Anyway, Mr

Belding is still here, and all of my stuff. I wouldn't have left them behind!' I hop over a cardboard box full of brightly coloured poster paints.

Peach purses her plump lips, a small frown gathering at the top of her freckle-covered nose. 'Be careful not to trip over again coming through here. Mrs Beam is having her meeting in the drawing room with the lady from the publisher. I don't think it's going well at all and disturbing them might make it worse.'

Drawing room? What is this, the olden times?

'Why isn't it going well?'

Peach's eyes flicker towards the 'drawing-room' door. 'I've only popped in and out with tea a few times but, from what I gather, the publishers *aren't* here to make an offer to reprint Matilda's books at all, they're here to tell her that they're absolutely *not* interested in republishing her books and that she should stop sending them letters about it. It seems they only sent someone in person out of respect for their history with her.'

'Oh, that sucks.' I feel a spike of sympathy. Publisher rejection. Grandma and I have that in common.

'It is an awful shame,' Peachy squeaks, fiddling with the end of her plait. 'Lord knows what we're gonna do now.'

'Something will come up, I'm sure. It always does.' I pat Peachy's arm briskly. 'As for disturbing them, don't worry about that. I'm a pro at this hallway now. Check it out.' I twist sideways in order to angle myself past a dismantled pewter bedstead and before I've even taken one step, some sticky-out part of my body nudges a wonky table, off the top of which a bowling ball comes rolling, dropping onto the floor with an almighty thud.

'Fuuuck,' I hiss.

Peach puts a palm to her cheek. 'Oh mah goodness.'

The drawing-room door immediately swings open and out glides Grandma, wearing a sage-green twin set and pale gold scarf-slash-shawl. She looks so relieved to see me, overwhelmingly so, until her eyes drop downwards and she spots the hot pink bra dangling from my wrist. Then her gaze travels slowly back upwards to what I suspect is the hairstyle of someone who has blatantly just been mega-shagged. She presses the back of her hand to her forehead.

'Where on earth have you been?' she says beseechingly. 'I thought ... I thought—'

'Sorry! I was just out, you know, running.'

'Running? Running away? Running *where*?'

'Just ... around. I like to run.'

She gives me the same worried look she was giving me yesterday. I cross my arms with a prickle of annoyance. And then, as if things couldn't get any more ridiculous, a head pops up from behind Grandma's shoulder. It's a familiar head with beautifully highlighted hair and a hugely impressed, dazzling grin.

'Jessica Beam? How wonderful! What a fabulous, abstract idea to use a bra as a bracelet. You're so creative!'

What the hell is Valentina Smith doing at Grandma's house?

CHAPTER TWELVE

A Good Woman is always poised. She must display a calm and graceful temperament, even when her temper is ruffled.
MATILDA BEAM'S GOOD WOMAN GUIDE, 1959

'I cannot believe it. I just *cannot* believe it,' Valentina is saying. 'I heard that beautiful voice and thought, could it be? Could sweet Jessica Beam of all people be here? And it *is* you!'

We've drifted into the drawing room and are now sitting round Grandma's teal silk ottoman, which holds a pewter tray full of fancy tea-making paraphernalia. Valentina confidently pours out tea into cups, as if this is her house and we are her guests. It occurs to me that Valentina Smith is the publishing big gun Peach mentioned was coming to visit Grandma today about her guides. The Southbank Press. Of course. Like Summer said, they publish everyone.

Except bloody me.

I nod my hello politely but don't return Valentina's smile. This woman made out like Summer and I were going to get a book deal and then backed out because I insulted her ex. All right, *accidentally* threw champagne over her ex. But still. She was so into the whole idea, and to just drop it because of the party, well, I think that's quite fickle.

'I'm afraid I do not understand,' Grandma sniffs, her liquid blue eyes flicking from me to Valentina and back again. 'You are acquaintances?'

'Oh, Matil, Jess and I are old friends.' Valentina tosses her perfectly tinted locks back with a warm laugh. 'Such a shame I can't stay much longer, because this – ' she points one finger at me and one at Grandma – 'really is just the most amazing moment. Grandmother and granddaughter! Jessica, you dark horse. You never mentioned your esteemed bookish heritage. Beam. *Of course.* I should have known! Both writers, both extraordinarily talented. Matil, can you believe that Jessica turned the Southbank Press down? I don't think I've ever been turned down before. I was awfully disappointed. I kicked my office fridge because I was so disappointed. Now it's broken. Just like my heart.'

Turned down? Wait, what?

'I didn't turn you down,' I say, outraged. 'You turned *us* down!'

Valentina's brows draw together. 'I told you at the party! It was damn near as good as a done deal. Of course, I *was* a little tipsy, but where books are concerned I never say anything I can't back up. When Summer said you'd decided to go in another direction, TV of all things, I was heartbroken. I thought we had a connection, you and I! No need to be embarrassed, Jess. I can't win them all, although,' she muses, 'I usually do ... '

I don't believe it. Summer really did screw me over. We *were* offered the book deal for *Summer in the City*, but she turned it down because some glossy American TV producer was interested and she didn't need me for that. She *would* have needed me for a book. What the hell? Disappointment claws at my empty stomach. What makes the whole thing worse is that there's not a bloody thing I can do about it.

'Jessica, you are a writer?' Grandma asks, leaning forward in her chair.

'I was almost a published one,' I mutter darkly. Bloody Summer.

'Jessica is a wonderful writer,' Valentina says cheerfully, and then pauses. 'Wait. Why did you not know that, Matilda? You're her grandmother.'

'It's a long story,' Grandma and I say at exactly the same time.

'I do love a good long story. What a shame I have to dash off. Perhaps you can tell me over a gin and tonic sometime, Jess? Ping me an email, we'll pencil it in.' She turns to Grandma. 'And once again, Matilda, I'm so sorry not to be able to make you a reprint offer.'

Grandma rises from her chair, worriedly kneading one thin hand into the other. 'Miss Smith, I *implore* you to reconsider. Women today really could learn a great deal from my books, from my years of expertise. The way they behave nowadays. No grace! No manners! No skills for the home! How on earth are they supposed to find a good man … ' She trails off and eyes the hot pink Wonderbra wrapped around my wrist. I unravel it and stuff it underneath my bum.

'Oh, Jess, do help me to explain this to dear old Matilda,' Valentina pleads, glancing discreetly up at the grandfather clock. 'Perhaps she'll listen to you. The Southbank Press can't republish her 1950s *Good Woman* guides because they simply would not sell in the year 2014. My hands are tied.'

Grandma's huge eyes are shining with tears behind her red-winged glasses. She looks so desperate. I feel quite bad for her. But Valentina is right.

'Sorry Matild – *Grandma*. I'm afraid no young woman I know would take notice of old self-help tips in this day and age,' I say gently. 'They're irrelevant. I mean, it's just not what we're thinking about any more.'

Grandma sighs, throwing her hands up in exasperation. 'You, my dear, are a woman of almost thirty and without a husband! The whole thing is unfathomable. It is ... *sad*.'

'Oi, I'm not sad!' I stand up from the sofa, indignant. 'I'm not "almost thirty" either. I'm twenty-eight. And aside from marriage being a generally daft idea, being single is my *choice*. I like the way I live. That's who I am. Young, single and ready to tingle. I'm a feminist and an independent woman and I love it. I work hard, I play hard, I party hard and do any bloody thing I want to, OK? That's the opposite of sad.'

'Bravo, Jessica!' Valentina claps. 'Bravo!'

'Oh dear me. Dear me.' Grandma presses both wrinkly palms to her cheeks. 'You mean to tell me that you *choose* to live this way? I thought this was just part of ... a terrible breakdown. Goodness. Does this mean that the colour of your hair is a considered decision and *not* a cry for help?'

I gasp. Beneath the teary eyes and worried glances, Matilda Beam has got an attitude and a half. And she's not finished yet. 'You have no job, Jessica. You have no home. You come to me for money, dear. Living the way you are living doesn't seem to be making you very happy at all.'

'Gosh,' Valentina says, thoroughly enjoying herself now. 'Gosh.'

'Leave my lovely platinum blonde hair alone!' I complain.

'I'm not super happy right now, admittedly. Things are quite shit, actually. But *in general* I am! I have more freedom and equality than you ever had. That's awesome. And it's not like you're in great shape now, either, is it? You're totally skint, you hoard all of your shit *and* you have a room full of porcelain dolls. I'm pretty sure that life tips from you would just not fly with the cool, fierce young women of today.'

Grandma gasps, two blotches of pink colouring her cheeks.

'I assure you, my tips are one hundred per cent effective in any day and age,' she sniffs, folding her long arms in front of her bosom.

'Er, I don't think so,' I grump back.

Valentina looks between us, a most entertained grin on her face. 'The familial resemblance is *uncanny*.'

My face buzzes with heat. I need to go for a run, shower, clear my head, get the hell out of here.

'Can I go now?' I indicate the door.

'I really must be going too,' Valentina says brightly. 'It was so lovely to see you both. A particularly wonderful surprise to see you, Jessica.'

As I open the door, Valentina close behind me, Grandma suddenly gasps and calls out, 'Wait! Both of you. Just a moment. Don't go! I can *prove* that my tips will work in this day and age. I have an idea! I will – I will *show* you how!'

Valentina's face melts into a sympathetic grimace. 'I really am sorry, Matil. I truly am. It's simply not possible. I hope that you can—'

'It is possible!' Grandma frantically shouts out over Valentina. 'Jessica here will help me to prove it!'

'Excuse me?' I say.

'Beautiful Jessica?' Valentina narrows her eyes for a moment before nodding. 'All right, go on.'

Grandma glances at me and takes a step towards Valentina.

'If we could use my tips to transform Jessica into the epitome of a Good Woman, then surely that would absolutely prove that the guides work and are worth republishing.'

'Well, that's the daftest thing I've ever heard,' I scoff. 'And pretty fucking presumptuous, to be honest.'

Grandma flinches at my swear, but ignores me and continues addressing Valentina as if I'm not even in the room.

'We would fix poor Jessica's look, work on her manners and poise, her feminine skills, how to behave around a good man . . . '

Manners? Matilda Beam is the one who needs a lesson in manners!

'My look is cool!' I cut in. 'And trust me, I have plenty of feminine skills. *Plenty*. Jeez.' I turn round once more to leave the room when Valentina calls me back.

'Hold on a second, Jessica.' She puts a finger to her chin thoughtfully. 'Continue, Matilda, I'd like to hear this.'

I stop short. Valentina is *listening* to her? I snort, shaking my head in disbelief.

Grandma goes on. 'We could use my first book, *Matilda Beam's Guide to Love and Romance*, to help find Jessica a good man who will fall in love with her.'

'And create a book about that experience?' Valentina ponders. 'So ... a dating bible? A *vintage* dating bible showing women how to use techniques from your guides in the modern day?'

'Quite.' Grandma nods slowly, sensing Valentina's renewed interest. 'Exactly that.'

'God, not vintage again,' I grump, trying to keep my patience. 'No offence, but surely everyone knows by now that vintage is just a trendy word for "old shit".'

'Actually, Jess, our most recent non-fiction bestseller was a wonderful vintage afternoon tea cookbook,' Valentina informs me with a wry smile.

Vintage afternoon tea cookbook? That might be the grossest, twee-est thing I've ever heard.

'The vintage angle is very hot right now,' she confirms. '*Clever* thinking, Matil.'

Valentina leaves me standing by the door and settles back down on the sofa, seemingly no longer in a rush. She pulls a pencil and a black Smythson notebook out of her handbag. She doesn't write anything in the notepad, but points her needle-sharp pencil in the air.

'Hmm. What about ... *How to Catch a Man Like It's 1955?*' she murmurs after a few seconds.

I look at her blankly. Grandma absolutely beams.

'It could work . . . ' Valentina narrows her eyes. 'A *brand new* book full of vintage dating tips, tried and tested from the wholly modern perspective of Jessica Beam. I like it. And, of course, the renewed interest would mean we could eventually rethink the reissuing of the original books.'

'Oh!' Grandma puts her hands to her neck, her cheeks flushed with pleasure. 'I love it!'

'Matil, in your opinion, how long do you believe it would take to snare the man?' Valentina asks.

'No more than two to four weeks if Jessica stays here at Bonham Square and we spend all our time on the project.' Grandma looks me up and down. 'There would be rather a lot to do, but we could condense it into a shorter space of time.'

'Wait a minute – hold up,' I interrupt, looking between them. 'You're saying you want me to stay here, in this house, for two to four weeks, change everything about the way I look and the way I behave, like some kind of science experiment, just to get some random chump to go out with me?'

'Not to 'go out' with you. To fall deeply in *love* with you,' Grandma says happily. Valentina smiles in agreement and scribbles something in her notebook.

I wave them away. 'And then you want *me* to write about it?'

'Yes,' they say as if it isn't an absurd, totally backwards, entirely humiliating proposal.

I glare at them both as if they're mental. The very idea of hanging about here for longer than the two days I had intended, learning this strange new grandma's version of manners and style, trying to chase after some bloke and get him to – puke – fall in love with me? It's literally abhorrent, the complete opposite of anything I would ever want to do with my time. Yes, I'd like to be a writer. Yes, I'd like to have a book deal. But not like *this*. I disagree with the whole notion of changing your entire self for a fella on a very base level. Nuh-huh. No way.

I spot Grandma's massive eyes fill with watery hope and my neck starts to prickle.

'Look, guys.' I back away in the direction of the door. 'Thanks a million for the offer and all, but, well, no thanks. I like my "look" and my "manners" and my "feminine skills" exactly as they are. Good luck with it, though. I'm leaving now. I need a shower and then I'm going to go run.'

'But didn't you just go running!'

'I like to run.'

* * *

Twenty minutes later, I'm out of the shower and dressed in my favourite running gear of lycra crop top and soft grey trackie bottoms.

I'm tying up the laces on my nice bright yellow trainers when there's a knock on the bedroom door.

'Jessica, may we enter?'

It's Grandma.

'You feisty duckling, Jessica, let us in. We want to talk to you.'

And Valentina.

What is their problem? I've just told them that I'm not interested in their idea. Why is Valentina even considering this? I thought she was so smart when I first met her at the Southbank Press. Turns out she's as batshit crazy as Grandma. I hurriedly throw myself onto the bed and burrow under the covers, pulling the blanket right up over the top of my head. If they think I'm taking a nap then they'll go away. No one bothers a napping person.

Except, of course, these people.

I hear the door click open and the muted footsteps of Valentina and Grandma walking across the carpet. Talk about invasion of privacy. Yes, I know it's not my house, but still, I could have been doing any number of private things in here. I could have been practising my withering glance in the mirror or having a wank. Jeez.

'Is she asleep?' Grandma says curiously.

I scrunch my eyes closed and pretend I am deep in the land of nod.

'Hmm. She's wearing trainers,' Valentina replies, 'A super pair of bold yellow trainers. I love them, Jess. I really do.'

Shit. My feet are poking out of the end of the bed. I casually tuck my them back in like the Wicked Witch of the East.

'Yes, I think she is awake and simply trying to avoid us,' Valentina declares.

'What odd behaviour.'

'Jess, we know you're awake,' Valentina says firmly. 'Matilda and I have been chatting about this new idea and we really are rather excited about it. *How to Catch a Man like it's 1955* will slot very nicely into my list. Especially since *Summer in the City* is sadly no longer an option.'

'And Miss Smith has already thought of the chap we could catch,' Grandma adds. 'A Good Gentleman by the name of Leo Frost.'

I splutter and choke, swiftly disguising it with a yawn/sleepy snuffle type sound. Leo Frost? What the sweet hell is Valentina Smith thinking of? He hates me. And I hate him. And Valentina hates him. Plus he'd recognize me in an instant.

'We'd have you in disguise, of course,' Valentina says as if she's reading my mind. 'And despite my personal experience with him, perhaps because of it, I believe he is a *perfect* choice. London's most notorious, eternally single, hard-hearted bachelor. If you could get a declaration of true love from Leo Frost, then the book would be a bestseller.'

'And my *Good Woman* guides would be reprinted. Jessica, my house could be saved! You could save everything.'

Emotional bribery to the max.

Valentina clears her throat. 'And, of course, there would an advance. Five thousand pounds on spec.'

Whaaat? Five grand? Five grand. I get a vision of my

bank account balance as it currently stands: twenty-three pence. *Overdrawn.*

I pop my head out of the top of the covers, meerkat style. Grandma's hands are shaking with anticipation.

'Five thousand quid?' I say, just to be sure.

'Initially,' Valentina replies with a confident grin. 'If it goes well then the possibilities are endless.'

I peer at Grandma. She's about half a minute away from squeaking.

'Does the dude *have* to be Leo Frost?'

'I can think of no one better. And surely you can see what a good story it would make.'

'Do I have to do it under my real name?'

'Yes. Matilda Beam and Jessica Beam. The family dynamic must be clear.'

'Er ... do we get to keep the five thousand even if the whole thing fails miserably?'

'Well, I'd very much hope that doesn't happen, but yes. That is how an advance works.'

Wow. Half of five thousand *guaranteed* for two to four weeks' work. No matter how futile this project is, no matter how much I will despise doing it, that kind of money is hard to argue with when you're in my position. That much money would get me to Thailand. Hell, it would get me to Fiji. It would be a leg-up, a fresh start. I picture myself beachside at sunset, sipping on half a coconut filled with pear cider, wearing a brand new silk jumpsuit and swaying in time to a soundtrack of Pink Floyd's *Dark Side of the Moon*. It's too much to turn down.

'All right. I'll do it.'

Grandma bursts into a decidedly unpoised round of tears and mutters 'thank heavens' and 'what a day!' before dashing out of the room to fetch the *Good Woman* guides. Valentina simply leans over the bed to shake my hand.

'Of course, I'll need the first twenty thousand words of the book within four weeks,' she says happily.

What the fuck have I just agreed to?

CHAPTER THIRTEEN

A Good Woman's skin must always be dewy, fresh and even. The perfect chap will recoil from dry or blemished skin, and what a pity that would be!

***Matilda Beam's Guide to Love and Romance*, 1955**

Grandma brings through a tall stack of jewel-coloured hardbacks and hands them over as if she's bestowing me with a solution to world peace before dashing back off to see Valentina out. I lounge on the end of the bed and select the top book on the pile.

Matilda Beam's Guide to Love and Romance

I put it to my nose and give it a sniff, instantly sneezing. It smells of old. Running my finger over the coarse, dark pink, cloth-bound cover, I open it up. On the front inside page is a black and white photograph of a woman sitting at a desk with a glass of champagne in one hand and her other hand elegantly extended to the camera to show off an art deco engagement ring. Presumably Grandma. She looks young, twenty or so. And she's hot! Beneath the, well, bitterness, my mum was really beautiful, but Matilda Beam is something else. I can't tell the exact colour of her hair from the monochrome image, but it's quite dark and styled in a gorgeously perfect wave down to her shoulders. She's raising an eyebrow and wearing a dress that flips out in the skirt, making her waist look absolutely minuscule. Underneath the image there's a little bio:

Matilda Beam (née Miller) pictured on the day she was engaged to Jack Beam, New York heir to the Delightex empire.

Delightex? The American bra company? My granddad owned Delightex? Woah. Why didn't Mum tell me that titbit? That's mega information.

Before she fell in love with Beam, Matilda was the toast of the New York debutante scene, receiving proposals of marriage from no less than three of Manhattan's most eligible bachelors! No doubt about it, Matilda Beam is a Good Woman. Read her story! Follow her tips! Land the man of every woman's dreams!

Three marriage proposals? Toast of New York?

I flick forward a few pages.

. . .

Never wear trousers on a date. A Good Man will appreciate shapely legs. But not too much leg, lest you be thought of as loose. Skirts below the knee, always.

I snort and think about my skinny jeans that are so tight you can see what I had for lunch yesterday. And the only skirts I have that go below the knee are my nighties. And most of them don't even manage that.

Nobody really likes a Chatty Cathy. Let your date take the lead in conversation and be sure to let him know just how fascinating you find him with an enigmatic smile and a few well placed throaty laughs. He will certainly enjoy being around you!

What? This can't be real. Are they going to expect me to *do* this? I can't quite figure out whether it's hilarious or horrendous.

I pick up the other books and leaf through them. There's everything from a *Good Bride Guide* and a *Good Mother Guide* to a *Good Housewife Guide*. Wow, Grandma wrote loads!

I examine the biography picture in the final book – *Matilda Beam's Good Woman Guide*: it's Grandma again. She's sitting beside a tall, handsome man in a suit with a cute, chubby toddler perched on her knee.

Matilda Beam sure is a Good Woman! Married to Jack Beam in 1955, she is the bestselling author of guides to life as a

Good Woman. The Matilda Beam Good Woman Guides are a staple in any home library, not just in Britain but in America, where Matilda's straightforward brand of charm and amazing results are renowned. Matilda Beam lives in New York with her husband, CEO of Delightex underwear, Jack Beam and their young daughter, Rose.

Wow. Mum lived in New York? I wonder how long for? Did she grow up in New York? Was she a *cheerleader*? Why did they return? Once again it occurs to me how much I don't know about her, about my history, and I experience a roll of guilt for not asking her more when I had the chance. I suppose that, at the very least, being stuck in this place for the next month will give me a chance to find out more.

Before I can think on it much further, the door bursts open and Grandma sweeps back in, closely followed by Peach, who is carrying a fresh set of fluffy cornflower-blue towels.

'Oh, Jessica. I couldn't be happier. You have answered my prayers,' Grandma chokes out. 'Valentina has asked that we keep her updated with our progress. She likes you a great deal, I think. Oh, what an utterly wonderful development.'

Peach echoes the sentiment with a small, pink-cheeked grin.

And then my worst nightmare becomes real. The pair of them engage me in an enthusiastic group hug. I hold my breath until it's over, which takes so long that my vision starts wobbling around the edges.

'A new friend,' Peach whispers to herself, quite intensely.

'Oh! Er, yeah.'

'I have such a lot to teach you, dear,' Grandma says breathlessly. 'I will teach you everything I know. Everything. You will be the perfect Good Woman. This time I will get it right.'

I have my trainers on. I could run out, escape right now and never look back ... except that I have nowhere to go and no cash with which to go there. Yet.

'Brill,' I say weakly when I've escaped their stranglehold on my body. 'Fine. Yay. Great. Hurrah. Just ... no more hugs, all right?'

They laugh lightly as if I am joking. But I am not joking.

* * *

After giving me a house key, the landline telephone number, and – due to my firmly enforced no-hugs rule – many joyfully teary arm pats, Grandma reluctantly grants me leave (on account of good behaviour) for my run, with instructions to meet her and Peach at Cafe Lucius on Kensington High Street for lunch at one p.m. prompt.

My run is a pleasant, sunshiny affair on the fancy-ass streets of Kensington and Chelsea, and I'm chuffed to discover that around here I don't have to keep my head down in order to avoid errant dog turds like I usually have to in Manchester. Silver linings.

I try not to think too much about what I'm going to be doing for the next month, the fact that I'm going to have to see the knob-prince Leo Frost again, how I now have to write twenty-thousand words in four weeks, or that when Grandma smiles she looks exactly like my mum. Instead I shove in my earbuds, turn up the Arctic Monkeys to full blast on my iPhone, and think about the money this project will earn and the freedom that could bring.

When I can run no more, I check the clock on my phone. Ten past one. Oops. I shuffle as quickly as I can manage, sweaty and breathless, to this Cafe Lucius. I spot Grandma and Peach sitting at one of the outside tables on the pavement. It must be about thirty degrees today but, as I approach, I notice that Peach is holding an umbrella over Grandma's head. With her free hand she gives me a small, shy wave.

'Oh, you're here!' Grandma says as I slump down onto a cast-iron chair beside them and catch my breath. 'And perspiring rather heavily. Never mind, at least you're here. Although, Jessica, you'll do well to remember that being late is never, ever fashionable.' She gives me a pointed smile.

'What's with the brolly?' I say, unwrapping my earbuds from around my neck and plonking them onto the table.

'The parasol protects Mrs Beam from the harmful rays of the sun,' Peach tells me, as if it's a normal occurrence for her to be holding a freaking parasol over someone's head. I wonder how long she's been holding it for. Her arm must be killing her.

'Yes, a Good Woman's skin must always be dewy, fresh and even,' Grandma echoes. 'The perfect chap will recoil from an ill-kept complexion.'

I snort. 'A guy who palms you off because you've got a spot or two? Sounds like a twat to me. I love the sun, I do.' I close my eyes, spreading my arms out and sighing happily as I bask in its soothing golden warmth. 'And anyway, we have amazing science-y light-reflecting foundation nowadays, you know. Hides everything.'

'A naturally clear complexion is the finest foundation,' Grandma insists. 'Such a lot to learn,' she mutters to herself.

'It's only skin.' I roll my eyes and take off my steamy glasses, cleaning them with a stiff linen napkin from the table. 'I don't know why you're getting so *put the lotion in the basket* about it.'

'Ah yes, lotion is a very good idea.' Grandma nods approvingly, missing my reference. 'We shall moisturize you as soon as we return home.'

We? Is this moisturizing of me intended to be some kind of group activity? I don't think I'm up for that.

Before I can verify her plans, a waitress comes out of the vine-framed cafe door and hands us thick cream menu cards.

'Oh yes, the wine list,' Grandma beams. 'A bottle of my favourite vintage champagne is in order, I think. One must always celebrate the good moments.' And then, as her eyes scan down the list, her nostrils flare.

I look at my wine list. Fucking hell, it's expensive! From what Peach said, there's no way Grandma can afford this: the cheque from Valentina won't clear for another few days, and even then she'll have to use that for this month's mortgage. Her cheeks pinken slightly.

'Gad, I really hate champagne,' I say, casually handing my menu back to the waitress. 'Do you guys mind if we don't get any of that?'

'Me too,' Peach agrees fervently, catching on. 'But I'd love some of the home-made lemonade, please.'

Grandma's lips wobble. She looks down at the table for a moment before closing the menu with a sigh. 'Oh, but of course I shan't have a whole bottle to myself. Lemonade for me too, I suppose.'

'Anything to eat?' the waitress asks, pencil poised.

Each of us orders the cheapest possible dish – a garden salad for Grandma and Peach and a side order of hand-cut chips for me. The waitress gives us a thoroughly irritated look before clomping back off into the cafe.

Grandma inhales sharply and immediately dives into her handbag – a real Chanel by the look of the gold clasps – and pulls out a little leather notebook and silver pen.

'Chop-chop then, we must get started,' she says briskly. 'Peach, you should telephone Mr Frost's secretary right away to find out his schedule. We need to know his whereabouts in order to orchestrate a *chance* meeting between he and Jessica.'

'Oh, don't bother with that.' I tap on my iPhone. 'He'll be here on Twitter – I can find out right now.'

'Twitter?' Grandma frowns. 'Is that a telephone directory?'

'No,' I chuckle, showing her my phone. 'Twitter is a social media site. Look! People update every few hours with their thoughts on the world, what their plans are, what they're having for breakfast, pictures of animals they like the look of.'

She shakes her head in wonder. 'How terribly self-indulgent.'

'It's right popular, Mrs Beam,' Peach says as the waitress brings out our lemonade. 'Martha Stewart is on Twitter, you know.'

'Dearest Martha is a Twitter?' Grandma looks confused. 'Whatever for?'

I shrug. 'It's hard to explain why it's so good. But it's brill, trust me. Aha! Here he is. Leo Frost, see?'

I click on his profile page, noticing that his avatar has been professionally shot. It's black and white and manipulated by one of those hyper-contrasted Instagram-type filters. In the photo, Leo Frost is wearing a sharp black suit and smoking a cigar. The Manhattan skyline looms behind him.

'Very handsome chap.' Grandma nods approvingly.

Peach squeaks. 'Oh my, what a beautiful man. He looks like that actor Tom Hiddleston.'

'He does not. Not really. He's an idiot, anyway.'

A wave of dislike rushes through me as I read Leo Frost's twitter bio: *Leo Frost. Woolf Frost ad agency. Artist. Thinker. Man.*

Ew. What an absolute turd. I can't believe I'm going to have to spend actual time with this knucklehead and, worse, pretend to *like* him. 'Ugh,' I hiss at the screen. Scrolling down past the hyperlinks and the conversations and the retweeted compliments, I see a tweet from four days ago.

'*Got it*,' I say in the manner of an FBI agent locating a perp. 'Leo Frost is going to a funfair tomorrow night. It's a pop-up retro summer funfair in Regent's Park. The event company who run it are a big client of the agency where he works, by the looks of it.' I Google speedily like a pro. 'The launch is tomorrow and Leo is a VIP guest.'

'Wonderful. The funfair is a perfect place to approach Mr Frost for the first time, especially on a balmy midsummer's evening. The scent of the cotton candy, the sound of young laughter ... ' Grandma sighs to herself and looks into the distance. 'My precious Rose always *adored* the funfair as a girl. She was ever so fond of the carousel . . . ' She trails off into her memories.

I blink. My mum liked the funfair? I think of her face, drawn and always tired. I can't imagine her anywhere near a funfair. At the doctor's, the benefits office, crying in her bed, at Morrisons, yes. Never a funfair. It seems like such a stark juxtaposition. And to hear Grandma describe her as happy? Mum was pretty much the *opposite* of happy.

I bite my lip, examining Grandma as she scribbles in her notebook. It strikes me once more that Mum had this completely separate life before I came along. She had a whole long, complex, funfair-going life that I know absolutely nothing about. To me she was just Mum, the person who took me to school (on the good days). The one who bought me books from the charity shop and wrapped them up in gift paper, even if it wasn't a birthday or Christmas. The woman I loved so much and wanted to make laugh and smile and be happy again. Didn't quite manage that, though.

'Why didn't you go to her funeral?' I blurt out to Grandma before I can stop myself.

Grandma quickly looks up from her notebook. A lock of her frizzy silver hair falls out of her chignon. She blinks rapidly beneath her red spectacles and opens her mouth as if to say something before closing it again. Looking around at the cafe tables surrounding us, she eventually opens her mouth again.

'I-I had ... a terrible ... chest infection,' she says slowly. 'Sadly, I was too unwell to go, I'm afraid.' I notice her hand shake a little. She notices me noticing and puts it on her lap underneath the table. 'Jessica, this is hardly the place to talk about such things.' She purses her lips. 'We've got a lot of work to do and only a little time in which to do it.'

What an odd response. I frown at Grandma. She looks back at me for a moment – her expression inscrutable – before her eyes slide away and she goes back to note-making.

I take a big gulp of my lemonade and try to clear my head. I don't like thinking about Mum. It makes my brain and my insides ache.

I wonder if it's too early for a glass of pear cider?

Why am I asking? It's *never* too early for pear cider. I signal over to the waitress.

UNTITLED

Rose Beam's Diary
26th April 1985ck date

What a night! The most important of all the events – Thom Truman and I kissed. And it was even better than I imagined. He has stubble, which I don't think I've ever experienced before. It made everything feel so much more grown-up. Before he kissed me, he stared at my mouth for what in reality was probably just a few seconds, but to me felt like an entire year. Wow. Before the kiss, I'd been to see him in his play at The Old Vic. He was wonderful. Far, far more powerful than the drip who played Romeo. Afterwards we, along with Victoria and Thom's friend John (an excellent Mercutio), went to a pub. Of course I've been to loads of pubs at university, but this one was different. It was down a little side alley and they had burly men on the doors. Inside, everybody seemed to know Thom. Not only that, they all seemed to love him. I didn't get the impression that the patrons were real Shakespeare fans, so it must have had something to do with his natural charisma, of which he has an absolute ton. By proxy, I was very popular too and the people were so lovely to me. Thom didn't leave my side all night, always making sure I was comfortable and that my glass was never empty. Later on, a few of us went into another room for a card game. It was all very serious and tense and I was an odd mixture of nervous and excited. Thom won and that's when he kissed me. He said I was his lucky charm! I think he might be mine too.

R x

CHAPTER FOURTEEN

A Good Woman does not indulge in intercourse until after the wedding ring is on her finger. After all, why should he buy the cow when he can get the milk for free?

***Matilda Beam's Guide to Love and Romance*, 1955**

Following my ill-timed funeral comment, the rest of lunch is stilted and awkward. We eat our food in silence, and as soon as we return home Grandma hurries off to her room for her afternoon nap. Peach is dispatched to town for various project supplies, and I'm given instructions to read the first two chapters of *Matilda Beam's Guide to Love and Romance*, paying extra special attention to a chapter entitled 'Making a New Male Acquaintance'. I go upstairs to my bedroom, drag the tub chair out onto my balcony and sit in the sun with the first of the guides, flicking forward a few pages to the correct chapter. I skim over the text, snorting at some of the more ridiculous suggestions.

. . .

Catch a Good Man's attention by 'accidentally' dropping your glove and allowing him to retrieve it for you.

Never talk about clothes with a Good Man – he is not interested in your new dress. Find out about what he is *interested in and only talk about that.*

Speak to your chap in soft, soothing tones, almost as if you're keeping a delicious secret.

I can't decide whether to laugh or throw the book at the wall in rage. What a lot of bollocks. May as well just remember to 'act like a wimp' and be done with it. I cast the guide aside and turn my face up to the sun, letting my eyes flutter closed. I try hard to keep it out of my head, but I can't help but think back to Grandma's reason for not coming to Mum's funeral. I might have been so drunk on tequila that I barely remember any of it and Summer might have had to drag me there, but I went. You don't miss a funeral. Not for a chest infection anyway. I can't help but think Grandma is hiding something. She was so cagey and cross afterwards. But why would she hide anything? And why, come to think of it, if she's so pleased to see me now, has she never tried to get in touch before? And *why* – while we're in a suspicious mood – does she think it's a reasonable choice to keep porcelain dolls at her age?

I make a mental note to ask her. Not in a blurty way like I did at the cafe – that was awkward and she closed up like a clam – but maybe just in a subtle, casual way when then mood is right. Even though the very thought of those kinds of deep conversations makes my brain itch to the max, I find that my curiosity about Mum and Grandma has been well and truly piqued.

I take off my glasses and prop my feet up on the rail of the balcony. I'll get back to revising that silly chapter in just a second. But for now, the sun feels damn good. I could almost be abroad. If only ...

* * *

'Jessica? Are you all right? Jessica?'

I come to with a start. I was having a lovely, almost hypnotic daydream about possible exotic travel options when all this shit here is done. I open my eyes to see Peach's anxious round head blocking out the sun. I wipe some drool from the corner of my mouth.

'Hey, Peach,' I say blearily. 'How's it going?'

'I got you contact lenses, like you asked,' she says, handing me a Specsavers bag.

'Awesome, thank you. I think I dozed off. What time is it?'

'Four.'

'Is it? You were in town for ages!'

'Matilda had a long list.'

She follows as I drag the chair back into the bedroom. It takes a moment for my eyes to adjust from the glare of the sun outside. I plop back down in the chair with a sleepy sigh. Peach points to the end of the bed. 'May I sit down?'

'Course – you don't need to ask. S'up?'

Peach stares down at her T-shirt and fiddles with the hem. 'I've been thinking.'

'OK.'

'I've been thinking that since you are here, and you said

that your friends had abandoned you, and I never had many friends in Alabama and I can't seem to find any here – I'm a little shy, you see—'

'No kidding.'

'I was hoping that ... '

'What?'

'Well, I reckoned that m-maybe we could be friends?'

'Oh.' I nod. 'Sure. Good idea. We are now friends.'

'Really?'

'Yeah, why not? Friends. It's official.'

Peach's cheeks turn blotchy pink as she stands back up from the chair and wanders off to the door. 'That's great. I'm right pleased. Don't worry about a thing, Jess, I'll organize it *all*.'

She dives off out of the room in a flurry of excitement.

Wait. *Organize it all?* What's she talking about?

'Organize what?' I call after her, but there's no answer. 'Peach? . . . Peach? . . . *Peach*?'

Nope. She's gone.

Why is everyone always so weird?

* * *

That evening at dinner, Peach keeps giving me bizarre, excited, conspiratorial looks, which I return with non-committal smiles. Grandma seems to be in a much better mood after her nap and is regaling us with really long and winding tales of her younger years: her debut into New York society, the dances she went to and the clothes she wore, and how every man who ever set eyes on her wanted to marry her and was totally in love with her, and how much I need to learn if I'm ever going to be anywhere near as amazing as the amazing Matilda Beam. Honestly. I thought

Summer was big-headed, but Grandma is something else. She's tearfully gushing about the time she renewed her vows with Grandpa Jack, and it's all very odd as I know none of the people she's talking about, even though some of them are apparently my family. I try my best to pay attention, but I end up zoning out a bit, and when the front-door buzzer goes, I quickly grasp the opportunity for respite and jump up from my chair.

'I'll get it!'

I hurry down the hall to the front door to find Doctor Jamie from last night (and again this morning – heh) standing there, hands in his white coat pocket, shuffling his feet.

'Hullo there,' he says, trilling the 'r' in his Scots burr. 'I said I'd call for you. So here I am. Calling for you.'

I smile. He's cuter than I remember him being. But maybe that's because of last night and the whole making me come three times thing. Hmmm. I wouldn't mind doing that again, actually – it's not like I've got any other plans for tonight besides hanging out with the fun twins in there.

'Can we go downstairs to the clinic again?' I ask without preamble.

'Fraid not' he replies, running a hand over his stubble. 'Doctor Qureshi is still there. He's working late tonight. I was thinking we could, ah, go for a bite to eat. I know a great Greek place not far from here.'

I pull a face. That's a bit date-y. I don't do dates. Dates lead to relationships and relationships lead to love and, as my mum always said, love leads to bitter hearts, and I don't plan on getting me one of those.

'I've just eaten.' I shrug.

'A walk then?' he asks with a smile. 'Kensington Square?'

'Tell you what ... ' I lower my voice. 'You go to the shop and get us some booze – Grandma only has sherry in and I think it's out of date. It's gross, either way – and then meet me at the balcony. Not the big balcony, because that one goes into the drawing room. The one above and to the left. That one's the one into my bedroom.'

'How will I get up there?'

'I dunno. Climb? It's not far. The one to the left, OK?'

'Sounds dangerous. Can't I just come in via the normal front door means?'

'Do you know my Grandma, Doc?'

'Um, not really. We occasionally say hello when we pass each other in the hallway.'

'All right, based on those brief interactions, does she strike you as the kind of woman who would let a bloke into her house for the purposes of making out with her granddaughter?'

'She does seem a bit old-fashioned ... '

I snort at the understatement.

Jamie looks unsure. 'Even so, climbing up that high still seems a little—'

'Don't be such a loser. It'll be like Rapunzel. Or the end of *Pretty Woman*.'

'Stop listing everything to do with balconies.'

'Or *Romeo and Juliet* ... '

'Fine. And then what will we do?'

I wiggle my eyebrows in what I think is a sexy way.

He nods once. 'I'll be back in ten minutes.'

* * *

I hurry back to the dining room and make my excuses to the dinner table.

'Boy, am I full!' I say, patting my tummy. 'And really sleepy. Super tired after all of today's ... excitement. I think I'll go to bed now.'

'But it's only eight,' Peach says, her sandy eyebrows dipping. 'I thought we could ... hang out. I... I hoped we could have iced tea in my room.'

'Can we do it tomorrow? I'm worn out.'

'Oh. Sure. All right,' she murmurs, looking back down at the table.

'Who was at the door?' Grandma says, putting her knife and fork together on her plate and staring at me through narrowed eyes.

'Oh, er ... Jehovah's Witnesses.'

'At this hour?' She peers up at the dining-room grandfather clock – the only working one in the house from what I can tell.

'Time of day doesn't matter when there are millions of souls to be saved.' I say solemnly.

'Deary me. Rest up, then, Jessica. Beauty sleep is most integral in the life of a Good Woman!'

'Of course, definitely, I totally agree!' I say cheerily. 'Bye!'

* * *

I open the bedroom balcony doors for Doctor Jamie and can't help but laugh when I hear him heave-hoing up the side of the wall. I wander out into the fiery evening sunshine and watch with amusement as he clambers over the rails of the balcony, a stripy plastic carrier bag dangling from his wrist and a look of genuine terror on his beardy face.

'Oh, bugger,' he pants as he finally gets his leg over the bar and tumbles onto the balcony with a thump.

'Smooth. Real smooth,' I tease.

'That was highly dangerous,' he huffs, red-faced. 'I'm wearing brogues. A bloke is not supposed to climb in brogues.'

'I'm not sure a bloke is supposed be doing *anything* in brogues.'

'Hey, lay off my brogues. Are you going to let me in?'

'Come on in then, little Joey Potter,' I chuckle, leading him through the balcony door and into the bedroom.

He brushes off his cords and hands me the carrier bag. 'Here you go, Dawson. Hello, cat.' He crouches down to where Mr Belding is smooshing his furry body up against Jamie's legs and gives him a soft behind-the-ear tickle.

I climb up onto the bed and dive into the bag, emerging with a bottle of red wine, which I proceed to open with the mini corkscrew Stanley knife thing Doctor Jamie has attached to his keys.

He unties his shoelaces, kicks off his brogues and joins me on the bed, shuddering as he notices the porcelain dolls. 'Christ Almighty, it's like a Point Horror book in here.'

'Creepy, right?' I take a swig from the bottle.

'There are so many of them. They're ... they're looking at me.'

'They are. Hatching evil plans, I reckon.'

Turning his back on the dolls, Jamie pulls out his phone and fiddles with it until some horrible tinny-sounding muzak starts to seep out.

I frown. 'What are you doing?'

'It's a "Sounds of The Saxaphone" playlist on Spotify,' he smiles. 'Just setting the mood.'

'What do you think this is, *Red Shoe Diaries*?'

He shrugs and tugs at the collar of his T-shirt. 'I like it.'

'Fine, fine. Just turn it down a little.' My eyes dart towards the door. 'My Grandma really can't know you're here. We're working on this kind of secret project together and I'm supposed to be in here getting my "beauty sleep". If she hears us, the proverbial shit will hit the fan.'

'A secret project?' He lifts a dark eyebrow. 'Intriguing.'

Hmm. Should I tell him about it? Can I trust him? What if he tells someone?

Oh, what am I worried about? He's just a nerdy doctor geek boy who is obsessed with hearts and wears brogues. Who is he going to tell, really?

'All right, I'll tell you.'

And so I tell him about the project, about Valentina Smith and the guides, and about Leo Frost and how Grandma reckons her romance tips will make him fall in love with me.

When I'm done, Jamie pulls a face.

'It's a daft idea, isn't it?' I chuckle. 'Ridiculous, really.'

'Yeah, it's kind of insane. Seems a bit callous on the guy. Frost.' His tone is disapproving.

'Oh, don't worry about him.' I wave away any notion of concern for Leo Frost. 'He's a massive twat. He deserves everything that's coming to him, trust me.'

'Hmm.' Jamie ponders, taking the wine from me and drinking some. 'But what if he actually, you know, falls in love with you? Surely it would destroy him to discover that you weren't who you said you were. That it was all some cynical experiment for a dating book. It seems a little heartless.'

'Jeez, he won't *fall in love* with me!' I laugh. 'It's not *actually* going to work, Doc. I only agreed to do it because I get two and a half thousand quid either way and I'm in no position to turn that down. He's some kind of womanizing, eternal bachelor anyway. *He's* the heartless one. Honestly, don't worry about Leo Frost!'

Jamie shrugs stiffly. 'If you say so.'

I feel a prickle of irritation. Pah. Why am I even explaining myself to a veritable stranger?

There's a bit of an awkward silence. I don't tend to mind awkward silences, but we haven't really got a great deal of time here.

I take my top off as an icebreaker. It works. Jamie dives on me.

* * *

Life might be strange and rubbish in general right now, but I'm engaging in some truly good sex and I thank the heavens for that. Doctor Jamie has tied my hands to the huge bedpost with the belt from his corduroys and has propped one of my legs over his shoulder. It's very effective indeed. So pleasant, in fact, that I can't help the squeak of delight that pops out of my mouth.

'Christ, Jess,' Jamie utters gruffly, biting my inner thigh and moving with deep concentration. 'Christ Almighty.'

He drops my leg, slides his hands underneath my bum, lifts me up slightly at the torso and goes deeper.

Oh my God!

I don't intend to say that out loud. But I do. Very loudly. And to my complete horror the door to the bedroom opens and Grandma appears. She's holding a tub of moisturizer in one hand, a glass of milk in the other, her mouth falling open in dismay. The worst, the most cringe-worthy thing of all, is that Jamie doesn't notice she's standing there. I wriggle about and try to clamber off the bed but my hands are literally tied. Jamie's still going, he's still going with the vigour of a bucking bronco! Grandma hurries backwards out of the room, slamming the door on us.

'Jamie, get off!'

He stops thrusting and scrambles off me to the edge of the bed. 'What is it? Are you OK? Am I ... am I too ... big?'

I give him my withering glance. 'My Grandma just walked in on us. Untie me!'

He removes the belt restraint with fumbling hands. I jump off the bed and cover myself up with the duvet.

'What? Old Lady Beam saw my arse?'

'She saw *everything*! Balls, bums, boobs. All of the B words. *Everything.*'

'Right. Oh, bugger.'

'Shit.' I bury my head in my hands. I didn't think true, deep embarrassment was an emotion I had any capacity for – I've never really experienced it before. But then again I've never had a seventy-seven-year-old long-lost relative watch me engage in a little light bondage. It feels highly uncomfortable.

I hear a weird noise and remove my hands from my face.

The weird noise is coming from Jamie. He's still naked, standing in front of the gigantic wardrobe, his face tomato red, his shoulders shaking up and down. He's bloody laughing.

'Stop laughing!' I hiss. 'You're a doctor. You're supposed to be sensible. I can't believe she walked in. She was bringing me milk, as well. Oh God!'

'I'm sorry,' Jamie splutters apologetically between blasts of laughter, picking up his grey cotton boxers from the floor and pulling them on as he guffaws noisily. 'I – ha-ha-ha – I'm really sorry, but you can't deny that this would all – ha-

ha! – make an excellent "how we got together" anecdote one day. Ha-haa!'

Got together anecdote?

Er, what does Doctor Jamie think is occurring here? I thought I'd been putting out a strictly casual vibe ... Have I not?

I glance up at him sharply.

'Um, not to ruin the mood, but you do know that this *thing* with us is just a no strings deal, right?'

He gasps, pressing a hand to his mouth jokily. 'You mean to tell me that ... that y-you're using me for my body?'

'Well, pretty much, yes. Sexual convenience, stress release, etcetera. Nothing more. Not anything against you, of course, you seem perfectly lovely and I can't deny that you have ... skills. I'm just not interested in anything more ... any *emotional* stuff, you know? I'm not that kind of girl. So you need to know that, if we're going to, like, see each other again or whatever.'

'I was joking, Jess,' Jamie retorts, a small frown playing around his mouth. 'I was just messing about. No strings, I get it.'

'Good.' I give a firm nod. 'That's all right then.'

CHAPTER FIFTEEN

The chap of your dreams will appreciate a neat whisper of a waist that can be clinched beneath his hand span. The largest part of the bust should be equal to the largest part of the hips and the waist should be at least ten inches smaller than either!

***Matilda Beam's Guide to Love and Romance*, 1955**

The next day, Grandma doesn't mention anything about last night and the fact that she may have seen my vagina, though she studiously avoids meeting my eye, which is absolutely fine by me. Tonight is the night of the retro funfair in Regent's Park where I'll be meeting Leo Frost in a 1950s disguise and attempting to charm him into asking me out on an actual date. I haven't looked less forward to something since I had to defrost the freezer last February.

Grandma has marked the entire day out for the purposes of making me over. Now ordinarily I love a good makeover – especially if it's in an eighties teen movie and involves some sort of perm, but I am filled with trepidation about this one. I don't want to change my appearance; it's already kind of all right, I reckon. But needs must, and I have agreed to take it like a woman.

We're starting my transformation with, as Grandma has kindly termed it, 'the ghastly situation atop my head', i.e. my hair. She and Peach have set me up in Grandma's huge bathroom in front of her big Hollywood mirror, which is framed by light bulbs and casts a sultry boudoir glow over us. I gaze at my long platinum hair extensions and feel a sinking in my heart. I love my fierce so-white-blonde-it's-almost-blue hair: people can easily spot me in a large crowd, and the sun reflects off my head, giving me a certain glow. I will miss that. I will not have a tantrum, however. No one ever won *America's Next Top Model* by having a tantrum on makeover day. Tyra never forgets, you see.

Peach fishes inside one of the shopping bags from her supplies trip and pulls out a home dye kit. After much debate yesterday, we decided to turn me into a fiery strawberry blond. Grandma was advocating for brunette because that was her hair colour as a young woman, and she felt it presented a classier look (whatever that is), but I refused. I have not been a brunette since I was seventeen, and there is no way I'm going back to that life. No way. So strawberry blonde was the compromise and still enough of a change from platinum to disguise me from Leo Frost.

All three of us start to take out my hair extensions, loosening the glue bonds with an acetone solution that Peach picked up from town. I feel sad as I watch my former hair being chucked into the bathroom bin. I spent a month's wages on that stranger's lovely hair. Peach and Grandma pull disgusted faces as they take it all out, the glued ends on occasion getting stuck to their fingers. It is pretty gross, admittedly, but no one was ever supposed to see this part of the process. Hair extensions are a very private thing.

The pair of them fuss about, pulling on heavy-duty marigolds and mixing up the dye. They carefully squirt it all over my head and rub it in. I watch the three of us in the mirror and wonder quite how I got myself into this odd situation with these odd people rubbing my head so enthusiastically. How many wrong turns must I have taken to get here?

'I trust you revised the chapter on making a new male acquaintance?' Grandma asks lightly, avoiding my eye in the mirror.

If revising means having a vague flick through last night to show Jamie before casting it aside so he could go down on me, then yes. Yes, I did.

I nod my head.

'Good. That's good, at least.' Grandma smiles a little and a sharp spike of guilt darts my chest. Must remember to look over the chapter properly before tonight. Ordinarily I'd write it on my hand as a reminder, but I don't have a pen. I take my iPhone out of my bathrobe pocket, open up the *Notes* app and create a new document entitled 'FROST'.

I tap out: *REMINDER FOR JESS: Read chapter on making male acquaintance.*

When the dye is rinsed off, the atmosphere in the bathroom becomes heavy with anticipation. Peach blasts my hair dry with an old sage-green hairdryer and then I face the mirror. I'm totally ginger. It's a pale, orangey-gold ginger. It makes my hazel-coloured eyes 'pop' and really sets off my Fake Bake. I like it.

Grandma turns to Peach. 'The tan will most certainly have to go.'

What?

'*Noooo!*' I yell in a Scottish accent. 'You can take my

freedom, you can take my hair, but you will never take my tan!'

Peach muffles a small laugh while Grandma shakes her head at me in astonishment, wide-eyed and open-mouthed. 'Deary me,' she croaks. 'Peculiar girl.'

They cannot take my tan away! My tan is what makes me *me*. If you asked someone to describe me in a word, they would say, 'One word isn't enough! I have to have three words and those words are Golden Fucking Brown.'

I pull a sad face as Peach dashes out of the room, returning with a bag of lemons and brandishing them in the air like a weapon. I know all about lemons. Lemons are the murderers of tans.

'Disrobe, please, Jessica,' Grandma commands, indicating the dressing-gown. I grumpily shrug off the robe, blatantly ignoring the sharp gasp of dismay that emanates from Grandma as she takes in my silver Wonderbra and non-matching turquoise knickers with the word 'Juicy' stitched over the backside in purple sequins.

I smile at her benignly. She looks away quickly and hurries out of the room, muttering to herself about appropriate undergarments.

Peach squeezes the lemon juice onto a sponge and starts scrubbing it all over my legs and arms. Ow. Bit by bit my beautiful tan fades away. Goodbye perfect tan. I am bereft.

'I *thought* we were gonna be mates,' I hiss at Peach as she makes me more and more translucent with her stoopid lemons.

'You will look wonderful, just wait and see,' she squeaks as she scrubs my ankles. 'And, Jess ... speaking of friends ... ' She pauses her rubbing and looks up at me shyly. 'In many of the movies I've seen, girlfriends often hang out and watch DVDs together as a way of bonding. They have popcorn and wine and do face masks and that sorta thing. I was thinking that when you get back tonight we would maybe watch a DVD together ... '

'Sure.' I shrug. 'Sounds cool. I love watching movies.'

Peach smiles and flushes pink, handing me a towel to wipe off the bits of lemon gunge all over my body. Grandma returns with three pieces of fabric and a dress bag.

I peer closer and notice that the fabric is some sort of underwear.

'Underwear? Why on earth?' I clutch my bum and my super-cool 'Juicy' knickers. 'Isn't the point of this that I'm supposed to be demure? Leo Frost is never going to see my knickers!'

'Jessica,' Grandma says with a calmness that seems to take a great deal of effort. 'Undergarments are the fashion *beneath* the fashion. They will streamline your silhouette.'

'My silhouette? What's up with my silhouette?'

Grandma looks me up and down and purses her lips. 'You are a little *wiry*. All that running, I suspect. I would like you to appear softer, more curvaceous. This – ' she holds up a piece of elasticy cream-coloured material that looks like some kind of Spanx skirt – 'is a Spirella 206 girdle. It will smooth out your shape, in particular lifting the derrière. And this – ' she hands me what looks like a very wide belt – 'is a boned waspie. It will create an *illusion* of curves, giving you a twenty-three-and-a-half-inch waist.' Grandma says this casually as if she's not just suggested something anatomically impossible. 'I had a twenty-three-and-a–half-inch waist on my wedding day,' she adds proudly.

'Yeah, well, Kylie Minogue has a *twenty-three*-inch waist,' I retort. So there.

'Twenty-four, actually,' Grandma replies promptly.

How does she know that?

I step into the girdle and watch forlornly as Peach and Grandma struggle to roll it up over my hips like a too-small condom. When it's finally in place, Grandma takes the waspie and wraps it round my waist.

It's a bit tight, actually. Really quite tight.

'Fuck!' I yell as they tug at the corset and I realize that my breath is being taken from me against my will. 'I thought you said I need the illusion of *more* curves?' I groan through the pain. 'This is stealing all my curves!'

'A Good Woman does not use such coarse language, Jessica,' Grandma says impatiently, pulling at the waspie. 'You will get used to it. It will be worth it. Beauty is often painful.'

Normally I'd agree – I've got eyelash glue in my eye on more than one occasion – but I feel like this is a wrong thing.

'Now we are going to hook it at the top,' Grandma says, panting with the effort of yanking and pulling the corset. 'Peach, I'm going to need your help. It needs to be just a little tighter.'

'Hook it? Tighter? It's not fastened yet? Oh, Jesus.'

'If we had more time we would have had a few practice runs to get your ribs used to the pressure.'

'Ugh. This kind of restrictive shit says a lot about why I'm glad I'm a woman today. I shouldn't be wearing *anything* that my ribs have to get used to.'

I feel myself go pale as Peach and Grandma tighten the waspie and hook the final eye, squidging my body into a shape it was not designed to be in.

'A bra too?' I huff as Grandma hands me the final piece of fabric – an odd, pointy sort of bra. 'Surely nothing on earth is as good as my Wonderbra?' I indicate my brilliantly pushed-up cleavage, so pushed up that it looks like I have Harry Hill and Harry Hill's twin brother comfortably tucked inside.

'This is not just a bra,' Grandma says, sounding vaguely like the woman who voices the M&S adverts. 'This is an original Delightex firming, lifting bullet bra.'

'Sounds dangerous,' I grump, still twisting with rib pain.

'It served me well for many a year,' Grandma says, a look of happy nostalgia flitting across her wrinkled face.

This is *Grandma's* bra? Ew. No. I cannot.

'You don't even know if it will fit!' I protest, eyeing the weird cone-shaped bra with horror.

'36C,' Grandma declares with conviction. 'All Beam women are.'

She's right. I *am* a 36C. God, please no. This is so wrong.

I reluctantly unclip my beloved silver Wonderbra and they turn away to give me my modesty, which I never have and don't currently require. I pull on the weird pointy bra and clip it at the back. As I turn back round, I seem to lose all spatial awareness regarding my breasts and knock Peach into the wall with my left boob.

'Oh mah goodness.'

'Shit, sorry, Peach. I'm all uneven! Let me look – I need to see this.'

Surely I must look like a member of the circus by now. Boobs like road cones and a waist circumference smaller than my thigh circumference.

'Just a little longer, Jessica, dear. Your look has to be perfect. A Good Woman is a *patient* woman.'

Grandma takes a suspender belt from the big drawer and clips it round my waist. Man, there are so many things wrapped around me and I'm not even dressed yet.

Grandma unzips the dress bag and pulls out a white cotton summer dress with a pale blue polka-dot pattern on it. The skirt is huge – all pleated and sticky-outy.

'This piece is my favourite Victor Josselyn dress. I wore it to my first ever mid-summer picnic with Jack. It's *perfect* for the funfair. It will show your figure while also being light, seasonal and demure.'

I take a closer look at the dress. It smells faintly of Chanel No. 5, the perfume my mum used to wear. I go slightly dizzy at the scent. *Don't think about that, Jess.*

I take a deep breath and recover myself, putting my hands in the air while Peach and Grandma pull the dress over my head.

Once they've buttoned up the gazillion buttons up the back, Grandma glides around me in a circle like a shark, huge eyes narrowed in assessment.

'Can I look now?' I tut, folding my arms in front of me.

Grandma nods once and gestures towards the mirror. 'Go ahead.'

I stiffly shuffle over to the large bathroom mirror, trying not to exert myself too much due to the pure danger of breathing too hard in this ridiculous get-up. I bet I look ridic—

Oh.

Wow.

There I am.

What I see before me is not a freak of nature, but sort of a more elegant version of Jessica Rabbit. My waist is tiny, but it doesn't look that peculiar, it just makes my hips and boobs look bigger – a quintessential hourglass. The shoe-string straps of the summer dress show off my now creamy-coloured shoulders and décolletage, and while the bare flesh of my breasts is covered up completely, they still look, and are quite literally, knock-out tits.

'Fair enough,' I say eventually. 'Maybe you're right about the look.'

'Well, of course I'm right about the look, Jessica, dear.' Grandma gives a nonchalant shrug, delicately pushing her red glasses up her aquiline nose. 'I'm Matilda Beam.'

UNTITLED

Rose Beam's Diary

5th May 1985

I spent every day this week with Thom. Mum and Dad think I've been doing extra hours at the gallery, but really I've been visiting Thom at his flat near the theatre. He lives with three other actors and he does not live well. There are no curtains at the windows and it's as if no one has emptied an ashtray in a month. But there's a scruffy energy about it, you know. Lots of expressive artwork on the walls and always hip music playing. Thom's room is in the eaves of the house. Mostly we just lie in his bed, guzzle red wine and talk about what we hope for. He comes from Manchester, and has always dreamed of being an actor in Hollywood. I'd like that too, I reckon. Perhaps one day we'll get to go together and become movie stars! Impossible, I know, but it's nice to dream, isn't it? On Thursday night I told Mum I was going to a Bach concert with Claire-Marie, but really Thom took me to a casino. I've never been to a casino before. It was brilliant fun until Thom lost one hundred pounds on the roulette. Luckily I have more than enough money in the bank to help him out. Of course, he hates the idea of taking money from me, but he only lost it because he was trying to show me a good time and I know he'll pay me back. Money means nothing when you're in love.

R x

CHAPTER SIXTEEN

Apply powder generously. Press on as heavy as can be and remove the excess with soft cotton wool. What a smooth and radiant look you have achieved!

***Matilda Beam's Guide to Love and Romance*, 1955**

The afternoon flies by in a manic flurry of dress-fittings, nail painting (an aptly named pale pink shade called 'Cotton Candy') and hair waving. I've been forbidden from removing the corsetry all day, and, as such, have just about got used to the fact that as long as I take super-shallow breaths and don't move too much *at all*, I will not die in this get-up. At four o'clock, Peach reluctantly leaves us to carry out a bunch of her chores around the house, while Grandma applies my make-up for the evening.

No sooner has she smeared on the first swipe of thick, musty-smelling foundation than her watery blue eyes make contact in the mirror for the first time all day.

'Jessica, dearest, now that Peach is attending to other

matters and it is just you and I, I would like to have a word with you about last night.'

Oh man, I was hoping she'd forgotten about catching me in flagrante delicto by now, or at least decided that the whole event was too mortifying to bring up.

'I'm, er, I'm dead sorry you had to see that,' I apologize earnestly. 'I'll put something in front of my bedroom door next time. Or maybe I can get a lock. I'll pick one up from B&Q this week.'

Grandma smooths the foundation over my face with a deft and sure touch.

She sniffs. 'I don't think you should see that man again, Jessica.'

Um, what now?

'Sorry?' I squint at her reflection. 'Are you kidding?'

She shakes her head. 'I am not a lady who *kids*. I simply think that if we are to embark on this project, it needs to have your full attention. Courting somebody new when you have already agreed to devote your time to seeking the affections of Mr Frost strikes me as a terrible idea.'

'I'm not *courting* Jamie, though. We're just having sex. No strings and all that. You don't need to worry, honestly, I can focus on the project just fine.'

Grandma's eyes widen. 'But a Good Woman must remain virtuous until marriage,' she gasps.

I snort. 'Bit late for that now.'

She purses her lips. 'Jessica, you will do well not to be so impulsive. To not give in so easily to your immediate desires – it's a sure-fire way to get yourself into trouble.'

I have known this woman for less than three whole days and she's trying to tell me who I can and can't sleep with? What the fuck? I inhale deeply and try to hold onto my patience, but I don't quite manage it.

'I'm a grown-ass woman, OK? Let's just agree that my room is my room and my free time is my free time and as long as I do what you say when it comes to *How to Catch a Man Like It's 1955*, then you have bugger all to worry about. Sorry, but it's really none of your business who I spend time with. Jeez.'

In response to my declaration, Grandma promptly drops the foundation tube onto the dressing table and starts to cry.

Oh dear.

Fuck.

I can't bear it when people weep in my near vicinity. Mum did it loads and I never quite knew how to make it stop. What do I do? My chest tightens.

'Matilda?' I stumble over the words. 'What's wrong? Why are you crying? Shall I, er, shall I get Peach?'

Her massive eyes spill over with tears that are magnified by the thick lenses of her glasses. 'I only want to help you, Jessica. You are here now and we are *family*. I *do* worry.' She grimaces, a look of guilt flitting over her face. 'Your ... your mother had the same impulsive nature, blindly followed her passions with no thought, and look what happened to her. If I could have made her listen to me, if she had just allowed me to guide her with my knowledge of how a woman ought to conduct herself, then maybe ...' She trails off with a heavy sigh.

'What?' I say, my stomach churning. 'Maybe she wouldn't have killed herself?'

Grandma gasps. My heart thuds.

'Look ... It wasn't like it was your fault, was it?' I say, awkwardly rubbing her thin arm. 'She was always mega depressed because of her broken heart. Because my dad left her and she couldn't get over it. Because she fell in love with the wrong person. It had absolutely nothing to do with you.'

Grandma sniffs, takes an embroidered cotton handkerchief from her blouse pocket and daintily blows her nose.

'Jessica ... you don't know ... '

She fiddles with the lace trim of the hanky, hand shaking.

'Don't know what?'

Grandma seems to have some kind of internal battle before exhaling heavily.

'You don't know... how pleased I am to have you here. Just tell me you won't see young Dr Abernathy downstairs. At least not until we've done our work here. This is *such* a wonderful opportunity for both of us. We must be focused. A Good Woman is always collected.' I absolutely don't agree.

But Grandma is clearly having a bit of a wobble right now.

Hmmm ... I suppose I could always meet up for awesome Jamie sex in secret. I mean, what Grandma doesn't know won't upset her and if it will stop her sobbing all over the place.

'Okay, G. I won't see him again.'

Grandma breathes a sigh of relief.

'You're a good girl, Jessica.'

* * *

Grandma continues to paint my face, occasionally saying things like, 'The complexion must be roses and cream', 'Elizabeth Arden's Flamenco will do wonderfully for a strawberry blonde in the summer time', and the best one, 'Apply eye shadow with a touch as light as a butterfly's wings'. She says each thing in a strange melodic voice, almost as if she's writing the tips in her head as she goes along. When she's done, she hands me a pair of ugly white cotton gloves with tiny little pearls stitched across the cuffs. I do not like them. I do not like them one bit.

'These beautiful gloves have given me much luck over the years. My own mother presented them to me on the night of my debut. It would mean such a lot to me to see you wear them.' Grandma smiles at me hopefully. What will happen if I say no to the gloves? Will she start crying again?

I harrumph and pull on the gloves. We meet Peach downstairs in the hall, where she's leaning against the stair banister, Mr Belding snuggled in her arms. She squeaks as she catches sight of my finished look for tonight. 'You look like Rita Hayworth!'

'Do I?' I sidestep an old film projector and a stack of *Good Housekeeping* magazines to get to the full-length gilt mirror by the front door.

Wowser. She's right. With everything put together – the hourglass shape beneath the summer dress, light rust-coloured hair in an extreme side parting and with thick waves (immovable thanks to a mega blast of hair-setting spray), my make-up both delicate and transformative – pink lips, long, curled lashes and creamy rose-red cheeks – I must admit the effect is quite startling.

Nothing at all like me.

If it wasn't for the fact that I'm off to see the knob-prince, I might even be quite excited about the prospect of a summery night at the fair.

'Remember, dear, keep it brief,' Grandma instructs as I leave the house. 'The aim of this evening is simply to bewitch and charm Mr Frost into obtaining your telephone number. Nothing more. No long conversations, Jessica. We need to train you up a great deal more before that. For now, simply look beautiful, be alluring and mysterious. Pique his interest enough for him to want to find out more about you.'

'Yeah, yeah. Keep my mouth shut and look pretty. Like feminism never occurred. I get it. Stop fussing.'

'It's all in the chapter you've been revising, so I'm sure you'll be fine.'

Oh fuck, the chapter.

I *knew* there was something I was supposed to do.

CHAPTER SEVENTEEN

A lady must never be over-confident or brash when meeting a gentleman for the first time. Ideally, she will be introduced formally, but if not, chatting about the weather is an agreeable way into pleasant conversation.

***Matilda Beam's Guide to Love and Romance*, 1955**

On the Tube, I spot a group of super-cool-looking twenty-somethings kitted out in elaborate fancy dress. A hunky blonde guy dressed as a Ghostbuster waves me over as if maybe I'm headed for the same costume party as him. *I wish.* He pretends to zap me with his proton pack and gives me a sexy wink. Hmm. Could I just sack off the Leo Frost thing tonight, make friends with this crowd and jolly off to whatever shindig they're headed for? That would be so much more fun and surely not quite as mental a way to spend my night ...

No.

I can't.

I agreed to do this. And we really do *need* that money. Not just for my escape fund but also for Matilda – on my way out of the house tonight I spotted a small stack of final reminder bills in the unopened post pile. She caught me noticing them and her lips wobbled.

I give the fancy-dress crowd a reluctant goodbye smile and get off the Tube to change at Piccadilly. When I arrive at Regent's Park, the sky is still light but the sun is low and raspberry-pink. A gentle breeze carries the deliciously sweet scent of candyfloss beneath my nose.

I wander onto the crisp, scorched grass and into the eye of the fair amongst a soundtrack of pulsing dance music, giddy laughter and jangling arcade games. I spot Leo Frost almost immediately. His rangy form pops up out of the crowd, glossy copper quiff shining like a beacon. He's wearing a pale grey suit with a dapper burgundy handkerchief in the jacket pocket. His suit pants are pretty tight. Pre-tty darn tight.

Leo Frost. Artist. Thinker. Man. Tightpants.

He's surrounded by besuited people – obviously big guns from the event company there to show him round the fair.

Seeing his uppity face lit by the colourful flashing lights of the fair only serves to flame my original dislike of the guy. Even the way he's standing – long nose in the air, chest puffed out – gets on my nerves. He thinks such a lot of himself. If it wasn't for him being a massive dick at the Davis Arthur Montblanc launch party, then Summer might not have sacked me or kicked me out, nothing would have changed and I wouldn't even have to be in this bloody absurd situation right now. It's going to take everything in my power not to betray how much his very existence annoys me, let alone pretend that I'm actually *into* him.

Right. Focus, Jess. Grandma said that all I have to do tonight is get Frost to ask for my phone number. I simply need to catch his attention in a sweet and ladylike manner. And the instructions for *how* exactly to do that are in the first chapter of *Matilda Beam's Guide to Love and Romance.*

Which I didn't properly read.

In fact, the only thing I can remember from the book is something about dropping a glove to get a dude's attention. That seemed to be very important...

I covertly follow Leo Frost as he walks around the fair with the event organizers, being careful to hang back at least a few metres so as not to come across as suspicious. Patting down my stiffly lacquered waves, I slip off the soft cotton gloves, enjoying the feel of the breeze on my now sweaty hands.

The group stops beside the coconut shy and the event organizers laugh super heartily at something Frost says. Chuh. As if anything he says could be *that* funny.

Right, Jess. Time to get tonight's task over and done with.

I take a deep breath, lift my chin and wiggle across the grass towards the coconut shy. Passing by Leo, I casually let one of the gloves flutter to the ground and continue on walking as if I'm oblivious to my lost property.

Less than five seconds after I drop the glove, I feel a light tap on my shoulder.

Yasssss! It worked! *Amazing.* Grandma is an actual genius.

I spin round, ready to bewitch Leo Frost with a delicate yet alluring smile.

Oh.

Somebody *has* picked up the glove, but it's not Leo

Frost. It's a chunky, middle-aged fella with a bushy black beard. He's holding a piece of rope, attached to which is a small fairground donkey. The pair of them smell, quite strongly, of manure.

'Oi, petal, you dropped your glove.' The man grins, handing over the glove. 'Here y'go.'

Well, that's it, then. The tips work. *Grandma, meet my new beau: the Donkey Man* .

Smiling politely back, I thank him and take the glove, noticing, as I do so, that there's a little brown mark on it. I try to tell myself that it's not donkey shit, but in my heart, I know it is.

I turn back and notice that Leo Frost and his cronies have abandoned the coconut shy in favour of a little shooting range behind the waltzers, where Leo is handed a toy gun and instructed to shoot the targets. He gets three bullseyes in a row. Of course he bloody does.

Bit by bit, I edge through the crowds, closer to the gun range, waiting patiently for a lull in their conversation. Then I slink by him once more, dropping the glove.

Where it lands on the wheel of a donut cart.

Noooo!

As inconspicuously as I can – which isn't very, considering my outfit – I dive over and swipe up the scrap of material, which now has a grass stain and some wheel oil on it too! As I'm examining it, I hear Leo Frost speaking from above me.

' ... yeah, she was easier than a two-piece puzzle, curves like you've never seen. Frankly, what choice did I have but to give her a quick ride before Martin took her back home.'

The men in the group all laugh, and one even slaps his back.

Ew. Who talks about women that way? What a disgusting, sexist turd. I cannot believe that Valentina went out with this bonehead.

I shake away my strong desire to forget this whole project and just kick Frost really hard in the shins. Instead, I focus on a final attempt to 'drop the glove'.

Closing one eye, I take careful aim – it has *got* to land in his field of vision if he's going to actually spot it – but right before I can drop the bloody thing, two bulky teenage lads dart past me, shoving into my arm. I lose my grasp on the glove and it goes flying through the air, landing perfectly on the shoulder of Leo Frost's slick grey suit.

It's all going wroooooong!

Before anyone can realize that I am the dirty glove flinger, I swiftly duck behind the candyfloss cart, out of sight and away from the scene of the crime.

Leo Frost and the event runners are mega horrified. Looking around in befuddlement, Leo picks the glove off between finger and thumb, smiles stiffly at the events people, and drops it into a nearby litter bin. He takes his burgundy handkerchief from his jacket pocket and dabs at his shoulder.

Brill. Well, Operation Drop the Glove has well and truly failed. Abort. Abort. Grandma said her mother – my great-grandmother – gave her those gloves, and now one of them is in the bin! Shit. I *have* to rescue it, but I can't until later; Leo Frost is hardly going to be charmed and bewitched by me if he finds me rooting around in a manky bin.

What the fuck am I supposed to do now? The only other thing I remember from the book is something about soothing voices. Speak to a good chap in a soft, low tone? Was that it? It sounds ridiculous to me. Either way, how can

I even attempt to make contact if he's constantly surrounded by all these funfair event organizers?

Aha!

As if divine intervention has answered, I notice Leo strutting over to the big dodgems rink at the centre of the fairground. He hands a ticket over to a steward and excitedly folds his tall frame into a lime-green bumper car. Realizing that this could be my only chance to talk to him one on one, I jog over – which is super tough in the girdle and is more of a speedy waddle, actually – and before one of the other events people can join him, I nudge through, stealth it past the steward and dive at the car, throwing myself into the driver's seat right next to Leo.

He jumps in shock and blinks at me as if I'm a mirage.

I gaze up at him from beneath my lashes. Please don't let him recognize me from the book launch. He shouldn't – I'm not wearing glasses or a onesie and my hair and make-up is *completely* different. I look nothing at all like the normal me. But still ... *pleeeease* don't let him recognize me.

I hold my breath.

No appalled shouting. No call for security.

Phew.

I exhale in relief and hold out my hand, eyeing Leo Frost in what I think is an enigmatic way. He doesn't get chance to shake my hand, though, because the rink lights start flashing on and off – our signal to drive. Music suddenly blares out from the massive speakers round the rink. 'Driving in My Car' by Madness.

Nice choice! OK, I can do this.

I gently press my foot down on the pedal and we slowly move forward round the track.

'Hiii,' I say to Leo in a nice, low, soothing-type voice. 'I'm—'

Crap! Who am I? I can't reveal my *real* name. He's only met me once, I know, but he might have an extra-good memory – I did chuck champagne all over him, after all. Cockwaffle, why didn't we think of this? I have to think of a brand new fake name and fast. I rapidly flick my eyes about the place for inspiration. *Ferris wheel, fortune teller, bouncy castle, portaloo... loo...*

'Loo, er, I mean ... Lucille,' I finish in my low voice. 'I'm Lucille.' I spot a little wooden food cart declaring itself: *Darling's Roasted Chestnuts!* 'Darling! Lucille Darling. I'm very pleased to meet you.'

'Yeah, hi, Lucille,' Leo Frost says absent-mindedly. I meet his eyes to see if I'm charming and bewitching him. They are focused entirely on my breasts, which are so pointy they're almost touching the steering wheel of the car. Pointy boobs for the win.

Right. Time to make some gentle opening conversation. I clear my throat. 'It's a *lovely* fair, isn't it? I do so love the—'

CRASH!

From behind, another bumper car smacks into us. Leo and I are thrown forward in our seats.

'Shiii—' I instinctively yell, but thankfully stop myself just in time. Instead I say 'Shimmy!' and give a little wriggle of my shoulders. Leo's eyes widen at my chest-wiggle. I whip my head round to give my withering glance to whoever bumped our car so hard. It's those bloody teenage boys from before – the ones who shoved into me when I was trying to drop the glove. One of them – a skinny doofus wearing a sleeveless vest that shows off a shit barbed-wire tattoo – does a 'wanker' motion at me with his hand. Absolute chumps. They laugh at my angry expression. I long to flip them the bird, but I'm pretty sure that's not in Grandma's guides.

I take a deep, calming breath and drive once more round the track. Turning to Leo again, I give him a simpering smile. *And then his phone starts to ring*. Checking the number, he answers it. Rude. He turns slightly away from me, talking into the phone. I hear him say 'dodgems' and 'account' and 'good show' but it's not fully clear because of the excited squeals of the other drivers and the sound of tinny fairground music blasting out around me.

BAM!

I'm jerked forward again by the teenagers and this time my left boob actually hits the steering wheel.

Ow. *Fuck.*

Right, enough is enough!

I side-eye Leo – he's clearly engaged in his phone conversation and paying no attention to anything else whatsoever. As delicately and subtly as I can, I turn round my car so that *I* am now in pursuit of the oafish teenagers.

'She's a fat cow. And old,' I hear Leo saying on the phone beside me. 'She's clearly of no use to anyone. Get rid of her, she's served her purpose.'

What the sweet hell? I can't believe my ears. Is he advising that somebody should be sacked because they're ageing and may have put on a few pounds? Ugh!

A dark flame of rage rises up throughout my chest, spurring me to step down on the pedal a little more forcefully. I block out the sound of horrible Leo Frost and chase after the horrible teenagers.

BLAM!

I bump into the side of their car with glee. The lads startle in fear.

'Serves you right, you little fuckers!' Is what I *want* to say. But a Good Woman would never say that. So I say it with my eyes. I say it so well with my eyes.

The teenagers gasp. Oh yes. The weirdly dressed woman with the nonsensically tiny waist is going to show you what happens when you mess with a Beam.

I whizz and dodge once more round the track – Leo still oblivious on his sexist phone call – and bash into the teenager's car again. I love the bumper cars! I can't help the giggle of joy that escapes me. I suspect it comes out as a little manic.

One of the teenagers whimpers, 'Muuuuuum'.

OK. Maybe that's enough. I reckon they've learned their lesson now. The chumps give me a very wide berth for the rest of the track and it's only when the cars slow to a halt that Leo finally ends his conversation, putting his phone back into his inside jacket pocket. Out of the corner of my eye I spot the event organizers approaching, ready to continue Leo's never-ending tour of the fairground. Dammit. I've completely missed my chance to bewitch and charm him. Fuck.

'Lucille, is it?'

I look up in surprise to see Leo's smug face staring at me.

'Um, yes. Lucille. Lucille Darling,' I reply in the breathy, soothing voice.

'I'm Leo. I have to tell you, that was some rather excellent dodgems driving you just did.' He grins, one eyebrow raised. 'You certainly showed those two little shits what for. I got caught up in an important call, but on the inside I was *very* much cheering you on.'

I laugh out loud in spite of myself.

'They *were* a tad raucous.' I say faux shyly, patting down my perfect hair.

'Yes, and of course one of them had a barbed-wire tattoo, which was quite reason enough for your fury.'

He holds his hand out to help me from the car. I take it, and as I step out I catch him checking out my bum, lifted considerably by the Spirella girdle. I smile at him as if I am mysterious and interesting and Good and refined and sexy and alluring and maybe a woman he could fall in love with. It's not an easy smile to perform. Is it working or do I look a bit crazy? I think it might be working. Leo Frost half smiles back, a spark of amusement in his green eyes.

'This is a little unorthodox, but ... would you like to accompany me to the Ferris wheel?' he says eventually, with a glance at his fancy-ass watch. 'Perhaps get a drink? I've some business to attend to, but then I'm free for a little ... fun.'

What the hell? It worked? I did it? It must be the boobs and waist. Or was it the soothing voice? Either way, he is *well* interested.

I recall Grandma's parting advice:*Keep it brief. The aim of this evening is simply to bewitch and charm Mr Frost into obtaining your telephone number. Nothing more.*

'I am so sorry, but I have a prior engagement this evening,' I respond, as if I really am utterly fed up about this made-up prior engagement. 'But you may have my telephone number to arrange a date at your convenience.' I bat my eyelashes and tilt my head to the side.

Arrange a date at your convenience? Where the fuck did that come from?

He smirks. 'Excuse me?'

I tuck a non-existent strand of hair behind my ear and bite my bottom lip. 'Would you *like* my telephone number, Mr Frost?'

He blinks in a mildly startled manner, then looks at me with interest, eyes travelling slowly over my body, pausing at my boobs and finally resting on my face. Ew. I try to hide my disgusted squirm.

He hands me his phone with narrowed eyes as if he's not quite sure why he's doing so. 'OK. Put it in, then, Lucille,' he says. 'I'll call you sometime.'

'Wonderful! I'll look forward to that,' I giggle. It's a real drippy, tittering giggle. I hate it.

He gives me a wide grin, showing off straight white teeth with a tiny gap between the front two. I will admit that, as grins go, Leo's is an impressive one. I can sort of see how so many less knowing and far more foolish women could maybe get a bit lusty for it.

I type in my number, gazing up at him serenely.

Leo Frost, you are going to get sooo played.

UNTITLED

Rose Beam's Diary

18th May 1985

Tonight Thom and I made love for the first time. It feels even too personal to tell you about, but I will tell you this: it was perfect. If I was in any doubt that Thom is the person I'm supposed to always see life with, tonight has totally changed that. Afterwards, we both cried and said that we were in love. Thom told me that when he is with me, it feels like someone turned the brightness up on his life. I love that.

He asked to meet Mum and Dad. I said it's too soon in our relationship, although that's not really the problem. My parents will hate him, and for no other reason than where he's from and what he does. I'm embarrassed by their snobbery. This can't be spoilt yet.

R x

CHAPTER EIGHTEEN

Telephone calls are not the place for long conversations – you wouldn't want to bore a good chap by going on and on! Keep chatter light, brief and to the point. Make sure your tone of voice is soft, alluring and interested.

***Matilda Beam's Good Woman Guide*, 1959**

As the final rays of blush-pink sun dip down over London, I make my way back to Kensington, a buzz of achievement quickening my step. I may have super messed up with the glove (which I later found in the bin, splodged with hot-dog juice and ketchup), and I definitely disliked every minute of having to speak to that sexist div Leo Frost again, but I did what I was asked to do: I made sure he absolutely didn't recognize me and I got him to take my number. Plus I didn't even have to read the whole chapter of Grandma's book! Go me!

As I arrive at Bonham Square, I notice Jamie lumbering out of the front door of the building, talking animatedly on his mobile phone. His doctor's coat is slung over his arm and he's wearing a faded khaki T-shirt that says 'Abernathy Canal Centre' on it above a picture of a barge.

When I reach him, he does a slapstick double-take at my outfit, signalling that he'll be finished in just a moment.

'All right then, snotface.' He smiles into the phone. 'Love you all the world. See you soon.'

'Snotface?' I raise an eyebrow once he's hung up.

'My nephew, Charlie. He's seven.' His dark eyes sparkle. 'Look.' He hands me his phone on which there's a picture of a skinny young kid in a Leeds United football kit. 'He's coming to visit me this weekend. Brilliant little bugger, isn't he?'

'Adorable,' I nod vaguely, even though, to me, Charlie looks pretty much like every other seven-year-old-boy on the planet.

'He's bloody obsessed with science,' Jamie chuckles proudly. 'I bought him one of those kids' chemistry sets for his birthday last year and it's his favourite thing. Well, after the Wii. And farts.'

'Oh. Cool.'

Jamie's smile drops a bit. It's not that I don't want to hear all about his kid nephew. Well, actually, I don't, really. But it's just ... what's the point? Family talk is for people in relationships, a way to bond by revealing intimate life details and shared experiences. And that's not what's happening here.

'Nice outfit.' Jamie gives me a pointed look.

I do a daft twirl. 'It's for Grandma's project. Stoopid, I know. I'm wearing a chuffing *corset*.'

'A corset, eh? Well, yes, that is ridiculous. Also ... kind of bloody sexy.' He takes a step closer so that we're only centimetres apart.

'It's actually mega painful,' I huff. 'Anyway, Doctor, we

shouldn't be fraternizing. My Grandma has *forbidden* me from seeing you again . . . ' He frowns slightly. I grin. 'But ... I reckon what she doesn't know won't hurt her.'

'Aha.' He steps closer, wrapping an arm round my restricted waist. 'Are you suggesting we run around in secret? Conduct an, um, elicit affair?'

'Something like that . . . ' I wiggle my eyebrows. 'Could be hot . . . '

'Would you like to start right now?' He trails his warm hand up my back, sending a shiver right to the pit of my stomach. 'The clinic's empty. We could get you out of that corset, if you like?'

'Oh God, yes please.' I rub my stomach in anticipation of the beautiful moment when I will be able to fully breathe out once more.

'Come on, then,' Jamie whispers, holding out his hand and glancing up and down the street with an over-the-top worried expression. 'Before someone spots us out here.'

He's such a plonker. I laugh and take his hand, dragging him inside to the clinic.

* * *

Carrying my plethora of vintage underwear in my arms (including the tights Jamie ended up ripping in his eagerness to get them off me), I sneak back up to Grandma's house at midnight, being careful to let myself in stealthily so as not to wake anyone. The house smells really strongly of popcorn. That's odd. I'm far too knackered to remove my make-up and so simply flop onto to the bed fully clothed, where I pass out in a matter of seconds.

It feels like my eyes have only been closed for a few

minutes when I'm awoken by a firm knock on the bedroom door.

It's morning already?

Noooo.

Grandma's voice is bright and breezy from the landing.

'Jessica, dear, rise and shine! We are most eager to hear all about last night! Breakfast is ready. Peach and I will be waiting downstairs. Do hurry!'

'Mnnghg.' I turn over to where Mr Belding is curled up beside me, purring like he doesn't even care that it's crap o'clock in the morning. 'You go downstairs, make an excuse for me will you, Mr Belding?' I ask him. 'Take one for the team, eh?'

In response he puts his cold nose against my nose and swipes his paw at my face.

Gad, why can't anyone just let me have a tiny little lie-in? Why? WHY?

With a sigh, I reluctantly climb out of the bed, change into tracksuit bottoms and a blue cotton vest and trudge downstairs. I blearily make my way into the kitchen and, plonking down at the huge oak table, pour myself a black coffee from the pot.

'How did it go?

'Was Mr Frost charmed and bewitched by you?'

'Did he take your number?'

'Where are my gloves?'

I am bombarded by questions. I take a huge gulp of coffee and rub my eyes. Then I do a really long stretch and a massive yawn just to wind them up.

'What happened, Jess?'

'Tell us, for heaven's sake!'

I raise an eyebrow. 'Oh, you know,' I say nonchalantly,

putting the coffee cup back on the table. 'Gave him my digits, didn't I?'

Peach laughs out loud in astonishment. Grandma tries to look unsurprised and cool but completely fails. Her eyes sparkle with excitement and two spots of pink brighten her high-boned pale cheeks. 'Which of my Good Woman tips was it, Jessica?' she asks. 'Which one worked?'

I bite my lip. I can't bloody tell her that I totally failed at dropping the glove. She'll probably start crying again. Instead I say:

'The glove! I dropped it and sauntered past Leo just like the book said to and he came right over. It was, um, it was like magic.'

She claps her hands together. 'And you managed not to curse?'

'I didn't even say shit. I was the very image of a demure woman.'

I tell them about the whole night, how I called myself Lucille Darling, about Leo asking to take me for a drink and how I said I had a 'prior engagement'. I conveniently leave out that I pretty much made a mess of it and the fact that he took my number was probably a fluke and nothing to do with Grandma's tips, possibly more to do with my unavoidable boobs and most amazing dodgems driving.

'I hope he rings soon,' Peach mumbles, spooning Tesco Value cornflakes into her mouth.

'Oh, he will,' Grandma tell us confidently. 'Though we will probably have to wait a few days.' She chuckles in a knowing way. 'Men do *not* like to diminish their power by telephoning a lady immediately, lest they appear over-eager.'

As it turns out, Matilda Beam is completely wrong on

that one. Because just twenty minutes later my phone rings. And it's Leo Frost.

* * *

Grandma and Peach hurry over to join me on the sofa as I press answer on my iPhone.

'Hello?'

'Good morning, Lucille. This is Leo Frost speaking.'

Leo Frost. Artist. Thinker. Man. On the phone.

'Hi there, Leo,' I say in the low, soothing voice. 'How *terrific* to hear from you. I do hope you enjoyed the funfair last ... '

I abruptly stop talking as I notice Grandma and Peach staring at me in horror. They gesticulate wildly, waving their hands up and down like mad people. What's wrong? What are they trying to say?

'Excuse me, Leo, please hold the line for just a moment.'

I press the secrecy button. 'What are you doing?'

'Your voice! What on earth has happened to your voice?' Grandma's chin trembles.

'Er ... it's a soothing voice. Like you said? Throaty and that.'

'It's much too deep! A soothing voice should be light and enticing!'

'What do I sound like?'

Peach grimaces, not quite meeting my eye. 'You sound sorta demonic. Like you might be planning to murder him.'

Grandma pats my knee. 'Soften it a little, dear. Speak to him as if you're keeping a *scrumptious* secret.'

I nod, clear my throat and try again, making my voice softer, higher and more melodic. I sound like a twat.

'Sorry about that, Leo,' I breathe, clicking the phone

onto loudspeaker. Grandma gives me a thumbs-up. 'What can I do for you?'

'Yeah, I thought we could get together. I have a dinner meeting this evening but I'm free as a bird afterwards. Coffee at my pad sound good? About eleven?'

Oh. My. God. I am well versed in the art of the bootie call and this is an outright boot-*ay* call. I didn't put out any of my usual super casual vibes last night, I'm sure of it. Must have been the boobs sending out a very specific kind of message. I don't know why I'm surprised – according to Valentina this is Leo Frost's M.O., after all.

'Just a moment, let me check my schedule.' I press secrecy on the phone again.

'He's bootie-calling me,' I hiss to Grandma and Peach

'*Bootie calling*?' Grandma squints. 'I'm afraid I don't understand.'

Hmmm. How do you explain a bootie call to a seventy-seven-year-old woman who still watches her movies on VHS tapes?

'Er ... he's not quite offering to take me on a date. I reckon he wants me to go to his place for ... *you know* ... '

'I don't know.'

'Um, well, let's just say that he wants to do to me what Oliver the gamekeeper does to Lady Chatterley.'

Grandma's mouth drops open. She snatches the phone from my grasp and presses her bony finger onto the 'end call' icon.

'What did you just do!' I yell, grabbing my phone off her. 'You hung up on him!'

'He's a cad, dear,' Grandma declares, calmly pushing her big red glasses up her nose. 'A very handsome, very wealthy and charming cad. Women don't hang up on him – the very fact that you just did will intrigue him, trust me.

When he calls back, tell him that you would love to meet him for an early dinner tomorrow evening – he won't correct you about his original dishonourable intentions, his manners are far too polished for that.'

'He won't blummin' call back!' I roll my eyes. 'This isn't the olden days, G. It isn't cute or intriguing or flirty when you hang up. It just pisses people off.'

The phone rings again.

It's him.

I blink at my mobile and eye Grandma with astonishment. She casually examines her perfectly painted fingernails as if this is no big deal.

'Woah.' Peach gawps at the phone.

I pick it up.

'Hello?'

'Ah, Lucille, we must have got cut off,' Leo says in his deep plummy tones.

'Oh dear, I'm so sorry about that. I got distracted and *completely* forgot you were on the telephone!' I giggle warmly. Grandma beams.

'Oh,' he coughs lightly. 'Right.'

'Now, about dinner. I'm available early evening tomorrow, I hope that suits? I'm sure a *gentleman* like you knows the *most* wonderful places to take a girl.'

I wait for him to explain that he wasn't exactly asking me out on a date. But he doesn't. Grandma was right. She was completely right! He's too well brought up to overtly correct my 'mistake', especially since I just referred to him as a gentleman.

'Um ... yes, well. I wasn't ... Yes, OK. I suppose early evening ... could work?'

'Divine,' I purr down the phone. 'I'm already looking forward to it.'

Like. A. Boss.

Completely oblivious to the cunning trickery that has just been performed upon him, one Leo Frost agrees to take one Lucille Darling for an early dinner date tomorrow evening.

I click off the phone and hold my hand out to Grandma for a high-five. She thinks I'm waving at her and waves back, a confused expression on her bespectacled face. Thankfully, Peach dives over, slaps my hand and saves the high-five. Phew.

It's on. It's on like donkey kong.

CHAPTER NINETEEN

It is not a lady's place to trouble herself with the financial matters of her family, but the man's. Trust your husband's judgement, always.

***Matilda Beam's Good Housewife Guide*, 1957**

The buoyant mood of the call with Leo Frost is dampened shortly afterwards when the door buzzer goes.

'I'll get it!' I yell, weaving my way down the hallway of doom and narrowly avoiding death via a precariously wobbling block of Japanese chopping knives balanced on a stack of retro board games. I tut and, carefully placing the knife block on the floor beside the other junk, answer the intercom.

'Yo.'

'Morning. Y'got a letter needs signing for.'

I buzz the postie up and open the front door. I see him – a stocky fella in shorts and a postman's cap – racing up the stairs. When he spots me, his young, tanned, smiling face drops in stark disappointment. Jeez. I know I look a bit manky in the mornings, but he could at least *try* to hide his distaste.

'Where's Peach?' he asks, handing me a letter addressed to Matilda. 'Has ... has she left her job? Are you her replacement?'

'Oh no, Peach is in the kitchen, I think. Would you like to speak to her?'

He pulls the lip of his cap down. 'N-no. Unless ... do you think she wants to talk to me?'

'I don't know. We can ask her?' I turn around to call Peach from the kitchen.

'No! No, don't.' He wipes a bit of sweat from his brow. 'It's cool. Just sign this, please.' He hands me a little machine and an electronic pen. I do a squiggle and take the letter from him.

'You want me to tell Peach you said hello?' I raise an eyebrow.

'Um, no. I'll see her tomorrow,' he mumbles, hurrying back off down the stairs.

'Bye then!' I call after him cheerily, but he's already gone.

Odd.

Moseying back to the drawing room, I peek down at Matilda's letter. Beneath the transparent part of the envelope I see the words:

Possession Action: Bonham Square.

Fuck. That sounds serious! And scary. Even the bold font they've used looks grumpy. I hand the letter to Grandma, who's sitting in her blue chair with her sewing box out, taking in the grey pencil skirt she wants me to wear for tomorrow's date with Leo.

'This letter just came for you!'

She barely glances up. 'Thank you, dear. Put it on the hall table, please. I'll get to it later.'

I picture the stack of unopened final reminder letters I saw last night.

'Er ... maybe you should open this one. I think it's important.'

'Yes, I shall ... later,' she answers vaguely.

'But ... '

Grandma looks up sharply, her face displaying the same frowny expression Mum used to give me when I asked her why I didn't have a dad, or spent my week's pocket money in one day. I stop talking and rub my neck. Why am I even getting involved? It's not *my* problem. It's not my business. In two to four weeks I'll be out of here, hopefully in another country.

But ... when you don't deal with letters like this, nasty people start turning up at your door. And that's not something that should happen to *any* old person, regardless of whether or not they're a blood relative. My stomach lurches just imagining the horrible scenario.

I rip open the letter.

Grandma's head darts up from her sewing, her mouth dropping open. 'W-what on earth are you doing? That's private! It's illegal to open someone else's post! Stop!'

'You haven't been opening your post for ages and you have to deal with this.' I unfold the bright red letter and read it, taking in the threateningly passive-aggressive tone, the phrases 'Notice of Possession', 'significant arrears', 'proposed payment plan'. Grandma casts the skirt aside and stands up, grabbing to take the letter off me.

I let her take it and watch sadly as she reads.

'Oh dear. I ... I ...' she starts, before plopping back down onto her chair and hanging her head.

Oh dear indeed.

'Hey, we can sort this, OK,' I say, swallowing hard. 'Don't get upset. It, um, it says that they need you to agree to a minimum payment plan. If you can keep up with it then they won't take you to court.'

Grandma removes her glasses and sighs, her eyes filling with tears.

'How on earth has it has come to this?' she mutters to herself before meeting my gaze. 'I can't bear to think about it, Jessica. I ... I was hoping that if I didn't think about it, it would go away. I told myself that I would deal with it all once my books were republished, but these people – ' she waves the letter about with trembling hands – 'are terribly impatient. And *very* rude.'

'Maybe if you just phone them up—'

'But Jack always handled the finances! It's the job of a Good Husband to deal with these things. *I* don't know what to do. Whatever will I do?'

Shit. I'm not exactly money-savvy, but my old-fashioned Grandma has no clue at all how to handle this. How can she have been so successful with her books and not have a grip on how to handle money and debt issues?

'I could get a part-time job?' I suggest.

I did bar work when I was travelling. There are probably loads of bar jobs in London.

'No,' Grandma sobs. 'We have to focus on our project with Valentina. That's the best chance of a decent income we have. And I can't ask you to pay for your Grandfather's mistakes. I simply cannot. Not when it's our fault that—'

There's a noisy crash from the hallway as Peach trips over one of the many pieces of junk in there.

'I'm all right!' she calls out. 'I just tripped over a whisk!'

A whisk? Why the hell is there a ... Then I get a brainwave.

'Grandma,' I say, sitting down on the sofa opposite her. 'I've got an idea. I think maybe we're going to have to sell some of your stuff.'

'Excuse me?'

'All that junk in the hall and in the attic. We could sell it, you know? I mean, you don't use any of it.'

'Those are my belongings! They have ... sentimental value.' She frowns at me as if I've just suggested she remove her own leg and sell that.

I roll my eyes. 'It won't mean anything to have eight different candelabras if you're living in a park.'

'Oh, good grief!' Grandma dissolves into another round of tears. Shit. I reach across and pat her shoulder.

'I'm kidding.' *Kind of*. 'But sentimentality is for suckers. You've got to be ruthless in these situations. Are you honestly telling me that you *need* all that stuff out there? There are two bowling balls by the front door. When was the last time you went bowling?'

Grandma looks at her knees. 'I believe it was 1978. But ... I might decide to go again. One day.'

'You won't! And what about the old record player? Some muso geek would probably pay a fortune for that.'

'I have a record player?' Grandma says in astonishment. 'I didn't notice that!'

'See! You don't even know half the junk you've got. We

could even sell all those porcelain dolls in my room too. They're really cree—'

'No!' Grandma interrupts fiercely. 'No. Not those. They stay put. Under no circumstances must those dolls be—'

'OK, OK, jeez! Not the dolls. *You* choose what we sell and we'll put it on eBay. I'm awesome at eBay. Last year I wrote such a good eBay description for a pair of platform boots that there was this *major* bidding war and they ended up selling for sixty quid. I only paid fifteen quid for them at the inside market and that was in 2003.'

'The Ee*bay*?' Grandma sniffs. 'Is that a jumble sale? Where is it situated? Is it in Zone One?'

'Oh, you have *such* a lot to learn, dear,' I say in a hammily imperious impression of her. 'Seriously, though. I'll show you how to do it. It's super easy, and it could maybe ward off the bailiffs, at least until we finish the project.'

Grandma takes a deep, quivering breath, her chin sinking to her chest. 'I have rather been burying my head in the sand.'

I shrug. 'Don't worry, shit happens – sorry – *rubbish* happens. But we've opened the letter now and that was the worst bit. We'll get it sorted, all right? It's going to be OK.'

In response, Grandma leans across, puts her liver-spotted hand on my cheek and gives me a small smile. 'Precious Jessica. Thank the heavens for you.'

UNTITLED

The day whistles by in a series of archaic behavioural lessons from Grandma. Because of the date with Leo tomorrow, and the likelihood that he'll take me somewhere mega fancy (see: pretentious), Grandma insists that I 'learn how to conduct myself at the table'. According to her, I 'eat like a rabid caveman'. Which is just not true. I eat like an adult human being. Who sometimes accidentally spills a bit of food on her boobs. But apparently I'm supposed to take tiny, delicate bites, like I'm some kind of fragile sad-act bird or a French woman. It's ridiculous. When we move onto 'correct use of cutlery', I tell Grandma that I've seen *Pretty Woman* a gazillion times and know all about the 'knives and forks from the outside in' rule. But she is insistent that we work from her guides which, of course, *also* instruct that 'cutlery should be taken from the outside, working inwards'.

Some of the more absurd tips we go through include:

Preserve a Good Man's pride by allowing him to pay the bill.

Wait to be seated by your dinner companion or the waiter. A Good Woman never seats herself.

Never engage with the waiter. Keep your eyes on your date and allow him to order on your behalf.

All of which make me laugh out loud *and* snort with rage in equal measure. At about five p.m., and satisfied that she has filled my head with more than enough useless information on how to make Leo Frost fall in love with me at dinner (because obviously it'll be boner city once I reveal to him my extensive knowledge of fucking spoon etiquette), Grandma glides off to finish her skirt sewing, and I set my laptop up at the big kitchen table.

Opening up a new word doc, I type out 'How to Catch a Man Like It's 1955' and underline it.

And then I stare at it.

For quite a while.

I haven't written anything other than *Summer in the City* blog posts in two years. When I was travelling I wrote rambling journals and essays and short stories at the drop of a hat. But writing about nothing but cocktail recipes and boutique hotels and Summer's Top 5 Skirts ... Ever! has left me woefully out of practice at anything more, well, *meaningful*.

Twenty thousand words in less than four weeks is quite a massive commitment when you think about it. Do I even know twenty thousand words? What if by some outlandish miracle I actually have to write the rest of the book? That's at least another sixty thousand words. How long will *that* take? Will I have to stay here? Wearing the corset every day until my ribcage gets smaller and smaller, until it eventually disappears and I die? Living with my watery-eyed Grandma and all of her many feels? Being reminded of my mum? My stomach churns nervously and I push the questions away into the farthest corners of my mind.

I change the font on the document title five times, eventually settling on good old Times New Roman.

Then I make a pot of tea really slowly.

Then I do my singing impression of Shakira just for my own amusement.

Then I look out of the window for a bit and think about Summer's TV show and if she will become the new Lena Dunham.

As I'm pondering this, Peach clomps into the kitchen, Mr Belding clasped to her chest. His tiny head is nestled cosily against her large T-shirt-clad bosom. She gazes down at him with a doting smile. They've bonded. He's going to be well peeved when he has to go back to Manchester and all that dressing-up for the Internet. Maybe I'll hold off telling Summer I nicked him for just a teeny bit longer ...

'Hey, Jess,' Peach squeaks.

I practically fall on her in an effort not to have to return to the computer screen just yet.

'Hey, lady P. What's occurring? Tell me all your gossip. All of it. Do you want a brew? A jammy dodger? What did you get up to last night?' I pour out another cup of tea.

Peach sits down at the table and arranges Mr Belding in her lap. 'I, um, I watched a movie. It was a shame you didn't get back home in time. I was really looking forward to watching it with you.'

Huh? *Oh.* I said I would watch a DVD with her last night! *That* was why I smelled popcorn when I got home. I bet she got us face masks as well. Crap, I completely forgot! Should have written it on my hand.

'Shit, I'm sorry Peach.'

She turns red, waving away my apology. 'Oh, don't worry. I know how busy you are with the project ... I was hoping you might be free this evening?'

I side-eye the word document on my laptop . 'Hmm ... What did you have in mind?'

'I don't know, maybe we could go out for a coffee? Like they did in the popular TV show *Friends*. They drank a lot of coffee together and always seemed to have a whole lot of fun and hijinks.'

I shrug. 'Hmm, how about we take it up a notch? We could go out for a few drinks? Maybe a boogie?' I shake my shoulders to demonstrate the boogie.

Peach's pale grey eyes light up at the idea, but then she shakes her head. 'Sounds expensive.'

'My cheque from Valentina cleared today ... '

'I can't let you do that. You need that money.'

'I do ... but I'm sure a few quid or so won't matter *that* much. It'll be my way of saying sorry for missing your movie night. And I'm kind of an expert when it comes to having a top night out on basically no dosh.'

'When would we go?'

I squint at the laptop for a moment longer. Then I gently snap down the lid with the tip of my forefinger.

'How's about right now?'

* * *

Grandma must be feeling generous because she doesn't seem to mind at all that Peach and I are going out dancing.

'You have worked hard today and every Good Woman deserves a little fun from time to time.' She gives me a benevolent look. 'Dancing is a truly *wonderful* way to keep one fit in an elegant and ladylike fashion.'

I wonder what kind of dancing she thinks we're going out to do? Probably the bossa nova or something. I don't correct her. While Grandma is cool about us going out, she absolutely insists on two conditions: one, that we pull a Cinderella and return by midnight so that I'll get a full beauty sleep ready for my date with Leo tomorrow, and two, that I wear my vintage underwear in order to learn how to '*move around more gracefully*' in it.

Peach helps me into the waspie, the girdle and the bullet bra, and though it hurts like a motherfucker, when I put on my skinny jeans and tight red Ramone's T-shirt, the curvy effect is kind of epically sexy. Peach changes into a cute green tunic, black leggings and a gauzy black pashmina and, together, we leave the house.

'Where shall we go?' I ask her as we amble through the hazy sunshine towards South Kensington tube station. 'Where are all the hip young kids of London at these days?'

Peach gives me a look as if I've just asked her to describe exactly how and why ITV's *Splash!* is still pulling in an audience. 'How should I know?'

'Um, haven't you worked in London for, like, five years? Don't you go out?'

She crosses her pashmina more tightly round her body and throws me an embarrassed glance. 'I usually just knit or read in my room. I don't know if you've noticed, but I'm a little—'

'Shy? Nooo. You're kidding me!' I peek across at her. Her shoulders are hunched, head down, mass of tumbling mousy curls hiding her gentle, round face. 'Peach ... have you *ever* been to a bar? A club?'

She gives a tiny quick shake of the head.

I gasp in astonishment. 'How old are you?'

'Twenty-six.' She sighs. 'In my defence, I grew up on a

farm in Alabama and left the US before I was legally allowed in any establishment that served alcohol. And then I got here and I never quite got the hang of meeting people. I went to the pub once. But that was just for a ploughman's lunch.'

I cannot believe it. This woman is twenty-six years old and she has never been to bar or a nightclub!

It's like my whole life has been leading up to this very moment. Going out is my *raison d'être*. Partying is my purpose. Peach could be my protégé. She's young. She's still got a few years left before she turns to the dark side of long-term relationships and babies and TV development deals and Farrow and Ball paint shades. I could teach her everything I know, and in doing so create the best going-out buddy of all time! At least for the next two to four weeks.

I grab her chubby hand in excitement and quicken our step towards the tube.

'Watch and learn, my little one,' I say with a mad smile. 'Watch and learn.'

CHAPTER TWENTY

Dancing with a chap is a terrific way to engage in chatter, while making the best of your figure. A Good Woman moves gracefully, elegantly across the dance floor. She avoids complicated or exuberant moves and always, always lets the gentleman lead.

***Matilda Beam's Guide to Love and Romance*, 1955**

'Here's to pear cider!' I hold up my bottle in a toast.

'And to the United States of America!' Peach adds, happily clinking her bottle to mine.

Following a cheap and tasty chippy dinner, then a pub crawl round Soho, we settle in to a small booth at Twisted Spin, a trendy basement club that the popular Love/London blog calls 'London's freshest indie and rock venue'. The music is well selected and loud – but not so loud that you can't hear anything else, the cider is reasonably priced, and it's got the kind of dark, sexy, industrial vibe that completely disconnects you from the outside world and all of its crap. Here is my utopia.

It's taken Peach a while to warm up – for the first hour or so our conversation was pretty stilted and mostly based on the recent heatwave and what types of weather we both liked or disliked or didn't mind. Thankfully, by the time we reached the third pub, the beers had loosened her up a little and she is, as I hoped, turning into an excellent going-out companion, if a *teensy* bit of an unusual one.

'Jess!' she yells over the sounds of Arcade Fire blasting out through the club speakers. 'Shall we think of a nickname for you?'

'Huh?' I squint at her.

'To call each other.' She muffles a burp. 'Like friends do. Everyone in *The Goonies* had a nickname and they were the best of friends. Chunk. Mouth. Data. I'm Lady P. What do you want to be called?'

Earlier, Peach confessed that she's always found it difficult to meet new people because of her social anxiety and shyness. As such, all her information on how to make friends seems to be based on TV and films she's seen rather than real life. With her beer-induced confidence, and in a bid to bond by finding out 'what makes me tick', she's been asking me a series of questions. Including what my favourite colour is (green), if I had any pets as a kid (no – Mum always said that it was extra responsibility we didn't need), and best and worst things that have ever happened to me (a question I gracefully avoided by suddenly needing a wee). And now she wants us to think of nicknames to call each other. So, yes, fairly odd. But between the bizarre questions and beneath the hunched shoulders, Peach seems funny and intelligent and sweet. I feel a bit bad that I probably won't be around long enough to develop the kind of deeper friendship she seems to be looking for. Besides which, even if I wanted to – which I don't – after what happened with Summer, I'm not sure of my capacity to be anything other than a 'super-cool fun-times' mate. But if Peach wants to practise being friends on me, I don't mind. Especially if it means a nice break from the *How to Catch a Man Like It's 1955* project.

'I don't know about a nickname, but I'll have a good think about it. I do know one thing, though, Peach,' I grin, taking a hefty swig from my bottle. 'It's about time we were dancing.'

Before I've even finished the sentence, Peach is out of the booth and shaking her sizeable backside over towards the dance floor. A Klaxons song blasts out across the club. At the opening riffs, she whips her thick curls around and starts air-drumming. I cheer and whoop, impressed by her unexpectedly awesome moves, before joining her on the floor, where we proceed to jump about the place like a couple of giddy fools.

I *knew* she had potential.

* * *

We dance for ages, and though it's kind of difficult to move freely bound up in all this underwear, it feels brilliant to let go and laugh and be silly and loud without judgement. We take a breather so that Peach can nip to the loo while I buy us another round of the delicious flavoured vodka shots that are on offer. Carrying the drinks over to a bench by the dance floor, I almost drop them when I spot, not two feet away and chatting to a crowd of glam people who look totally out of place in this club, Summer.

As in *my* Summer.

What the actual fuck? Why is she at Twisted Spin? And what the hell is she doing in *London*? Summer spots me and does a double-take, her eyes widening in an expression of shock that I'm guessing mirrors mine exactly.

'Jess?' I can't hear her but I see her mouth my name. She stalks over, icy Mojito in hand, looking extra amazing in a tiny white playsuit and towering nude patent heels. She nudges her way through the other revellers to get to me.

Great.

I was having such a lovely time too. What the chuff am I supposed to say to her? Could I just forgo all civil conversation and mini-pinch her instead? I mean, surely she deserves it for being such an absolute turd.

No. Violence is never the answer.

When Summer reaches me, she air kisses both of my cheeks, something she only ever does when she's had a few drinks, and even then only with people she doesn't know that well. We used to greet each other with a cool fist-bump.

'I can't believe you're here! It's sooo good to see you!' she chirrups, casually wiggling her almost-prizewinning bum to the music. She's acting as if she *hasn't* recently ruined my life, like she *didn't* screw me over to get a TV show and then kick me out of my home. 'What are you doing in London? How long have you been here for? I'm here for meetings about my show.' She thumbs at the crowd of shiny people she just left. 'Those guys are from the production company. They're *great*. Just, like, so clever and super full of ideas for the SITC brand.'

'Oh,' I say flatly, casually bopping my head to the music in a way I hope indicates how little of a fuck I give and how so *not* jealous I am.

'Yeah, I'm not sure this club was quite the best place to bring them, though.' She grimaces. 'Love/London said

Twisted Spin is one of 2014s freshest indie and rock venues, but it's actually a bit of a dive, isn't it?'

I roll my eyes.

'So we'll probably end up at Soho House anyway. That's where all these TV and film types hang out. Anderson always said it was his favourite place to go for a drink in London. He's in town, you know? He's doing Graham Norton this week, so he might be there tonight. Not that I'm bothered or anything. I'm with Holden now, *obviously*.'

Why is she telling me this? I give her a blank look and neck my shot. And then Peach's shot.

'You look different,' she announces, taking in my new strawberry blonde hairdo and tiny waist with narrowed eyes, a flicker of something – annoyance, maybe – crossing her pretty features.

'It's for a project I'm working on.' I say stiffly.

'A project? What project?' She looks surprised. What did she expect? That I'd be wallowing in a corner without her?

The opening riffs of Arctic Monkeys' 'Do I Wanna Know?' kick in and we adjust the speed of our casual half dancing, half standing accordingly.

'It's nothing,' I say. 'Just a writing thing.'

As if I'm going to tell her about working with my grandma. She'd love that.

'Oh. *Good for you*. I'm super glad you've found something to do.' Her enthusiastic intonation is entirely unconvincing. 'I was *really* worried about you. You just took off without saying goodbye. Where have you been stay—'

'Yeah, I was overwhelmed by all your worried calls and texts, there were so many of them, practically a *mountain* of messages from you.' I shake my head, irritation making my teeth clench.

Why is she even talking to me? Does she not realize she's done anything wrong? How dare she try to act like everything is A-OK?

'Look, Summer,' I say, with the best withering glance I can muster in my tipsy state. 'I'm on a night out with a friend and we're having a really fun time, so I should—'

'Who? You don't have any friends.'

Do not mini-pinch her. Do not mini-pinch her.

'A new friend, actually. So, you know ... bye. Good luck with your TV show. Forgive me if I don't watch it.' I spin round on my heel, preparing for a dramatic exit, but Summer grabs the top of my arm and pulls me back.

'The show just happened, Jess,' she says, eyes wide. 'I didn't, like, plan it. It was an opportunity that came up for me and I simply couldn't turn it down. I mean, you wouldn't have enjoyed it anyway – it's a *lot* of responsibility. I did you a favour, really, not involving you. After everything, why can't you just be happy for me?'

I throw her off my arm. 'You're a liar!' I hiss in disbelief. 'I *spoke* to Valentina Smith. I know you turned the book deal down. You met Seth Astrow at that launch party and you knew exactly what you were going to do. You completely screwed me over! At least have the fucking decency to own it.'

She looks guilty for a brief moment, but before she can respond, Peach stumbles back from the loo and into the conversation with a guffaw.

'Sorry I took so long in there! I met a nice lady in the toilets and we got to talking. She has a little cat too!' She gives a tiny hiccup. 'She showed me a picture on her phone but it was a little cross-eyed and nowhere near as cute as Mr Belding.'

Busted.

'Sorry, what did you just say about Mr Belding?' Summer frowns, looking Peach up and down. 'Who are you?'

'I'm Peach Carmichael,' Peach answers brightly. 'Jess's BFF. Nice to meet you.'

'Jess?' Summer glares at me. 'Why is this strange, random person talking about Mr Belding? Where is he? Do you know where he's gone?'

Now it's my turn to look guilty.

'Actually, I've got Mr Belding, Summer,' I admit, huffing through my cheeks. 'I ... took him when I left.'

'What?' Summer's face contorts into an uglier version of itself, all pretence of niceness vanished in an instant. 'You *took* him? You took our cat? Who does that, Jess? Who the fuck steals a cat?' She sniggers. 'That's messed-up, even for you. I mean, I knew you had issues, but ... *wow*. I've had Holden looking everywhere for him. You better bring him back. My Instagram traffic has really dipped since he's been gone. I almost had more followers than fucking Carol Vorderman and now they're dropping like flies.'

She's unbelievable.

'Mr Belding doesn't even like you!' I bellow angrily. 'You dress him up in clothes he hates and make him pose for pictures for hours on end. It's no life for a kitten. It's no life at all.'

'Yeah,' Peach squeaks suddenly. 'He's happy staying with us!'

She's right. Mr Belding *is* happier with us, or at least with Peach. And I quite like having him sleep on the pillow next to me. I quite like it a lot.

'I don't think so.' Summer throws Peach her frosty glare. 'Cool new friend, Jess.' She smirks.

Peach gasps, her rotund cheeks colouring.

Summer looks at me with a faint sneer of pity and superiority. It's a familiar expression. At that moment I realize that's how Summer has always looked at me. Like she's better than me. Like I'm her ridiculous sidekick; there to do her work, to roll her eyes at, to have one over on, to feel better than.

Not any more.

'Who chose Mr Belding from the RSPCA, Summer?' I ask her with as much calmness as I can manage.

'What's that got to do with anything? He *belongs* to us both.'

'It was me. I chose him. You were busy getting your hair dip-dyed, if I remember correctly. You phoned me from the hairdresser to remind me that I had to get the most photogenic one. And who signed the adoption papers?'

'That doesn't mean a thing!'

'Doesn't it? I don't own any of *Summer in the City* because I didn't sign anything, remember? But I did sign the papers for Mr Belding. So *technically*, he's mine. And ... I'm giving him his freedom.'

I lift my chin. I am Jessica Beam – brave and noble rescuer of Internet cats in captivity.

'You can't do that!' she splutters. 'You ... can't!'

I shrug. 'You know what, Summer? I think I just did.' I turn to Peach and link her arm through mine. 'Come on, Lady P. Let's ... let's blow this joint.'

I've never, ever said *let's blow this joint* before, but I heard it on a film once and it seems the kind of hard-core thing you should say at a moment like this. Peach links my arm, a look of blatant admiration on her face. And with that, we strut out of the club, leaving Summer staring furiously after us.

* * *

In an effort to re-buoy the mood of the night, Peach and I end up in a late-night karaoke bar, wailing 80s power tunes until the small hours. Of course it works – there's nothing a bit of 'Love Is a Battlefield' at full blast cannot fix. It's past curfew when we get back to Bonham Square, munching on greasy kebabs from a dubious nearby takeaway and quoting our favourite jokes from 30 Rock.

In order to avoid waking Grandma by even attempting to navigate the hallway of doom, we scramble up from the bottom windowsill to my bedroom balcony instead, clutching onto the cast-iron railings for dear life. Jamie was right. This is much harder and more dangerous than it looks. Luckily, Peach manages to yank me up quite easily with her mega farm-girl strength.

'I think this was the besht time of mah life,' she whispers as we tumble into the quiet, darkened bedroom, trying to muffle our laughter like a pair of giddy teenagers. When the single working grandfather clock echoes throughout the house, chiming three times, Peach laughs even harder. 'Three a.m.,' she breathes in delighted disbelief. 'I feel alive! I feel like I can achieve anything! What a night!'

I grin back at her. In spite of the unexpected and grim altercation with Summer – maybe even because of it – it *was* a pretty damn good night, all things considered.

Once Peach has drunkenly wobbled off to bed, I pick Mr Belding up from the stripy tub chair where he's lazily stretched out beside Felicity, the world's most ominous looking doll.

I give him a merry smile. 'You're my cat now,' I tell him, wonkily carrying him over to his spot on the pillow. 'And, as Felicity is my witness, I promise you this, Mr Belding: you will never, *ever* have to wear shit cat clothes again. I ...' I take a deep breath. 'I release you.'

Mr Belding doesn't respond per se, but I like to think I can see a smidgeon of relief cross his furry face.

I am so drunk.

CHAPTER TWENTY-ONE

A Good Woman must always be enthusiastic. Even when faced with an unsavoury situation, it is always best to put on a happy face.

***Matilda Beam's Good Woman Guide*, 1959**

The next morning, Grandma is in an offensively brisk, go-getting sort of mood and fully expects Peach (pale of cheek and maybe still a bit pissed) and me (a complete shadow of a woman) to follow suit. Now that she's agreed to clear out some junk, she wants us to tackle the hallway of doom *immediately* and find all the things we might be able to sell on eBay.

On the one hand it's great, because it means that I got through to her yesterday and we might be able to put off the bailiffs for a little longer, but on the other hand it's completely shit, because Peach and I are experiencing a level of hangover that you can only cure by lying absolutely still for a long time while someone nice feeds you Fanta through a straw while making sympathetic mewing noises.

I *really* wanted to go for a run before starting any work – it's the next best medicine after lying still all day – but Grandma insisted that all the running is probably making my calves bulky and mannish and that I should only exercise by doing gentle stretches instead. Which is bollocks. Gentle stretches are for losers. I love running and don't plan on giving it up for anything or anyone, regardless of how muscular my bloody calves get. However, where *How to Catch a Man Like it's 1955* is concerned, I promised I would stick to Grandma's rules, so – added to sexing it up with Jamie – pounding the pavements is just another thing I will have to do in secret.

By mid-afternoon, Peach has vommed twice, I have dozed off once and we have, against all odds, managed to sort, label and photograph almost everything in the hallway. We've come across some absolutely cracking stuff, including three gorgeous copper pans, an antique Tunbridge chess set and loads of retro vinyl records. Apart from a silver pocket watch that belonged to Jack (which she cried over for twenty-five whole minutes and declared she would take with her to the grave), Grandma's been fairly stoic about what we get rid of. I'm pretty impressed with how staunch she's being about it. I do find it a tad odd that we haven't discovered anything of Mum's within the hallway junk – after all, she lived here for years. I don't ask why, though, in case Grandma bursts into uncontrollable tears again, something I can barely handle even without the cracking headache and dicky tummy.

When it's time to start getting ready for tonight's date with Leo, I'm dusty, super pukey and beyond shattered. I've never done this much work on a hangover before. It would be so much easier if I could just cancel this evening's 'date', have beans on toast for tea and go chill with Peach and Mr

Belding on the sofa instead. In this pitiful state, I haven't a clue how I'll manage to stay awake, never mind remember the endless Good Woman tips Grandma has been trying to drum into my brain. Thankfully, Leo, being the hollow-hearted scoundrel that he is, probably won't care if I'm a little quiet; he seems the type to like his women pretty and passive. I'm banking on the theory that as long as I look hot and act super impressed and interested in everything he has to say, he won't notice that I am rougher than a badger's arse, and I'll get through the evening with no major issues.

* * *

The Strand is bursting with busy people leaving work, ties loosened, hair askew and crumpled suit jackets slung over their shoulders as they hurry down the busy London street. I could not look more out of place, for tonight Grandma has dressed me in an extra-scratchy charcoal pencil skirt and a dusky pink blouse which has been super tightly tucked into the skirt to show off my squidged-in waist. My hair has been curled into a soft femme fatale wave which keeps falling over my left eye and getting in the way. Choking me is a knotted dark pink and violet Liberty print neck scarf, and the worst thing of all is that Grandma has made me wear a fucking hat. It's some little mauve cap affair with a tuft of white lace at the front. The whole get-up is tight and uncomfortable and really hot (in the temperature way, not in the sexual way).

I arrive at Woolf Frost early and, with a tired and wholly self-pitying grumble, push open the massive doors to the building. The agency offices are huge and 'old money' – all oak panelling, low-lit lamps and ugly burgundy chester-field sofas. I wander over to the reception area, where the young receptionist is gathering her belongings, ready to leave work. I bet *she's* off out with her mates to do brilliant fun activities like a normal twenty-something girl on a Friday night.

'I'm here to meet Leo Frost,' I explain, stifling another yawn. 'I'm a bit early.'

The receptionist rolls her eyes. 'Third floor, second door on the left,' she reels off in a monotone as if she's given these instructions to many a woman here to meet Leo Frost after work. I wish I could tell her that I'm not *really* one of his conquests, that I know so much better than the trail of women whose hearts he has already stamped upon – I hate the pitying look she's throwing me.

'Cheers,' I say instead.

Outside his office, I take a big breath, try to ignore the increasingly queasy feeling in my stomach and fix a fascinated smile on my face. It's Lucille time. Yay.

I knock gently on the door.

There is no answer.

I knock again, a bit harder.

Still no answer.

I push open the door and step into a large, bright office. The walls are plastered with framed print adverts, all of which I recognize from magazines and billboards. There's a definite theme to Leo's work – it's all hyper macho, with lots of shadowy, mechanical tones and bold, aggressive typography. That ridiculous Drive Alive ad takes centre stage above an expansive walnut desk, the diamond bikini woman pouting vapidly down at me as if she's wondering why the sweet hell she forgot to get dressed this morning. Frost isn't at the desk but sitting at a tilted graphics tablet facing the sunny open window. His broad back is to the door, a pair of silver Bang & Olufsen headphones squashing down his dark ginger quiff. He's furiously moving pencil over paper and tapping his feet against the floor in time to whatever music he's listening to. He has absolutely no clue I'm here.

'Hiiii,' I say as loudly as I can while trying to keep my voice soft and soothing.

Of course he doesn't hear me. I wander over towards him and my eyes widen in surprise as I spot what he's drawing. It's a delicate line sketch of an old man in a rickety fishing boat, head resting wearily in one hand.

Wow.

I'm reluctant to admit it, but it's actually really great; completely different from all the framed crap on the walls.

Hmm. Maybe I should let Leo know I'm here before he turns round and catches me mere inches away, silently watching over him in my hat.

'Hello, Leo?' I tap him lightly on the shoulder.

He jumps at my touch, pulled from his reverie, and drops his pencil on the wooden floor where it lands with a clatter.

'*Fuck me*! Oh ... yes, Lucille. Hi.' He recovers himself, pulling off his headphones and quickly arranging his face from fearfully surprised to devilishly confident. He takes in my outfit with a mildly amused but definitely lusty glance. Gross.

'Sorry to interrupt your work,' I coo. 'I got here early and the receptionist told me to come right up. I hope you don't mind.'

'Not at all,' he responds smoothly, waving my apology away. 'Would you like a swift drink before we head to dinner?'

'Mmmm, yes, please,' I say enthusiastically.

I'm not sure that Grandma would be too impressed with me drinking booze before dinner, but I feel so rotten, and hair of the dog might be just the thing to perk me up and ease this persistent sickly feeling in my belly.

Leo strolls over to a glass bar cart in the corner exactly like the one Don Draper has in *Mad Men*. That's probably why he bought it, the chump. He swiftly mixes two Martinis and hands one over to me. I take it, and we sit down together on a dark green chesterfield.

I bat my eyelashes up at him and smile.

He smiles back.

I return the smile even harder.

We sip our drinks, just smiling at each other like a right pair of dickheads.

He scooches closer to me on the sofa, his eyes travelling over every inch of my face like he's super fascinated by it. What's he playing at? *I'm* supposed to be the one doing the fascinated looks. He brazenly stares me out and, although I'm usually the queen of stare-off competitions – I can go two whole minutes without blinking – I suspect Grandma would want me to let him win. So I wimp out and let my eyes slide away first.

The whole just looking at each other and not talking thing is creating some tension that I'm not entirely comfortable with.

I bet this is one of his 'moves'. I bet Leo Frost thinks it's sexual tension he's creating here. It's *not* sexual tension. I just don't know what to say to him. I need to say *something*, to have an actual conversation if he's going to see this date as anything other than a means to a shag. But I have no clue what to talk about – Grandma hasn't paid a great deal of attention to the verbal contents of the dates as yet, beyond telling me to be impressed with everything he says and interested in the things he's interested in. Although she *did*

mention something about the weather being an agreeable way into conversation.

OK.

'My goodness, it's sooo warm out—' I begin.

I'm interrupted by the door flying open and banging loudly against the wall, making the room shake slightly. A bit of my Martini plops over the side of the glass, wetting my hand. A tall, silver-haired, expensive-looking man strides into Leo's office. He's wearing a sharp navy blazer, tan slacks, and a mightily pissed-off expression on his distinguished face.

'Leonardo, for heaven's sake, bloody Sasha in copy is on at me again about the bloody brand concepts for Longchamp. Have you finished then ye—' The man pauses when he spots me in the room. 'Oh. I didn't know you had company.'

He gives me the exact same lascivious look that Leo did when he met me at the fair.

Barf.

'This is Lucille Darling,' Leo says stiffly, sitting up a tad straighter in the chair. 'Lucille, this is my father, Rufus Frost.'

The great and powerful Rufus Frost, owner of Woolf Frost.

'Gosh, I'm so pleased to meet you,' I simper at Rufus Frost, politely holding a hand out for him to shake.

'My, my, you are *quite* the little head-turner, aren't you?' he drawls, not shaking my hand but instead giving it a wet old kiss. He smells of cigars. Now my hand probably smells of cigars. Maaan. 'A rather lovely specimen indeed,' he finishes, looking me up and down and nodding with approval like I'm a freaking vase he's considering for purchase.

Cringe city or what. Leo's dad is even worse than him! As if I didn't already feel vomtastic enough.

I muster every ounce of composure I have in order to give a 'flattered' giggle and not punch this dude in the balls. It's really tough for me. I take a gulp of my Martini.

Leo coughs. 'Apologies, Father, I'll send the brand concepts across to Sasha by midday tomorrow, OK?'

Rufus doesn't reply, spotting Leo's drawing on the tablet and picking up the piece of paper with a smirk.

'Ah, *doodling* again, I see!' He shakes his head, turning his smirk onto me and holding up the picture between finger and thumb. 'What are your thoughts, little Miss Darling? A man in a boat! Hardly Rembrandt, is it?'

Woah, that's cold!

'We should probably be going, Lucille,' Leo says, rubbing his hand across the back of his neck.

'You're wrong, Mr Frost,' I grumpily blurt out to Rufus before I can stop myself. 'I think the drawing's ace, actually.'

Oops. A Good Woman probably does not blurt. I don't think she's says 'ace' either.

Mr Frost's smirk twitches slightly. 'Yes, well, I expect a layman might be fooled. Good to meet you, sweetheart, have a pleasant evening.' He gives me a politely dismissive smile and turns to Leo with a frown. 'By tomorrow, son.' He points to the boat drawing. 'The company doesn't pay you to idle about.'

He strides out of the room and I try to hide my appalled expression from Leo. I mean, I don't like *him* either, but that was très uncomfortable.

Leo drains the remainder of his drink and clanks the glass back onto the bar cart.

'Let's go to dinner, shall we?' he suggests, running his

hand through his quiff, nostrils flaring. 'We can pick up a cab on the Strand.'

'Yes,' I agree, following him out of the office. 'That sounds like a *super* idea.'

* * *

'Don't mind my father,' Leo says tightly once we're outside and he's flagging down a taxi. 'He can be a little ...'

... bit of a douche?

' ... heavy handed,' Leo finishes with a mirthless smile. 'But then that's why he owns one of London's most respected ad agencies, I suppose. He's not a bad egg. Just a bit of a tyrannical one.'

'Oh, of course, I understand.' I nod fervently like a Churchill insurance dog.

'It's not often that someone disagrees with him ...'

'Maybe not to his *face*,' I mutter with an eye-roll.

Shit. That just slipped out. What is wrong with me tonight? This hangover is totally putting me off my game. I glance up at Leo, ready to apologize, but he's grinning down at me, green eyes glinting with amusement.

'So ... you really liked my drawing?' he asks lightly.

'I really did,' I confirm, hamming up my response with a deeply impressed gaze.

'Why?'

Hmm ... I don't think 'I just liked it, all right?' will cut it as an answer here. I think about why I did like it.

'It was ... pure,' I answer after a few seconds, shrugging a shoulder.

Leo stares across at me for a moment, an indecipherable expression on his snooty face. Then he looks at his Tag

Heuer watch, which probably cost him the same amount of money as a car.

'Do you like coffee, Lucille?' he says eventually, hand stroking his lightly stubbled chin, eyes to the sky as if he's forming an idea.

'Do I!' I respond in a pleasant tone. *A Good Woman must always be enthusiastic.*

'Well, that decides it.' He nods once and, to my surprise, he stops trying to catch a cab. Instead, we continue walking down the street.

Where are we going? I thought we were getting a taxi to the restaurant? We cross over the busy road and walk a little further until we reach a small coffee house. The blue neon sign in the window flashes *Little Joe's Java... Little Joe's Java.*

'Here we are,' Leo announces brightly.

Huh? This is not an amazing fancy restaurant. Where is the amazing fancy restaurant he's supposed to be taking me to?

'Here?' I ask uncertainly.

Leo grins, loosens his tie and – swiftly undoing the top button of his shirt with one hand – steps forward to hold open the door for me.

I remain on the pavement for a moment. Grandma said he'd be taking me to a restaurant. I learned all that stuff about how a Good Woman behaves at the table! I learned *nothing* of what a Good Woman is supposed to do at the coffee house!

Befuddled, I follow Leo inside, where I'm hit by the overwhelming scent of roasting coffee beans – which is usually one of my most favourite smells, but tonight, with this annoyingly icky tummy, is not quite so pleasant.

Little Joe's Java is indeed little, warm and packed out to

the rafters. Low, tatty velvet sofas, and plump battered beanbags are dotted here and there, filled with artistic, alternative-looking folk squashed up against each other. Everyone is facing towards a little spotlit stage at the back of the room. I follow their gaze to where a man with wispy chin-length hair, wearing a tight black turtleneck, is speaking into a microphone. Is he ... reciting *a poem*?

'I love the open mic poetry night here,' Leo grins as we make our way to a tiny free table in the corner. He holds out a chair for me and signals to the waitress.

Leo Frost. Artist. Thinker. Man. Into poetry?

'Er, terrific.' I try to look excited. 'I ... adore poetry. I adore it such a lot.'

I'm totally lying. Poetry is the *worst*, and that's coming from someone who did an English Lit degree. Why did he bring me here? Ugh. I feel really sick too, and this coffee smell is making it worse. Tonight is not going as Grandma said it would *at all*.

Just as the waitress approaches to take our drinks order, my phone beeps with a text. It's from Peach.

I'm as sick as a dog! Do you think it was the kebab last night Hope y'all are OK? Love, Lady P. x

The kebab! Fuck, is that why I feel so sick? I mean, it must be – I've never felt this rough after a night out before.

As if in response my stomach gives an almighty gurgle.

Oh no.

CHAPTER TWENTY-TWO

Form a bond with your intended by being interested in the things he enjoys. It may not come naturally, but with practice you will learn to love his hobbies as much as if they were yours.

Matilda Beam's Guide to Love and Romance, 1955

I spend the next forty-five minutes delicately sipping water, trying not to chuck up and attempting to be mega interested in open mic poetry. All the people at Little Joe's Java are so excited to be here, and Leo is the most excited of all. He really does love it, clapping enthusiastically after every performance and nodding like he *gets* what they're all spouting on about. Why did Valentina not tell me about this hobby of his? Did she even know? It's absolutely not what I thought he'd be into. Sensitive sketches and poetry aren't usually the kind of thing you'd associate with arrogant, sexist ad men. I'm so confused.

When (thank God) it's interval time, I lean over to Leo.

'So how long have you been coming here?' I ask curiously.

'A while,' he replies, taking a sip of his espresso. 'Though never with a girl, come to think of it.'

What did I do to deserve this hell?

I put a hand to my chest.

'What did I do to be so lucky?'

He looks thoughtful for a moment. 'I'm not sure. I suppose you seem a little ... *different* to the girls I usually date . . . A little *alternative.*' His eyes flick up to my tufty lace hat and across my powdery face. 'I thought you might enjoy a more unconventional scene.'

He thinks I'm *alternative*? This was not the intention. Stupid quirky hat. I try to hide my bewilderment and appear as enthusiastic as I can possibly be.

'Oh, yes, I *am* enjoying it,' I purr, looking around Little Joe's Java with wide eyes as if there is nowhere in the world I'd rather be. 'Open mic poetry is *wonderful*. I – I come to these places all the time. I'm thrilled you brought me here. Thrilled with a capital T.' I peek up at him through my lashes. He seems to like my fake excitement so I carry on. 'Yes, if I'd known we were coming to a spoken word event, I'd have, er, signed up to recite myself! It's so ... brave and, um, expressive to share your *soul* on stage. To, um, connect with strangers. It's so ... er ...' What were they always saying in poetry lectures at uni?' ... so avant-garde!'

Leo slowly nods as if I've just said something dead insightful. He slips a hand round my waist, rests it on my ribcage and moves his thumb in a slow circular motion that my body, annoyingly, does not immediately reject.

'Lucille Darling,' he says, looking at me in an odd, appraising sort of way. 'Aren't you an unexpected pleasure?'

'That I am,' I reply with an alluring, mysterious throaty laugh. 'That ... I am.'

He pulls me in close as yet another amateur poet takes to the stage.

Despite being completely miserable, totally unprepared and on the verge of puking like a mofo, I seem somehow, in the most unlikely of circumstances, to have piqued Leo Frost's interest.

* * *

This date is going fairly well. Because of the performance nature of the evening, we thankfully don't have to talk too much so I try to zone out, sip my water and deep-breathe until the night is over and I can shuffle off back to bed and rub my belly. But just when I think I might be about to pull this whole evening off like a boss, I'm thrown a curveball.

And it's a massive one.

'And now, everyone, we come to the improv poetry portion of our evening,' the goateed host says into the mic. The crowd make an 'ooooh' noise. 'The part of the night when members of our audience come up on stage to recite a little something off the cuff.'

Oh man, there's *more*? But we've heard so many poems already. I look around at this crowd in disgust, huffing as discreetly as I can. These people are so obsessed with poems. They can't get enough of poems. There's no escape. I am in poetry purgatory.

The MC picks a little piece of paper out of a hat.

'OK, guys, first up to share some improvization with us is ... Lucille Darling.'

Because Lucille Darling is not my real name, it takes a second to sink in.

What. The. Fuck?

No.

I spin round to Leo in horror. He's smiling excitedly. 'I put your name in when you were using the ladies' room. You said earlier that if you'd known we were coming here you'd have got up. Well, now's your chance.' He looks so pleased with himself. Like he's done me a favour. What a turd!

Leo Frost. Artist. Thinker. Man. Turd.

What will I do? My eyes flick towards the door. I can hardly leg it, can I? Especially not when it's taken everything I have to get this far without letting on how unwell I feel. If I run away now it will all have been for nothing. The whole thing. Shit.

Leo stands up and gestures to the audience in much the same way he did at *The Beekeeper* launch when everyone slow clapped his disapproval of me.

'Let's give Lucille a round of applause!' he calls out in his smooth, deep baritone.

'I don't ... '

'Just close your eyes, Lucille,' he says earnestly. 'Let it flow, you'll be super.'

Balls.

The audience clap and click their fingers heartily.

No one could ever describe me as shy, but my knees have gone proper wibbly. Leo seems really into the idea of me going up there. And Grandma said I must be as enthusiastic as possible.

Stop being a sucker, Jess. Just get it done.

I slowly get up from the table and straighten my pencil skirt, trying my best to ignore the acid swishing around in my stomach. Then I totter over to the stage and hold out my hand so that the MC can help me up.

I take the mic, squinting as the spotlight dazzles my eyes.

OK. It's only a poem. A tiny little poem. I just need to say some random words together and pretend that they make sense to me. Then I can go home to bed where I belong. Right. Random words ...

I take a deep breath and try to focus.

'Um ... Hacky sack,' I whisper into the mic.

Shit. No. That's what Freddie Prinze Junior says in *She's All That*. I can't have *my* poem be about a hacky sack too. The audience think I'm making a hilarious ironic joke and roar with laughter.

'Ha-ha,' I agree.

OK. Poem time.

'*Rain-soaked sky*,' I croak out, my throat suddenly dry and flinty. Leo smiled and nods to encourage me, his auburn hair glowing out from the crowd.

'*Oh why ... Oh why. Why did you have to... let her fly?*'

What am I even saying? I blink at the audience. They don't look impressed at all. I don't blame them. This *sucks*.

I try to close my eyes like Leo suggested.

Er ... '*Empty spaces*,' I go on. '*Silent places, blurred faces. Stop the weeping. Leave her sleeping.*'

I cough.

'*It's ... a, um, puzzle, I'll never know. I can't reach, I try to grow. Now... she's left me here alone... My Rose.*'

Rose. Mum. My eyes quickly flicker open. I swallow hard. Where the *bloody hell* did that come from?

The audience, sensing that I'm finished, start to clap half-heartedly.

I feel sick.

It's hot in here.

I drank so much last night.

That kebab was uber greasy.

My head is killing me. The coffee smell is too strong.

I think I have to ...

'Puke,' I whisper.

Knocking the mic stand over, I jump off the stage and race right past a startled-looking Leo Frost and into the ladies' room. I reach the loo just in time to hurl like I've never before hurled in my life. I hurl like a champion.

I hear Leo's deep voice from outside the cubicle.

'Lucille?'

Shit!

I grab some loo roll and lightly dab at my mouth, trying not to smudge the pink lipstick Grandma so carefully applied earlier. I feel absolutely rotten. I'm never drinking that much flavoured vodka or eating a dodgy kebab again.

'I'm OK,' I say as brightly as I can manage, which isn't very. 'Just something I ate!' My voice is all shaky. I wonder if Leo Frost heard me puking?

I reach up, unlock the door with shaking hands and peek round it. He's grimacing. Yup. Definitely witness to the vomming.

Fuck. *Fuck.*

Well now I've completely ruined it. I'm pretty fucking certain that a Good Woman must never chuck up in the near vicinity of her intended chap.

It's over. The project is over. There's absolutely no way to come back from this.

I yank off Grandma's ridiculous hat with a sigh and rub my hand over my face.

'Look ... Leo, you might as well, you know, leave. I don't mind,' I sigh heavily, dropping all pretence of Lucille. What's the point? I mean, he's hardly going to want to see me again after I made a right tit of myself on the stage and then extravagantly chundered in front of him.

Man, I feel rough.

Leo Frost steps towards me, his rangy frame filling up the tiny ladies' room. He crouches down and undoes the tight Liberty print scarf from around my neck, takes it off, folds it neatly and tucks it into his shirt pocket.

'Might get in the way,' he says reasonably.

Before I can respond, my stomach lurches horribly. I turn back to the basin and throw up again. God, this is the worst fake date in the history of the universe ever.

But then the weirdest thing happens. Leo leans over, gathers up my hair and gently sweeps it back from my face so that it's away from the toilet. He patiently holds it there until I'm finished.

When the contents of my stomach are flushed away, I flop back against the wall and take long, steady breaths. Without a word, Leo hurries off to get me a glass of cold water. When he returns, he hitches up his fancy suit trousers slightly and sits on the floor beside me. Thankfully, it's a clean floor.

I rub my stomach and puff the air out through my cheeks, taking the glass of water from him with a mumbled thanks.

'You can't *possibly* have any more left.' He raises an eyebrow.

Grandma would be horrified if she saw that my grand first date with Leo had ended up on a flipping toilet floor. She would cry, for sure.

'We ought to get you home,' Leo says in a low voice. 'You're certainly not going to get better in time for our next date by hanging around in a coffee-shop bathroom. Though, as bathrooms go, it's not a terrible one. A rather good selection of reading material, in fact.'

He points up at the scrawled graffiti on the cubicle wall.

Wait ... did he just say *next date*?

Whaaat? He's still interested after everything that's just happened?

I don't understand . . .

Unless ... God, it must have been all my enthusiasm about the poetry. Grandma must have been right. By pretending to be super interested in what *he's* interested in, I've totally hooked him in. I've hooked him in so well that he's overlooked the puking. Woah. Matilda Beam might be magic.

I blink in surprise. So... the project *isn't* over?

I clear my throat and gaze up at him. 'Oh, Leo,' I croon in the slinky Lucille voice. 'You are soooo thoughtful.'

And we're back.

* * *

Leo arranges for a Woolf Frost town car to take me back to Bonham Square, and when I get there Grandma is eagerly awaiting my return.

She jumps up from her chair as soon as I enter the drawing room, *Lady Chatterley's Lover* clattering to the floor. Huh. She's taking her sweet time with that book. I wonder if she's just rereading the filthy bits like I do.

'How did it go, dear?' she asks,super eagerly. 'What happened? I've been waiting for you to get back!'

I flop down onto the sofa and sprawl out, completely drained of all my energy.

'Frost took me to a coffee house.'

Grandma blinks. 'Not to dinner? How ... unusual.'

'It was a poetry night.'

'Poetry?' Grandma pulls a face. 'Poor you.'

If I wasn't so ill, I'd laugh.

'Did he try to kiss you?' she asks hopefully.

Hmm. I think he might have done if I hadn't just barfed up. Grandma doesn't need to know that, though, it'll just bum her out.

'He did,' I lie. 'But I turned so it landed on my cheek, just like the guide said. He's asked me out again for Thursday night.'

'Oh, how wonderful!' Grandma claps her hands together. 'I am so pleased, Jessica. You're doing so well. So well. Remember, you must write down what happened for the book. The sooner we have something to show Valentina the better.'

Oh yeah. The first twenty thousand words. I'd forgotten about those. Blerg.

Grandma peers at me worriedly through her big red glasses. 'Are you all right? You look a little peaky.' She reaches across and flattens the back of her cold hand against my forehead.

'I feel a bit sick' I say – the understatement of the century. 'Nowt to worry about, though. Just a dicky tummy.'

'Hmm,' Grandma murmurs. 'Peach has been unwell too. Perhaps it's a bug of some sort.' She pats my knee. 'Get yourself to bed, dear. I'm sure the pair of you will feel *much* better in the morning. *Everything* looks better in the morning.'

UNTITLED

Rose Beam's Diary
8th June 1985

I can't remember if I mentioned that Mum and Dad are renewing their marriage vows . . . Anyway, they are, and as the party date draws closer, Mum is in full Good Woman mode. Anyone would think she wasn't busy enough, what with her official Matilda Beam WI appearances and the endless interfering in MY life. As much as her fussing-about annoys me, I can't help but feel excited about it. They love each other so, so much and there's no doubt that it will be the most stylish event anyone in London has seen in a long time. If there's one thing I can't deny, it's that Mum knows how to throw a gorgeous party. They're holding it in the private gardens opposite our house on a dusky summer's evening. Dad was fitted for his new suit today and he looked so handsome and excited. I wish I could tell them both about Thom, but it just feels too soon and they'll probably wig out about the whole thing. I know they can't forbid me from seeing anyone, I am an adult after all. But I couldn't stand it if they were unhappy with me in any way. Despite my moaning about them, they dote on me. I don't know. Maybe I'm underestimating them. Maybe they'll see how happy Thom makes me and know that it's the right thing for us to be together.

CHAPTER TWENTY-THREE

There are few things that a good night of sleep cannot remedy. Life always looks better in the morning!

***Matilda Beam's Good Mother Guide*, 1959**

Grandma is so wrong about things being better in the morning. I didn't believe it was possible to feel any worse than I did last night, but I absolutely do. I've been up with belly-ache for most of the night and now I'm groaning in bed while Grandma fusses about, taking my temperature and bringing me sachets of dehydration powdery stuff every hour.

Peach is worse too. We've been texting each other from our respective sick beds, wishing all sorts of evil things onto the owner of that dodgy kebab house. Namely, that he eats one of his own bastard kebabs.

I really hate being unwell. Being unwell means you have to stay still. And when you stay still there are no distractions, no fun, and all the things you don't want to think about start to seep into your brain and take over. I was never ill, growing up. There's simply no time to be poorly when you have a poorly mum to look after.

I try to distract myself by going online. I open my Facebook app to see if anyone, anyone at all, is wondering where I am, how I am or what I'm doing. But there are no messages or posts at all for me, just a friend request from Peach Carmichael, which I accept. I look at my newsfeed. There's a status from Betty in Didsbury – she's planning Henry's birthday party. And, oh, there are a few photos from Amy Keyplass – all her newly painted skirting boards. I scroll down further and see that Summer has posted a number of particularly passive-aggressive status updates.

Summer Spencer

The cheek of particular people is unreal. #fuming

Summer Spencer

You give and you give and some people just take. Have learned my lesson. #movingonup #blessed

Summer Spencer

thinks that certain people will get what's coming to them. Karma's a bitch, folks. #noregrets #karmachameleon #thekittenismine

With an exasperated eye-roll, I log out of Facebook and

swipe onto Google, where I idly type in 'Leo Frost'. To be honest, I'm a tiny bit freaked out by what happened last night. Leo wasn't at all what I thought he'd be like. The entire night was pretty unexpected. Yes, he's a twonk in general – he was snobbish and horrible at *The Beekeeper* party, and I overheard him being completely sexist at the retro fair – but the whole poetry thing, the fact that he wasn't a dick when I puked up, his git of a dad and that gorgeous drawing . . . I didn't, you know, *hate* him.

Google displays a few articles about Leo Frost the advertising wunderkind and his rise to the top, under the helm of the powerful and ruthless Rufus Frost, how he's just been nominated for a London Advertising Association award – one of the youngest people to ever be nominated. I already read those fluff pieces when I first researched him a few days ago, so bypass them and check out the numerous gossip sites, where Leo is regularly spotted at cool bars and events and hanging out with celebrities. I flick onto Google images. There are a few pics of his print adverts – stark, steely artwork for cars, golf clubs, beers, man stuff!, but mostly it's paparazzi shots of Leo with various modelesque-looking women on his arm. Oh look, there's one of him with Valentina. They're leaving a club and she's kissing him on the cheek while he grins arrogantly into the camera.

The way his lips are curled in this photograph, his cupid's bow sneering upwards ... He didn't seem at all like that last night.

Maybe he's got an evil twin.

Maybe not – this isn't *Sunset Beach*.

Confused, I press my phone icon and dial Valentina's number.

After three rings, she answers.

'Jess? Is that you?'

'It's me.' I sit up in bed, prop a pillow behind my back and take a sip of water.

'Jess, my sunshine pudding, how *are* you? How goes my pet project? I'm so excited about it.'

'Um, all right, I think ... I was actually calling because I went on the first proper date with Leo Frost last night.'

'Hold on, I'm at lunch, it's noisy, let me just head outside.'

I hear her apologizing to whomever she's with, and then the sound of her heels clip-clopping across a wooden floor.

'I'm back. Go on. Tell me. How did it go? He's a fucking terror, isn't he? So charming. Such a prick.'

'Well, that's kind of why I'm ringing, Valentina. Leo Frost is a goon, obviously, no diggity, no doubt, but he wasn't, well, he wasn't a total dick. He wasn't what I was expecting at all ... '

'He schmoozed you with fancy dinner and expensive wines, I expect? Did he bring you extravagant gifts? Exotic flowers? Artisan chocolates? Tell you your face is sweeter than honeydew? It's easy to be swayed by those things, believe me, but—'

'Well, no, that's the thing. He didn't do any of that. He didn't take me to dinner. He seemed like he was going to, but then he changed his mind and took me to a poetry night instead. At some little coffee house.'

There's a pause on the other end. 'Poetry? Jesus.'

'I know, right?'

'Hmmm.' I hear her long nails tapping against the phone. 'He never mentioned poetry to me when we were seeing each other. He tried to get you into bed, of course?'

'Um, no. Ew. But I have been putting out the "not that kind of girl" vibes like Grandma's guides tell me to.'

'Gosh ... He must be trying out a new move. It has to be

that. Leo is a shark whose only goal where women are concerned is to get them into the sack and then to heartlessly dump them when he's feeling bored or tied down. Maybe he's changing up his M.O. . . . How curious. Keep your wits about you, sweet, naive Jessica. It's you who must hold on to the upper hand. Stick to Matilda's tips and remember who you're dealing with. Keep me updated, OK? I have to go back to lunch now, but let's speak soon, and Jessica, remember ... Leo Frost is not to be trusted.'

She speaks as if I'm going off into battle. Wow. Poor Valentina. He really did pull a number on her.

I say bye and press the 'end call' button.

Leo Frost. Artist. Thinker. Man. Not to be trusted.

So it's all an act? He's being what he thinks I want, just to get me into bed? Kind of like what I'm doing to him ...

I picture Leo gently taking my scarf from around my neck, holding back my hair. The whole kind and sensitive act. How he told me to close my eyes and 'let it flow' when I got on stage. *And I blummin' did.*

Oh, he's good. He's really fucking good.

* * *

At about five p.m., there's been little improvement in my condition and, according to her texts, it's the same for Peach. Grandma is dashing from my room to Peach's and back again to bring us fresh water and soothing platitudes. I'm watching *You've Been Framed* on the iPhone in-between trips to the loo and feeling incredibly sorry for myself.

When there's another knock at the door I expect it to be Grandma bringing more dehydration sachets, but it's not. It's Jamie. He trails in, followed by a small boy in a Leeds

United football kit and clutching a football under one arm. Dashing in behind the pair of them comes Grandma, who hurries over to feel my forehead for the gazillionth time.

'Jessica, dear, the doctor's surgery isn't open on a Saturday so I took the liberty of telephoning Dr Qureshi downstairs. Unfortunately he wasn't there, so young Doctor Abernathy here – ' she says his name with a wrinkle of the nose; to be fair she has seen his balls – 'has agreed to take a look at you and Peach in order to check that nothing more serious is occurring here. I shall, ahem, leave you to it, Doctor Abernathy.'

Her chin wobbles for a moment and then she bustles out of the room.

Jeez.

'Um ... hey?' I say with a sigh. 'I'm all right, really. Sorry she rang you, we just ate a shifty kebab the other night is all. She's a bit of a worrier.'

The young boy darts over to the balcony door and gazes out onto the big park opposite Bonham Square. 'Woah, I can see for ages up here!' he yells with glee.

'This is Charlie, my nephew.' Jamie grins proudly.

Ah, yes. He did say his kid nephew was coming to visit this weekend.

'I was showing him around the clinic when Old Lady – um, Mrs Beam called to say you were unwell. Say hello to Jess, Charlie.'

'Hello, Jess,' Charlie says shyly, wandering back over from the balcony to get a good look at me in all my pukey glory. 'What team do you support?'

'Oh, um. Well, I don't know ... ' I eye his top. 'Leeds United?'

Right answer. Charlie's punches the air and Jamie laughs at my quick thinking.

'Aw, cool, a cat!' Charlie skips over to the tub chair where Mr Belding is stretched out beside Felicity the doll. He kneels down on the carpet and gently takes Mr Belding's paw into his own little hands.

'You play nicely with the cat, Charlie,' Jamie says in a soft burr. 'I'm just going to examine Jessica here so we can make her all better.'

Charlie nods solemnly.

'I'm fine, honestly.' I roll my eyes. 'There's no need for you to—'

Jamie shuts me up by sitting down on the side of the bed and shoving a temperature stick in my mouth. He pulls a stethoscope from around his neck, slipping the cold metal up the back of my nightie. This is weird.

'OK, your pulse is a little fast, but not weak, so you're probably not dehydrated.'

He takes out the temperature stick and examines it. 'No fever.'

Pushing lightly on my shoulder so that I lie down, he flattens his palm against my stomach and has a good feel about. I think about the last time he had his hands in that area. I drift off a little into that far more pleasant memory.

'How are your stools?' he asks brightly.

And straight back to earth I tumble.

'Go away!' I sit up and push him off. 'I'm fine. I *told* you – it was a kebab and too many beers.'

He laughs, rubs his hand over his beardy face and stands up. 'Yeah, you're all right. Like you say, just a wee case of food poisoning. Plenty of fluids, OK? And only dry toast to eat until you stop spewing.'

I shake my head. 'Nice terminology, Doc. Fine. Fine. I have my orders.'

He leans closer to me on the bed and kisses my cheek.

'Gerrof.' I shrug him away. 'I'm gross.'

'Get better, you. I'll see you soon ... in secret?' he whispers, giving me a knowing grin. And then in his normal voice. 'Come on, Charlie. Our next patient awaits.'

Charlie quickly jumps up from the floor, startling Mr Belding who proceeds to screech and dart into the air, knocking Felicity off the tub chair and onto the floor, where her melancholy face loudly smashes into three sharp pieces. At the noise, Charlie starts crying. Really loudly.

I jump up worriedly in the bed. Jamie hurries over to Charlie. 'Woah, watch your feet, buddy!' he warns, scooping the kid up into his arms and looking at him with a tenderness that makes my neck prickle.

'Sorry about that,' he says with a grimace once he's calmed Charlie down via lots of hugging and shushing. 'Kids, you know.'

I don't know.

'Oh, don't worry about it.' I breezily wave him away and pull a pissed-off Mr Belding onto my lap. 'I'll clean this up in a bit. You go and see Peach. Thanks for coming. It wasn't awkward *at all*.'

He hovers by the door looking worriedly down at the broken doll.

'Go! It's fine. It's just a doll!' I say with a shrug. 'Honestly, it's really no big deal.'

* * *

Oh, but it is a big deal. It is apparently a *very* big deal. When Grandma spots smashed-up Felicity on the floor, she almost crumples down there with her. I thought I had seen the worst of Grandma's emotional meltdowns, but I hadn't. I really hadn't.

'Shit, I'll clean it up, OK?' I crawl quickly to the end of the bed in horror. 'I was just, you know, waiting for a fresh burst of energy before I did it. No! Don't cry! It was a total accident.'

Grandma gathers the body of the doll up into her arms, holds it to her chest and bawls. She doesn't even notice that I said shit.

Fuck.

'We'll get a new one,' I try. 'I'll pay for it. I'll get one today.'

Grandma slowly sits down on the chair. She takes a shaky breath.

'There *are* no new ones,' she mutters, delicately straightening Felicity's pinafore.

'I'm sure they sell them at Argos,' I say brightly. They always sell that sort of tat at Argos. 'I'll have a look, shall I?' I grab my phone from the side table and open up the Internet icon.

'You don't understand. This was Rose's doll.'

'What?' I drop my phone onto the duvet. These were Mum's dolls? I knew she was unstable, but ... porcelain dolls?

'These are *all* her dolls,' Grandma sobs, indicating the many creepy porcelain dolls positioned around my room. 'Jack and I bought her a new one for every birthday since her first. This one is the last one we gave to her before she ... '

Grandma dissolves into tears.

'Before she what?'

'Before she left. And now it's gone. Broken, and I cannot fix it. I will never be able to fix it.'

My eyes scan the large room, counting out the dolls.

Including Felicity, there are twenty-five of them. One a year for twenty-five years.

Mum was twenty-five when she got pregnant with me.

That can't be a coincidence. Shit, was I something to do with why she left Matilda and Jack?

I'm not sure I even want to know the answer. It never does any good to dwell on the past. But suddenly I'm really, really curious.

'Um, why ... why did Mum leave?' I ask lightly, the crawling sensation already making its way over my head. I clench my fists and ignore it. 'I mean, she never talked about her life here, about you or Granddad Jack. Was it ... ' My voice goes unusually small. I swallow. 'Was it because of me? Was it my fault she left? Because, you know, she was pregnant with me?'

Grandma meets my gaze, blinking as if she had momentarily forgotten I was in the room. She takes a sharp breath, removes her specs and fiercely wipes the tears from her eyes with her embroidered hanky.

'Of course not, Jessica,' she says, speedily dabbing at her nose and attempting to be brisk. 'Your mother left home because she ... she wanted to be independent. It was *nothing* to do with you, dear. Nothing at all. You mustn't think that.'

I frown. I don't want to push her and I really don't want her to cry any more, but ... something doesn't add up.

'But ... if she left home because she wanted to be independent, then why did you guys never speak? Why have *we* only just met? Why—

Grandma interrupts me with a gasp. 'Goodness, is that Peach I can hear? Is she ... is she calling for me?'

I scrunch up my face. I hear nothing.

'Yes. Yes, I do believe I hear Peach.' Grandma picks up

the pieces of Felicity and clutches them close to her chest. 'She must be very unwell. I must go and see to her right away.'

'Wait—'

Grandma ignores me, dashing out of the room super quickly. From the hall she calls, 'Rest up, dear. We have a busy week ahead. Lots to do!'

If I wasn't already sure that Grandma was hiding something about my mum, I'm certain of it now.

And I'm going to find out what it is.

UNTITLED

Rose Beam's Diary
12th June 1985

Mum has invited the Pembertons round for the vow renewals a week on Saturday. I know that she intends to tout me out like I'm some kind of prize cow for sale – she even gave me a pair of gloves she claimed she wore at some silly debut she had a hundred years ago. Gloves in summer. Christ. It's not like I can have a tantrum either as she is so looking forward to the party and I don't want to ruin her light mood. It's never going to happen with Nigel and me. I've tried telling her a million times, but she insists that I give Nigel a chance because he's a 'perfect gentleman' and that the notion that love happens at first sight is ridiculous. Well, I know it's not ridiculous because I fell in love with Thom the first moment I saw him and he with me. I already know, in my heart, that I'm supposed to be with him. And that's why I've invited him to the vow renewals as my guest. It's earlier than I would like, but my hand has been forced. And I reckon this will be the easiest scenario in which to introduce him. Such an important party means my parents won't cause a scene. They'll be polite enough to really meet him properly. Thom's nervous, bless him. I wanted to tell him that of course he shouldn't be, but I'd be lying. I'm nervous too.

CHAPTER TWENTY-FOUR

A man needs to feel that he can share his innermost thoughts and desires with his sweetheart. Show your potential by encouraging your chap to talk about himself. Be attentive to his emotional needs and quicker than you can say 'diamond ring' he will see you as his greatest confidante!

***Matilda Beam's Guide to Love and Romance*, 1955**

Over the coming days, I try again to broach the subject of my mum with Grandma. On Sunday afternoon, while demonstrating how to list items on eBay at the kitchen table, I casually ask her once more why she and Mum didn't speak to each other for all that time. Grandma avoids having to answer by feigning a sudden terrible headache that 'must have been brought on by the ghastly lights of the computer machine'. On Monday afternoon, I try to catch her unawares after her nap. I wait patiently outside her door until she wakes up, and when she blearily comes out of her room, I corner her and ask what exactly happened the day my mum left. With wide eyes and sleep-rumpled hair, she stutters that she's can't quite remember, that it's not a good time, that I mustn't worry and that she's suddenly very tired and, come to think of it, 'rather needs a *second* afternoon nap'. Then, blinking rapidly, she shiftily retreats backwards into her bedroom, closing the door firmly behind her.

I try to push the unanswered questions away – I'm usually so good at refocusing my brain – but they continue to whizz and flutter around my mind like cheap glitter in a shaken-up snow globe. On Monday night, once everyone has gone to bed, I skulk downstairs and search the house for clues. I rifle through drawers and dressers and cupboards trying to find old letters or pictures, any evidence at all of my mum's time here and what might have happened for her to become so disconnected from her own parents. But beyond the dolls and a single framed photograph of my mum as a teenager in a demure-looking party dress, I discover precisely bloody nothing. Once again, I find myself wishing that I'd asked Mum about her life when I had the chance. Maybe if I'd known more, if I'd forced her to tell me what happened, helped her to fix it, I could have stopped her from getting so ill.

By Wednesday, I decide to hang fire on my secret investigation because life gets all kinds of busy and, to be honest, I'm grateful to be distracted from the unsettling Mum thoughts. Having listed all the hallway junk on eBay, we're (thanks to my amazing descriptions) inundated with buyer bids, and in-between waking up early to squeeze in secret runs and sneaking out late to meet Doctor Jamie for sexy rendezvous at the clinic, I spend most of the days managing auctions, requesting feedback and packing up items for Peach to take to the post office. I read some more chapters of *Matilda Beam's Guide to Love and Romance* when I can, watch Grace Kelly movies with Peach, and, under Grandma's instruction, learn how to walk as a lady – shoulders back, arse tucked in, nose up, short, delicate swaying steps. So like a twat, basically.

I try my best to get some words down for *How to Catch a Man Like It's 1955*, but time seems to slip so easily away from me and I don't manage to do anything more than an opening chapter.

But I will.

Definitely.

The days race along, and by Thursday it's time for my next night out with Leo. Despite my asking, he's refused to give any clue as to what we'll be doing, beyond asking that I meet him at the Fourth Plinth in Trafalgar Square at six o'clock. Based on the fact that I didn't have a bloody clue what to talk to Leo about on our last date, I ask Grandma for advice as she's getting me ready.

'Of course, the aim this evening is to get Mr Frost to open up to you,' Grandma declares as she wraps my pale ginger locks up into pin curls, securing each one with a purple crocodile clip. 'Very early on, he needs to see you as someone with whom he can share his hopes and his dreams. A confidante. A partner!'

Hopes and freaking dreams? Wow. That sounds super heavy. I don't know much about second dates, having never been on one before in my life, but that seems like a dead intense topic of conversation. Shouldn't we be talking about *Great British Menu* or, I don't know, favourite childhood toys?

I frown at Grandma in the bulb-framed bathroom mirror. 'Isn't that a bit pushy? I mean, won't it scare him off?'

Grandma laughs out loud, her hand paused on my

head. 'A Good Woman *is* a little pushy from time to time, dear. Men don't know what they want or what they need. It is our job to show them. Subtly, of course.' She gives me a benevolent look. 'People love to talk about themselves, Jessica. All anyone really wants is to be heard.'

But ... I'm no good at that. I'm no good at emotional stuff and listening and seriousness. I never have been. When you let people tell you their deep feelings, they expect you tell them *your* deep feelings too. They call it sharing. And then you have to think about your emotional shit and everything gets sad and complicated.

'On second thoughts, can I not just stick to being fake-fascinated by him instead?' I try. 'He seems to really like that.'

Grandma tucks a strand of wiry silver hair behind her ear and gracefully shakes her head with a chuckle. 'Of course he likes that. But I'm afraid we don't have a great deal of time to do this, and tonight we need to deepen things a little. You *must* get him to open up, Jessica. Ask him lots of questions about himself. Prompt him to reveal his heart's desires to you. Be a good and sincere listener and he will see you as a serious contender.'

I pull a face. 'Contender? For what?'

'Why, for *love*, what else? Trust me.' Grandma pats my shoulder and takes a tub of Pond's cold cream off the countertop, ready to moisturize my face for the hundredth time this week. 'Millions of women have taken my advice on how to make a man fall in love. I know *exactly* what I'm doing.'

I cross my arms and grumble into the mirror. A whole entire night aimed at discovering Leo Frost's hopes and dreams. Awesome!

Not.

* * *

'Wow.' Leo smiles broadly as I do my new, slinky 'lady' walk to where he's waiting for me at the Fourth Plinth – which is currently topped with this mental sculpture of a cockerel blaring ultramarine blue in the hot sun.

'*Wow*,' he repeats, drawing the word out across two syllables, green eyes taking in every inch of me with undisguised lust. To be fair, Grandma has done a cracking job tonight. I'm wearing another sundress, this time a saturated coral-pink colour that nips right in at the waist and with little cap sleeves instead of spaghetti straps. My feet are encased in turquoise Mary Jane high heels, and balanced on my nose is a pair of huge winged tortoiseshell Chanel sunglasses. With my pin-curled hair framing my elegantly made-up face, I'm totally channelling a 1950s bombshell – less goody-two–shoes Doris Day, more smoking-hot Ava Gardner.

'You look good too,' I purr, briefly tilting my sunglasses down with my forefinger. It's true. Leo is dressed down in a fitted navy blue polo shirt that shows off his broad shoulders, and tan chinos that demonstrate the admittedly pleasing shape of his bum. His quiff is still perfectly coiffed and dickhead like, but out of the dapper suit he looks different. Less ... dapper.

I hold onto the memory of Valentina's warning. Leo Frost is *not* to be trusted. He's probably dressed like this because he *knows* how hot it looks. Well, I know better, so who's the sucker here?

Leo Frost. Artist. Thinker. Man. Sucker.

'I got you a gift,' he grins, reaching into the back pocket of his chinos.

Aha! This is what Valentina *said* he would do. Give me

extravagant gifts in order to 'woo' me into bed. Must be something small if it fits into his back pocket. Jewellery? A Eurostar ticket to Gay Paris? A little origami heart that he made all by himself?

Leo pulls his hand out of his pocket and gives me ... a small white paper bag?

I tentatively take it from him and open it up. There's nothing inside. He's given me an empty paper bag.

Huh?

Oh!

All at once, I get the joke. It's an aeroplane sick bag. It's not an extravagant gift at all. Leo Frost brought me a sick bag! I laugh out loud in surprise and make a great show of tucking the bag carefully into my purse. *Well played*, I think suspiciously. Leo laughs back gleefully and offers me his arm.

'So, where are going tonight?' I ask, delicately linking arms with him as we wander past the fountains in the square. 'I've been looking forward to this evening all week long.'

Leo points over towards the National Gallery.

'Right there,' he says, eagerly leading me in the direction of the steps. 'There's a private viewing of a newly acquired Van Gogh collection and I've got tickets.'

Van Gogh?

Shit.

If there's one thing I know even less about than poetry, it's art.

Gad, why can't he just take me to dinner like a normal person? Or a rock concert. I'm ace at rock concerts – I can mosh like nobody's business. Except for that one time when I tried to crowdsurf but the crowd was a bit sparse and it was essentially just one meaty-looking guy holding me up in the air for a bit.

I frown discreetly to myself. Art. Leo Frost has gone and thrown me another bloody wild card. I only just got through the poetry night without letting the Lucille veneer slip and revealing Jess underneath.

How the fuck am I going to manage this one?

CHAPTER TWENTY-FIVE

A Good Woman is sophisticated and cultured. Make sure you are well versed in the topics of fine art, classical music and great literature. A good chap will appreciate a partner who won't merely listen to his thoughts on the world, but who will understand them too.

***Matilda Beam's Good Housewife Guide*, 1957**

I am so out of my depth. The exhibition is full of posh artsy people sipping the requisite vintage champagne and talking about the Van Gogh paintings. They're using words like 'vigorous' and 'rhythmic' and 'urgent' to describe them. The paintings are incredible, I'll admit, but these people act like they're about to have mega multiple orgasms over them. I think the pink-cheeked woman standing over by *Sunflowers* just did. I'm not quite in that place yet.

As we make our way from painting to painting, I try hard to do as Grandma instructed and ask Leo about himself on a more substantial level. But each time I do, we're interrupted by somebody he knows: clients from Woolf Frost, many, many women – some who seem to love him and some who very definitely hate him, all of them ridiculously beautiful – and even a reporter from the *Telegraph*, there to cover the event and extra keen to get a picture of me and Leo looking thrilled to be here.

'Nooo!' I yelp as the photographer points his big camera towards my head.

If my picture is in a national newspaper then someone will recognize me for sure. They might spill the beans and then the project would be in jeopardy. I can't risk it. Not now.

But my plea comes too late, because the photographer has already papped us. Dammit. Grandma's careful disguise has been enough to fool Leo Frost, but what about people back home? The people who know me in real life. They'll be able to see through the hair and contacts and clothes and pointy boobs in a second.

Leo raises his eyebrows. 'You don't like having your picture taken for the press?'

I fiddle with the collar of my dress. 'Um, no. I'm, er ... I don't.'

He narrows his eyes and half smiles in an approving way. 'How refreshing.'

Whipping another two flutes of champagne off a passing waiter, he hands one to me. I sip meekly, pretending to be part of the champagne conspiracy. On the other side of the room, a white-haired man wearing bright red trousers spots Leo, waves enthusiastically and starts to make his way through the mob towards us. Before Leo notices this guy and I have to stand next to him looking pretty while he has another boring conversation about golf and centre-spreads and his turd of a dad, I dart right in front of Leo, peeking up at him from beneath my eyelashes.

'It's hot and crowded in here, don't you think? Would you mind if we went somewhere a little ... quieter for a while?' I bite my lip. 'I'd be ever so grateful.'

Leo eyes me with concern. 'Of course. Are you all right? It should be pretty empty upstairs. C'mon.'

He grabs my hand and we dodge back through the crowd, out of the Van Gogh room and towards the lifts. Once the doors have closed, Leo asks:

'A good idea to get away from the hubbub. Any particular painter you'd like to see? They've got a wonderful collection here.'

My mind goes blank.

I can't think of *any* painters. Not a single bloody one!

I know them, but now that he's asked me I can't remember any of their names? Except for Van Gogh, who we just saw.

I tense up and tap my fingers against my chin. 'Hmmmm, let me seeee ... '

And then, right as I'm about to make a total chump of myself, I get a miracle of a brainwave. Teenage Mutant Ninja Turtles. *Teenage Mutant Ninja Turtles.* Weren't they named after magnificent painters?

'Donatello!' I almost yell in relief.

Turtle power.

'Oh, I don't think they have any Donatello in right now,' says Leo.

I scrunch up my face. 'What a shame. Well ... um, Leonardo then.'

Leo grins, immediately pressing the button for the Sainsbury Wing on level 2. 'Da Vinci, my namesake. Good choice. The National Gallery hold a fantastic assortment of Renaissance art.'

'Super.' I breathe. '*Super*. Renaissance art is my *favourite* kind of art.'

Leo's eyes widen in pleasure. 'Mine too!'

When the lift doors open, we're intercepted by a bespectacled, besuited man with a long, studious face. I think this is the art world's version of a bouncer.

'Hi, Terence,' Leo says, heartily shaking the man's hand. 'Only me. Thought we'd get a breather from downstairs.'

'Don't you ever go 'ome, lad?' Terence winks. Leo winks back.

I can't believe the cheek! I should have known. Of course Leo brings all his dates here, probably perfecting his sensitive, artistic persona until some fool falls for it. Well, it won't be this fool! He's wasting his time and he doesn't even know it.

Terence guides us through a huge archway and into a high, white-walled room filled with gold-framed paintings. He glances down at his watch. 'I can only give you fifteen minutes tonight, chief. It's just me up 'ere tonight.'

When Terence has left, Leo leads me over to one of the paintings. He takes great big confident strides across the floor and I have to totter quickly in the Mary Jane's to keep up with him. I miss my trainers.

Right. Alone at last. No one to interrupt us. For fifteen whole minutes. I'm going to have to work super fast.

Hopes and dreams time. Do it.

But ... I can't just blurt out the question, can I? *Hey, Leo, what are your biggest hopes and dreams for life?* It would be too obvious. And creepy.

I start off lightly.

'So, Leo,' I say in my soft voice. 'Please do tell me a little more about your work. I know you're in advertising, but what exactly is it that you do at Woolf Frost?'

'Well, I'm Artistic Director there,' Leo replies brightly, his voice echoing in the large empty space. 'Which is basically a souped-up way of saying that I work with copywriters and artists to generate concepts for client briefs and such. My specialism is print media. It's not as popular as it once was, but I really enjoy working on a tangible page.'

I nod deeply in the way Grandma showed me. Soooo interested.

Leo Frost. Artist, Thinker, Man. Soooo interesting.

'How long have you been there?' I ask, taking a sip of my champagne. Blerg.

'Gosh, ages. I started straight after uni at St Andrews, actually – my dad owns the company so I had an 'in'.' He raises his chin slightly. 'But I worked my way up on merit and spearheaded the recent Mercedes Campaign. *Drive Alive*.'

Drive alive. That shit advert again. Yuck.

When I don't respond Leo prompts,

'Do you know it? The Drive Alive advert?'

Hmm. I'm not sure my skills are quite up to pretending that I thought that ad was anything less than gratuitous, nonsensical crap. Surely the rage would shine through my skin like E.T.'s heart does in *E.T.: the Extra Terrestrial*. Instead I shake my head 'no'.

'I'm afraid I don't,' I simper apologetically. 'But I'd love to see it.'

'I'll show it to you sometime. I'd be interested to know your opinion – it's had a pretty mixed response.' He laughs to himself, as if remembering something. 'You know, I was at a book party the other week when this woman barged up to me out of nowhere and told me how awful she thought it was!'

Oh God. *He's talking about me at* The Beekeeper *launch.*

I actually stop breathing.

'Oh dear.' I squeak in an uncanny impression of Peach. Fucking hell. I wouldn't say I *barged* up to him . . . did I? 'How awful for you!' I simper. '*Anyway—*'

'Yeah, I sort of blew up at this woman. I felt bad about it afterwards – I'd lost a client at work that day and I was getting a terrible cold, so I was in a foul mood already. The funny thing is that the bit of the advert she was most offended by – the model wearing a gratuitous diamond swimsuit – wasn't even my idea, it was my father's! And I kind of agreed with her that it was ridiculous.'

My jaw drops open. I can't believe it. Leo Frost felt bad about being so rude at that party. He had a cold. The diamond bikini wasn't even his idea.

'Oh, I'm sure all your ads are *wonderful*,' I say evenly, trying not to betray my surprise.

'It does its job, I guess,' Leo shrugs, pausing in front of *Portrait of a Musician*. 'It *has* managed to snag a nomination for a London Advertising Association award, so it can't be all bad.'

I already know about the award nomination from my Internet research, but feign shock and pleasure at just how clever my date companion is.

'Wow!'

Leo shrugs in a very good impression of a modest man. 'There'll be one of those ridiculously showy black tie ball and dinner events. It's my first time being nominated so, you know, pretty exciting stuff.'

'That's so impressive.' I clap my hands together. 'Your father must be very proud of you.'

At the mention of his dad, Leo swallows hard and swiftly changes the subject. 'Tell me more about *your* work, Lucille?'

My work? Eek. I can't exactly tell Leo that I'm a writer. He might make the connection to the publishing party and realize I'm the girl who called him a knob-prince. This is too important to just make up on the spot – it's something I definitely need to check with Grandma.

I pretend to be distracted by one of the paintings.

'This one's beautiful,' I say, staring up at a painting entitled *Virgin on the Rocks*. As I look closer, I realize that it *is* amazing. Breathtaking, actually. I don't know why – it might be the intricacy, the attention to detail, or the way the skin of the subjects glows; I don't quite know how to describe it, not being an art ponce like Leo Frost.

'I love it,' I murmur.

Leo gives me a sidelong glance. 'That was my mother's favourite too.'

'*Was?* Did she change her mind?' I laugh lightly.

'I mean, it was her favourite painting before she died. She named me Leonardo after the artist. I come here a lot to look at it. More than I should, probably.'

My breath catches in my throat.

Leo's mum died?

I didn't expect that. It doesn't quite fit into the 'charmed life' theory I had worked up for him.

'God, I'm sorry,' I say instinctively. It sounds empty and not nearly enough to express that I know exactly how it feels. He gives an almost imperceptible shrug, and his eyes flicker with an emotion I recognize instantly. One I've seen when I look in the mirror for too long. Loss.

'My mum died too,' I say, plopping down onto the bench behind us. 'When I was eighteen.'

I shouldn't have told him that.

I tell no one that.

I don't even know him.

'Fuck, I'm sorry to hear that, Lucille. I was young too – fifteen.' He sits down beside me and smiles grimly. 'Sucks, right?'

Taking hold of my hand, he gives it a brief squeeze. It feels warm and strong. My chest tightens. I know I was supposed to delve a bit deeper with Leo tonight, but this feels like much too much. And though he might be the only person I've ever met who even slightly gets what it's like to lose your mum, after all is said and done, he's a stranger. And I'm not supposed to be telling him real stuff about myself. I pull my hand away from his and place it neatly in my lap. I need to lighten the melancholy mood that seems to have spilled over the room like oil. But I don't know what to say. What the bloody hell do you say when someone tells you about their dead mum. I've never been on *this* side of that conversation before. Ordinarily, if this were real life, I'd just do one. But this is a job. I made a promise to suck it up and stick it out.

'Well, she'd be proud about your award nomination,' I say with a smile.

Leo fiddles with the stem of his champagne flute for a moment. 'You know, I'm not sure she would. She loved my dad fiercely, but always hated commercial art, said it was soulless . . . ' He turns to face me. 'Want to hear something ridiculous?'

'Always.'

'I sometimes worry that my mother would be disappointed to know I joined my father in the ad business. Like I've let her down somehow.'

'Not ridiculous.' I shake my head. 'Mums have a way of getting under your skin like that, even when they're not there any more. And you love what you do, don't you?'

'I'm *good* at what I do, I suppose. You know, my mother always wanted me to be an artist. I won a school painting competition when I was fourteen and I'd never seen her quite as proud of me.'

He looks wistful for a moment. I think of that boat drawing.

'So why don't you do that then?' I shrug. 'Be an artist. If that's what you love. You're talented enough.'

Leo laughs out loud, a blast of a laugh that makes me jump. He runs a hand through his hair, mussing up the front of the quiff so that it loses its rigidity. 'Ah, no, that's just a pipe dream, the thing I think about before I go to sleep. Not something for real life. My drawings are just a mess-about, and I'm doing all right at Woolf Frost. Dad intends to give me the company one day and, well, no man turns his nose up at an opportunity like that. Everything's lined up for me. I'm a very lucky man.'

He gives me a confident grin. It's the grin he was doing in the paparazzi shots I saw. But it falters slightly.

'Just because things are handed to you doesn't mean you have to accept them.' I say quietly. 'And we both know that life's too short and too unpredictable not to grab the things you really want.'

I think about what I really want. A lovely beach villa in a faraway place. But the image blurs a little in my mind, not quite as vivid as it usually is.

Leo nods slowly.

I examine his haughty features, the slightly long nose,

high cheekbones, matinee-idol jaw, long-lashed, clever green eyes, all thrown off balance by the slightly sad frown between his eyebrows. Hmm. Is this part of the act? Some kind of 'troubled soul' play to get me to shag him? Based on what Valentina told me, anything is possible where this guy is concerned ... But surely he wouldn't use his mum's death for that. Not even the worst kind of dickhead would do that.

Leo leans in and nudges me with his shoulder. 'So, was Rose your mum?' he says in a low voice. 'The person in your poem?'

My heart suddenly starts to beat faster. Too fast. I'm not up for this question. I'm really not up for talking about my mum with Leo Frost of all people.

'What do you know, I think our fifteen minutes are up!' I say, so forcefully that it bounces off the walls and echoes back at us three times. I get up from the bench with a dazzling smile. 'We should probably go back downstairs,' I say more softly. 'Wouldn't want to incur the wrath of Terence!'

'Oh.' Leo looks startled. He stands up and follows as I head back out of the archway. 'Yes, of course. Terence can be quite frightening when he's not obeyed. Hulk-like, in fact. Perhaps a conversation to continue another time then?'

Not if I have anything to do with it.

I don't say that, though. Instead I nod fervently like the open and sincere confidante I'm supposed to be.

As we take the lift back down to the ground floor, I ponder about the aim of tonight's date. To get Leo Frost to tell me about his hopes and dreams.

How the sweet hell can I do that when he seems to have given up on them?

UNTITLED

Rose Beam's Diary
21st June 1985

The vows were so beautiful tonight. Seeing how much love Mum and Dad have for one another made me realize that it was the right decision to be honest about Thom. He showed up to the party wearing a stiff, clearly borrowed tuxedo. It was odd seeing him in something non-colourful, and I could tell as soon as he arrived that he was uncomfortable to the max. I introduced him to my parents as my boyfriend, and although Mum flared her nostrils, it played out exactly as I had hoped and no one made a scene. Dad shook Thom's hand and invited him for dinner tomorrow evening. Thom was thrilled, as was I. Nigel Pemberton spent the whole party giving me meaningful looks. Thom thought it was hilarious and we couldn't stop giggling about it. Poor old Nigel.

CHAPTER TWENTY-SIX

If you have followed my advice as instructed, it is likely that more than one Good Man will want to be your sweetheart, and thus you will have to turn someone down. Do so with sensitivity, kindness and respect. The heart is delicate and must be treated as such.

***Matilda Beam's Guide to Love and Romance*, 1955**

When the Van Gogh event is over, we amble out into the warm night, back through Trafalgar Square and onto the bustling road to wait for the town car that Leo has ordered to take me home. As we're waiting, I watch the nearby fountains, now illuminated with brightly coloured lights. The twinkling running water is almost hypnotic, and not helped by the champagne I ended up drinking in an effort to extinguish the uncomfy feelings ignited by the deep-and-meaningful earlier on. I huff to myself, the sound of it getting lost in a sweep of evening breeze.

Leo slowly spins me around, reaches forward and nicks

the sunglasses from where they're resting on the top of my head. He props them onto his face. They look ridiculous.

'Lucille, do I look hot in these?' he asks casually. 'I *feel* like I look hot.'

'You look very hot,' I say wryly.

'I knew it.' He walks a little down the street, doing an exaggeratedly masculine 'T-bird'-type strut in the big winged Chanel sunglasses. A middle-aged tourist couple walk by. 'Evening,' Leo says in his deep, plummy voice. 'Lovely night for it.'

The couple scurry away, muttering about London and deviants.

I giggle. I really don't intend to genuinely laugh at anything Leo does, but . . . I must admit he's kind of funny. And it's such a bloody relief to laugh after the sad-sack tone upstairs in the Da Vinci room.

Taking the sunglasses off, Leo hands them back and stands right in front of me.

'I like you,' he says matter-of-factly as a red bus whizzes past behind him.

'Oh, Leo, I like you too!' I return immediately in the wimpy breathy voice.

He grins, green eyes narrowed. 'You're different. I mean ... different from anyone else I've ever ... '

Screwed over?

' ... dated. I love how comfortable you are with yourself. You're unique and, and, *alternative*.'

Alternative. There's that word again. Shit, he thinks because I'm dressed in vintage clothing and acting delicate and old-fashioned that I'm some kind of manic pixie dream girl. A sweet Zooey Deschanel -type in quirky dresses and hats. If it wasn't so off kilter it would be hilarious.

I gaze up at him, feigning modesty. 'Thank you. That's *very* sweet of you.'

He steps closer to me, tucking one of my curls behind my ear. 'I mean it, Lucille. I like how ... how real you are. There are so many phoneys in this town, people who only care about money and status, where they can be seen with you and who your bloody father is. You're ... not like that. You're just you. Do you know how refreshing that is?'

Oh God.

'And I don't want to get all Tom Cruise on the sofa right now,' Leo goes on, shoving his hands deep into his chino pockets, '*especially* when we've only met each other three times, but ... I thought I ought to tell you, just, you know, how much I like you. And, well, I don't feel that way a lot. Or ... ever. That's it, really.'

Taking his hands back out of his pockets, he grabs one of mine and moves his forefinger back and forth across my palm. Then he shrugs slightly and gives me a bashful look. 'Do you think that's absurd?'

Either Leo Frost is the world's greatest actor or ... is he *nervous* right now? He seems sort of nervous.

I get a weird feeling in my chest. A fluttering. Like acid reflux, but not entirely unpleasant.

Leaning forward tentatively, Leo moves his head towards mine. His mischievous eyes flicker to my lips and he half grins. I look at *his* lips, arrogant and full, red and ... annoyingly inviting. He wraps his arm around my lower back, swiftly and confidently pulls me in so that we're waist to waist, and with his other hand tilts my chin upwards. I move my face towards his, closer, closer and then ... right at the last minute, I turn my head so that his kiss lands squarely on my cheek.

Just in time. Phew.

Phew. Definitely phew. Right?

My back stiffens as I realize that I don't feel entirely 'phew' about halting his kiss.

Did I *want* to kiss him? No. Of course not. He's a moron. A sexist pig. Mean slow-clap starter. Breaker of Valentina's heart.

Leo recovers from my rejection admirably, taking out his phone and checking on the whereabouts of the town car.

I look at his mouth again as he talks on his mobile.

It's a nice mouth. Arrogant, yes, but also kind of, well, gorgeous.

Fuck.

Why can't I stop looking at Leo Frost's mouth?

Don't be a dick, Jess. It's just smoke and mirrors. He's handsome in his blue polo shirt, there's a heatwave, you've had champagne, maybe he's not quite as terrible as you thought he'd be and maybe he's got a bit more depth to him than you expected but that does not mean you fancy him. It fucking does not.

Leo catches me staring at his mouth and grins widely. I quickly look away under the guise of searching my purse for some non-existent thing.

When he's put the phone down, he asks, 'Are you free tomorrow evening, Lucille? Tonight has been very me-centric and I'd love a chance to find out more about you.'

'Yes, I'm free,' I say at once.

But as Lucille or as Jess, I'm not entirely sure.

Suddenly, I feel nervous too.

* * *

I ride the town car back to Bonham Square with a very niggly feeling indeed. It feels like butterflies, but not in the nice way. To be fair, I did drink loads of champagne and maybe just need to do a massive burp. I hope so.

I flashback to Leo Frost looking sad about his mum in the gallery, making me laugh by the fountain, leaning in to kiss me. Then I think about what it would have been like to kiss him. I bet Leo Frost is dead good at kissing . . .

No.

I do not like Leo Frost.

I pull a face at my treacherous brain. Stoppit, brain.

I try to get a grip of myself. Maybe Leo Frost releases a higher than average amount of testosterony, pheromoney-type chemicals, and I'm sniffing them out and my body and brain are simply reacting to that in a normal human way. There's no other reason for almost kissing him. Or . . . maybe, without even realizing it, I'm falling victim to the Leo Frost power? To the magnetic power that Valentina and Summer were talking about at the David Arthur Montblanc party? Maybe this is Leo Frost's magic – confident and charismatic twat on the outside, sensitive and pained soul of an artist on the inside. Maybe this is his *thing,* how he captures his hearts before he chews them up and spits them out.

I make a mental note to call Valentina again in the morning and find out more about what he was like with her. I need back-up.

When the car reaches Grandma's building, I thank the driver and get out. Lifting my head, I walk determinedly across the street.

As I approach the door, I see the downstairs lights are on. Jamie is at the clinic.

See. *That's* what I do. I like Jamie. I have casual sex with Jamie. I don't get bizarre nervous sensations about Jamie and that's the best way to be. The safest way to be.

Ugh. I feel all kinds of weird. My heart is racing. I do not like it. This feeling needs to do one and fast.

There's only one thing for it.

I hurry up the steps of the building, storm into the lobby and knock hard on the clinic door. Jamie answers immediately, almost as if he was waiting for me.

'Hullo, Jess,' he starts with a warm smile. 'How was your ni—'

'Let's have all the sex.' I interrupt, pushing him back inside the clinic and slamming the door behind us. 'Now.'

* * *

There. That's better. I can breathe again. Lovely, casual fun sexy times with Jamie and no horrible overthinking things and fancying the wrong people. As I'm pulling my sundress back on, Jamie says, 'You want to go for a walk?'

I shrug. 'Why not?'

Doing a circuit of the park will be a good way to wind down. I've not managed to get a run in today; besides, I don't quite feel up to relaying tonight's date to Grandma and Peach right away. I'd rather not think about it at all, if possible.

Jamie and I mosey around Bonham Square's leafy private park, the welcome breeze cooling down our hot and sweaty bodies. I probably look a right state, pin curls messed up, mascara down face, dress buttoned up haphazardly. That's the cool thing about hanging around someone casual like Jamie – I don't care what I look like. He's my buddy. My sex buddy.

'I got asked out today,' Jamie chuckles as we amble past a rose bush in full bloom. 'By a patient!'

See? He got asked out and he's comfortable enough to tell me. Cool, casual sex pals. That's what it's all about.

'Wit woo!' I tease, elbowing him. 'Is she nice?'

He shoves his hands in his pockets. 'She's nice. Her name is Kiko.'

'Cool name.'

'She's Japanese. She comes for a check-up about her mild arrhythmia every few months. I couldn't believe it when she asked me if I wanted to go out for a drink. Right in reception, in front of the other patients!'

I laugh with him. 'So . . . what did you say?'

'Um, no. I said no.'

'Aw, that's a shame. Did you not fancy her then?' I ask.

'I told her I was already seeing somebody.'

'Huh?' I scrunch my face up. Jamie stops walking, pausing by a huge old oak tree rustling gently. 'What are you doing, you plonker, why have you stopped walk—'

'I said no to Kiko because . . . I'm seeing you.'

I snort. 'You used me as an excuse? Well played, my friend.'

He doesn't respond. Just looks at me intensely, a bit of breeze ruffling his curls.

He's not kidding.

I shake my head. 'But we're only hooking up, right? No strings, etcetera. Remember? You're free to go on a date with whoever you choose. It's totally, totally cool with me.'

Of course it'll be a bummer not to have access to his man parts whenever I need them but . . . I can live with that. Definitely.

Jamie takes hold of my hand. 'Surely you don't *really* think that, Jess. That this is still just "hooking up".'

I take my hand back, confused. 'What you talkin' 'bout, Willis?'

Jamie frowns – it doesn't suit him. 'You said no strings two weeks ago, Jess, but we've seen each other pretty much every day since then. Ergo *seeing each other*. This is, um, clearly more than just sex. I know you know that. I know you *feel* that.'

What the fuck is happening? I peer at Jamie to see if he's telling a joke, if he's going to reveal that this is some ridiculous prank for shits and giggles. But he looks serious. Very serious indeed.

Oh, balls.

He's only gone and attached.

Jamie Abernathy has sodding emotionally attached to me like a foolish, feeling leech. I thought I'd made things super clear to him? I definitely did.

With an exasperated tut, I whirl around and start power-walking back through the park, past a bed full of gawky looking daffodils and in the direction of Grandma's building.

'Where are you going now?' he asks, following me.

'Doc, when I said I wanted something with no strings, I meant it. I still mean it.' I huff out through my cheeks. 'Nothing has changed. Sex is ace, we have a giggle, but nothing more.'

'Why nothing more? More would basically be what we're doing now but with a little more, I don't know, conversation. I don't get why you don't—'

'I'm – I'm busy. Really busy right now.'

Jamie catches up with my power-walk, stumbling slightly on a grid. 'With your project? You don't want to even try to take things more seriously with me because of that guy you're hanging out with for your project. Frost? Was that his name? The guy you're *tricking*?'

I stop again and put my hands on my hips. 'No, it's

nothing to do with that! And even if it was – which it isn't – that's none of your bloody business.'

We reach the door. Jamie goes to get it for me, but I dart in front of him and yank it open furiously. I spin round to face him.

'Say yes to Kiki,' I sigh. 'Maybe she can give you what you need.'

'Kiko.'

'Kiko then. Look, I like you, Jamie. I *really* like having sex with you, but this – ' I indicate the pair of us – 'is . . . is nothing more . . . and it never will be. It's time to cool things off.'

Jamie stands there in the lobby. He doesn't say a thing. Just glows with anger? Embarrassment? High blood pressure? I don't know.

I can't bear to be there with him any longer, witnessing this unasked-for change of heart. It makes me feel horrible and guilty and, well, really fucking confused.

'You – you didn't stick to the rules, you turd,' I spit, my voice breaking unexpectedly.

Then I run up the stairs two at a time, tripping over twice in my heels, and let myself into Grandma's, leaving Jamie staring forlornly after me.

What's happening? First I get weird attractions to Leo and then Jamie gets weird feels for me.

It must be a full moon tonight. Maybe all this odd behaviour has something to do with the tides and the stars or some shit. I hurry over to the upstairs hall window and peer out into the night sky desperately. But the moon is not full. It's just a boring old crescent moon.

I creep down the hallway of doom, which is now completely empty of junk and no longer doom-like, up the stairs and into my room. Angrily stripping off my clothes and underwear, I have a quick shower, towel-dry my hair and climb into bed beside Mr Belding. The sooner I can get to sleep, the sooner these unsettling feelings will bugger off.

But sleep doesn't come for ages. I even go back downstairs and make myself some lightly warmed milk, but it doesn't work. Then I listen to some gentle sounds of the ocean on my iPhone, but that doesn't work either. I end up lying awake, tossing, turning, thinking, stewing and wondering until the early hours of the morning.

CHAPTER TWENTY-SEVEN

Falling in love with your chosen chap can feel like flying – enjoy this sensation, you have certainly earned it. But do be careful not to lose your head. A Good Woman must remain focused on the goal.

***Matilda Beam's Guide to Love and Romance*, 1955**

After approximately two hours of sleep, I wake up at six a.m. and immediately call Valentina.

'Hello?' comes a bleary voice. Valentina sounds half asleep. I thought all successful people woke up very early? That's what Summer always said whenever I slept in past ten a.m.

'Yo, Valentina. It's Jess. Sorry to wake you, I'll bell again later.'

'Jess? I'm awake, stay right there.' I hear some shuffling about and Valentina clearing her throat. 'Jess Beam, you delicious kitten. Lovely to hear from you. How are things?'

'I had another date with Leo last night.'

'Great, did he take you somewhere fabulous this time? The Ivy? He's very fond of the Ivy—'

'No, we went to the National Gallery.'

'Oh! Really? He always visited the gallery alone when we—'

'Look, I wanted to ask you, Valentina, did Leo ever talk to you about his mum?'

'No, no he didn't. He rarely shared anything of his past, as I remember. Why do you ask – wait . . . did he . . . did he talk to *you* about his mother?'

'Yup.' I put the phone onto loudspeaker and place it on the duvet beside me.

There's a gasp on the other end. 'Gosh, that's very unusual. He's such a closed book of a man.'

'Did he talk to you about his art?'

'His art? What art? Do you mean his adverts?'

'No, his sketches.'

'Leo *sketches*? Sketches what?'

'I don't know, I only saw one. Of an old man in a boat.'

'A man in a boat? Was it good?'

'It was amazing.'

'Gosh, Jess. Gosh. He never told *me* he liked to draw, not in six weeks. And he shared this with you? *On your second date?*'

I nod, even though she can't see me. 'We talked about it a bit, yes. And then he told me he liked me. That he found me *refreshing*. That he's never, um, met a woman like me before. Is this normal?'

There's a pause. And then, in a very excitable tone of voice, Valentina says, 'It is *not* normal. This out-of-the-ordinary behaviour can only mean one thing.'

'What's that?'

'Matilda Beam's 1950s romance tips must be working.

They must be working *magic*. I suspected they might, but this is beyond! Matilda must be thrilled. Wow. Keep on doing what you're doing, clever Jessica,' Valentina continues happily. 'The scoundrel Leo Frost deserves everything that's coming to him.'

'Does he? Does he definitely?' I ask, a slight spike of guilt darting through my chest.

Valentina laughs knowingly, the sound of it blasting out of the loudspeaker and echoing through my room. 'Oh, he might be showing you a different side now, Jessica, but think of all the women before you. The ones whom he cast aside, treated like trophies, did *not* show his sketches to. You're doing this for them. For women all over London. Be strong. You are a warrior, Jessica. A *warrior*.'

I think about all those broken hearts. Broken hearts are dangerous things. I think about my mum's broken heart.

'OK,' I say firmly, punching my fist down onto the duvet.

I am Jessica Beam – noble and true hunter of cruel, hard-hearted knobheads with really nice mouths.

'And write,' Valentina urges. 'Write it all down for me. Everything. Write like the wind, my love!'

'Yes. Will definitely write like the wind. Thanks, Valentina.'

'It's my pleasure. Keep me posted, duckling.'

'Will do.'

'And Jess?'

'Yeah?'

Her voice goes kind of low and growly.

'Annihilate that rat.'

'Yep. Fo sho. I'll do my best.'

Hanging up, I turn to Mr Belding, who's languishing across the end of the bed.

'What the fuck I got myself into?' I ask him, raising my hands to the air.

He answers by licking his own butt.

'You are of no use,' I grumble, and head to the bathroom for a wee.

* * *

The weird nervous feeling I had last night has settled back in and I really need to clear my head. Nothing like a good top-secret run to do that.

I change into my running gear and sneak downstairs as quietly as I can. I know where all the creaky floorboards are now, so I hop and step over each one like I'm doing an Irish jig.

In the downstairs hall I bump into Peach coming out of the kitchen, wearing a long pale yellow dressing gown, hands clasped around a mug of coffee, corner of toast hanging from her mouth. Damn. I thought everyone was still in bed.

Peach gasps in surprise. 'Jess, you're up early! What's happening? Is something wrong? Are you unwell again?'

Then she spots my lycra-wear and trainers and frowns.

'You're going running? But I thought Matilda told you not to run on account of your masculine calves.'

I roll my eyes and do some stretches, holding onto the stair banister for support. 'My calves are awesome, OK, there's nothing wrong with them. Running makes me feel better. Don't tell her you saw me sneaking out, will you?'

'You want me to keep your secret?'

'Do you mind? Grandma will just be upset if she finds out, and she's had no major meltdowns for two whole days now. It would be cool to keep it that way.'

'Our first official secret,' Peach almost whispers, smiling to herself. Then she puts her coffee cup down onto the side table and inhales through her nose. 'I *will* keep your secret, Jess. In fact, I'll come with you on your run. I will *participate* in the deception.'

'Oh, no, you don't have to do that. I trust you.'

'I would like to.'

'But ... I run alone. I run hard.'

'You don't *have* to run alone any more,' Peach says reasonably. 'You have Lady P now. I will run with you. I'll get changed right now. Meet you outside in five minutes.'

I try to think of a reason to protest, why I should go running alone. But it's super early and my brain isn't all lit up yet, and I can't think of the reasons. I nod my assent and Peach flies past me, lumbering quickly up the stairs to get changed.

* * *

Five minutes after setting off on our run, I am full to bursting with the reasons I usually do this on my own. Top of the list is the fact that running is my lovely alone time, peace and quiet, a time to think and listen to my music and focus on nothing but the steady pound of my heartbeat and the feel of the air whipping at my skin. Peach has other ideas about what a run is. First of all, she thinks that 'run' is a euphemism for medium- to slow-paced walking with a stop-off for frothy coffee along the way. Secondly, Peach wants to talk on our run. She wants to talk a whole lot. Since our night out at Twisted Spin, it's like Pandora's box has been opened and a new, chattier Peach is starting to emerge like a butterfly from a cocoon. Which is great. It's awesome that she's starting to feel more confident – her shoulders aren't as hunched, she's mumbling less, it's fab. But I'm still the only person she feels comfortable talking to, which means that everything she wants to say out loud, she says to me. And after twenty-six years of barely talking to anyone, there's a lot of stuff she's feeling the need to share. By the time we're halfway down Kensington High Street, I've zoned out a bit.

'. . . and then at senior prom it was all planned out, but Lyle lost the room key and the mood sorta fizzled. And I never quite got around to it. And that's the story of why I'm still a virgin. Then in 2004 I decided—'

My mind zones back in immediately. 'Wait – what?' I stop outside Marks &Spencer's and turn to Peach. 'What did you just say? You're still a virgin?'

Peach nods. 'I sure am. Not for lack of wanting, just lack of opportunity, I guess.'

'Wow,' I breathe. I lost my virginity at eighteen. On Summer and mine's first night out together at uni, actually, the week after my mum died. I can't imagine having reached twenty-six without doing it. Sex is ace. How does she get her kicks? How does she cheer herself up? I examine her curiously.

'I have got my eye on someone,' Peach grins, taking a hefty gulp from her water bottle.

'Who? *Who?*'

She fiddles with her ponytail of frizzy curls. 'Gavin.'

'Who is Gavin?'

'Our postman, duh!'

Aha, the stocky blonde fella.

'He's cute,' I say approvingly as we cross over to the other side of the road.

'I know.' Peach smiles wistfully, her round cheeks pink. 'But he's sorta shy too. I've been taking all that eBay stuff for delivery so I've seen him lots at the post office recently, but we've never managed to say more than a few words to each other. I wanted to ask you a favour, actually.'

'Go on.'

'I feel more . . . confident when you're there, if you know what I mean? Like I can talk a little easier.'

I don't know quite what she means, but nevertheless, at her words, I get a tiny flutter of pleasure in my chest.

'So I was hoping that the next time Gavin came around with the post, you would answer the door with me. I wanna ask him out for a date and I don't know if I'd be able to do it unless you were standin' by me.'

I laugh. 'You're going to ask him out? That's awesome.' I give her a high-five. 'It'd be my pleasure to stand there creepily looking on during that intimate moment. Oh God, Peach, you should totally tell Gavin that you want his special delivery. Ooh, I know, ask him if he's got a big package for you. *Please* ask him that.'

'Should I really ask him that?' Peach's gentle grey eyes widen solemnly.

'Er, no. No, I'm kidding, Peach. Don't say that . . . at least not yet.'

'You're weird.' Peach guffaws to herself in a vexed way, as if *I'm* the peculiar person in this duo.

'Can we do some actual running now?' I moan, hopping up and down on the spot. 'We've got barely any time left and Matilda will be awake soon.'

'Of course,' Peach pants, joining me in a couple of star jumps. Then she stops. 'But first, let me tell you *all* about my life in 2004. It was January fifteenth, and the opening day of Alabama's world-famous national peanut festival . . .'

I take off into a sprint.

* * *

Later that morning Grandma and I gather in the drawing room to tot up our eBay earnings. I get comfy on the sofa, place my laptop on my knees and call out figures to Grandma who, from her favourite blue chair, adds them all up on a massive old-as-time calculator.

As I get to the last sold item – an old Tiffany table lamp – I peek up at Grandma in excitement for the total. I watch her face, waiting for the smile to appear, the look of relief to soften her taut, worried features. But that doesn't happen.

'We didn't make enough,' she says in a small, dejected voice.

'Whaaat?' I jump up from the sofa and dash over to look at the calculator. 'How? We sold so many things? People were going crazy over that stuff. This calculator is an antique – it must be broken!'

'There's nothing wrong with the calculator. We simply do not have enough for the minimum payment.' Grandma's lips start to wobble. Shit. She's going to cry again.

I frantically recheck the numbers and add them up myself. Grandma's right. We've made a fair amount on eBay, but not nearly enough for the stupid bank's extortionate minimum payment.

'In ten days they will take me to court,' Grandma says in a panicky voice. 'I'll be evicted! I will lose my home, my memories, everything I have worked for.'

Argh, she's spiralling off. Not again . . .

'Stop crying!' I say firmly. 'It won't help.'

Grandma looks up at my strong tone and frowns.

'A Good Woman is never callous,' she sobs.

I huff.

'Well, a Modern Woman gets on with the shit that life

has thrown her without melting down. Let's be practical about this.'

It is not often that I play the role of sensible person in a situation. I feel like I'm wearing a costume.

Grandma hangs her head, her wispy hair falling over her face.

'You can do it,' I urge, pouring her a small cup of tea from the tray on the ottoman and handing it over to her. 'You are Matilda Beam. Mega bestselling writer and romantic magician. You are the person who managed to get me to take out my hair extensions. If you can do that, you can bloody well sort this out.'

Grandma takes a sip of her tea. 'Your hair *is* much lovelier now,' she weeps.

'I wouldn't go that far,' I tut, patting my gingery locks. 'OK. So. Peach mentioned that you have some things in the attic. Shall I go up there, have a look through and see if there's anything else we can sell on—'

'No!' Grandma interrupts, plonking the cup of tea back down on the silver tray with a clatter. 'No, no. The attic is empty. There's nothing in there. Nothing.'

I definitely remember Peach saying that there were so many things in the attic she could barely get the door open.

I narrow my eyes at Grandma. She avoids my gaze.

She's lying.

I make a mental note to check out the attic as soon as I get chance.

'Because there's *nothing* to sell in the attic,' Grandma continues, rising from her chair and wandering over to the drawing-room window. 'I think the best thing to do in this short time is to speed up the *How to Catch a Man Like It's 1955* project.'

'Speed up? How?'

'Leo has shown a very definite interest in you. We ought to increase the time you and he are spending together in order to get to our conclusion at a faster pace and secure the deal with Valentina as quickly as possible. Once we have a full contract, I can show that to the bank as proof of future income. Perhaps then they will be a little more lenient. You have a date with Leo this evening, don't you?'

Pretty much all I've been worrying about since last night. Well, that and Doctor Jamie and his annoying change of heart. Ugh. I nod and take a sip of tea.

Grandma wanders back over to her chair, straightens her skirt and sits back down. 'Then tonight, it is time for your first kiss with him.'

I splutter out my tea. 'I have to kiss him tonight? But the guides say I'm not supposed to kiss him until date five.'

Grandma gives me an approving glance. 'You *have* been reading them! You're right, my guides do advise that. But we are in an unusually time-sensitive situation. And a first kiss is a powerful thing. It can do the job of ten dates when it comes to forming a bond with your intended.'

At the mere thought of kissing Leo Frost, my cheeks burn up and my neck itches.

I do not like Leo Frost.

Spotting my blush, Grandma smiles a little. 'Oh, Jessica, I know a first kiss is a lot of pressure, but don't worry. I will teach you how it is done.'

I sputter out my tea a second time. 'Er . . . what?'

Grandma dashes over to her TV cabinet and opens up the glass doors, selecting a bundle of videotapes from her collection, including *Gone with the Wind*, *Breakfast at Tiffany's* and *From Here to Eternity*.

She taps the old plastic case of one of the films. 'Everything you need to know is in here.'

UNTITLED

Rose Beam's Diary
22nd June 1985

Thom showed up for dinner forty-five minutes late and with a black eye. I almost turned him away at the door, but Dad came through and saw he was here. I didn't get much chance to ask what had happened before Mum came bustling out to take his coat, but from what I gather he owed someone some money and was late with the payment, so they beat him up. It's fricking barbaric, the way some people behave. Seeing his beautiful face interrupted made me feel sick to my stomach. Mum and Dad studiously ignored the bruised eye, and for once I felt proud of their faultless manners. And although the Beef Wellington was a bit cold (I didn't mind – I've been so queasy with nerves these past days), all in all, lunch was pleasant. Dad asked lots of questions about Thom, what his father did, what his plans for the future are. Nothing they haven't asked Nigel flippin' Pemberton. Thom did his best, and I'm certain he charmed Mother with his outlandish tales of the theatre. How could he not? He's the most charming person in the world, and clever with it. Later on, Thom went for drinks in Dad's study while Mum and I did the dishes.

After Thom left, I was all giddy and excitable and asked Mum and Dad what they thought of him. Dad said he seemed like a pleasant chap and Mum said he was very handsome, but she said it with a very odd look on her face. Then they disappeared to bed without saying much else. They're not fawning over him yet. Yet! But there's time to convince them! At least they've stopped going on about stupid Pemberton. Hurrah!

CHAPTER TWENTY-EIGHT

Ladies, there is nothing in the world quite like the first kiss of a new romance. It is a crucial moment in a burgeoning relationship and, if done correctly, can decide your entire future together. Prepare your lips with a soft balm the evening before the intended kiss. Be passionate, but respectful. French kissing or nibbling is not advised at this stage.

***Matilda Beam's Guide to Love and Romance*, 1955**

By the time I meet Leo that evening, my head is full of romance and kissing and Burt Lancaster, who was actually really mega hot in his prime. I didn't even get chance to sneak up to the attic to search for any Mum clues because the entire freaking day was filled with Grandma's favourite sappy romance movies, pausing and rewinding and replaying the moment that the hero and heroine kiss so that I could learn how it's done. It was ridiculous. I am the *queen* of kissing. I have probably done more kissing than anyone else in all of London. And even if I wasn't an expert kisser, people kiss loads differently nowadays. They don't *Hollywood Kiss*. They snog and grab arses and, you know, slip in a bit of tongue.

While I'm waiting outside Ladbroke Grove for Leo to arrive, my mind flits to Jamie. He tried to catch me on my way out of the house tonight. He dived out of the clinic door in his white doctor's coat, stethoscope dangling from one ear, and said in this unusual anguished sort of voice, 'Jess, we need to talk.'

But I pretended I didn't hear him and legged it past and out onto the street, where I ran and ran until I reached the Tube station. Now is so not the time to deal with Jamie and his misapprehension about what 'casual shag' means. Especially not now that I have to speed up the project so that Grandma doesn't get turfed out of her home.

I smell Leo before I see him. The scent of ginger and rosewood mixed with freshly laundered cotton.

Keep cool, Jess. Think of the women he trampled on before you. You are a warrior, remember.

'You look amazing,' Leo grins, shaking his head slightly as if he can't believe his eyes.

Tonight I'm wearing a dress that I think has been inspired by a sailor. It's a white shift dress with a pleated skirt, gold buttons and a blue anchor-patterned scarf tied round the collar, which accentuates my ridiculously sticky-out boobs. My hair has been gathered up into a white ribbon-tied ponytail that swings and bounces chirpily as I move. And, on account of it being the hottest day of the year so far and the fact that I must not, under any circumstance, catch any semblance of a tan, Grandma has insisted I use her white antique lace parasol to shield myself from the scorching rays. A fucking parasol. A member of the public has absolutely *got* to point and laugh at me tonight.

If they don't then something very wrong is going on in this world.

Leo doesn't even raise an eyebrow at the dorky parasol. He probably thinks it's part of my 'alternative' style.

'Hi.' I give a simpering wave and try not to notice that he's wearing a faded Van Halen T-shirt beneath the sharp navy blazer. Leo Frost likes Van Halen too? I assumed he'd be into gentle piano jazz or Savage Garden or some crap.

I do not like Leo Frost. I don't. I don't.

'Where are we going?' I ask pleasantly as we walk together down Lancaster Road.

'There's a showing of *Grease* 2 on at the Electric Cinema,' Leo informs me. 'That's where we're going. I know it's a bit niche, but I always thought it was a far superior film to *Grease 1*. And it's a really cool cinema.'

Must. Remain. Ladylike.

Grease 2 is only in my all-time top list of favourite films. I cannot believe he's taking me to a showing of *Grease Fucking* 2.

'I love 80s films,' I say, marvelling at how much better this is going to be than a boring old dinner, and then feeling confused that I'm so excited about this date.

'80s films are the best films,' Leo agrees as we walk down Portobello Road. 'I have this huge collection of DVDs.' He pulls an over-the-top cocky face. 'I'm actually a bit of an expert, you know.'

'Oh *really*. Have you seen *The Breakfast Club*?' I ask.

'Standard.'

'*Better Off Dead*?'

'That film made me take up skiing.'

'OK . . .' I narrow my eyes. 'You can't possibly have watched . . . *Teen Witch*.'

'*Au contraire*.' He rubs his hands together. 'Check it

out.' And then, to my utter surprise, Leo Frost starts to do the horrendously painful 'Top That' rap from *Teen Witch*, complete with ridiculous dance moves.

'I'm hot, and you're not, but if you wanna hang with me, I'll give you one shot, top that!'

Oh my God. What is he doing? He looks like an absolute loser!

But it's really, really funny.

I laugh out loud as Leo raps super enthusiastically. Members of the general public cross the street to avoid him and a student starts filming him on her phone. I laugh so hard that I feel like my corset's going to burst. Leo notices me clutched over with laughter and a flicker of pride flits over his face. Then he makes his moves even more hammy and outrageous.

I try hard to collect myself, to stop laughing and hold on to what Valentina said this morning, to be a warrior, to think about all the women Leo fooled before me. But the more he raps and dances and completely embarrasses himself in the pursuit of making me laugh, the more her warning sort of fades away.

* * *

Leo snuggles up to me in one of the Electric Cinema's back-row sofas. At first I feel awkward sitting so close to him, the lengths of our bodies squished up against one another, but with one of my favourite films playing and Leo's arm slung round my shoulder, I eventually relax into it. During 'Cool Rider', Leo runs his hand over my thigh, sparking off some very particular feelings in my lady business.

I do not like Leo Frost. I do not.

I grab hold of his hand tightly so that at least I know

where it is, but then he moves his thumb across my palm in a very suggestive way and that feels awesome too.

I do not fucking like Leo Frost.

I spend the rest of the film twitchy and on edge about the fact that I'm squashed up next to Leo in the dark, and nervous about the moment when I have to kiss him and the worrying suspicion that I might actually like it.

* * *

When the end credits roll, I jump up from the cinema sofa in relief. Leo suggests we take a pleasant stroll through nearby Holland Park, and I agree wholeheartedly. A nice boring walk in the daylight. Much safer than a cosy, low-lit cinema.

On the way to the park, Leo dives into a nearby off-licence, where he picks up a bottle of Chianti and a tube of plastic cups. The sun is still quite high in the sky, and so I flip open my parasol and twirl it around as we wander into the park's entrance. I spot a family of squirrels darting about near a huge oak tree, and a baby one scrambling up the tree with a nut so big that it keeps dropping it. We laugh, take the mick out of the squirrel and mosey past the young families and couples enjoying the last dregs of the day's sunshine.

'So,' Leo says brightly as we walk side by side down a tree-lined path. 'Tell me more things about you, Lucille.'

Fuck! With everything that happened with Jamie last night, and Grandma being upset today, I totally forgot to ask about what my fake job should be. Shit. I can't fudge this again!

Think, Jess. What the chuff would a well-to-do girl from Kensington with impeccable manners and enough time to wear a hairstyle that takes over two and a half hours to prepare do for a job?

'I'm . . . a socialite!' I blurt out.

Why? Why didn't I just think on it a little longer. Fucking *socialite*?

'Gosh, really?' Leo raises his eyebrows sharply in astonishment. 'I haven't heard of the Darling family.'

Shit. He *knows* all the socialites in London. They're probably all his mates. He knows I'm not one of them.

'Oh, the Darlings are based in Lancashire,' I say as confidently as I can. 'Farmers, you know. I—'

'Farmers? My best friend Alistair is in farming! What kind of farming?'

'. . . Cows?'

'Alistair breeds cows! Sadly, he's just had to put his favourite one out to pasture. She was getting a bit old.'

Hmm. Something about that rings a bell. The thing Leo said about 'getting rid of a fat old cow' at the funfair.

'Was the cow fat too?' I ask.

'Yes, actually! How did you know?'

'Oh, um, it's common.'

Oh my God. Leo was not being sexist at the funfair. He was talking to his friend about an *actual* old fat cow. I peer at him, eyes narrowed.

'So what do you enjoy doing with your time, Lucille?' he asks.

'Oh, well, I like to read,' I reply. Which is true. 'And . . .

Dancing, pear cider, copping off, rock concerts, Pot Noodles, stand-up comedy, sexy times, Netflix, partying like a champ . . .

I run through my list of favourite things, but none of my real hobbies are very socialitey at all. What the hell do socialites like to do? I squint and search my brain for ideas.

And then I get a vision of the end pages in one of Summer's celebrity tat magazines. Socialites are always hanging out at fancy events for charity.

'I'm . . . a philanthropist.'

Leo stops mid-walk and gives me an astounded look. 'Wow. I had no idea. That's fantastic.'

'Yes,' I say nobly. Leo is mega impressed by my good grace, my selflessness. 'I'm *passionate* about charities.'

'What charities do you aid?' He takes hold of my hand and swings it as we walk past a young family having a picnic.

'Uh . . . um . . .' My brain scrambles frantically for an idea. My brain is shit. 'Er . . . well . . . er . . . squirrels,' I say slowly, nodding in a meaningful way.

Cockwaffle. Of all the amazing charities I could have said, why the fuck did I make one up. *About squirrels.* Stupid squirrel family that I thought was so cute before. I look backwards and throw the squirrels my withering glance. They are whizzing up a tree trunk and don't even notice.

'Squirrels?' Leo repeats with the raise of a ginger eyebrow.

'Oh yes,' I say fervently, a vague feeling of panic beginning to circle my chest. I have no blummin' clue where I'm going with this. 'I, um, I think squirrels are very important to . . . er . . . to this life. People think they're cute and that's all there is to it. But squirrels . . . um . . . they don't always have it easy.'

What am I saying?

'No?' Leo asks with a great deal of interest. 'Why not?'

'Well, squirrels need nuts, but . . . in the winter there's too much snow and they can't find the nuts. Our charity . . .

well, we distribute bags of nuts so that the squirrels don't go without.'

'What is your charity called? I'll make a donation.'

'Thank you!' I breathe. 'It's called . . . well . . . it's called, erm . . . Squirrel's . . . Nut . . . Sacks? Um, Squirrel's Nut Sacks.'

I look across to Leo and see that he is politely stifling a laugh. I act nonchalant.

Fucking hell, why is my mind so disgusting. Why is nut sack the first nut-related thing that comes into my mind? I am so gross.

'I must say, it sounds very niche,' Leo says with an amused chuckle. 'I had no clue that anything like that existed, but I suppose squirrels need advocates like any other woodland creature.'

'They really do. It's an issue very close to my heart.'

Leo gives me a sidelong smile. 'You certainly are one of a kind, Lucille Darling.'

I grin faux shyly and twirl my parasol some more. And then, out of nowhere, Leo properly yanks me behind a big cherry tree. What is he doing? He pulls me close to him and stands very still. Is this it? Are we going to kiss now? Did my passion for squirrel welfare get him hot?

My heart starts to hammer in my chest. What is it playing at? I look up at Leo to see if he's going to kiss me, but he's peeking out behind the tree, an absolutely mortified look on his aristocratic face.

Frowning, I peep round the tree too and see a tall, statuesque woman with gorgeously highlighted blonde hair jogging down the path in designer sportswear with a cute little Yorkshire Terrier attached to a lead.

Leo moves us further round the tree and out of sight as

the woman jogs past. When he spots her face, his expression of terror melts away.

'Who's that?'

Leo gives me a grimace. 'It's actually no one. I thought it was an ex, but I was mistaken.'

Ah. He thought it was an ex. No wonder he wants to hide. Did he think she was one of the many women he has fucked over? Chuh. And there I was getting all wibbly about the prospect of a kiss. I mentally punch myself in the face.

'Oh,' I say casually. 'Why did you hide?'

Leo runs a hand over his stubble. 'Yeah, that was really embarrassing of me, wasn't it? Sorry about that. I . . .' He trails off, looking uncomfortable.

'You can tell me,' I purr. Let's see him wriggle out of this one. 'You can tell me anything. Shall we sit down?'

I point to a nearby wooden bench. We head over to it and plonk down. Leo opens up the wine and pours out two paper cups.

'I thought it was Katie, my ex-fiancée, ' he says eventually, watching as she jogs off out of sight. 'I *really* didn't want to her to spot me.'

Huh?

'You were *engaged*?'

That juicy titbit was not on Google. And Valentina definitely didn't mention it.

Leo takes a large gulp of his wine. 'A long time ago.'

I look up at him curiously. 'Why didn't you get married?'

He inhales long and low.

'I . . . well, I actually caught her fooling around with my father.'

What the hell? Ew. That is a concept so gross that I

want to swear out loud, but I have to keep up the soothing voice.

'Oh dear,' I gasp. 'That's horrible! Why on earth would they do *that*? Sorry, that's very nosy of me. You don't have to tell me if you don't want to.'

'I don't mind,' he says. 'It's pretty mental, isn't it?'

'Um, yes. Pretty mental,' I agree, wide-eyed with horror.

'It happened years ago – the summer after I'd left university,' Leo explains, taking another gulp of his drink. 'I had this ridiculous idea that I was going to travel Europe, try to become an artist on my own dime without the help of family money.' He rolls his eyes and laughs mirthlessly. 'Katie and I had been dating for about a year and she wanted me to join Dad's company – she had her heart set on a very particular sort of lifestyle and thought me being a Frost would afford her that. When she realized that I was going to focus on art, intended to live by simple means, she completely lost interest in me. Thought she'd have a crack at my dad instead.'

'But why would he . . .'

'My father is many great things, but moral is not one of them.'

I think of the way Rufus Frost looked at me when we met at Leo's office. Barf.

'I caught the pair of them drunkenly pawing each other in the downstairs bathroom during a family barbecue,' Leo explains, his voice low. 'The two people in the world who I thought had my back lied to me. I had to forgive my father – I've not exactly got an abundance of family to pick and choose from – but we've never *quite* recovered from it.'

'That is so, so rubbish,' I say, taking the bottle of wine and topping up our cups. No wonder he just freaked out.

Leo's pale face flushes crimson, the frown between his

eyebrows deepening. 'Apologies, Luce. I didn't expect that to happen. This grimness is not what I had in mind for today.'

'God, don't apologize.' I lean back against the bench. 'It must have been a relief to go travelling after all that.'

'I didn't go in the end. After everything that had happened, such a romantic notion suddenly seemed idiotic and childish.'

I nod thoughtfully. 'So . . . have you had many girlfriends since Katie?'

Leo shakes his head and drains his drink. 'Not really.'

'No?'

'I mean, I've dated women. Lots of them. So many, in fact, that I'm painted as some sort of womanizer in the press.' He pauses and gives me a wry smile. 'I don't know if I should be telling you this – not exactly helping my cause, am I?'

I do my Lucille giggle. 'I like that you're being honest with me. So . . . *are* you a womanizer?'

He shrugs. 'I hate that word. But honestly? Yes, I was. I was a bit of a dickhead for a while, actually. Since Katie, I've had this issue that every woman I meet has an ulterior motive. Whether it's my family money, or this ridiculous notoriety of being a 'playboy', or the column inches and being seen in the right places. God, that sounds arrogant, doesn't it?' He pulls a face. 'What I mean is that it's been easier to live up to the press and become this caricature of myself rather than to open myself up to another situation like Katie.'

'You haven't seemed like a caricature to me,' I say honestly.

Leo gives me a warm smile which completely softens his aloof features. He moves closer to me on the bench and, up close, I notice that there's a light sprinkle of freckles dusted across his patrician nose. Cute. My stomach dips.

'That's because you're different, Lucille.' He takes my paper cup from my hand and puts it, with his, on the twig-covered ground beside us. He leans sideways against the bench and pulls me towards him. 'You knew nothing about me when we met at the funfair,' he continues, his voice husky. 'You had no idea who I was. No expectations or motives.'

I swallow guiltily. He hasn't a freaking clue.

It occurs to me that the reason for Leo's arrogance, his past behaviour is not as simple as him just being a massive twat. It's more complex than that. He has this history, this awful thing that happened to him, that hardened him, made him push people away. I get it. Not that it's forgivable, but maybe if Valentina knew this she'd understand it more, feel less angry at him, understand why he acted the way he did.

'I feel like I can be myself with you,' Leo murmurs, stroking a finger up my cheek. 'Like I can share the real me. And I haven't felt like that for so long.' He tucks a strand of hair behind my ear. And then, cradling my head in his other hand, he leans in and, ever so softly, plants a kiss on my lips.

As his lips make contact with mine, my eyes widen in shock.

Oh.

Leo presses my body to his and runs his hand across my lower back as the kiss deepens.

Oh no.

A sigh of pleasure escapes me, and in response Leo pulls me even closer, kisses me harder. My stupid head starts to spin wildly, my idiot heart thuds out of time, and every dumb nerve ending in my body zings and fires. What the fuck is happening? I suspected I might like it when he kissed me but . . . not like *this*.

I run my hands up to the back of his neck, it feels warm and soft and vulnerable and strong beneath my fingertips.

Completely losing it, I cling onto Leo and he clings onto me.

This is how the men and women kissed in Grandma's movies.

Like they never wanted to let go.

And I think it might be the best kiss of my whole entire life.

I pull back and it takes me a few seconds to come to. Leo laughs out loud.

'Woah,' he says, like that might have been the best kiss of his whole entire life too.

Oh fuck.

I like Leo Frost.

UNTITLED

Rose Beam's Diary
9th July 1985

I'm pregnant.

Frankly, I'm bloody terrified. I don't know what to do. I've tried ringing Thom but there's been no answer. I went to his house after work today but nobody was in. I hope he's OK, especially after what he told me about those horrible brutes he owes money to. I can't think straight about this, I need to talk to someone. Hang on, Mum is calling me downstairs . . .

CHAPTER TWENTY-NINE

A chaste kiss in public is acceptable, anything more than that slips into the realm of 'heavy petting' and that sort of behaviour is highly uncouth.

***Matilda Beam's Guide to Love and Romance*, 1955**

Leo and I make out on the bench for a very hot and steamy twenty minutes, and it is *so* good that I completely forget where I am, who I'm with and what I'm supposed to be doing. Or not be doing, as the case may be. A grumpy park keeper interrupts to inform us that there has been a complaint from a young family passing by and that we should not be fornicating like this in a public place. Giggling like idiots, we leave the bench and carry on walking round the park. For the whole rest of the way around, we chat about anything and everything, and every five minutes we look at each other and burst into wild laughter for no apparent reason. Like we can't quite believe how good we are at kissing one another. At how amazing that felt. My adrenalin is pumping. He won't let go of my hand. This is ridiculous. I am ridiculous. But . . . the way his body just felt to my body. It wasn't simple randiness in the usual way when I fancy someone. It was *kablam*!

When Leo pushes me up against a sycamore tree for another round of kissing, I participate willingly. I care about nothing else other than how excellent it feels – like I'm melting into a puddle of warm, buttery awesomeness

Leo Frost. Artist. Thinker. Man. Jess melter.

'Oh, Lucille,' he groans, nuzzling my neck.

My eyes fly open.

I jump away from the kiss.

Lucille.

Lucille.

This is not real.

It's fake.

Leo thinks he's kissing someone entirely different. He's not kissing me like that. He's kissing Lucille.

I mentally shake myself. I have to get a fucking grip, and fast.

'Lucille, what's wrong?' Leo says, his eyes flashing with concern as I back away from him.

'I . . . I need to get home. I'm running late,' I mutter, nodding quickly as I scan the park for the nearest exit. 'It's time to go now. I have to get my, er, my beauty sleep.'

Leo chuckles. 'Oh no, is that like *I need to wash my hair?*'

I laugh too, but it comes out as a bit manic.

Leo takes hold of my hand again. 'We could go back to my place?' He gives me a wolfish grin.

My vagina says yes. YES.

'No!' I yell. 'I really do have to go or I'll . . . be late.'

'Late for what?'

'Er, work. Yes. I have lots of work to do . . . for my charity. For the squirrels. Urgent squirrel business. Bye. Bye now!'

And before he can convince me to stay with another one of those other-worldly, mind-fuck kisses, I spin round, tuck Grandma's parasol under my armpit and race off out of the park.

* * *

In desperate need of cooling off, I decide to jog back home to Bonham Square. It's not easy in these high heels and I keep tripping up as I go. God knows what I look like, trussed up in this weird sailor dress with my pointy boobs, stumbling through the fanciest streets of London holding an antique lace parasol and angrily muttering 'fuck . . . fuck . . . fuck . . . balls . . . fuck' to myself every few steps.

My head is in a massive mess. A twisty whirl of confusion. What is going on? All my life I've been very, very careful not to get too giddy about a bloke. God knows, Mum's warnings about letting people get too close to hurt you scared me off for life. I thought I was way smarter than that.

But I'm not.

I'm an idiot. A fool. A sucker. A chump. An idiot fool sucker chump.

I've been so convinced that Leo Frost is a turd, and was so focused on behaving like a made-up person around him, that the real me has been left defenceless, and now I think I've got . . . feelings.

Feelings. Urgh. I can feel them, these feelings. Whizzing around my insides and making me feel excited and scared and worried and super horny and like there might be something to look forward to, maybe.

But it's a lie. There isn't anything to look forward to here. The only reason Leo has *got* feelings for me is because he thinks I'm this 'alternative' vintage posho who likes poems and Renaissance art and is super fascinated and amazed by every single blummin' thing he says and does.

Even so, he's surprised me and . . . I *like* him.

But I can't. Not now. Not when I've spent my whole life avoiding this very situation.

I think about Mum. About what she told me on the day I left for university, just six months before she . . . well. She stood on the doorstep of our house, eyes swimming with tears, and put her hands firmly on my shoulders.

Never give your heart away, my darling. If you lose it, you might not get it back, and then there's nothing left. Don't be foolish like your mum. Trust me.

I clench my fists tightly as I hurry towards Grandma's house.

This is dangerous. These *feelings* are dangerous.

Ugh, I acted like a sappy fool back in that park. I didn't even recognize myself, getting all melty like that. What was I thinking? I *wasn't* thinking. I can't risk it. I can't risk ending up like Mum.

I inhale sharply and blow out steadily in quick succession, trying to focus.

There's only one thing for it.

I can't see Leo Frost again.

I have to call off the project.

* * *

I'm completely ready to storm into Bonham Square and

demand to Grandma and Peach that the project is over. That *How to Catch A Man Like It's 1955* is simply no longer a possibility, that there have been creative differences, that they are just going to have to figure out their problems without me, that everything is not my responsibility, and why all of a sudden is it supposed to be my responsibility?

When I get to the drawing room, the door is slightly open. Peach and Grandma are hanging out on the sofa watching *Scott & Bailey* on the telly.

Grandma is sipping from a little tumbler of sherry and fidgeting with her blouse collar. Peach – Mr Belding sprawled comfortably on her lap – keeps peeking towards the window, probably wondering when her friend will return. Grandma gasps, riveted, as Suranne Jones nicks a goateed criminal. Peach giggles at Grandma's reaction and tickles Mr Belding's belly.

This is their life.

With a lurch of the stomach, I get a sudden vision of Grandma clutching onto the railings of Bonham Square as burly bailiffs ransack the place, kicking her out onto the street. Then I picture Peach, interviewing for a room-mate position at some rough, crowded, flatshare in Peckham, and the amount of anxiety that living with new strangers would cause her.

My shoulders slump as I come to a stark realization.

I think I have feelings for *these* people too.

I smack my own head. *What* is going on? I'm turning into a right loser.

I watch Grandma and Peach watching the telly. Two weeks ago these people were complete randomers to me. And now . . .

Oh, who am I kidding? I *can't* bloody call off the

project. I can't let them down. Especially not because I'm scared of how I feel about a boy I barely know. I rub the back of my neck and take a deep breath.

Dammit.

Right. Change of plan. The only thing I can do in this horrid situation is to try and ignore these ridiculous feelings for Leo sodding Frost. To keep my head down, work super hard on the project *as* Lucille, get Leo to declare his love for me as quickly as is humanly possible, write those stupid first twenty thousand words, get this book deal, write the rest of the book, save the world and *then* do one. Maybe to the Caribbean. Then I will send Leo a letter of apology for tricking him for cash and my heart will be safe and I'll live happily ever after, alone on a beach.

I sigh to myself, and at the sound of it, Peach notices me in the doorway. She jumps up from her chair in excitement. 'Jess!' she says happily, as if I've been stranded on a desert island for a month. Grandma gives me a huge smile. Never before in my life have two people been so genuinely pleased to see me.

'Hello, dear,' Grandma says. 'How did it go?'

'Did you kiss him?' Peach asks.

I kick off the high heels and plop into Grandma's blue chair. 'I did.'

Grandma presses her hands to her cheeks. 'Oh!'

'What was it like?' Peach says eagerly.

It changed everything.

'Erm . . .'

I can't tell them the truth about that kiss. They can't know how complicated it has made stuff, how ridiculous I am, how I've totally let the side down by thinking that Leo Frost's kiss was possibly the best kiss I'll ever have, that I reckon under his clothes he has a body to rival Ryan

Gosling's in *Crazy, Stupid, Love*, that he loves *Grease* 2 and knows all the songs even better than I do, that he got me a sick bag and knows exactly what it feels like to lose your mum, and rapped in public to make me laugh, and is brilliant at drawing, and those eyes, and he smells so delicious, totally grown-up, like rosewood.

'. . . smells,' I say a tad dreamily, wandering off into my reverie.

'Does he?' Peach says with interest. 'He smells?'

'Oh.' I come back to earth instantly. 'What? Um . . . Yep. He . . . smells disgusting. He reeks. Like a rubbish tip.'

Grandma blinks. 'He looks clean on all the googly pictures we saw.'

'Well, of course that's what he wants you to think,' I say with a cocky look that belies my wibbling insides.

I have no clue what I'm talking about. I'm so messed up right now. Stupid Leo and his stupid game-changing mouth.

'Gosh,' Grandma says, wrinkling her nose. 'I suppose you never really know about a person, do you?'

'Nope,' I say. 'Don't worry about it. I'll, er, slip him a Trebor mint next time. Spritz him with deodorant when his head's turned.'

'When is the next time?' Peach asks.

As if on cue, my phone rings. It's him. My hands shake a little and I drop the phone onto the rug. *I'm nervous.* What a loser. Peach gives me a suspicious look. 'Answer it, Jess.'

I nod slowly, pick up the phone and press the loudspeaker icon. 'Hello,' I say evenly.

'You're not in bed yet? What about that beauty sleep?' Leo jokes.

'Oh, you,' I titter, as Lucille as can be.

'I just wanted to call and tell you that I had a really, really great time today, Lucille. Really bloody great.'

Grandma presses a hand to her chest, while Peach does a big thumbs-up.

'Me too,' I choke out.

'You darted off so quickly, I didn't get chance to ask you . . .'

'Ask me what?'

'Well, the thing is, it's the London Advertising Association ball on Saturday, and I was hoping you'd come with me, as my date.'

At the mention of a ball, Grandma gasps in delight, shoots up from her chair, opens up the liquor cabinet, takes out another two glasses and fills them up with sherry. When I've agreed to attend the ball and the call is finished, she hands Peach and me a glass each.

'I think somebody is smitten!' she exclaims excitedly.

'Who? What?' I hiss. 'Who now?'

'Mr Frost,' Grandma says, giving me an odd look. 'Sounds like the scoundrel is smitten with you. Or with Lucille, as the case may be.'

'Oh. Yeah. Definitely.'

'We are *exactly* on track. You are an absolute marvel, Jess. I must admit, I had my doubts, but you have been an excellent student.' Her eyes fill up. 'I'm so proud of you.'

She's proud of me.

Nobody has ever said that to me before.

Grandma reaches over and pulls me into a hug. She gives me a little squeeze and I expect the uncomfortable itch that usually occurs at public emotion to make its way over my body.

But, to my surprise, it doesn't come.

CHAPTER THIRTY

Avoid first date awkwardness by embarking on a double date. Not only is it fun to dine out with chums, the conversation is sure to never run dry!

***Matilda Beam's Guide to Love and Romance*, 1955**

I'm having a freaky dream – about a ghost wearing a corset, having an arranged marriage with Michael Carrington from *Grease 2* – when I'm woken by Peach shaking my shoulder. Her big farm-girl hands are much stronger and more aggressive than I think she realizes. I push her off before she dislocates something.

'Ow! Jeez, Peach,' I mumble, rubbing my sleep-crusty eyes. 'This better be an emergency.'

'Gavin's here!' she breathes.

'Huh? Gavin?'

'The postman,' she reminds me, with just a touch of exasperation. 'He brought a package that needs a signature.

I didn't order anything, and I know Matilda didn't. Was this your work?'

I grin innocently because it *was* me. I knew she'd put it off, so I ordered a little something online that would need signing for.

'Is it a big package?' I say drowsily. 'A big, hard package?'

Peach frowns. 'Hush. You said you would come and stand by me when I asked him out. For support. Come on!'

I sit up in the bed.' Er . . . can I at least get dressed?' I indicate my sleep-hair and old AC/DC tour T-shirt-slash-nightie.

'No, *now*, you promised.' She throws me what I think is her version of a withering glance. It's a slight, sweet, pursing of the lips. 'Lady P needs you,' she says solemnly.

Gad.

I down some water from the glass at the side of the bed, pull on my dressing gown and reluctantly trudge downstairs behind an extremely fidgety Peach.

We get to the front door, and sure enough, there is Gavin the postman in his shorts, holding a small parcel in his hands.

'He's got a tiny package,' I whisper to Peach.

'Quit it,' she hisses back, turning to Gavin with an overly bright smile. She looks weird. 'Hiiiii, Gavin. H-hii.'

'Um, hi.' He raises a curious eyebrow at my presence.

'Yo,' I wave sleepily. Don't mind me!' Taking the small oblong box off him, I sign the little electronic box thingy. We all look silently at each other for a few seconds.

I nudge Peach with my shoulder and give her an encouraging look.

'Ah . . . yeah, Gavin, I was . . . I was . . .' she starts, her full cheeks turning a shade of deep ruby red. 'I . . .'

'Peach. W-would you . . .' Gavin begins, trailing off with a look of pure embarrassment. 'Uh . . .'

Oh no.

We stand there for another thirty seconds while the pair of them make increasingly fumbled attempts to ask each other out. *This* is why alcohol was invented.

Peach turns to me with an embarrassed grimace, her shoulders hunching right back up to her ears.

It's time to invoke my fourteen-year-old self.

'Gavin. This is my beautiful friend Peach.' I indicate Peach. 'Do you wanna go out with her?'

Gavin laughs nervously and furiously nods his head, his little red baseball cap wobbling a bit.

'And Peach, do you want to go out with Gavin?'

'Y-yes.' Peach beams.

'Awesome.' I nod firmly, grabbing a pen from the side table. 'Gavin, write your number on here.' I hand him the package.

He scrawls down his number with slightly shaking hands.

'I . . . I . . . I'll call you,' Peach eventually gets out, her voice as squeaky as it's ever been.

'Cool,' Gavin replies, smiling shyly at Peach. 'See you. Bye, Peach.'

'Bye Gavin!'

'Er . . . bye,' I say pointedly as he races off back down the stairs. He doesn't look back, just hurries off out of the building. I tut. What am I, a ghost?

When he's disappeared from sight, Peach whoops with relief.

'Phewee! I can't believe it, he said yes!'

'Well, course he did.' I wiggle my eyebrows. 'Looks like *someone's* gonna get laid!'

I'm winding her up, but she smiles dreamily in response.

'I can't wait!' She holds her hand up for a high-five, which I take up enthusiastically. 'I can't wait to get laid. Things are finally starting to happen for old Peach Carmichael!'

I stuff the unopened package in the hall dresser drawer along with the rest of the post, and after making a couple of brews, Peach and I wander out onto the drawing-room balcony, where we lean against the railings and look out over the perfectly manicured park opposite. It's another sweltering morning and the heat makes the distant skyline throb and flutter.

I gulp down my strong coffee, enjoying the zing of the caffeine coursing its way through my body, and tilt my face up to the sun.

'So where do you think you'll go on your first date with Gavin?' I ask her.

I wait for an answer, but it doesn't come

'Peach?' I open my eyes and glance over at her. She's staring over the balcony, her cup of coffee halfway to her mouth as if she's in a trance. 'Peach?' I repeat loudly. What's she doing? 'Earth to Peach!'

'A first date,' she says, a tremor in her voice.

'Huh?'

'I'm gonna have to go on a first date with Gavin. Alone.'

'Yeaahhhh . . . Wasn't that sort of the point of, you know, just asking him out . . .'

Her nostrils flare and she nods rapidly. 'Sure, but . . . I was so excited that he said yes, I didn't think of the reality of the situation. I'm *awful* on first dates, Jess. Terrible. I've only been on one of them in the past six years, and my hands shook so much that I accidentally knocked over the candle on the restaurant table and set fire to my date's menu. Then, at the end of the date, when we were supposed to kiss – ' she looks down at the floor, her chubby cheeks blazing – 'I broke wind real loudly and my date heard. I was so nervous. It was mortifying.'

I laugh out loud and then stop just as quickly when I realize that she's not kidding.

Panic-faced, Peach puts her mug on the balcony ledge and starts taking big gulps of air. Then she sinks to the floor, presses two fingers to her throat and starts counting under her breath.

'Are you OK?' I say, sitting down with her.

'My pulse is racing. Oh God. I can't do it. I have to cancel the date I just made with Gavin. It's not worth it. I don't *need* to have sex, do I? I can live just fine without it. It's probably not even that good anyway. I mean, how the fiddle can I do this? You just saw what happened out there. *You* had to talk *for* us! I'm not ready . . .'

'You are,' I say firmly. 'You're just having a teeny bit of a wobble. All dates are a bit awkward at first, and then you just sort of relax into it. Honestly, by the end of the night you won't even know why you were worried!' I gently take her hand away from where it's pressed against her neck. 'Calm down. You'll be ace.'

She looks up at me, wide-eyed. 'But I can't do it alone. You . . . you have to come with us, Jess.'

'What? On your date? No!'

'Yeah. I feel better when you're there.'

I grimace. 'Wouldn't that be a bit . . . third wheel.'

'No, no. I just need a buffer. You *have* to come. I reckon I'll mess everything up on my own.' She starts flapping her hands at her face as if to cool herself down – she's having a full-on panic. 'Say you'll come with me, Jess. I might never get this chance again! Please? Please!'

Oh God, she's totally losing her nerve. She can't back out now.

'Look.' I quickly pat her shoulder. 'Why don't you, I don't know, why don't you come to the ball? I'll see if Leo can get a couple of extra tickets. That way, you have me there as a buffer, but it'll be a less awkward group situation.'

She swallows hard, her breathing starting to slow down. 'OK . . . That would work. Are . . . are you sure?'

No. I'm not. But I don't know how long I'll be hanging around here for, and if she chickens out on Gavin now, she might never get to have sex, ever. I can't be responsible for that. I wouldn't be able to live with myself.

'Yeah, it's no worry,' I assure her brightly. 'It'll be nice and busy and much easier than a one-on-one dinner-date with the guy.'

Peach takes a deep breath and gives me a small, shaky smile. 'Oh, I don't know what I'd do without you, Jess.' She grabs my hand and sandwiches it between both of hers. 'I'm so, so glad we met. Because of you, things are finally starting to get better.'

On the outside I cross my eyes at her in a 'don't be so soft' kind of way, but on the inside, for the third time in three days, I get a happy tingling feeling. I think this is what they call the warm fuzzies.

Jessica Beam, you need to get a grip.

* * *

Something terrible is happening. Since kissing Leo Frost, it's like the floodgates have been yanked open and all the mushy feelings have been coming thick and fast, like projectile spew, but even more gross. On Monday I let Grandma hug me again, and on Tuesday *I* hug *her*. I have many long conversations with Peach about her upcoming date with Gavin at the ball (Leo was totally cool about them joining us), and I actually listen to her anxieties about what they'll talk about and give her advice about sex, like, you know, a real friend would. If I wasn't already worried that my hard shell is softening too much, Grandma and Peach point out my slightly gooey mood at dinner on Wednesday night.

'Gosh, if I didn't know how much you despised Mr Frost, I'd almost believe you were a little giddy about him!' Grandma jokes breezily, to which I choke on a pea and splutter, 'No, *you* are,' before angrily stabbing my fork into the chicken breast.

All these untypical behaviours only reinforce the fact that I'm obviously in an increasingly dangerous situation here. Which makes it all the more vital that I keep my head down, get *How to Catch a Man Like It's 1955* over and done with as quickly as I can, and leave this place before the *feelings* get any worse. Because if I let things fester I'll have no armour left at all, and before I know it I'll become one of those people who cry over John Lewis ads or develop an interest in unicorn-related paraphernalia, or fall for a man who knocks you up, then shatters your heart, leaving you depressed for the rest of your life until you simply can't deal with it any more . . .

So in the days running up to Saturday and the London Advertising Association Awards ball, I try my absolute best to focus and be the very model of a perfect vintage woman. I revise the Good Woman tips, use Pond's cold cream on my face every single night, avoid Jamie downstairs like a criminal avoiding capture – though I'm on my bedroom balcony at Thursday lunchtime when I spot him outside the clinic with a pretty girl who I assume to be Kiko, and that makes me feel a bit weirded out – I barely go running at all, practise *waltzing* with Grandma, and I even manage to write ten thousand words of the book. When I send them to Valentina she responds with an email that simply says:

I smell a bestseller.

Which I show to Grandma, who, as expected, bursts into noisy, happy tears.

So everything is going exactly according to plan. And soon I'll be done with all of this, loaded, and safely on a plane to somewhere lovely and warm and exotic and far away.

On my own.

Which is definitely for the best.

Definitely.

* * *

All week long, Grandma busies herself tailoring one of her old ball dresses for me to wear on Saturday. She does this super privately, in the manner of Dexter preparing a kill room. Apparently she 'wants it to be a lovely surprise for me'. As if I could ever get giddy over something as sappy as a freaking ball dress.

Except that, to my dismay, I do.

On the afternoon of the LAAA ball, I'm chilling on the bed, intermittently playing bejewelled blitz, writing words for the book and Googling 'help – how to stop sudden and unwanted mushy feelings seeping in?' when Grandma knocks on my bedroom door.

'You may enter!' I call out, speedily deleting my search history and closing the lid of my laptop.

Grandma bustles in, holding a cream padded clothes

hanger that displays the most gorgeous piece of clothing I have ever seen. Even more beautiful than my sequinned 'Juicy' knickers. I think I actually gasp out loud at the sheer beauty of it.

The ball dress is palest ice blue, with a silk, strapless, boned bodice that flares out onto a layered tulle skirt, stopping at mid-calf. At the gathered waist there's an intricate band of silver lace, so subtly embroidered that you can't see it unless you're up close. It's fucking amazing.

I dart over and touch the silk bodice – it feels cold and smooth beneath my hands, like the jumpsuit I was going to wear to *The Beekeeper* launch. People like me don't get to wear dresses like this. People like me don't care about wearing dresses like this! But it's an incredible dress. The kind of dress Summer would fist-fight someone to get her hands on.

'It will look wonderful with the strawberry blonde of your hair,' Grandma beams. Then she glances at her watch. 'Which we should perhaps make a start on now. We haven't a great deal of time, and it *must* be perfect. Chop-chop.'

She carefully hangs the dress on the big wardrobe door and sashays downstairs to the kitchen where she has laid out all her rollers and brushes and setting lotions and potions and make-up like she's holding a vintage cosmetics jumble sale.

Tonight, Grandma has decided that I will wear my hair in thick, smooth waves with an extreme side parting à la Veronica Lake. While I idly watch Netflix on my iPhone, she hums Doris Day songs and spends ages rolling my hair up into huge rollers, setting it with the hairdryer, and smoothing it down with hair serum before spritzing on enough hairspray to hold it in place during an apocalypse. I avoid choking to death by lifting up my vest and using it to cover my mouth and nose. As Grandma paints on my make-up (black liquid-lined eyes, curled eyelashes and crimson lips), I try to concentrate on the task at hand and not what Leo might look like in a tux.

When my hair, make-up and nails are complete, Grandma helps me into the vintage girdle, corset, a strapless version of the bullet bra and then, eventually, the dress. I hurry back downstairs to the big mirror in the hall, Grandma trailing excitedly behind me.

'Fuck,' I whisper in response to my reflection.

On this occasion, Grandma pretends not to hear me curse. To be fair, if she swore she'd probably say the same thing right now.

Because I look unreal. The crystal blue of the dress looks crazy with my cream-pale skin and rust-gold-coloured hair. My make-up is flawless, my hair is even more so, my neck looks longer, my waist even smaller, there's not a false eyelash, patch of tan or pot noodle stain in sight.

I look like someone else entirely.

I *am* Lucille.

I think of Leo's reaction when he sees me and get an excitable flip in my gut.

Then I mentally mini-pinch myself. *This is fake. Must not get carried away. Keep focused.*

Peach gallops down the stairs.

'Oh, heck, Jess. You look like you're going to the Oscars.'

I spin round and laugh out loud in delight. Peach looks epic. Her usually frizzy dark blonde hair is all shiny tumbling curls, pinned up at the back with tiny jewelled clips. She's wearing a gorgeous midnight-blue taffeta ball-gown, a matching satin wrap draped round her shoulders. The colour of it looks amazing against her glowing pink skin.

'You look awesome,' I say to her. 'Gavin will be speechless.'

Peach's smile plunges into a frown. Shit. I forgot that Gavin being speechless is a very real possibility.

'I'm kidding!' I speedily correct myself. 'And anyway, even if things are a bit stilted, remember – I will be there to lubricate the wheels of conversation. Don't worry.'

'Promise?'

'Fo sho.' We fist-bump, at which Grandma gives us both a puzzled shake of her head.

Grandma fusses with my hair again, smoothing down any flyaway strands with her thin hands, and my mobile trills once to let us know that the town car Leo ordered to pick us up is waiting outside.

'Remember, Jessica,' Grandma says as we head to the front door. 'Tonight, you are representing Leo on his most important night of the year. You must be the very image of elegance. The woman every gentleman at the ball wants to be with, the woman that every other woman *longs* to know the secret of. How you conduct yourself tonight could make or break the entire project.'

I pull a face. 'Jeez. No pressure then.'

Grandma takes hold of my hand and gives it a squeeze. Her magnified eyes are, once again, teary with emotion. 'I believe in you, dear'

Ugh. Another warm and fuzzy fast approaching. I give her a swift kiss on the cheek. It leaves a crimson imprint, adding a shock of colour to her translucently pale skin.

'Thank you, G. Thanks for the belief. Cool. Awesome. OK.'

I quickly open the dresser drawer and grab the package that Gavin delivered the other day. I tear off the jiffy bag to reveal an oblong box wrapped in shiny navy giftpaper.

'What's that?' Grandma asks.

'Oh, um ... it's just a ... a mascara I bought. I'll open it on the way.' I stuff the package into my silver and pearl clutch. The end of the box pokes out of the top. Grandma frowns suspiciously. Ignoring her, I turn to Peach, who's clasping her evening bag, eyes wide with nervous terror about her first date with Gavin. Her first adult date ever.

'Let's do this thang,' I yell, though it comes out sounding a little weaker than I intend it to.

'Have fun!' Grandma calls, as if this is a real, genuine social event for us and not just part of our wicked plan.

When we're halfway down the stairs, Grandma leans out of the door.

'Wait! Wait!'

Peach and I spin round, wobbling on our heels. 'What is it? Have we forgotten something?'

Grandma looks down at her feet. 'Um, The Facial Book thing you like on the Internet?'

'Yeah?'

'How do I . . . locate that on the online computer machine?'

'You want to go on Facebook?'

Her lips wobble. 'I might.' She lifts her chin. 'I don't know yet.'

Peach and I look at each other in astonishment and laugh out loud. Loads of bizarre things have happened these past few weeks, but Matilda Beam social networking might just be the weirdest one yet.

I hastily issue Grandma instructions on how to access Facebook on the computer machine and hurry back down the stairs, through the lobby and outside.

Shitballs. Jamie's there. He's pacing up and down the

pavement in his doctor's coat, talking into his phone. Probably to Kiko.

When he spots us, he ends the call then drops his mobile, clumsily catching it just before it hits the floor.

'Hello, Doctor Abernathy!' Peach says brightly.

'Hullo!' he responds, shoving his phone into his trouser pocker. His eyes flicker towards me. He coughs. 'Hi, Jess.'

'Hey!' I give an awkward wave. This is weird. I've extra carefully avoided him all week. I have no clue what to say. Peach looks between the two of us curiously.

Jamie swallows hard. 'You're so beautiful,' he says eventually in a soft, low voice.

'Why, thank you!' Peach responds, beaming. She smooths down her taffeta skirt. 'You are too kind, Doctor.'

'We should probably go now!' I take Peach's hand and drag her out to the waiting car. 'Take care, Jamie! Bye!'

'Yes ... bye.'

I know Jamie watches us as we leave, but I don't look back.

CHAPTER THIRTY-ONE

Only one woman gets to be the belle of the ball. Make every effort to ensure that lady is you.

***Matilda Beam's Guide to Love and Romance*, 1955**

By the time we reach Christ Church in Spitalfields – where tonight's awards are being held – I'm freaking exhausted. Peach totally clammed up again when we picked up a very-cute-in-his tuxedo-but-clearly-shitting-himself Gavin from his flat in Hammersmith, and he wasn't much better either. They smiled nervously at each other in greeting and mumbled a bit before conversation completely halted and it got all kinds of awkward. Which I didn't particularly mind, but Peach was dying. In order to fill the silence and make it all a bit less uncomfy, I talked and talked the whole way here. As agreed earlier with Peach, I pretended to Gavin that Leo always referred to me by my middle name – Lucille – and that's what he should call me too, rather than Jess. Then I talked about the heatwave and how hot it's been and thank God for the car's air conditioning. Then, when conversation ran dry, I basically turned to commentating throughout the entire journey like some kind of glamorously dressed personal tour guide. 'So here, we pass a local McDonald's. Very busy indeed, as is to be expected on a Saturday evening.' Etcetera. Exhausting.

At the venue, we get out of the car, hand our tickets in at the entrance and make our way to the Nave as instructed by one of the very dapper stewards. When we enter the ball space, all three of us gasp in awe. What a room for a party! It's a converted church: the ceiling is sky-high and ornate. The room is bordered by swish oak panelling and thick, Tuscan columns, all uplit with pink and purple lighting. It's completely majestic and exciting. The place is already busy, and the atmosphere is throbbing with expectation; an excellent big band plays Ella Fitzgerald numbers at the front of the room, guests in fancy tuxes and luxurious ballgowns mill about the huge dance floor or chatter at one of the huge round tables that are topped with extravagantly colourful flower centrepieces, twinkling lights weaved in-between the leaves.

'Wow,' Peach breathes. 'I've never seen anything like it!'

'I know!' I look around in astonishment. 'They've seriously gone all out. My stomach flips with excitement against my will.

'Listen, guys, I'm going to go and find Leo. He said he was arriving with his work colleagues, so he must already be around here somewhere.'

Peach's eyes widen in horror at the prospect that I might be leaving her alone with Gavin so soon.

'Don't worry,' I assure her. 'You two go to the bar, and I'll find our table, OK?' Gavin takes a deep breath and musters every drop of courage he has within him to say, 'Come on, Peach, let me buy you a drink.'

Before they leave, I grab Peach by the arm and whisper in her ear, 'A shot of tequila will make things easier, OK! Loosen you both up a bit. You're ace, Lady P. Just chill out and pretend you're talking to me. Come and find me in a bit.'

Peach nods fervently and I wave her off as they rush over to the bar in search of a little liquid courage.

As I scan the room for Leo, my insides tilt and churn in anticipation of seeing him again. What if my resolve fades and I just dive in for another one of those kisses? What if he wants to make lurve to me tonight? How will I have the willpower to say no? Ugh. I need to get this bloody thing finished. I can't stand feeling so all over the place.

'Lucille!' Leo's familiar deep tones sound out from behind me.

I spin round elegantly to face him. Leo presses a hand to his chest as he takes me in. 'Fuck,' he whispers, leaning in to kiss me lightly on the cheek. 'You look incredible, Lucille. I knew you would, but this is something else. *You* are something else.'

I giggle shyly and to my horror it's not a completely fake giggle. So I'm basically a person who giggles now? Argh. I fix Lucille's enigmatic smile determinedly on my face and clear my throat. 'Gosh, you look rather wonderful yourself, Leo.'

I'm not lying. He's wearing a sharp black tuxedo with a crisp white shirt and black bowtie. His hair is styled more naturally than the super-perfect quiff, a bit mussed-up around the front. His eyes sparkle in a way that I'm sure is reserved for just me.

How did I think he was weird-looking when I first met him?

He's lovely-looking. Gorgeous-looking.

Hmm, I wonder what he looks like in the buff? I bet his willy is a really good one.

Argh. Danger-thoughts.

Must change the subject.

'This is quite an event isn't it?' I purr, indicating the extravagantly opulent room. My eyes widen in awe as I notice Daniel Craig stroll past us towards the bar as if it's completely normal that he's here with the non-famous folk.- 'Bond,' I squeak. Now there's someone who definitely looks good in the buff.

'Ah, it's just the brands showing off,' Leo chuckles, as if James Bond hasn't just breathed in the same air as us. But then, he *is* super used to hanging out in celebrity circles. 'They bring their famous spokespeople so it all looks more glamorous and important.'

At the back of the room I spot Benedict Cumberbatch – God, is there any event that guy doesn't attend? And ooh, there's Claudia Winkleman. I like her. I like her fringe.

Leo reaches into his inside pocket and pulls out a tiny grey velvet box. 'Not a sick bag this time,' he grins. I take the box from him, rub my thumb over the soft velvet and open it. Nestled inside is a tiny diamond and sapphire brooch in the shape of a Ferris wheel. It's unusual and lovely and exactly to my taste.

'Wow,' I gasp. 'You . . . you really shouldn't have.'

'I wanted to!' He lifts the brooch out of the box and carefully pins it onto my dress. 'Something to remind you of the night we met.'

'I love it,' I say truthfully, shame squelching around in

my belly at the fact that he's bought me this amazing present under entirely false pretences.

I reach into my clutch bag and hand Leo the package I brought with me.

'What's this?' he says, his eyes twinkling with surprise.

'You're not the only one who can bring gifts to a date, y'know.'

Bemused, Leo tears open the navy giftwrap and opens the lid of the oblong box, peering inside.

He laughs out loud. 'A paintbrush!'

'It's a good one. The website says it's fine-pointed and the tip is made of Kolinsky sable,' I mumble, embarrassed to find that I feel suddenly shy. Why did I bloody get him a paintbrush? It seemed like a cool, funny idea last week. Now, at a fancy ball, and him having just given me a diamond brooch, it feels all kinds of meaningful and romantic. I cough. 'I just thought you could, you know, paint some stuff.' I shrug casually. 'Do some art . . . things.'

Leo stares at the brush for a second, fingering the tip of it before pressing it to his chest. 'Thank you, Luce,' he says quietly, looking at me in an intense, serious sort of way that tickles my skin. Then he tucks the box into his inside pocket and leads me towards our table. As we make our way through the bustle, I notice that everyone's eyes are on me. Not in the way they were the night at *The Beekeeper* launch, like I was a subject for ridicule, but with interest, envy, lust, wonder. It's a weird sensation, and not an entirely pleasant one, either. I feel a bit like I'm on show, like I'm a doll to be admired. Like . . . *Felicity*.

But still, I'm here to do a job, so I do it; I smile and simper graciously as guest after guest says hello to Leo, congratulating him on his nomination, predicting that he's a shoe-in to win it, how they just looooove his Drive Alive ad . . .

Despite Leo making every genuine effort to include me in the conversations, it occurs to me that apart from an appreciative or envious glance or polite hello, no one is paying any real attention to me. No one asks me any questions about myself. I am, quite simply, arm candy.

We eventually make it past all the advertising suck-ups and reach our table. Leo introduces me to the people already sitting down.

'Lucille, this is Martin, our copy man. Martin has the most amazing Ferrari you've ever seen. I'll have to take you out for a ride in her soon. She runs like a dream.'

'Of course!' Martin says cheerfully.

I frown slightly as I get a flashback of Leo making a sexist comment at the fair, talking about giving someone curvy a ride before Martin took her home. Was he talking about a *car*? Man alive, I really have got the wrong end of the wrong stick about Leo Frost. I was so quick to judge him . . .

He introduces me to two more people from the senior team at Woolf Frost and their partners, who all seem nice and friendly, if a little formal. Then he reintroduces me to the fourth table-dweller – bloody Rufus Frost, the world's douchiest douchebag – who calls me Lucy and kisses my hand again with his gross old cigar-stinking mouth. Spew.

'Wait – where are your friends?' Leo asks. 'Are they still coming?'

I peer over towards the bar and spot Peach and Gavin deep in conversation. The tequila shot must have worked! Peach is laughing at something he's saying, her hand rubbing his forearm. Ha! I might just leave those too alone a little longer – they're clearly managing just fine without me.

'They're here – they must be in the crowd somewhere!' I say innocently. 'I'm sure they'll catch up with us later.'

We take our seats and Leo pops open one of the many bottles of vintage champagne that are sitting in huge buckets on each table. He pours everyone a glass and clears his throat to make a toast. But before he can get a word out, his dad interrupts, his exceedingly plummy tones blasting across the table like a foghorn.

'Here's to a win for Woolf Frost,' Rufus drawls, holding his glass up to the centre of the table.

'And Leo,' I add, before I can stop myself.

Oops. I didn't mean to blurt that. But something about his dad just winds me up big-time. Especially now I know how he betrayed his own son. Rufus Frost sneers a little and reluctantly agrees with my correction in a bored voice. 'Yes, of course . . . And to Leo.'

Leo gives me a pleased wink. 'Cheers, guys!'

'Cheers!'

I drink my champagne, the sweet buoyant bubbles lightly dancing on my tongue. To my surprise I don't entirely dislike the taste of it tonight.

I take another sip.

Am I . . . Am I starting to get a taste for vintage champagne? Shit, am I now part of the champagne conspiracy?

God, what is happening to me?

* * *

Perhaps I shouldn't have advised Peach that a tequila shot to loosen her and Postman Gavin up was a good idea. Because they clearly haven't limited themselves to just the one. Our table is having a very sensible conversation about the work of all the other nominees,when Peach finally leaves the bar, dragging Gavin over by the arm. I can tell just by looking at her that she's pissed – she can barely walk in a straight line and her blinks are lasting longer than usual. Shit.

'LUCILLE!' she calls with a totally hammy wink. 'There you are. And this must be Leeeeeooooo. Luscious Leo.'

Oh, Jesus. How many shots has she had? Gavin's cheeks are flushed and shiny, his bowtie already undone and hanging limply round his neck. They can't have had that many, surely? We've only been here for fifty minutes.

'Good evening, kind sirs and ladies,' Gavin says with a weird old-fashioned bow. Crap, how many shots has Postman Gavin had?

Balls.

Leo laughs. 'Peach and Gavin, right?' He stands up to kiss Peach on the cheek and shake Gavin's hand warmly. 'I'm so glad you guys could make it.'

'It's a party . . . in a church!' Peach giggles, using her hand to cover a burp. She reaches over and takes one of the bottles of champagne off the table. 'Is . . . is this *free*?' she asks, already popping it open, the cork whizzing precariously close to Rufus Frost's ear.

'It is,' Leo replies, grabbing a couple of glasses from the table for Peach to pour the golden fizz into. He hands one to Gavin, who knocks it back instantly and holds the glass back out for another.

'Partay!' he yells, punching the air, which makes everyone else at the table wince with distaste.

Eep. If they drink much more I'm in real danger of things going awry. God, why did I think it was a good idea to bring them? I was trying to be nice, but it was a stupid, stupid plan.

'Come on!' I say breezily, standing up from my chair so

rapidly that it makes the table shake. 'What say we dance?'

'Great idea!' Leo agrees, draining the rest of his drink.

'Come on, you two,' I gesture to a swaying Peach and Gavin, taking their flutes away and placing them firmly on the table. They sulk in response.

'Come on!' I repeat, in the same voice I use when I'm trying to get Mr Belding not to take a dump on Grandma's carpet. 'Come on now! That's it!'

My coaxing works and they follow me towards the dance floor.

As the four of us inch our way through the happy crowds towards where the other guests are dancing, I hang back and grab Peach by the arm.

'We'll catch you up in a second,' I call over to Leo and Gavin. 'Just a little ladies-only chat.'

When the two of them are out of earshot, I pull Peach over to one of the huge columns surrounding the room.

'You're fucking pissed,' I grumble, folding my arms huffily.

She hiccups. 'I'm not. I only had five shots. And look, now Gavin and I are getting along famoushly. He's really, really, really nice. He likes to hike on the weekends. And his favourite colour is blue. Like my dress. It's like we're meant to be!'

I see that she's been grilling him twenty questions-style like she did with me on our first night out at Twisted Spin. I wonder if she's assigned him a nickname yet.

'I love you, Jeshicaaa,' she grins, closing one eye to focus on my face. 'You're my besht pal. I won't dump you for Gavin, you know. I'm not that kind of friend.' Then she pulls my head down to her sizeable bosom and pats my hair with her big meaty hands.

'Ow, gerrof! And it's Lucille,' I hiss, removing my head

from her boobs. 'You're supposed to call me *Lucille.*'

'Lucille – oh, yeah. Sorry.' Peach nods sagely and rubs her eye, causing a bit of mascara to splodge onto her cheek. I flick it off. 'You're actin' a little uptight,' she pouts. 'Thas not like you. It's not *who you are.*'

She's right, I'm usually chillin' like Matt Dillon on penicillin. But tonight I *am* uptight. I'm super on edge. There's just so much a stake now. Part of me genuinely wants to be here, on a night out with Peach and Leo (not too bothered about Gavin, to be honest) having fun. The other part of me just wants to do one, so I don't have to acknowledge the complicated situation I've managed to get myself into.

I peek over towards Leo, who is awkwardly dancing with Gavin on the dance floor. It's a pretty slow song, so they're just sort of swaying from side to side and making small talk.

'No more booze, all right?' I say to Peach sternly and sounding a lot like Grandma. 'Your innocent body won't be able to handle it and we've got work to do. We can't risk any slip-ups. Think of Matilda. How important this is to her.'

'I won't slip up! I wouldn't do that to you, because you're my person, like Cristina Yang and Meredith in *Grey's Anatomy*. I love *Grey's Anatomy*. Do you, Jess? D'you love it?'

'Peach!' I hiss. 'Listen to me!'

'Fine. Fine. I'll jusht have one or two more drinks, maybe five more drinks. That's all.'

Jeez. Is this what I'm like when I've had a drink? Is this why Summer used to get so mad at me?

I try to keep my patience. 'Promise me you won't drink any more.' I plead, putting my hands on her shoulders.

Peach throws me a look as if I'm being a huge spoilsport, shakes my hands off her shoulders and stalks off to find

Gavin. With a sigh, I follow her, reaching Leo just as the band starts up with a big-band version of 'Some Kind of Wonderful' by the Drifters. Leo's face softens when he spots me. He takes me into his arms and together we glide across the dance floor in a waltz, just like Grandma taught me. At first I move stiffly, trying to remember the steps, trying not to tread on Leo's feet, but he has obviously had a great deal more practice than me and sweeps me across the dance floor effortlessly, making me look like I know what I'm doing. It's like something from a film. I'm basically Baby Houseman right now.

'I like your friends,' Leo grins, nodding over towards Peach and Gavin, who are shuffling from left to right, arms wrapped around each other like a couple of thirteen-year-olds at the youth club disco. 'Most people at these kinds of events are so bloody serious. It's nice to see someone having fun.' As he says this, he twirls me under his arm. It makes me dizzy, but in a pleasant giddy way.

'They're great,' I tell him, feeling guilty about getting grumpy at Peach. 'Though I don't really know Gavin, to be honest. Tonight's his first date with Peach.'

'Ah.' Leo nods slowly. 'That makes sense. While you were chatting with Peach before, I'm pretty sure Gavin called you Jess!'

Oh shit.

Act natural.

'How bizarre,' I say steadily. 'He's a little tipsy, I think.'

I glance over to where Gavin and Peach are dancing, now grabbing each other's bums and squeezing them in the manner of someone squeezing a stress ball. They are well on the way to being wasted.

I manoeuvre us a little further away from them on the dance floor, just in case.

I squint up at Leo. Does he suspect something? He doesn't seem to . . . But I can't risk it. I need to distract him from all thoughts of Gavin calling me Jess, I need to eradicate that memory from his mind. At least, that's my reasoning for what happens next. I tilt my head up and to the side, my eyes flicking down to Leo's mouth. He takes the hint like a champion, immediately leaning towards for a kiss.

Our lips meet.

KABLAM! POW! YESSSSSS!

If there was *any* doubt in my mind that the kissing we did in the park was anything other than a fluke, that has now been completely obliterated. Because this kiss is even better. Leo weaves his hands up into my hair, his tongue slipping gently into my mouth. My entire body relaxes into it, and if I didn't know that it was something that only happens in romance novels, I'd swear my knees go weak.

Fuck. I should probably stop kissing him now. When I kiss him, everything gets complicated. The *feelings* get stronger, making me all wibbly and dazed and stupid.

Have to stop kissing him.

But I *can't* stop kissing him. Things feel, I don't know, better when I kiss him. Calmer. Like medicine. Just a little longer will be all right, won't it?

I don't know how long Leo and I kiss on the dance floor for. I lose all concept of time. It could be two minutes, it could be two hours. I don't even care.

'Well, well, well. Don't you two look cosy?' comes a familiar voice from behind us.

My blood runs cold. I break off from Leo, my eyes flying open.

Standing there, and looking like the cat that got the cream, is Summer.

CHAPTER THIRTY-TWO

If you are in love with your chap, tell him. There isn't a Good Man in the world who doesn't like to hear that he is adored by a Good Woman.

***Matilda Beam's Guide to Love and Romance*, 1955**

I literally can't speak. My heart is thudding so hard, it must be making my boobs jiggle with the force of it. What the hell is Summer doing here? What's she going to say? My mouth loses all moisture in an instant. My tongue won't work. I stare at her, open-mouthed. Leo gives me a puzzled look.

'Lucille? Are you OK?'

'Hi, Leo.' Summer leans in and gives him a kiss on the cheek like they're the bestest of friends. She looks amazing in a long, red clingy dress, her dark hair piled stylishly on top of her head.

'Hi?' Leo says, unsure.

'Sooo lovely to see you again. We met in Brooklyn last year?' Summer reminds him. 'I was with Anderson?'

'Oh.' He nods with recognition. 'Anderson, right. Yes. Good to see you. What brings you here?'

'I'm with Anderson again actually!' She points over to the back of the room, where I spot Anderson Warner wearing an electric-blue tuxedo. He's grown a huge beard and is chatting to a couple of corporate-looking types.

'He's here with the guys from Saatchi & Saatchi,' Summer explains. 'They've just signed him to be the face of the new L'Oréal beard conditioner range in the UK. Massive beards are so in right now.'

I swallow. 'Are you two . . .'

'Maybe, yeah. He's been in London doing promo and, well – ' she flicks her hair back, even though it's all pinned up. It makes her look like she's got a tic – 'we just couldn't stay away from each other. We've always had this amazing magnetism.'

I suspect it was more a case of her stalking him, sending him nude selfies until he relented. I wonder how Holden took it. Probably crying into his lumberjack shirt, listening to She & Him on repeat. Poor sod.

'You look lovely,' Leo says politely. He seems to sense that I'm uncomfortable and gently winds his arm round my back.

'Thanks,' Summer says, turning around slightly so we can get a good look at her almost award-winning bum.

'You look lovely too, *Lucille*,' she enthuses.' Soooo super different. It's an *amazing* transformation.'

Huh. She just called me Lucille? What's she playing at? What does she know?

Shit. If Leo wasn't here I'd just tell her to fuck off. But I need to remain demure while telepathically telling her to fuck off. I try to do it with my eyes. She just smirks in response.

'Yeah,' she goes on. 'I saw you guys in the *Telegraph* last week, in that piece about the Van Gogh acquisition. I couldn't believe it when I saw you together. *Leo Frost with the latest in a long line of romances, Lucille Darling.*' She does actual air quotes. Was she always this much of a twat? 'I was totes shocked. You should have told me you were dating, *Lucille*.'

Fuck. I didn't know that article was out, that there was a picture of me in the newspaper. Dammit. She clearly knows I'm pretending to be someone else. Is this why she's here? To spill? To get me back for nicking Mr Belding?

'How do you two know each other?' Leo asks as the band segues into a smooth-as-silk version of 'Fly Me to the Moon'.

'Oh, we're old friends,' Summer laughs in a hollow way, and then lowers her voice. 'I know *all* her secrets!'

SHIT.

Leo nudges me, gives me a naughty grin 'Lucille's secrets? Well, now I'm very intrigued . . .'

Summer rubs her hands together. 'Oh, I know them all. For example, Leo, did you know that . . .'

I completely freeze, every muscle in my body locking. It's all going to come crashing down. Everything. Right here, right now.

I don't know what I'm more worried about, the fact that the project will be ruined after all this effort, or the fact that Leo will no longer be able to look at me like he's looking at me right now – like I'm the coolest, most interesting woman in the world.

Just as Summer is about to reveal some horrible truth

about who I really am, the band stops playing and a voice booms out over the speakers, cutting Summer off.

'Ladies and gentleman, please take your seats. The London Advertising Association Awards are about to be announced.'

Leo grabs my hand. 'Looks like it's time. Good to see you again, Summer.'

Summer's confident smile drops slightly. 'Yes, definitely. I'll come find you guys later.'

Not if I have anything to do with it.

With a last stony glance at Summer, I follow Leo to where we hurriedly take our seats as an air of excited anticipation settles over the room. There are two empty spaces at our table. Peach and Gavin's spaces. I squint, scanning the rapidly emptying dance floor for them. Where the hell have they gone?

'Wow, I'm actually a little nervous,' Leo laughs, squeezing my hand under the table.

'You'll be great,' I say in the soothing voice. 'Good luck.'

'Luck has nothing to do with these things!' Rufus Frost sniggers from the other side of the table, signalling over to one of the stewards for more champagne. I throw Rufus my most subtle withering glance. Leo kisses me on the neck. I lean into him and rest my head against his shoulder.

Summer, about four tables away, stares at me as I do this, one eyebrow raised. I lift my head back up instantly. Shit. She's totally gunning for me. As soon as the awards are announced, I'm going to have to come up with some way to get Leo out of here, and fast. I can't risk Summer talking to him again. Or Peach. Or Gavin, for that matter, wherever they may be. This is Def-Con 5 and I have to rescue our mission.

We sit through thirty minutes of really boring awards

for things such as Best Use of Typography and Best Utilities Branding. The lights are dimmed, so no one notices as I drift off a little.

'And now we come to the award for Print Campaign of the Year . . .' the host booms into the mic. I feel Leo sit up a little straighter beside me and that pulls me out of my daze. I wipe away the little bit of drool that has puddled at the corner of my mouth.

'This is it!' Leo whispers.

The host opens up a folded red card, and reads the result.

'And the winner of LAAA's Print Campaign of the Year goes to . . .'

Leo squeezes my hand even tighter.

'Leo Frost at Woolf Frost for Drive Alive!'

How? How?

Despite my befuddlement that anyone could think that that advert is anything other than ridiculous, I cheer and clap along with the rest of the room.

Leo pulls me up from my chair and bends me over his arm for an extravagant Hollywood Kiss that leaves me breathless, before jogging to the stage area to collect his award.

'Wow,' he laughs into the microphone, examining the silver trophy. In his hand. 'Not in a million years did I think I'd be winning this. Especially not when I'm up against such incredibly talented competition. Thank you so much to the incredible team at Woolf Frost for your hard, smart work and huge thanks to the LAAA judges for voting for me.'

We all clap.

Leo takes a deep breath.

'I've actually had quite a journey these past few weeks.

Some revelations about my work and, well, about the direction of my life, I suppose. Some of you, well, most of you, will know me as something of an eternal bachelor.'

There's a polite laugh from the audience and a shout out from the back by someone who says, 'That's putting it bloody lightly!', which gets an even bigger laugh.

'All right, all right!' Leo holds up his hands, grinning, his eyes searching me out.

'Three weeks ago, at a client funfair, Lucille Darling jumped into my dodgem car, and, at the risk of sounding cheesy, into my heart.'

The audience go *aaaah*. I turn a bit red and take a sip of my drink.

'Not many people can stand up to my father,' Leo continues, getting another laugh from the audience. 'But Lucille is one of them. She's also unusual and creative, a passionate philanthropist who's not afraid to be herself, to be different from the crowd. It's a complete bonus that she's also the most beautiful woman I've ever seen in my life. What I suppose I'm saying is that . . . Lucille, you've changed me. You've lit me up. And in front of the press, in front of my peers, in the interests of being as bold and as honest as you . . . I want to tell you . . .'

What . . . What does he want to tell me?

'That I . . . I think you're kinda terrific.'

I throw my head back and laugh out loud. 'I think you're kinda terrific' is a line from *Grease* 2.

As the audience burst into applause, Leo hurries down off the stage, races over to me, swoops me out of his chair, up into his arms, and spins me round with glee. I laugh into his neck, and as he puts me back down, he leans in close and whispers into my ear.

'I love you, Luce.'

I stop mid-chuckle.

What?

He *loves* me?

Is this a joke?

I peer up at him. He's staring tenderly down at me, and not at all in a jokey way.

God. I can't believe it.

Matilda Beam's tips worked, and Leo . . . loves me?

Does this mean that we did it? That the experiment has succeeded?

Wow. *Wow.*

I expect to feel a surge of relief. Finally, I can go back to Grandma and Valentina and tell them that, yes, *How to Catch a Man Like It's 1955* has worked. I don't have to see Leo again, I don't have to risk any more of these dangerous *feelings*.

But I don't feel relief. I feel happy and fizzy and guilty. Really fucking guilty. And a bit sad, like I've lost something, which is stupid, because you can't lose something that is based on a lie.

Leo loves me.

And . . . I think, shit, I think I might love him. Fucking hell. I don't know what to do. I can't love Leo Frost. Surely it's impossible after only three weeks. Not to mention the fact that he thinks I'm someone completely different. *And* the fact that *I* don't fall in love.

Is this how love feels? Like the most amazing, inconvenient fucking nightmare?

At my hesitation, Leo searches my face, his expression melting from one of joy into one of nervousness.

I open my mouth to respond. I think I'm about to tell him that I love him too when, suddenly, Postman Gavin appears in front of me, a concerned look on his boyish features.

'Peach is really drunk and I'm worried. She needs you. She's in the cloakroom.'

Oh no.

'Take me to her,' I say immediately.

As Leo blinks in confusion, I throw him an apologetic shrug before dashing off with Gavin to find my friend.

Gavin hurriedly leads me to the small church cloakroom. He waits outside while I go in to where Peach, massive ballgown pooled in the space around her, is sprawled on the floor under a rail of coats, head leaning dozily against the wall.

'Peach, are you all right?' I squat down to her level.

'I don't feel too good,' she groans, mascara smudges smeared on her cheeks. 'Am really drunk. Think it was the tequila.'

Damn right it was the tequila. This is my fault. I shouldn't have told her to have a shot. I knew how nervous she was tonight. I should have kept a better eye on her. How could I not have predicted this?

'Everything is spinny, so spinny.' Her eyes close slightly. She's absolutely fucked. Shit. Is this the state I used to get myself into?

'We need to get you back home,' I say, helping her to her feet.

'Bed.'

'Yup. That.'

Outside, Gavin is waiting on a bench in the church foyer. He looks worried, and decidedly more sober than he did earlier. 'Are you all right?' He hurries over to us, taking Peach by the arm. She leans against him, swaying from side to side.

'Just a bit too much to drink. She's all right,' I reassure him. 'Listen, I've got to go back in to get my handbag.' I cast my thumb in the direction of the Nave. 'You guys sit down there – ' I point to the bench – 'and I'll be back in a sec.'

Gavin nods, rubbing Peach's back as he helps her over to the bench.

Right. OK. Bag. I dash back into the ballroom. I move quickly through the bustle and towards our table, when I spot Leo sitting there deep in conversation with Summer. She's showing him something on her mobile phone. His cheeks are red, his handsome face is stony.

Oh my God.

He knows.

He knows.

I halt right in front of the table, my hands starting to tremble.

The pair of them look up at my arrival. Summer gives me an innocent smile. Leo looks at me in astonishment, blinking furiously, his eyes watering.

'Leo, I can explain—' I start, but before I can even finish my sentence, he's shot up, his chair toppling over on the floor behind him.

'I don't want to know,' he says in a strangled voice, darting right past me, his head down to the floor.

I turn back to Summer, my whole chest thudding hard.

'What did you say to him?' I hiss.

Summer shrugs delicately and picks up her champagne flute. 'The guy just publicly told everyone he's infatuated with you. He deserves to know the truth. That you're the woman in the onesie who humiliated him at *The Beekeeper* launch. That – for whatever bizarre reason – you're lying to him and pretending to be someone else. That you're not exactly the demure woman you're painting yourself to be.'

She chuckles to herself. 'Though maybe I shouldn't have shown him the picture of you mooning someone on that night out in Leeds last year. He seemed pretty shocked about that one . . . hashtag *awkward*.'

'You're a fucking nasty piece of work,' I spit, grabbing my bag from under my chair and racing after Leo.

'You cause destruction wherever you go, Jess!' She calls out after me. 'You really need to sort yourself out!'

I flip her the bird and dash back out into the lobby, where Peach is dozing on Gavin's shoulder. I spot Leo slamming out of the front doors of the building.

'Hold on right there,' I shout over to a puzzled-looking Gavin, as if he's a dog and I'm telling him to *stay*. 'Don't go anywhere. I'll be back in a second.'

* * *

When I get outside I can't see Leo, but I do spot three town cars from the company he hires lined up on the road. He must be in one of them. He's got to be.

I open the first car door.

'Leo?' I pop my head in. The car's empty apart from a sleeping driver, who jumps up in shock as I bellow right inside his earhole.

'Sorry!'

I race to the second car.

'Leo?' I call again. But this car's just got Benedict Cumberbatch inside, tapping something out on his phone. He looks furious at my interruption. 'Excuse me, this is a private vehicle,' he says imperiously.

'Oh, bloody fuck off, Benedict,' I grump, throwing him my mightiest withering glance.

He stutters furiously and I slam the door on him.

I go to car three.

Leo has to be here.

I yank open the door. There's no driver, but there Leo's in the back seat, staring forlornly at his trophy. He looks up at me, his eyes steely. I slide into the car and close the door behind me.

'I'm so sorry,' I choke out. 'I am so, so sorry.'

He looks absolutely gutted. I've made such a huge mistake. As soon as I found out about his past, as soon as I realized that he wasn't all bad, as soon as I thought we might be developing real feelings for each other, I should have put a stop to the whole project. I should have come up with another way to get the money for Grandma. I'm such an idiot.

'Why?' he asks me, his lovely moss-green eyes now distressed and desperate. 'Why would you not tell me that we'd met before? That your name is – is *Jess*? I don't understand. Was I really so rude to you that night at the book launch that you felt like you had to pretend to be someone else.'

Fuck. All he knows is that I'm not who I say I am. I have to come clean.

'It was for a book,' I say quietly, embarrassed.

His eyes widen in horror. 'What?'

'We wanted to write a book about how my Grandma's 1950s romance tips would work in the modern day. And . . . we chose to try them out on you.'

'Who's we?' he asks in dismay.

'Um, me, my Grandma and . . . Valentina Smith.

He blinks. 'Your Grandma? And Valentina? My *ex*. She put you up to this? Fucking hell, what is this?' He puts both hands to his head.

'I didn't think that you'd fall for me. Or, well, for

Lucille. Valentina told us you were a sleazy eternal bachelor!'

Leo shakes his head. 'What the fuck? This is sick. I told you I regretted the way I treated my exes. I apologized to Valentina so many times. I told her when we first hooked up that I wasn't looking for anything serious, that I was seeing other people. But she still got angry when I didn't want to commit. I felt shitty for hurting her, I said sorry a million times, but she didn't want to know, told me that I was evil. I'm not evil. I don't deserve this!'

'I didn't know you'd apologized,' I protest. Valentina left that bit out. I reach out to touch him, but he shoos me away as if I'm a fly.

'I can't believe you would take part in her getting some sort of fucking revenge on me.'

'It wasn't revenge,' I urge desperately. 'I didn't think you'd actually *like* me . . .'

His voice breaks. 'Well, I did.'

'God, I like you too,' I plead. '*More* than like, Leo, but it's complicated. I've never—'

'Get out,' Leo interrupts, his face stony, his usually amused eyes flat and hard.

'Just let me explain, Leo,' I try. 'I think I might be falling in lo—'

'GET OUT!' He dives across me and throws open the car door. 'Please, Luce . . . Fuck, I mean whatever your name is.'

I nod slowly, gathering my bag from where it's laid on the car seat beside me. 'I'm so sorry,' I whisper, climbing out of the car. I turn back to say something else, anything else, that might make this better, but Leo's already slammed the door closed. He's gone.

I stumble, dazed, back into the Christ Church lobby. It feels like I'm walking through water.

'Are you all right?' Gavin says when he sees me. 'You've gone as white as a sheet.'

His voice sounds echoey and far away

'I'm fine,' I swallow, pulling out my phone to call a cab. 'I just want to go home.'

* * *

Peach dozes the whole way back. Gavin, now fully sober, is back to his awkward, shy self, though he does keep checking to see Peach is all right.

After dropping Gavin off at his flat, we drive back to Bonham Square. I can't get Leo out of my head. The expression on his face in the car. Betrayal. I don't think I'll ever be able to forget that.

Back home, Grandma is tucked up in bed. I know Peach would be distraught if Grandma saw her in this state, so I help her up the stairs as quietly as I can and into my room. I make her down a pint of water, help her to get changed into a nightie and tuck her into my bed, turning her over onto her side.

I get in beside her. She murmurs something that sounds like 'sorry'.

'Don't worry, it'll be OK,' I whisper, stroking her hair away from her face.

But I'm lying. Because the truth is, I don't think any of this will ever be OK.

CHAPTER THIRTY-THREE

Every Good Woman ought to pursue a partner of equal or greater breeding and education. This is the person with whom you will spend your life, raise your children. They must have the means to take care of you, else you will be destined for a life of strife and financial worry.

***Matilda Beam's Good Bride Guide*, 1956**

I can't sleep.

Every time I start to doze off, I think of Leo and my heart lurches and wakes me up. And when it's not that bringing me out of sleep, it's Peach turning over in the bed and lobbing me in the face with her arm.

With a sigh, I climb out from beneath the duvet and pace around my room, halting when I feel a sharp prick in my toe.

'Ow!' I hiss, grabbing my foot and hopping up and down. I pick the offending shard out of my foot. It's a tiny piece of porcelain from when Jamie's nephew Charlie knocked over Felicity.

I gape at the rest of the dolls. Mum's dolls. I wonder if this sad aching I have inside is the feeling Mum had all the time? Is this what drove her over the edge?

I check the time on my iPhone. Two a.m.

Pulling on my dressing gown, I creep out onto the upstairs landing and peek up at the attic door, spotting a little rope cord dangling from it. Reaching on tiptoes, I pull the cord down as slowly as possible and unfold the wooden ladder super quietly.

As I step onto the first rung of the ladder, it gives a massive creak. I freeze. If Grandma catches me sneaking up here after she told me not to, she'll have a right paddy, and tonight has already been quite craptastic enough, thank you.

When, thirty seconds later, it becomes clear that Grandma didn't hear the creak and I'm safe, I carefully climb the rest of the way into the attic and close the hatch softly behind me. I sneeze instantly. Urgh, it's so dusty up here, I can smell it!

Feeling along the wall for the light switch, I find it and flip it on. The attic is illuminated by the glow of a bright, bare bulb dangling from the rafters. I shake my head as I see boxes and toys and papers and old trophies and books and more boxes. *Attic is empty* my arse. Grandma was totally lying. I pluck a trophy from where it's balancing on top of an open cardboard box and look at the inscription.

Kensington Young Ballet Competition. Winner Rose Beam.

And then I pick up an old school blazer with a label sewn into the collar.

Property of Rose Beam, Class 4 Blue.

Woah. This is all Mum's stuff! No wonder I never saw any around the house – it's all crammed in here!

Opening odd boxes, I rifle through them eagerly. There

are school reports, a signed theatre programme from *Romeo and Juliet*, old shoes, tape cassettes, half-used bottles of perfume and a few disco flyers for a club called the Blue Canary.

Then I spot – half covered by a turquoise stripy duvet cover – a large black trunk nestled in the darkest corner of the attic. I traipse over, muffling another sneeze as I dislodge a couple of teddy bears which proceed to fall off the top of a cardboard box and bop me on the head. Sitting down cross-legged in front of the trunk, I yank off the duvet cover, bunch it up and chuck it over to the other side of the attic. Then I slowly lift open the lid of the trunk.

Inside, there are envelopes and folders, old magazines and letters. Then I notice, buried beneath all the paper, a small pile of brightly-coloured patterned notebooks.

Frowning, I grab the notebook on top of the stack and open it up.

The first page is scrawled with large, looping script in the kind of thick blue ink that can only come from a fountain pen. I recognize the handwriting in an instant.

It's Mum's handwriting.

Rose Beam's Diary

My hands start to shake.

Rose Beam's Diary
9th July 1985

I can't write properly, my hands are shaking so much. Dammit. I need to breathe but I can't catch my breath.

I've just been downstairs as Mum was calling me. She was sitting in the drawing room with Dad, and they both looked so serious. I thought they were going to tell me that someone had died. Before I could ask who, Dad told me to sit down. Then he said that I wouldn't be seeing Thom any more. At first I laughed because I thought he was doing one of his stupid jokes, but then Mum started crying and completely wigging out and I knew that they were serious. Dad told me that he'd had one of his friends look into Thomas Truman's background and he'd found out that Thom is a known gambler with a string of debts who was obviously using me for our money. I told Dad how ridiculous he was being because I know all about Thom's card playing, but that he loved me and that it was real, true love. Thom paid me back every penny of the money I lent to him and I told them so.

And then Dad told me the worst thing anyone has ever said in my life. He told me that last night he went to see Thom at his house and offered him twenty thousand pounds to leave London and never see me again. According to Dad, Thom took it without a second thought. I don't believe it. I can't believe it. Dad said they hadn't spent all this time, effort and money to bring me up well, only for me to marry a layabout who was after the family money, that something scandalous like this would ruin the family's hard-earned reputation. Mum dashed over to hold me, but I pushed her away. How has she let this happen? She just sat by Dad's side, agreeing with everything he said like she always bloody does.

At that point I ran out of the room and out of the house.

I got the Tube to Thom's house. John answered. As soon as he saw me, his face crumpled. And then he gave me a note. From Thom. I tried to open the envelope but my hands were shaking so much that John had to do it for me. The note wasn't even worth being in an envelope. It simply said, 'I'm sorry.'

I asked John where Thom had gone and he claims to have no idea. How could I have been such a fucking idiot.

Rose Beam's Diary
10th July 1985

I went to the theatre to see if anyone knew where Thom had gone. Apparently he phoned in his resignation last week, and everyone is very upset that he's let them down. They don't know the half of it.

Rose Beam's Diary
12th July 1985

I've been in my bedroom for two whole days and only now have I stopped crying. I think I'm physically all out of tears. Mum keeps knocking on the door, trying to bring me food and warmed milk, and each time I tell her to fuck off. I've never used bad language in front of my parents before. But now I don't care. They mean nothing to me. I want to tell her what she's done. I want to tell her that I'm pregnant, that I'm having Thom's baby and that she's ruined everything. But she doesn't even deserve to know. Dad doesn't deserve to know. They are toxic and old-fashioned and cruel . . . And Thom . . . I've made such a fool of myself.

I need to get out of here. I have three thousand pounds in my bank account. I'll leave tomorrow. I'm finished here. They will never know my child. Never.

Rose Beam's Diary
15th July 1985

This will be my last entry. I'm going to throw this diary away. I'm going to throw all of them away . . . I want nothing to remind me of this life. I'm done and I won't ever come back. See ya.

Rose x

I spend over two hours looking through Mum's diaries, hardly able to believe what I'm reading. *This* is how Mum's heart broke? This man, my father, used her and left.

The words blur in front of me as I take in what happened. The only thing Mum ever told me was that my dad left us before I was born. Does he even know I exist? And Grandma. Her and Granddad Jack paid this Thom money to leave Mum. Because of their snobbishness. Because of the Beams' reputation. It's horrible. A wave of pity engulfs me. No wonder Mum didn't trust people, no wonder she was so bitter and depressed. The people she trusted and loved most in the world did one over on her.

My heart hammers rapidly as I place the last of the diaries carefully back in the trunk. Coming up here was a bad idea. What did I expect to find? Why did I choose to look now, after all the drama that's happened tonight? Jesus, my life is just one bad fucking decision after the other.

I feel so angry. Angry at myself. Angry at Grandma. Now it makes sense why she's been so cagey. Of course she doesn't want me to know that it wasn't just a man who broke Mum's heart. It was her. Her and Jack. That's what she was talking about when she said she was 'redeeming herself'. She thought that by taking me in she could make it all better.

Adrenalin courses through my body, making me feel like I'm about to explode. And there I was thinking that Grandma might actually be OK. Feeling pleased that she was proud of me.

I fiddle absently with the cuff of my dressing gown and watch as the dust particles glisten in the light, flying all around me, never seeming to reach the floor. I think of my mum. Of growing up around somebody who never wanted to hug, never wanted to talk about love, cried so much, stayed indoors all the time. I think of sitting on the floor of the library when Pam called to tell me that Mum couldn't even find it in her to face life any more.

Grandma lied to me. Big time.

* * *

On the way back down from the attic, I'm not quite so careful as on the way up, and I hit not just one creak, but three. Grandma dashes out of her bedroom, her silver hair a wild halo, a look of fright on her pale, wrinkled face. When she realizes it's only me rather than a burglar, her taut face relaxes.

'Oh, Jessica, you gave me a terrible fright! Goodness, how was the ball? Did you have a wonderful time?' Then she realizes where I've just been. 'Wait . . . what are you doing up there? I told you not—'

'You lied to me,' I cut in, stepping off the bottom rung of the ladder, my voice shaking. 'You let me think that you had nothing to do with why she was so unhappy. But it was *all* your fault. Yours and Jack's.'

Grandma sways slightly. 'That's not wha—'

'I've just read her diaries! She was in love, properly in love, found her – her *soulmate*, and because you didn't think he was up to your standards, your precious Beam fucking standards, you paid him to leave her. And she never ever got over it.'

'Good grief, 'Grandma whispers, her bottom lip starting to tremble. 'I was going to tell you.'

'Oh really?'

'Yes. I was going to explain everything. When the project was over.'

'Ah, yes, your precious project. Well, congratulations! Leo Frost said he loved me, so, you know, hip, hip, hoorah. Only he found out what we'd been up to, how we'd been lying to him, and he's devastated. I should never have trusted you.'

Grandma wrings her hands together. 'After she left, Thomas came back.'

I blink. 'What?'

'He came back four days later to return the money. He told us he was in love with Rose and realized he'd made a mistake. Your grandfather sent him away, told him that Rose had to decided to go and live with family in New York and that he must never, ever darken our doorway again. I felt horribly guilty.'

My throat aches with something, I'm not sure what it is. 'My father came back and you never told her?' I whisper in disbelief.

Grandma starts to sob even louder. I hate it. My first instinct is to make her feel better, but she doesn't deserve it. Because of her snobbishness, my mother lived her whole life believing that the person she loved took money to abandon her. And he didn't. He did love her. Maybe if she'd known, she wouldn't have . . .

'Jack forbade me to tell her. He was my husband. I had to listen to him.'

'She was pregnant, for fuck's sake!'

'We didn't know that until after we'd sent Thomas away. I only knew when I found Rose's diaries in an untied trash bag behind the outside bins. By that time it was too late.'

I run my hands through my hair. I can't believe it.

'She lived her entire life believing a lie. It ruined her!'

'I'm know, and I am sorry,' Grandma cries. 'I thought I knew what was best for my daughter. If she had only listened to my advice, she wouldn't have got involved with such an unsavoury man in the first place. Let herself get pregnant out of wedlock.'

I shake my head. 'You're unbelievable,' I spit, standing up. 'I knew you were old-fashioned, but that's just absurd. How can you not see how awful and judgemental that is?'

The back of my eyes sting. I need to get out of here.

'It's my biggest regret,' Grandma says in a small voice. 'The entire thing destroyed Jack. He started drinking heavily after Rose ran away, he lost control of Delightex, our entire fortune went, he became cold and distant. Her leaving with his grandchild, cutting all ties, refusing to even speak to us again . . . it shattered me, but it killed him. He had his heart attack less than two years later. Believe me, I've felt sorry for it every day of my life. I tracked Rose down after Jack passed. Found both of you in that tiny house in Manchester. When I got there, she screamed and lashed out at me. Said that if I loved her at all I would never contact her again. What could I do, Jessica? I didn't know what to do. So I knocked on the door of your next-door neighbour—'

'Nosy Mrs Farraway?' I whisper.

'Yes, Mrs Farraway. And I offered to pay her if she would send me monthly updates on how the two of you were faring. That's how I found out that Rose had . . . that she had . . .' Grandma trails off, her face crumpled with upset.

I try to swallow, but there's a huge lump in the way.

'If you knew she'd died then why did you never come to her funeral?' I ask, my voice cracking slightly with anguish. 'Why did you never try to find me?'

'I did go to her funeral.'

'What? You're lying. You didn't.'

'I *did*, Jessica. I was standing right at the back, behind the other guests. I saw you there with your friend. You were . . . a little worse for wear.'

I get a flashback to Mum's funeral. How I drank half a bottle of tequila beforehand, how Summer basically had to help me stand upright. So wasted, I didn't even know Matilda was there.

'Why didn't you come and talk to me?' I spit. 'Things could have been so different. I was alone. I had no one.'

The tears roll down Grandma's face, plopping off one by one onto the collar of her cream dressing gown.

'I wanted to, Jessica. I wanted to very much. But when your mum passed, I received a letter from her solicitor instructing that I should never try to make contact with you.'

'Well, what do you call this?' I scream, indicating the pair of us.

'I didn't seek you out. You came to me. I couldn't turn you away. You needed someone.'

'No, *you* needed someone. Someone to manipulate. Someone to do your bidding and do your stupid project. Well, congratulations. It worked. I'll write the book. Your house will be saved. Yippee for you.'

'I don't care about that. Maybe I did, but I don't now. I only care about you.'

'Someone who cared about me wouldn't have put me in the situation I was in tonight. I feel like shit about what I've done. We've really hurt somebody.'

Grandma looks down at her shaking hands. She's getting really distressed.

My stomach rolls and lurches horribly. 'Look, I . . . I have to go,' I gasp.

'Where?' Grandma says, horrified. 'It's half past four in the morning!'

'Anywhere, just so long as it's well away from you.'

I hurry to my room in a daze, grab my phone, and with shaking hands that keep missing the keys, dial the first number that comes to mind.

After four rings it answers.

'Hello?'

'Can I come stay the night?' I ask without preamble.

'Yes,' is the simple, short reply. 'Shall I pick you up?'

'No, it's fine. I'll get a cab.'

I quickly call a taxi, grab my laptop, put on my trainers and race past a loudly sobbing Grandma to wait outside for the taxi to take me away from here.

I just about make it out of the building when the tears I've been holding in for so many years finally start to fall.

CHAPTER THIRTY-FOUR

Disappointment is inevitable in this life. But a Good Woman can overcome most things by weathering the storm with patience and good grace.

***Matilda Beam's Good Woman Guide*, 1959**

It's weird, this crying business. It's like Pringles – once you pop you can't stop. And I literally cannot stop.

The taxi driver is polite enough to pretend that he doesn't notice as I cry and snot and wail in the back seat. I don't even have a tissue, so the sleeve of my dressing gown is now in a pretty gross state.

Eyes blurred with this onslaught of tears, I get out of the taxi at Edward Street, Bayswater, where Jamie is waiting outside his front door, huddled up in a blue towelling bathrobe. He looks at me in horror as I, in my dressing gown and trainers, hobble towards him, barely able to stand up because I'm crying so hard.

'Jess? Are you hurt?' he asks, leading me inside. 'Are you in pain?'

Yes. And yes.

'S-s-s-orry,' I get out through shaky breaths. 'I had a really bad n-night and haven't cried in t-t-t-ten yeeeears, so there's quite a l-lot of iiiiiit and it's freaking me o-o-out.'

We enter a clean, plainly decorated living room, darkened by closed curtains.

'Sit down,' Jamie says, pointing to a floppy, comfy-looking couch. 'I'll go and put the kettle on.'

I plop onto the sofa, noticing a box of tissues on the low coffee table in front of me. I grab the entire box of tissues, plonk them on my lap, pull a load of them out and press them all over my wet face to dry the tears. I repeat this, as needed, until soon enough all the tissues are used up. 'Bring some bog roll,' I call to Jamie in the kitchen.

Jamie comes back from the kitchen holding two steaming mugs of tea and a loo roll under his arm. He stumbles slightly on the edge of the rug and a bit of tea falls onto his bare foot.

'Ouch.'

I accept one of the mugs from him and take a big slurp. The tears are falling so fast that they plop, one after the other, into the tea. Putting the mug down onto the coffee table, I grab the loo roll from Jamie and use it for more face-mopping.

'I'm sorry,' I sigh shakily, 'to wake you. I didn't know who else to phone.'

'Don't worry about it,' he shrugs, sitting down next to me, hands cupped around his mug, stifling a yawn. 'So you want to tell me what's happened?'

I nod and take a deep breath. Then I tell Jamie the whole sorry story.

* * *

An entire roll of toilet tissue, three more cups of tea and an hour and a half later, I've told Jamie everything: about Mum, and my dad who I've just found out is called Thomas Truman and might not even know I exist, about Grandma lying to us. And then I tell him about the ball, about Leo finding out about the project, how he told me he loved me. I leave out the bit that I think I might love him too. When I'm finished, my face is almost red raw from the tears and my nose is full-on blocked.

'What should I do?' I ask him. 'I don't want to feel like this. I've spent my whole life protecting myself from feeling like this. How do I make it stop? I need to make this crying stop. I hate it! I'm Gwyneth Paltrow!'

'You just have to let it happen. You'll stop crying when you're ready.'

'What?' I say in horror, a fresh round of tears squeezing their way out. 'That's it? I just have to wait for it to stop on its own? I'm going to get dehydrated!'

Jamie smiles slightly, stands up and holds out his hand. 'Come on.'

'What? Where?'

'Let's go to bed.'

I goggle at him. I knew he was randy, but wanting a shag now, after everything I just told him?

'To sleep,' he adds, noticing my irritation. He yawns and I catch it, my mouth stretching sleepily.

'Ugh.'

'You can't sort any of this out until you've got some sleep,' he says kindly.

I nod, wipe my nose and follow Jamie through a hallway and up some beige carpeted stairs. From one of the rooms, I hear the sound of a bed squeaking along with a bunch of muffled sighs and moans.

'My room-mates,' Jamie grimaces. 'They sometimes start early. Come on, I've got earplugs.'

Jamie's room is large and clean, with blonde hardwood floors and lots of medical textbooks lined up on Billy bookcases. It looks like a student bedroom, which, I suppose, is what it is, after all. I notice lots of pictures hung up above his desk. Pictures of Jamie with family members and friends, a few of him with his nephew Charlie. I feel a rumble of self-pity in my stomach. I wonder what it must have been like to grow up like that. Surrounded by a normal, loving, functional family.

Jamie takes off his dressing gown to reveal, underneath, his tartan boxer shorts and a grey T-shirt that says 'Bazinga' on it. He climbs into the bed and I crawl in beside him, noticing that the duvet cover smells nice, like washing powder. I curl up into him and he flings his arm over my body. It's comforting and safe. Almost immediately he gets a boner.

I jump away and turn round. 'Jamie!' I scold, wiping my nose. 'Inappropriate much?'

'Sorry,' he says. 'Natural reaction.'

I sniff and turn back round, snuggling my head into the pillow.

'Unless . . . it might make you feel a bit better?' he adds.

He's right. It probably would make me feel a bit better. Things are easy with Jamie. There are no weird whizzy feelings, no heart thumps and melting. No . . . love.

'Thanks, Doc. But I just want to get some sleep.'

Jamie leans down and kisses the back of my head. He hands me a packet of neon-yellow earplugs, which I eagerly shove in to drown out the noise of his amorous room-mates. Less than thirty seconds later, I'm asleep.

* * *

I wake up the next morning to the sound of my mobile ringing. My throat is raw and sore, my head is pounding. I feel like I've got a shitty hangover and I barely had anything to drink. I turn over, but Jamie isn't there. I grab out onto the bedside table for my phone. It's Valentina. Probably calling to see how the ball went. Shit.

'Hey,' I answer dazedly.

'Jess, my lavender puff, how are you?

'Er ... '

'Listen, I'm afraid I've got some rather upsetting news.'

I quickly sit up in the bed, which makes my head pound even harder. Ow.

'What's wrong?'

'Unfortunately, first thing this morning we received an injunction notice from Rufus Frost regarding *How to Catch a Man like it's 1955*.'

'What? I don't understand?'

Valentina's voice comes crystal clear through the speaker of my phone.

'He has said that if we try to release the book, he will sue the Southbank Press.'

'But . . . we weren't going to use Leo's actual name in the book?'

'Yes, but we were going to *imply* it – he was our "eternal bachelor". Which would have been fine, but now there's a picture of you together in the *Telegraph*, and after his public declaration last night – which is on all the industry blogs and before you know it the gossip columns will stumble onto it – it will be clear who we're talking about. I'm afraid it's just not worth the hassle for us. And even if we could slip past it legally, Rufus has said that Davis Arthur Montblanc would never want to be part of a company who upset his nephew. And Davis Arthur Montblanc is our most important author.'

My stomach sinks. After everything that's just happened, there's not even going to be a book? This whole thing was for nothing?

'I can't fucking believe this,' I mutter into the phone, feeling the tears well up again. 'Why did you not think of this beforehand?'

'I know, pickle. It's *such* a pain. I had *such* plans for the book, and you did *such* an amazing job on the scoundrel.'

'He's not a scoundrel, Valentina,' I respond angrily. 'He told me what happened with you guys. He behaved badly, I know, but he apologized to you. You didn't tell me that. And you conveniently forgot to mention that he was completely honest with you about not wanting anything serious. You let me believe that he was cruel and heartless when he wasn't. He was just a bit of a tit. He didn't deserve *this*.'

Valentina gasps. 'I truly thought that *How to Catch a Man Like It's 1955* was a fantastic idea for a book,' she retorts. 'I still do. I make all my publishing decisions with nothing but absolute integrity. I'm highly offended that you, my beautiful protégé, would think that I—'

'But you chose Leo Frost as an example, Valentina. And that was purely because of your past with him. Admit it!'

Valentina goes quiet on the other end of the phone.

'Fine . . .' she sighs eventually. 'I *may* have let my personal feelings about him cloud my judgement a little.'

'You definitely did,' I grumble. 'And now we're all paying the price.'

Valentina's voice wobbles, less confident than I've ever

heard it. 'I . . . I really liked him, Jess,' she says softly. 'And, well, I'm afraid I'm not used to not getting exactly what I want. I don't understand why he didn't want to be with me. I'm super. A successful, strong and attractive woman with everything going for her . . . You're right, he did apologize to me, but that didn't change the fact that I was humiliated. Everyone in London knew we were dating, and everyone in London knew that he was screwing other women.'

'And you wanted him to be taken down a peg or two. You used me to flaming do it! I was your Patsy!'

'I didn't think it would turn out like this,' Valentina protests. 'And you're not exactly innocent in this! After your initial misgivings, you went along with fooling Leo very easily.'

I object to that statement, but she's right. I was *so* quick to believe that Leo Frost deserved to be tricked. It all fitted in nicely with every theory Mum had about men and relationships. I was just as ignorant when Mum told me that my dad was nothing more than a lousy charlatan – I didn't ever question that there was any more to it than that.

'I am sorry, Jess,' Valentina says eventually, her tone sincere. 'I truly am. I think you've got a bucketload of talent, and I truly hope that somehow we'll get to work together in the future.'

I sigh a heavy, sad sigh. 'Please will you tell Matilda about the injunction? I . . . I can't face her right now.'

'Of course. It's the least I can do.'

'Thanks.' I swallow hard. 'Bye then, Valentina.'

I end the call quickly and immediately burst into tears once more.

* * *

I cry into the pillow for another twenty minutes before I get the energy to go downstairs and find Jamie. He's sitting at the big kitchen table, sipping coffee and poring over a notebook. I glance at the clock on the wall and notice it's eleven a.m..

'Are you not supposed to be in work today?' I ask.

He shrugs. 'I pulled a sickie.'

I pour myself some coffee and join him at the table.

'You didn't have to do that.'

'Ah, any excuse I can get.' He smiles. 'How you feeling?'

'Rotten,' I answer, telling him all about the phone call I just had with Valentina.

'Is there anything I can do to help?' His face is sympathetic. 'Anything at all.'

Instantly, a thought occurs to me.

'There is something, yes,' I say, draining the rest of my coffee.

'Whatever you want.'

'Will you drive me to Manchester?'

* * *

Half an hour later we're zooming up the motorway. Due to the fact that I don't have any of my clothes, I'm wearing my pyjama bottoms and one of Jamie's T-shirts. Jamie is trying his best to cheer me up with a selection of horror stories from his course at medical school, and by singing me Led Zeppelin songs because his car radio is broken. I try my best to lighten up. I hate not being light. But I can't do it. All I can do is cry, and when I'm not crying, I think about how shit my life is, then I eat crisps, then I cry again.

When my phone rings, my heart leaps as, for a split

second, I think that it might be Leo returning one of my many missed calls. 'Hello?' I say, my voice squeaking.

'Jess, where are you? Are you all right?'

It's Peach. Her voice is all croaky. She sounds as rough as toast.

'Yeah, I'm all right,' I say. 'I'm just sorting out some stuff. Are you OK?'

'I'm so sorry about last night. I feel like such a jackass. I only woke up about an hour ago. I'm never drinking tequila again. And now Matilda is crying. She won't stop crying. What the heck is going on?'

I give Peach the highlights of the events that have played out over the last twelve hours: about Leo and mum's diaries and Valentina. When I'm finished, she starts crying too.

'Lord, I'm sorry, Jess. I could have helped you last night. Instead I was passed out in bed like a damn fool. I am a terrible friend.'

Ordinarily I would take the piss out of her for getting so wasted, for drooling all over Gavin. But I just haven't got it in me today.

'We've all been there,' I say instead. 'Is . . . is Matilda all right?'

'I don't know. She's locked herself in her room. I can hear her crying in there and listening to old doo-wop songs. I don't know what to do. You need to come back.'

My neck itches. 'I can't, Peach. Not right now. Will . . . will you look after her for me?'

'Of course.'

I swallow.

'And Mr Belding too.'

'Sure. He's right here on the bed with me, snug as a bug.'

'I'll be in touch soon, OK. You go and get some Berocca. And some Monster Munch.'

'All right.'

She sounds sad.

'And Peach.'

'Yeah?'

'You're not a terrible friend . . . you're, well, you're my best friend.'

And the realization that that's the truth, that, out of all this, I have met Peach, is enough to stop me from crying. For fifteen minutes, anyway.

* * *

When, around three hours later, we pull up at our destination, Jamie turns off the engine and unlocks his seat belt as if to get out of the car with me.

'I need to do this on my own,' I tell him with a small smile.

He nods, opens up his glove compartment and pulls out a textbook called *Cardiac Imaging*. He holds it up. 'I'll be right here.'

My whole body vibrating with nerves, I open the car door and climb out. I walk through the huge cast-iron gates and down a path bordered with trees and neatly tended shrubbery. I've only been to this place once in my life – ten years ago – but many times in my head. I walk the route as easily as if I'd been here just yesterday.

When I arrive at Mum's headstone, my chest squeezes. My neck and scalp start to itch so much that it burns, and my heart seems to slow right down.

I plop down on the grass and reach forward to touch the

smooth marble of the stone. It's warm from the afternoon sun.

I take a breath.

'Hey, Mum,' I say, placing my hands back in my lap. 'Sorry I've not been for so long. Or ever, really. It's been . . . well, everything's been a bit fucked–up, to be honest.'

I pause. The silence is deafening.

'I've been staying with Grandma Beam. I know now that you didn't want me to, and after reading your diaries last night, I understand why you never talked about her or Granddad Jack. But I found something out and I thought you should know . . .'

The tears start to fall again, and this time I don't try to stop them – I'm getting pretty used to them now.

'Grandma told me that Thomas – my dad – came back for you. He didn't take that money. Four days after you left, he returned and tried to give it back. Granddad Jack sent him away and told him you were living with his family in America. Otherwise I'm pretty sure he would have found you. And then, who knows how things would have turned out.

'I'm not sure yet, but I thought that maybe, at some point in the future, I might try to find him. Would you mind that? I mean, it seems that he's not exactly the shithead we thought he was, and, well, I feel like maybe he should know that I exist. I don't know . . .

'Mum, you always told me that love ruins you. That relationships are dangerous, that I mustn't open myself up to hurt. And I've carried that with me for my whole life. I've been so frightened of ending up like you that I've always tried not to care about anything or anyone. But then I moved in with Grandma, and I know she's crazy, but I started to care about her. And Peach, her assistant, who's also a bit nuts, well, I care about her too.

'And then I met a man. Someone that makes me feel the way I'm guessing Thomas made you feel. Like there was something to look forward to. Someone who I really, really just wanted to *know*. I fought against it, I told myself it wasn't possible, because I didn't want to end up like you. But it all went wrong and I feel properly like crap anyway. But I also feel something else too. I feel alive. Not because of booze, or parties, or sex, which – don't get me wrong – are still on the top of my list of favourite things, but because I allowed myself to feel so many good things about another person. And he, even if just for a little while, felt that way about me too.

'So anyway, I just wanted to come here to tell you that Thomas loved you. I think if you'd known that, things might have been different. And I hope that wherever you are now, you feel better.

'I love you, Mum. And I miss you. I miss you fucking loads. But it's time for me to live by my own rules. Love might end up breaking me. But I need the chance to find that out for myself, in my own way.

'Well, that's it, I guess. It was . . . It was really nice to talk to you, Mum. I won't leave it so long the next time.'

I touch the pale grey marble one more time, rubbing the tips of my fingers against the indentation of Mum's name carved into the stone. Then the sky rumbles and I jump slightly as it starts to piss it down for the first time since this summer heatwave began. As the heavy raindrops soak through my T-shirt and pyjamas, my breathing starts to calm, and then, all at once, I feel something inside me slot back into place.

I think it might be my heart.

* * *

On the way home, I gaze out of the window at the other cars driving alongside us and feel calmer, lighter than I have done in a very long time. The ring of Jamie's phone brings me out of my dozy trance. He flips a switch so that the phone call goes through to his headphones.

'Hello,' I hear him say. His eyes flick to me for a moment. Then he says, 'Oh, nothing . . . just going for a drive . . . no-one . . . I don't know when. Um . . . yeah, maybe. I'll call you soon. Bye.'

He ends the call. The tops of his ears have turned pink.

'Who was that?' I ask.

'Oh, just, um, Kiko,' he shrugs casually.

Kiko? He just totally palmed her off.

'I can't wait to meet her,' I say lightly.

He gives me a look. 'Really?'

I nod. 'Really. I . . . I want you and me to be friends.'

He chews his lip for a moment. 'Friends . . . with benefits?'

I smile, despite myself. 'No. I meant what I said the other week. And . . . well, I kind of have feelings for someone else. Not that anything's going to come of that, but . . . I want to be honest with you, and the truth is, I really like hanging out with you. And I'd really like it if we can be friends. Proper friends.'

He sighs long and low. And then he coughs: 'Does that mean we're going to have to brush each other's hair and talk about, um, Jared Leto and stuff?'

'Yes. If it were 1998 . . . Actually, those sound like awesome friend activities in 2014, too. So yes. We will have to do those things.'

'Well, that's fine by me, Jess,' Jamie says, pulling into the inside lane and speeding up. 'To be honest, I never really fancied you anyway.'

I can't help but laugh.

'Thanks, Jamie.' I grin, putting my hand on top of his and giving it a squeeze.

And then, when he starts up with a rousing chorus of Metallica's 'Enter Sandman' , I join in.

CHAPTER THIRTY-FIVE

Forgiveness is living proof of true love.
***Matilda Beam's Good Woman Guide*, 1959**

I stay on Jamie's couch for the next couple of weeks because the mere thought of even seeing, let alone talking to Grandma makes me feel irate and sad all at the same time. Peach drops my stuff off in Bayswater and calls me with regular updates about Mr Belding (as happy as ever) and Grandma, who's apparently pretending to be all right in the day, showing round potential buyers for her house, but then spends the nights crying. Which makes me feel kind of terrible.

I meet Kiko once or twice when she comes to see Jamie. At first she's a little wary of my friendship with him and the fact that I'm sleeping on his sofa, but I soon warm her up with my sunny disposition, and I really think there's a chance that, at some point, we'll become actual mates. Kiko even helps me to pick out an age-appropriate present (a bubble-making machine) for the first birthday party of

Betty's son Henry, which I travel down to Manchester for. Don't get me wrong – the whole thing was super boring – but the fact that I turned up and endured two hours of screaming kids made Betty so surprised and pleased that it was totally worth the pain, and she's since sent me a Facebook invite for a house party she's planning on having in September.

Speaking of Facebook, Summer is on there more than she's ever been. Now that she's back with Anderson, she's forever posting selfies and statuses about their 'amazing love' and how she's #superblessed to #haveitall. I try to be Zen about the whole thing, but the truth is that what she did at the ball was so needlessly mean that seeing her smug face all over the Internet just winds me up. So I unfriend her. And then, on the day she's set to announce the cast of her new TV show (which, annoyingly, *Stylist* magazine are calling the most hotly anticipated show for 2015) exclusively on *Summer in the City*, I log into the site using my password and send every page link on the site to a YouTube video of Rick Astley's 'Never Gonna Give You Up' in a sort of mass Rick Roll. I do it every day for a week until she finally pegs on that it's me and changes the passwords. But by that time her reputation as a tastemaker has already been sufficiently dented and there's a headline in BuzzFeed that says 'Summer Spencer's Bizarre New Obsession with Rick Astley', which makes me howl with laughter.

I attempt, a lot, to get in touch with Leo so that I can apologize properly. I ring him a gazillion times, but it goes straight to voicemail. I email him, but apart from my regular newsletters and one lovely offer of 'great and joyous wealth' from a Nigerian prince, my inbox remains woefully empty. I even turn up at Leo's apartment one night, hold my iPhone above my head (I couldn't locate a boom box) and blast out

Peter Gabriel's 'In Your Eyes' like John Cusack does in one of Leo's favourite 80s films. But Leo doesn't appear to be at home, and an exhausted-looking woman on the next floor up leans out of her window and tells me to stop being so selfish and shut the fuck up, else she'll call the police. To which I profusely apologize and shuffle away sadly.

I try to accept being frozen out by Leo. He's well within his rights to never want to speak to me again – after all, I massively lied to him. I even pretend to myself that I don't care that much, that it doesn't *really* matter, that I'll get over it soon enough. But I'm not sure that's true. I think constantly about his usually dancing green eyes full of betrayal, his gorgeous confident mouth downturned. Then I think about what he's doing right at that moment, if he's thinking of me, who he's hanging out with, and if they're laughing together. These inconvenient thoughts keep me awake almost every night. Eventually, when I can no longer bear the notion that he might never really know how sorry I am, I wake up one Friday morning and catch the tube to the Strand. I blast open the doors to Woolf Frost and march determinedly up to the receptionist.

'I need to see Leo Frost immediately,' I say firmly.

The receptionist glances up from her computer, a bored expression on her young face. We met last time I was here, but she doesn't recognize me in my normal clothes and glasses, my hair scraped back into a messy bun.

'He's not here.'

'Where is he? I need to see him. It's urgent,' I say, urgently.

She shrugs idly, grabs a packet of Maltesers from under her desk and opens them really slowly.

'Hello?' I prompt.

She tuts. 'He left the company. Resigned a week ago now.' She munches delicately on a little sphere of chocolate.

'What? He *resigned*? Why?'

Her eyes scan the reception area and she lowers her voice. 'Are you a client?'

'No. I just need to talk to him. Where is he?'

'OK, well, you didn't hear it from me, but there's this rumour that Leo Frost left the company to become an artist. Silly sod. Old Rufus is fuming! I hear Leo's gone to France for a couple of weeks. Wants to paint the sea there, or something.' She giggles to herself and rolls her eyes as if she thinks the whole thing is clearly the action of a wuss. And a month ago I might have thought exactly the same thing. But I think about the paintbrush I gave to Leo at the ball, and though my heart aches at the fact that he's not even in the country, a warm, light feeling sparkles in my chest and I can't help but smile to myself.

Leo Frost: Artist.

* * *

Leaving Woolf Frost, I wander down to Little Joe's Java. The place is much less busy than when I was here for the poetry night, and a lively samba-style music plays over the low din of late-morning customers. I order a cappuccino with extra whipped cream and ask the barista if he can lend me some paper and a pen. He cheerfully hands over a letter-headed notepad and a blue bic, and I take a seat on one of the squishy sofas. I start to write.

Dear Leo,

. . .

So I've been trying to get in touch via all the usual ways, but obviously you haven't wanted to hear from me – totally understandable, but I hope that when you get back from France you'll read this and know how truly sorry I am.

I was in a bit of a weird place when I agreed to take part in this project – I'd just lost my job and my home and was in search of a fast buck, plus my Grandma really, really needed my help. I was under the impression that you were some kind of sexist, womanizing shithead, and although that's not exactly an excuse for fooling you, it made the decision to do it so much easier. To be honest, our altercation at The Beekeeper *launch didn't help; I genuinely thought you were a massive prick.*

And then we spent this amazing time together. And I saw that behind that cocky, arrogant exterior was you. You. This kind, open, creative, gorgeous, sensitive man who wasn't at all what I thought he would be. And I was so afraid of how that made me feel. Like you, I have a bit of an issue with commitment, and I didn't want to admit that I might be falling for you because it's never happened to me before, and I really never planned on it happening at all.

A lot of what you saw (and liked about me, I hope) was really me. Jess Beam. Everything I said about your artistic talent was me. Loving 80s teen movies – me. Dodgem-driving like a maniac – me, telling that poem on the stage– me. Those kisses. Those kisses that I know you know were the best kisses either of us have ever had, ever. That was me.

. . .

The thing is, Leo, while so much in my grandma's Good Woman guides is rubbish anti-feminist crap that instructs women to be passive, subservient sidekicks to men, they do have a few good points. They taught me to be more patient, to really listen, to be more enthusiastic about new things and to, well, open myself up to a person for more than something uber casual. You were that something more. You are that something more.

I'm so sorry I hurt you. You didn't deserve it and I'm gutted about the way things have turned out.

Anyway, I'm rambling now probably, but I just wanted to explain things and to tell you how shitty I feel and how sorry I am about lying to you.

Love, apologies, and mega best-of-luck wishes with your artwork,

Jess.

X

P.S. If your grumpy upstairs neighbour tells you there was a creepy lass blaring 'In Your Eyes' outside your house, that was me. Sorry.

P.P.S. I'm not at Bonham Square any more, so if you do, by any chance, want to get in touch with me, my email is msbeambastic@mail.com

* * *

The novelty of being at Jamie's house with nothing to do but Rick Roll Summer and think about Leo, while barely getting any sleep because of his roommates' sex noises, soon wears off. And when Peach invites me out for lunch one sunny Tuesday, I fall on her invitation as if she's just offered up a naked and ready-for-action James McAvoy .

I travel to Le Petit Cafe in Kensington and wait for her to arrive. It feels weird not having seen Peach every day, and I find myself genuinely excited to catch up with her.

So imagine my shock when it's not Peach who walks through the cafe door, but Grandma. She glides in, tall and graceful in her dusky pink suit, her hair tied back in a chignon, her huge red glasses propped neatly on her nose.

Fucking Peach. She's completely set me up! And to think I was just having such lovely thoughts about her.

I grumpily stand up from the table and gather my things to leave.

'Please stay, Jessica,' Grandma asks, her voice cracking. Sighing, I sit back down. As she joins me at the small wooden table, I get a waft of her Chanel No. 5 and my eyes instantly fill with tears. I wipe them away fiercely.

I miss my Grandma.

But I'm so mad at her too.

'I've moving out of Bonham Square,' she informs me, discreetly signalling over to the waitress.

'I know. Peach told me.'

'I'm *downsizing*. To an end-of-terrace in Dulwich.' The waitress comes over and takes our order for tea. 'It's not quite Bonham Square, but it's bright and spacious and in rather a nice area.'

'Good. That's good.'

'I wanted to see you,' she says, 'to give you this.'

She takes a crisp white envelope out of her purse and hands it over.

Frowning, I open it up.

It's a cheque made out to the Mental Health Foundation. There are rather a lot of zeros on the end of the hand-scrawled number. I gasp.

'Woah.'

'I was wrong to ask you to get involved with the project.' Grandma sighs heavily. 'I should have known it was not your job to fix my problems. I thought that my house was the only thing I had left in the world. And by trying to save it, I lost what was most important to me . . . and that's *you*. Downsizing has left me plenty to spare. I thought that perhaps we could donate this in honour of Rose.'

She sobs slightly as she says my mum's name.

'I'd like that,' I nod quickly, the words catching in my throat. I swallow my own sob down. 'Thank you.'

Grandma takes a cotton hanky out of her handbag and dabs at her eyes with trembling hands.

'You haven't lost me, you know,' I say eventually. 'I'm just really, really pissed off at you.'

She opens her mouth instinctively, ready to tell me off for swearing, and then closes it just as quickly.

'I'm so sorry I . . . *pissed you off*.' She reaches over and takes hold of my hand. 'I've been very selfish. So consumed with self-pity and grief. I couldn't bear for you to see me the same way as your mother did. I thought, when you came through my door, that I had been given a second chance. And then I ruined it by involving you in my troubles.'

The waitress arrives with our tea. Grandma adds milk and I add sugar, but neither of us takes a sip.

'I'll never forgive myself for what I did to your mother,

Jessica. And however badly you think of me, I want you to know that I think that of myself. Please say you'll forgive me.'

'I forgive you, G,' I say immediately.

And I realize that I really do. None of us are innocent in this whole disaster; we've all been absolute turds in one way or another. Mum wasted so much of her life being angry and resentful. I don't want to do that. I can't do that.

Grandma exhales steadily and picks up her teacup in still slightly shaking hands.

'Peach tells me you've been wanting to go travelling. I'd like very much to pay for you to do that, Jessica. Where . . . where do you think you might like to go?'

I look at Grandma's wrinkly face and I realize how much I've missed seeing her every day, how nice it's been to have someone – however nuts – to care about what you're doing, how used to it I've become. Hmmm. The idea of travelling alone to Jamaica or Thailand or anywhere else really far away doesn't seem quite as urgent as it once did.

And then I laugh because suddenly I know *exactly* where I want to go, and it surprises the fuck out of me.

'I was thinking maybe . . . South London?' I suggest, taking a gulp of tea. 'I dunno, maybe somewhere like Dulwich.'

Grandma frowns for a second before she realizes what I've just said.

'With . . . with me?' She puts a hand to her chest. 'You mean at my house?'

'Yeah.' I grin. 'If you'll have me, obviously.'

'Oh, Jessica.' She sobs out loud, which makes a few of the other diners turn to give us super-annoyed stares. 'I *will* have you!'

'Oi, take a picture, maybe it'll last longer!' I shout over

to the staring customers, which makes Grandma chuckle and turn pink.

She presses a palm to her cheek. 'I can't believe it! Say you'll come back today, dear? I'll have Peach prepare the spare room. Well, your room now!' She looks over her shoulder and calls to the waitress at the cafe counter. 'Cake, please! We simply must have cake to go with our tea!'

'Cool.' I laugh, calling over to the waitress to cut me a bigger slice. 'I do have a few conditions, though.'

'Go on?'

'You have to promise me no more girdle-wearing, I go running whenever I want, we tell each other the truth from now on and . .. you never, ever, buy me a porcelain doll.'

Grandma holds her bony hand out in a flash. 'Done.'

* * *

I get back to Jamie's with a spring in my step. He's thrilled to hear I've sorted things out with Grandma. In fact, he seems a little too thrilled.

'Jeez, thanks a lot,' I say when he eagerly offers to help me pack my stuff.

'I've enjoyed having you here,' he grins. 'It's just . . . you're a little . . . messy.'

'I'm *creative*,' I protest. 'There's a difference, man.'

He lifts last night's plate of half-eaten lasagne off the coffee table. 'Yeah, very creative. I'm a medical professional. I have to think of the hygiene.'

I roll my eyes. Upstairs, I grab a black bin bag and start stuffing my clothes into it while Jamie doesn't so much help as stand there watching. When I'm all done he calls me a taxi and we wait out on his doorstep for it to arrive.

'Will we stay in touch?' Jamie asks quietly, kicking at the pavement with the toe of his Converse.

'We'd better do,' I say, nudging him with my elbow.

He runs a hand through his curls. 'Good.' He nods. 'Good.'

As the taxi pulls up at the curb, I yank Jamie in for a hug. 'You've been brilliant to me,' I whisper. 'And I'll never forget it.'

'I . . . I . . .' he starts, then sighs, his cheeks turning red. I don't know what he's about to say, but I interrupt it just in case it's what I think it might be.

'See you soon, Doc. And say bye to lovely Kiko for me.'

'Yeah. Yeah, I will do.' His shoulders slump for a second before he opens the boot of the cab and helps me to put my bags inside.

'Well!' I smile. 'See you soon, I guess. I'll ring you. Maybe we could go for a drink. Kiko too.'

'Sounds great . . .'

'Fab.'

'Be good, Jess,' he says tenderly, his cute face stretching into a warm smile.

'Never!' I yell, climbing into the cab and slamming the door behind me with a clunk.

The engine starts up with a roar, and as we trundle down the road I wave madly at Jamie through the back window. He waves back until eventually the car turns a corner and I can't see him any more.

CHAPTER THIRTY-SIX

The most important step a Good Woman can take in seeking enduring love is to first love and accept herself, with kindness, respect and honesty.

MATILDA BEAM'S FACEBOOK STATUS, AUGUST 2014.

Grandma and Peach – Mr Belding snuggled in her arms – are waiting for me on the doorstep of the Victorian terrace in Dulwich, grinning like fools and looking, for all the world, like family. I pay the cab driver, grab my stuff and race inside, where I'm immediately presented with tea and given a tour of the house. Grandma is right – this place is no Bonham Square, but in the world of normal, not mega-rich people like me, it's spacious and airy and full of lovely cosy period features. The pair of them lead me up two flights of stairs to my room – a huge attic space with big open windows at either end and ramshackle oak beams across the ceiling.

'What do you think?' Grandma asks, pink-cheeked and expectant.

I plonk onto the old bed, breathe in the fresh air sailing in from outside and smile.

'It feels good to be home,' I say simply.

'Ooh, Jess!' Peach squeals, coming to sit beside me on the bed. 'I almost forgot to tell you, I *finally* thought of a nickname for you!'

Oh God.

'Go on?'

'I hope you like it, I really think it's the right choice, but just tell me if you don't and we can think of something el—'

'Just tell me, Peach!'

'OK, the nickname I have chosen for you is – ' she expands her arms and grins a mad, buck-toothed grin – 'Lady ... J! What do you think? Do you love it?'

Brilliant. Fucking brilliant.

* * *

Over the next month or so, my life settles into a lovely routine – something I've never really had or wanted before, but something I find brings me a sort of peaceful feeling inside. I get myself a part-time job at a small second-hand bookshop in Dulwich, where I serve customers every weekday afternoon from midday to five – it's ace; the patrons are sweet and chilled and I get to read all the books whenever the shop is quiet.

When I'm not working, and when Grandma is not studying for the Finance Management course she recently signed up for, we write our new blog, *Matilda and Jess*, together. Yup. We've started a blog of our own all about the

Good Woman guides. It's not just from the angle of meeting a man, though, but all about our opposing views on what it means to be a Good Woman, with lots of stuff about fashion, feminism, lifestyle and career. We've had a fair few clashes in opinion, and Grandma insists that she controls the entire Facebook page, but other than that it's going really well and we're building a steady, loyal audience of readers.

I still spend a lot of time partying with Peach (who, sadly, ended things with Gavin. Once he started actually talking to her, she realized he didn't exactly set her lady business alight, so she's still looking for the right first person to have sex with), but the difference these days is that, while I have a shit-ton of fun, I don't get quite so messy that it affects everything else good in my life. It feels great to finally be taking control of what I'm up to, to not be the fuck-up in every room, to be working towards being a writer in my own way. I think that maybe I'm starting to figure out who I want to be, outside all the crap in my past. And I really like the way that feels.

As busy as things are, I still find the time to check my emails a gazillion times a day, hoping that Leo has responded to my letter or is even back in the country. But there's not a peep from him, not even on his social media pages, and I slowly start to get to grips with the fact that it really is over and I should probably start moving on.

I'm sure the ache in my chest at missing him will go away soon.

It has to at some point, right?

* * *

It's a hot, rainy afternoon in August and I'm lounging on my bed in the attic, working on posts for *Matilda and Jess*, when my mobile rings.

'Hello?' I say.

'Jessica? Kitten-paw? Is that you?'

It's Valentina. What does she want?

'It's me,' I answer.

'Did you get the envelope I had biked over to you?'

'Oh, I'm not in Bonham Square now, I'm in Dulwich.

'I know, duckling. Matilda sent a delightful notecard with the new address. It should be with you now.'

'What's going on?' I frown as I make my way downstairs.'What have you sent over?'

'Well, Jess, about an hour ago I got a letter from Leo Frost.'

I pause on the stairs. 'What?' My stomach dives to my knees.

'And you are not going to *believe* what it was.'

'What? What was it?' I hurry down the rest of the stairs and to the front door, where I rifle through the post pile. There it is. A white A4 envelope addressed to me. Peach must have signed for it on her way out to the shops.

'Have you found it?' Valentina asks impatiently.

'I'm just opening it!' I say, my hands shaking.

I carefully peel open the top of the envelope and pull out a small stack of papers. The top sheet of paper is a photocopy of a release form. It's signed by Leo and it states that he's giving us permission to use his name in *How to Catch a Man Like It's 1955*.

My heart starts to beat even faster.

'Oh,' I whisper into the phone.

And then I look at the other pieces of paper, and what's on them makes me drop the phone on the floor, where it lands with a thud. Because on each new piece of paper is a detailed, delicate line drawing. The first drawing is of me and Leo in a dodgem car. The next is of me in that weird, tufty hat, on stage at Little Joe's Java poetry night. There's one of Leo and me in the Da Vinci room in front of *The Virgin on the Rocks*. The sketches are intricate and breathtaking.

I rustle through to the final piece of paper in the pile. It's a drawing of me on the night of the London Advertising Association Awards ball. It seems Leo has remembered every detail of what I looked like that night, right down to the embroidering on the dress and the Ferris-wheel brooch. At the bottom of the drawing he has scrawled the words 'For Jess'.

I swallow down the lump in my throat and pick the phone up off the floor with barely working hands.

'Valentina, are you still there?'

'I am.' She sounds bemused.

'I don't understand,' I whisper. 'Why ... '

'Not only has Leo agreed to publication of *How to Catch a Man Like It's 1955*, but he's offered to illustrate it too.'

I laugh out loud. What does this mean?

'Perhaps he's got a heart after all,' Valentina says. 'Shocking. I never thought it possible. I heard he left Woolf Frost. Perhaps agreeing to this is his way of sticking it to his father and the company? Either way, everyone here is thrilled, such a high-profile man as Leo wanting to be involved. We're already talking about a sequel. Of course, I'll need those words from you as soon as possible. We want to strike while—'

'I can't believe it. I can't believe he did this.'

'It looks like you've brought something special out in Leo, Jessica. Something I never had a hope of doing. But that's OK. The heart wants what it wants, and I happen to have my eye on a delightful British actor I've seen at lots of parties lately. He's very famous, so I can't share anything more right now, but let's just say that *the game is afoot.* Shall we make plans for lunch? I'll tell you all about it then and we can—'

'So Leo's back in the country,' I blurt, not able to concentrate on anything Valentina's saying because my heart is pounding so loudly in my ears.

'Seems so!' she says.

He's back.

'Valentina, do you mind if I call you back in a bit?' I say, feeling a bubble of laughter rise in my throat.

She chuckles. 'Of course. Go to him, sweet Jessica. Go to him.'

And so I do.

* * *

I arrive at Leo's apartment block in the Docklands sweaty and breathless, my cheeks red, my hair clinging to my forehead, my purple vest absolutely soaked through. I knock on his door, clutching the photocopied drawings in my hands. I look down at them for the gazillionth time and bounce with pleasure.

The door opens, and there Leo is. He's dressed down in a plain white T-shirt and jeans, his ginger hair wet from the shower.

My whole body twinkles at seeing him.

'Hi,' I say, panting heavily after running here from the Tube station.

Leo looks at me evenly, betraying no emotion.

I take a deep breath and lift my chin.

'So, the thing is, Leo . . . I'm a woman who likes to go out to nightclubs and rock concerts. I eat Pot Noodles any chance I get, and I don't always change my socks. I've slept with lots of people, I'm not ashamed of it and I don't think I should be either. I really didn't like your Drive Alive advert – I'm sorry, but it is shit. I love wearing a nice comfy onesie and I don't really wear quirky hats and gloves. My mum did die.' My voice wobbles a bit. I clear my throat and soldier on. 'And it's the worst thing that ever happened to me. I'm still trying to get over it, and I don't know if I ever will, but I'll keep trying. I don't know much about poetry and art, but I'm open to learning about it. I swear a lot. A fucking, fucking lot. My grandma is a bit crazy. I really do love your drawings.' I clasp the drawings I have to my chest. 'And I think it's awesome and bold that you left your job to become an artist. I have some fairly hefty commitment issues, but I'm working on them. And I've never been sorrier about anything in my life than what I did to you . . . So, well, that's me in a nutshell, pretty much. Oh wait, there's one more thing ... I love you, Leo. I fucking love you.'

I look up into his extraordinary eyes. The eyes I know so well, but don't really know at all yet. They crinkle at the corners as his face breaks out into a huge grin.

Leo holds out his hand, his eyes travelling over my face as if he's trying to imprint it onto his brain.

'Hello, Jess,' he says. 'I'm Leo Frost. I am really, really pleased to meet you. I've heard great things.'

I laugh out loud, smiling so much that I think I might pull a muscle in my face.

'I'm Jessica Beam. Jess.' I take his hand and shake it.

'It's good to finally meet you, Jess,' he says softly, his voice breaking with emotion as he utters my real name.

He pulls me inside his apartment, weaves his hands up

into my hair and kisses me in the way that makes every single part of me glow. And I know, without a shadow of a doubt, that *this*, right here, is what love feels like.

'Would you like a drink?' Leo asks when we eventually pull apart.

'Yes please,' I reply, as I go with him into the kitchen, a massive dopey smile on my face. 'You got any pear cider?'

THE END

Dear Reader,

Hello!

Thanks so much for reading Jessica Beam's adventure. It took me a while to get this book exactly how I wanted it to be and I'm really proud of the result. I hope it made you laugh and that it took you away from your worries for a little while.

Reader reviews are massively helpful to an author. Especially authors like me who don't have the budget of a big publisher behind them. These reviews help to bring attention (and sales, of course!) to my books, but also help other readers to figure out whether they might enjoy what I write!

If you enjoyed reading LESSONS IN LOVE AND ROMANCE, I would be very grateful if you could spend a few minutes leaving a review. Even a really short one would be amazing. I read all of them and I vote up my favourite ones like some kind of creepy review stalker.

Thank you very much, and until the next book!

Kirsty x

YOU CAN READ MORE KIRSTY GREENWOOD BOOKS!

Yours Truly
Big Sexy Love

To sign up for new release updates, monthly giveaways and a free short story from Kirsty, add your name to her newsletter!

ACKNOWLEDGMENTS

It's been quite a journey, writing this book, and it wouldn't have been possible without this whole bunch of tremendous people.

My sincere thanks to:

Hannah Ferguson, super-agent, who is the perfect blend of wisdom, patience and encouragement. Thanks also to the excellent Marsh Agency team.

My editor and friend, the wicked smart Caroline Hogg, who, in the most awesome way, wouldn't let up until this book was the best it could possibly be. A most outstanding lady.

The clever people at Pan Macmillan including sales marketing and editorial teams. Particular thanks to Natasha Harding, Jeremy Trevathan, Eloise Wood, Jodie Mullish and Juliet Van Oss.

James Annal and Lloyd Jones, for creating the gorgeous original paperback cover.

Team Novelicious, for being the most brilliant bunch of book nerds I could ever hope to know.

Kerry Hiatt - such a fantastic Novelicious editor and saver of bacon on many occasions!

Poppy Dolan, Rosie Blake and Holly Kingston , for inspiring me with your mega talent and allowing me to work with you.

Leah Graham for giving me the loveliest, most encouraging beta read. Praise from you is high praise indeed!

The fabulously passionate book blogging community who have been incredibly supportive from day one, especially Victoria Stone, Kevin Loh, Lynsey James, Kirsty Maclennan, Steph Pegler, Eve Chong, Amanda Moran and Bronagh McAteer.

Andy and Angie - for your wonderful and consistent support.

For their uplifting encouragement - Dawn Dacombe, Nick Jones, Ben Holmes and Sharon Dudley.

Cesca Major - the loveliest person I've yet to meet and just the best email companion through this whole writing adventure.

For making me a happier human - Mary Holmes.

Mum, Dad, Lynette, Nichola and Tony - my noisy, absurd, beautiful, funny, heroic gang, who inspire me every single day.

Edd, beautiful man, for being my true constant in a crazy-ass year.

Finally, a big thanks to you readers. Hearing from you is the dopest thing about this job. I really hoped you enjoyed hanging out with Jessica Beam.

ABOUT THE AUTHOR

Kirsty Greenwood is an author of fast-paced, fearless and funny romantic comedies. She is also the founder and editor in chief of Novelicious.com.
She lives between Manchester and London, never without her laptop and a head full of made-up people.

To sign up for new release updates, monthly giveaways and more from Kirsty, add your name to her newsletter. The signup link is on her website!

www.kirstygreenwood.com

Printed by Amazon Italia Logistica S.r.l.
Torrazza Piemonte (TO), Italy

12613289R00235